OF STARS AND TIDES Copyright © by Locklyn Blake

www.locklynblake.com

Instagram: @locklynblake

TikTok: @locklynblake

Cover Design and Book Design by Franziska Stern

www.coverdungeon.com
Instagram: @coverdungeonrabbit

Author Photography by Tia Trapuzzano Photography @photosbytiaco

Hardback ISBN: 979-8-9880784-0-1 Paperback

ISBN: 979-8-9880784-1-8

eBook ISBN: 979-8-9880784-2-5

First edition 2023

THE DIVINE PROPHECIES
BOOK ONE

LOCKLYN
BLAKE

To my parents, who taught me to believe in myself without falter.
I owe all that I am today to them.

Out of the night that covers me,
Black as the pit from pole to pole,
I thank whatever gods may be
For my unconquerable soul.

In the fell clutch of circumstance
I have not winced nor cried aloud.
Under the bludgeonings of chance
My head is bloody, but unbowed.

Beyond this place of wrath and tears
Looms but the Horror of the shade,
And yet the menace of the years
Finds and shall find me unafraid.

It matters not how strait the gate,
How charged with punishments the scroll,
I am the master of my fate,
I am the captain of my soul.

"Invictus"
by William Ernest Henley

ARIES · FIRE
MANIPULATION · FIRE

TAURUS ·TELEPORTATION ·
EARTH

GEMINI · POWERS
UNKNOWN · AIR

CANCER · FORCEFIELD
GENERATION · WATER

LEO · STRENGTH ·
FIRE

VIRGO · PRECOGNITION ·
EARTH

LIBRA · TELEKINESIS ·
AIR

SCORPIO · POISON
MANIPULATION · WATER

SAGITTARIUS · WEAPON
MANIPULATION · FIRE

PISCES · WATER
MANIPULATION · WATER

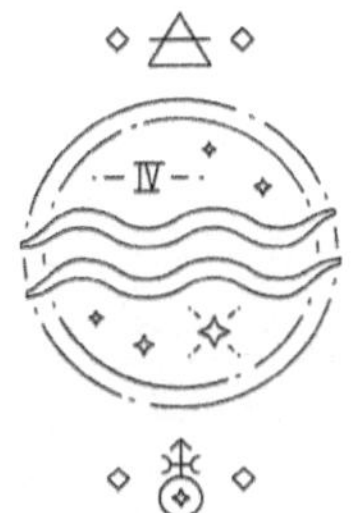

AQUARIUS · WEATHER
MANIPULATION · AIR

CAPRICORN · SHADOW
MANIPULATION · EARTH

APOTELESMA

(ADJ.) THE EFFECT OF STARS ON HUMAN DESTINY

Hero Stamos was no stranger to death.

His heart thudded in his ears, echoing the pounding of his heavy boots across the wet pavement. Shadows danced viciously in every corner of the dark alleyway, growing as impatient as he was for the slaughter to begin.

Grazing his hand over the hilt of his sword, he rolled his shoulders in anticipation. A smirk curved his lips, his confidence amplifying with each stride. It had always been a game to him: kill as many demons as he could and complete the mission as fast as possible. This time, though, the orders were different.

The girl.

He slowed as he neared the end of the alleyway, his footsteps softening. Wind caressed his face as the smell of fresh rain and spilled liquor wafted through the air—the signature scent of New Orleans, his home. He peered through the darkness, scanning for the slightest hint of movement. The demon lurked somewhere in its depths, hiding as it awaited its fate at Hero's hands.

Come out, come out, wherever you are . . .

His nose twitched. The stench of the demon's latest victim emanated from its skin, and hatred surged through Hero's veins. He willed himself to take his time with this one, to make it suffer, just as it had done to so many innocent mortals. It was nothing more than a filthy beast, a bloodthirsty monster. *Death.*

His sword gleamed as he emerged from the camouflage of night, offering himself as bait.

Gotcha.

The demon's eyes shone like the fires of the Underworld, searing with red-hot anguish. They alone illuminated Hero's battlefield for the night: the concrete boulevard. His raven-black jacket clung to his tense muscles, all the power of a Leo surging through him.

Strength. Force. Vitality.

The rush of exhilaration he'd grown to love erupted as the crimson beams flashed at him, a silent acknowledgment that the fight had commenced.

Lifting his chin, Hero took a deep breath, jaw clenching and fists tightening around the metal in his hands. He readied his sword with ease.

The demon emerged from the darkness at last, its bones cracking and reforming with each dastardly step. Hero ignored the chill snaking up his spine at the sound of its claws scratching across the concrete, like a knife dragging across a ceramic plate. Its humanoid body rippled toward him, and in the gleam of the stars above, Hero could see the scales and burns and scars that covered the beast. The demon grew, towering over him, its shadows following suit.

Razor-sharp talons lifted into the air and swiped at Hero in a fury. He dodged, swinging himself around to the demon's other side. Narrowing his eyes at the beast through his soaked curls, Hero grinned.

A game. That's all it is.

He'd trained for this moment since birth, every muscle and vein in his body screaming at him to fight. Nothing else in the world made sense to him but words of action. His mother's voice echoed in his ears: *"You're a loyal soldier, Hero. Kill the demons and protect the mortals. Fight harder. Fight stronger."*

Tonight, his mission was clear: he had to find the girl before the demons did, and he had to find her alive—nothing more, nothing less.

His ragged breathing masked the whistle of an arrow shooting past him. The demon bared its teeth as it snarled in pain, the arrow protruding from its leathery skin, green blood oozing from its torso. Hero trained his eyes on the raging beast, awaiting its next attack as metal clanked on the balconies above him. He'd drawn the demon toward the archer, serving it to her on a silver platter. While Hero might have been the stronger of the two siblings, Artemis would always be the better fighter, ruthless in the field, and never missing a single target. *A Sagittarius.* Although younger than him by a few years, Artemis had made sure her skills made up for every lost second, and they hardly ever went into a fight without each other, the perfect balance between strength and precision.

Artemis soared through the sky, her body crunching to absorb the impact when she landed next to Hero.

"Thanks for keeping it distracted until I got here," she said, grinning like a feline as she rose to her full height. Nockingtwo more arrows into her bow, she released them rapidly at the demon's leg. The demon screeched, but Hero knew better than to feel anything other than pure malice for such a vile beast. It was their job to send it right back to the trenches of Tartarus, where it belonged.

Hero locked in on Titus crouching on another balcony and nodded his head. Titus jumped, landing with a grunt, and plunged his black spear into the demon's back. The resistance of its scaly skin gave way as Titus pushed unflinchingly deeper, slicing its spine as blood pulsated out onto the pavement, the demon roaring in a fury at the new attack.

"Titus, let go!" Hero yelled.

Too late. The demon reached around, digging its claws into Titus's arm. Titus emitted a deep scream, blood sputtering out of the wound as the demon lifted him by his flesh and flung him across the alleyway. His body hit a brick wall, his head smashing backward with a sharp crack before his limp figure slid to the ground. The bloody spear dropped from his hand.

Hero's heart froze in his chest.

"Over here!" Hero shouted to lure the demon away from his friend. Arrows soared through the air as Artemis laid her claim to the creature.

Hero watched apprehensively as Titus finally shoved himself off the ground, spitting blood as his body swelled with rage. His injuries healed instantly, the blood slipping back into his arm as his cells stitched themselves back together within seconds, leaving no evidence of any harm.

Hero's gaze descended on the beast. He ignored the light breeze against his forehead as he took a taunting step toward the demon, provoking it by swinging his sword around and cracking his neck.

No way out now, scum.

He had more than enough strength to take on the demon alone, as he'd done so many times in his life. But his team had their routine down now: distract and attack.

Bow and arrows now discarded, Artemis sliced her way through the demon with her daggers, predicting its every move, the pure adrenaline of the fight taking over. She could sense a blade of grass moving toward her, let alone a giant beast, which made it easier for Hero in battle; he didn't have to worry about her as much as he did the others. His sister had only been injured once in the field, just a small cut to her cheek—his fault more than hers, although he'd never admit it out loud.

They weren't mortal, after all, but they also weren't immortal. Their lives danced somewhere in between.

Artemis's dark braided hair flung around freely in harmony with her body's movements. She threw herself into the air, spinning around and kicking the demon back to Hero. They'd practiced this move hundreds of times until they perfected it. It stumbled on its clawed feet, its attention now on Hero.

Distract.

The demon followed Hero's sword in a pattern, anticipating his next strike, waiting for the fight that would never come. Teasing and taunting—that was the beauty of working with his team: the games, the chase. His tongue glided over his teeth.

Attack.

Creeping up behind the demon, Titus slid his metal spear deep through its abdomen and out the other side. It threw its head back in agony, screeching into the night sky—and with one final swing of his sword, Hero beheaded the wailing beast. Its head hit the ground, rolling across the pavement as green blood spurted out of its lifeless body.

Triumph filled Hero's veins as he caught his breath, brushing the splatters off his face as the demon's gleaming eyes dimmed to darkness. The beast dissolved into the ground moments later, evidenced only by a telltale cloud of rising black smoke.

Hero chuckled as he wiped his blade clean and placed it back into his scabbard. "You and Elijah need to work on your kills." He turned to face Titus, puffing out his chest. "I'm five ahead of you guys, and there are only a few days left in the month."

"I'm waiting until the last minute, so all your hopes and dreams of not having to do laundry come crashing down on you all at once," Titus countered, holding his hands up as he revealed his master plan. "And hey, not my fault I had the disadvantage of being thrown into a wall either."

Abruptly, their coarse laughter faded as their ears pricked up at the sound of footsteps nearing the alleyway's entrance. Whipping around in anticipation, their hands flew to their weapons, readying themselves for their next fight. Hero knew the demon would only be the first of the attacks tonight. Nothing had been normal about this mission, from the mystery visions Nyssa had received, to tracking the location of where their mission—*she*—would be.

His shoulders tightened when he saw the rest of his team rounding the corner instead. Hero had instructed Nyssa and Elijah to stay in the car and not venture out unless something went wrong, due to Nyssa's condition—yet here they were. Hero's hand fell from his sword's hilt as he ran to meet them, Artemis and Titus following close behind.

Nyssa stumbled to the ground. Her black hair flowed around her face as she clutched her skull in agony, her jaw clenching as she held in her screams, the occasional shrill finding its way out. Her chin lifted at their approach, and her normally dark eyes flashed a vibrant green as her body convulsed.

Elijah winced next to her as she clutched his arm even harder, but he refused to move, and Hero knew that her suffering tormented Eli more than he'd ever let on.

As if a switch had been flipped, Nyssa's body suddenly fell loose, her eyes fading back to sweet and wise. "I found her," she gasped between heaving breaths.

The girl . . . our mission.

She lifted her shaking fingers to the street. "I saw her in my vision just now. She's out there, walking toward Echo's Club." She looked at Hero. "We have to do this together—all of us, or it won't work. The Seekers are coming."

Seekers.

Seekers were shadows trapped within the shell of a human body. They were the darkness—the sky without stars, the bleak curves and crevices of the world, the death coiling around each breath. They were a sort of demon vagabonds, living underground or in abandoned parts of the world, known to possess and kill humans. Often such events would surface as a strange death seen on the news, or a disappearance where the body was never found. Hero could count the number of times he'd encountered a Seeker on one hand, one being on a night he'd *never* forget.

But why come out now? Why for this one girl?

Nyssa groaned as she clutched Elijah again.

Hero balled his hands into fists at the sight of his friend in such pain. She'd been this way for days; her visions hadn't given her a moment of peace, plaguing her with her cursed gift. Yet she always reminded them that it was worth it. She'd told them of the silver-haired girl in the red dress she'd seen in her vision so many nights ago. Without them, the girl's fate would remain one of darkness and death. And now, with the Seekers coming . . .

Hero scanned Nyssa's face, taking in each wince of pain. "Come on, we have to get her before it's too late," he said, his voice strained. He glanced between Nyssa and his sister before his attention was diverted to where the mortals stumbled through the street a few meters away from them, not registering a sliver of their existence. The blessing and the curse of being a Zodiac—always living in the shadows, their true selves hidden.

"I can do this," Nyssa croaked out, the side of her mouth curling in the most pathetic way. She locked eyes with Elijah. "Take care of the Seekers; Artemis and I've got the girl," she told them, lifting her chin.

As she'd predicted, a crash erupted from the end of the alleyway. Shards of glass rained down from the windows above as cloaked figures leaped out in harmony, landing with their hands on the ground, one knee bent.

Hero took off running toward their new threat without a second glance; Titus and Elijah trailed close behind. They had to honor their mission, no matter what. If the demons or Seekers found her before they did, the entire night would be a waste. There was no more time for talking or for letting himself care; after all, *weapons don't weep.*

They halted a few feet away from the Seekers, careful to keep their distance. Hero reached for the hilt of his sword, drawing it out in one swift movement, ready for battle.

Black smoke seethed around their enemies, seeping from the Seeker's bodies as they planted their heavy boots. Large hoods covered their faces, hiding themselves from ever truly being seen, yet their leather fighting attire contoured the human figures they held possessed. It made Hero's blood boil to think about the poor souls entrapped inside, being controlled by such evil, forced into committing such unspeakable acts.

Hero clasped his sword, his other hand clenched into a fist. Titus leveled his hand to the ground as water droplets rose at his command, and Elijah's arms burst into flames. The Seekers drew their blades, waiting.

The mere fact that the Seekers, a threat they'd rarely encountered, would come out for this girl heightened the stakes of the mission to an entirely new level. They had to save her.

CHAPTER I

LACUANA

(N.) A BLANK SPACE; A MISSING PART

The morning sun gleamed brightly through the window, teasing Cassie's skin with the summer awaiting her. Only the sound of her fingers tapping away at the keyboard broke the silence.

She glanced at the time. Sixteen minutes until the deadline. Her back tensed as tiny beads of sweat made their way down her forehead, each one ticking like the hand of a clock. Her computer held the last document attached to her life back in California, the last step keeping her from her future.

It was time.

The corners of her mouth pulled up in anticipation as she uploaded her transfer documents and pressed send.

Cassie exhaled. It was official; she had switched colleges. Her life before was now a closed chapter. She'd done it, all on her own.

The ringing of chimes shattered the stillness. She dove onto her small twin bed, fumbling around in the tousled sheets until she found the source of the unrelenting noise beneath her pillows. She grabbed her phone from its hiding place. "Hello?"

"Happy birthday, sweetheart!" her father sang.

"Oh, hey, Dad. Thank you!" Her stomach turned the moment her words echoed into the phone, and she forced herself to swallow the bile rising in her throat. She sat upright on her bed, trying to remain calm, ignoring the pounding in her chest. He sounded so foreign. She tried to picture his kind blue eyes, the wrinkles decorating them . . . Her heart ached.

"So, what's the big plan tonight? Stephen taking you somewhere special?"

Stephen. Stephen was now her *ex*-boyfriend. She'd never felt that true spark with him. Worse, she always felt anxious and on edge around him, but also *bored*. It wasn't love; she knew that. Not the one she longed for, anyway. She'd broken up with Stephen before she moved, but she couldn't tell her dad that. She couldn't tell him anything.

Forcing herself to sound normal, she said, "Uh, yeah. We're going out to a karaoke bar on campus. Should be fun." Cassie glanced over at the limited-edition novel her father had given her the last time she'd seen him. She had yet to read it. Instead, she wrote poems based on the guilt she felt for the web of lies she'd spun. She found it easier to think of people, places, and things as poetry, as fiction. She could capture a moment in words, granting it immortality, a stability her tumultuous world had never known. She'd long yearned for a home she truly belonged in, a large group of friends, and a family that was whole. Cassie wondered if she could find it in New Orleans with her best friend, rather than a half-day drive from the town she felt too much loss in, at a college she only attended to make her dad happy, and to be close to him.

She loved her father, but it was always just them. She didn't have any living grandparents, her mom had passed away when she was young, and she had no siblings. It was fine, really—but a small, guilty part of her felt as if something were missing. She often found herself daydreaming of having that big family, the one where she had her mother back, along with those grandparents, and maybe some siblings . . . And, if she was listing fantasies, she also yearned for a love so epic that it could star in a novel. But she was starting to believe that wasn't part of her path, that maybe those things would never show in her lifetime, and that she wasn't as lucky as others. Not this time around, anyway.

Still, she was learning to be content with her life here with Quinn, in a new city. It was a change, and that had to be good enough for her.

"You know, I should come over soon and visit—"

"No!" Cassie yelled abruptly. Then she composed herself, blurting out, "I'll drive down in a few weeks, so I'll see you then." Never mind the fact that she'd sold her car weeks ago to pay for her move.

"I can't wait, kiddo!" he exclaimed. Cassie could hear his sweet smile through the phone, and yet it felt like a sharp blade entering her chest, steeped in the poison of guilt. "I'm super proud of you for making it into the summer program. Just . . . just promise me you'll be safe tonight, okay? Don't drink too much, and keep an eye out." His tone had turned stiff as a board. It had become a habit of his, as with most parents, forgetting how old she was.

It had been just the two of them for so long, she questioned if it *was* wrong to be so far away from him, and trying to balance what she wanted with what her father wanted was making her dizzy.

But he wasn't the one lying.

At least the part about the summer program wasn't a lie—just the *where.*

When she'd brought up the mere idea of moving to somewhere like New Orleans, her father grew uneasy, a sadness rippling through him. He'd suggested a college at least in the same state, and after many discussions—or rather, arguments—she complied. She'd been accepted into a rigorous English course that she admitted she'd liked and enjoyed for a few years, yet somehow it didn't feel *right,* as if it were a shoe half a size too small, or too big.

She couldn't explain it; she felt drawn to New Orleans, even only by seeing it through the screen of her phone. So, without her father knowing, she'd applied to the summer program in New Orleans, and she couldn't ignore it when the acceptance letter came in, also offering her a place for her final year too. She would only have to lie to her dad for one year; that was it. Quinn already lived there, so the apartment was sorted out, and everything else just seemed to *fit*.

Cassie called it fate. And she loved almost every second of it.

Her hand went to the emerald resting on her chest—the one object that had remained constant throughout her whole move—but her fingers flinched in response. Instead of the cool, smooth surface she'd expected, it was as if she'd touched a hot stove. A deep burning pain broke out in her fingertips, and reflexively she released the gem, only to have it swing back onto her chest, searing her skin.

Cassie yelped in pain. Leaning forward to keep the necklace from touching any part of her body, she reached behind her neck and quickly undid the clasp. The necklace fell onto her quilt—which, to her surprise, didn't burn beneath it. But the gem dulled, she noticed. It wasn't as bright, as significant as it once was. It seemed lifeless. Dead.

She studied her fingers, mesmerized by the skin pulsating under the rose-colored burn. A heartbeat. Life.

"Hello? Cassie, are you okay?" her dad pressed.

Cassie's consciousness pulled back into reality as his words finally registered. "Yeah, I just got an electric shock. I'm fine," she lied again, shifting in her bed. "I've gotta go, but I love you lots, and I'll call you in a few days." She grimaced when she heard the slight twinge of disappointment in her dad's voice as he said his farewells.

It took all of Cassie's willpower not to let any tears fall once she hung up. The line between choosing the right path for herself and being an honest daughter had blurred so much that she couldn't tell which was right or wrong. Instead, she focused on her breathing, trying to steady herself one inhale at a time, reminding herself with each exhale that her lies were for a worthy cause.

Cassie touched her burned chest, wincing at the tenderness. This was the first time she'd taken the necklace off in years, and she felt naked without it. She would toy with it whenever she was nervous, she would make sure every outfit she wore matched with it, and on some nights—the especially hard nights—she would talk to it. She'd tell it about her day, which boy she had a crush on, why she and Quinn had fought. It was almost a part of her by now. She shivered from the bareness.

For a moment, Cassie wondered if her mom's spirit had used it to burn her for lying to her dad, it being her necklace and all. Placing her head in her hands, Cassie rubbed her face and tried to move on. *Weirder things have happened, right?*

Getting out of her warm, comfy bed, she tried to shake off her anxiety and walked over to her vanity table. She plopped onto her chair, and the mirror answered as she willed a small smile onto her face. Staring into her gray eyes, she blinked, the same smile dissipating as she found herself unable to stop questioning it.

Why did the necklace burn me?

Her fingers lifted to her chest, brushing over the skin to find no pain or bump of a scar. She looked at her chest in the mirror, then at her fingers. She remained untouched, a blank canvas.

The cool air hit her teeth as she sucked in sharply, then chuckled. Maybe she *was* going crazy, and maybe it *had* been an electric shock. The memories danced in her mind, mixing reality and fiction.

A knock on the door broke Cassie from her thoughts. Before she could even respond, Quinn shoved the door open and bounced into her room, her hands filled with a bottle of bubbly liquid and two half-filled glasses of orange juice—a perk of now living with her best friend.

Cassie always admired how Quinn could look so beautiful at any time of day, her light brown skin free of any imperfections, and her coiled hair always so full of life. It might have been because Quinn herself was always so full of life.

"It's time to celebrate!" Quinn squealed, jumping knees-first onto Cassie's bed.

Cassie giggled at the sight, lifting her eyebrow at the bottle, then turning to look mockingly at her bare wrist as though she were checking the time.

Quinn groaned. "It's your twenty-first birthday! This is the best excuse *ever* for drinking in the morning," she argued as she popped the bottle open, foam dripping everywhere. She topped off both glasses with the sparkling wine.

Cassie took the drink happily and clinked it against Quinn's before sipping her mimosa. The sourness of the orange and the cool bursting of the bubbles was a welcomed taste, blotting out, for a moment, all her worries, like the shadow of the moon blocking out the sun during an eclipse.

Quinn's eyebrows bunched together, and then she reached over to lift something off the bed.

Cassie's heart stopped as she watched the golden chain she knew so well tangle between Quinn's fingers. "Wait!" she yelled, pushing herself off her seat as the emerald of her necklace landed in her friend's palm.

But nothing happened—nothing at all. No burn, no pain.

Quinn's face scrunched in confusion. She awkwardly laughed a bit before softly saying, "Sorry—I know it's your mom's necklace. I just saw it behind me and didn't want to sit on it."

"No, I'm sorry. I overreacted," Cassie said shakily, sitting back down. "I, uh, just didn't want it to break." Her thumb drifted over her finger, where the burn mark once lingered minutes ago.

"Why'd you take it off?" Quinn asked. "I don't think I've ever seen you without it on."

A lump formed in Cassie's throat. She swallowed hard and said, "I didn't want to wear it out tonight, in case I lost it." *More lies.*

Quinn leaned over the edge of the bed to hand Cassie the necklace. "Anyway, before this turns into a sob-fest, we have a full day of drinking ahead of us, and a wild night out. I'm not letting *anything* ruin your birthday."

Cassie pinched the necklace by its chain and gently set it down on the vanity. She wanted to push away all the negativity, all the shadows surrounding her, and celebrate with Quinn, as she deserved.

"Cheers to that." Cassie tilted her glass over to Quinn's once more, clinking in the harmony of a new beginning.

Quinn gasped, jumping off the bed in a rush. "I almost forgot! I stayed up all last night working on your present, so you better not hate it," she said in a mock threat, pointing her finger at Cassie. With that, she pranced out of the room, only to return seconds later, holding a stunning red dress in front of her body.

Cassie leaped out of her chair, her jaw slack as she let her gaze drift over the fabric, taking in all the small details trailing up the silk. "You made this? For *me*? It's beautiful!" she gasped. Her fingers glided around the material in awe. It was tighter and shorter than any of her other dresses, but a voice inside of her told her to be daring, pushing her to live a little and wear it.

ONEIRATAXIA

(N.) THE INABILITY TO DISTINGUISH BETWEEN
FANTASY AND REALITY

Light rain cast down on them, tickling Cassie's face as they walked down the street toward the club. The clicking of her heels against the pavement slowed as she neared a closed bridal shop, the crowds of people passing her by as she paused to brush away her dampening hair.

Finally able to check her reflection, Cassie startled at what she saw. A person stood inside the darkened shop, staring back at her—not a mannequin, but a *woman*, moving and breathing. Yet despite Cassie's twisting stomach, she found herself compelled to look as her gaze remained glued to this stranger . . .

A weird feeling overcame her then, as if she'd once known this person, or perhaps even passed her on the street one day, but she still couldn't quite see her shadowed face. Cassie dipped her head to the side, wanting to study the figure more closely, yet as she did, the person inside copied her. Lifting her arm, she moved her hand in the form of a wave, wanting to test her shadow further. The woman followed as if she knew what action Cassie would take before she knew herself. Her mouth dried as she tried to take a step back, but she found herself nearly paralyzed, as though this woman had a hold on her.

Her arm registered a slight pain as her body was pulled to the side, guiding her free. Quinn's face came into view. "Come on! We don't have the time to admire ourselves all night!" she exclaimed, slurring her words as she prodded Cassie in the ribs with her elbow, oblivious to what had happened.

Cassie squinted behind her as Quinn hooked their arms together, trying to catch one more glimpse of the stranger. "Did you see her? The . . . the woman in the window?" Her thoughts ran faster than she could have even put down on paper.

Quinn huffed. "You mean your own hot bod in that amazing dress I made you?" Her eyes rolled.

Cassie shook her head. "No, there was someone else in there, I swear." A shiver crawled up her back, cold and unwelcoming, as though warning her of a darkness lurking all around. She wrapped her arms around her body, rubbing her hands up and down to make it go away.

"I'm pretty sure no one was there," Quinn said, her voice suddenly laced with concern and a bit of confusion. But in seconds, her face lit up, and she snapped her fingers. "Oh, I know! You're getting the New Orleans creeps! I've seen all kinds of spooky stuff here. These streets are haunted by witches, ghosts; you name it." She laughed it off like it was nothing. "But . . ." she said, drawing out the word, "it's probably just your mind playing tricks on you."

Cassie knew without a doubt that what she'd seen was real, whether Quinn believed her or not. Something was happening to her; she could feel it in her bones, in her stomach. It had been there this morning too, with her necklace. And it was wrong.

It was *dark*.

Her steps quickened as she unhooked her arm from Quinn's, walking ahead. She tried to take stock of what the figure looked like. It—*she*—had long jet-black hair, and her eyes were a shining . . . purple? The starry blanket of the night and the busy crowds had made it hard to see much else, yet the sensation of familiarity stayed with her. She didn't like it.

As she glanced skyward, neon red assaulted her vision. Echo's Club.

Quinn approached from behind, knocking her arm against Cassie's. "Hey, I don't know what happened back there, but if you saw someone, I believe you." She sighed. "I just want us to have fun tonight. We're finally in the city together, like we always wanted."

Cassie knew she was right. They'd spoken about moving here together since they were kids, and now that she could finally join Quinn, it was a milestone worth celebrating. And it *was* her birthday. "It's forgotten," she finally said.

Quinn squealed and clasped Cassie's hand to guide her to the door flanked by bouncers. Cassie, despite herself, took one last scan around, filtering through the crowd on the street. She couldn't quite get rid of the persistent suspicion that there were eyes on her, watching her . . . but she had to let it go.

Easier said than done.

The loud, pulsing beats of the music paired with the flashing strobe lights were a welcome distraction as the two girls walked in together, the overwhelming heat hitting them in waves. Cassie watched the half-dressed dancing bodies desperately groping each other, each move laced with alcohol and tomorrow's regret.

They bought their drinks and struggled their way to the middle of the dance floor. The mix of the overwhelming music and the vodka worming its way through her system was nothing short of euphoric. *Ecstasy.* Cassie let her mind go, tilting her chin up as she focused on the strobe lights infiltrating her vision. Her body moved effortlessly along with the bass line, the vibrations ricocheting through her bones.

"Can I borrow your phone? Your camera's better than mine!" Quinn yelled over the music, holding her hand out.

Cassie slipped her phone out of her bag, passing it over. Quinn turned her body around, held the phone in the air, and smiled as the flash captured the moment.

Cassie blinked as her sight reformed, watching Quinn's face twist at the phone screen.

"What's wrong?" she asked.

Quinn pouted. "There's a weird glare. It ruined the photo!"

As Cassie peered at the screen, the music suddenly faded from her ears, pitching into a deafening silence. Everything around her blurred, passing her by in slow motion, as though she weren't in the club anymore, but on another plane, in a different universe, peering into her life as an outsider.

"I'll be right back," she muttered to Quinn.

Bodies slammed into her as Cassie made her way out, her heart pumping in her ears. She needed to escape. Her chest rose and fell, her breathing quickening as her shoves became harsher, the crowd threatening to swallow her whole.

The cool air hit her skin in a tortured comfort as she emerged from the dance floor, exhaling in relief. Stumbling to the bar, she gripped the sides of the counter-top and bent her head, studying the tips of her high heels.

The glare from the photo . . . It came from her eyes—the same purple eyes the woman in the window possessed, as though she were following her, haunting her.

A chill raked up her spine as the feeling of someone watching her came over her once more. Pushing herself off the bar, Cassie peered over her shoulder.

Two women were staring at her from a few meters away, their eyes wide, as if they'd located their prey and didn't want to scare it off with sudden movement. The dim lighting made it hard for Cassie to see who they were, but deep down, she had an odd sense that all the insane things that had happened to her today somehow led back to them. Then, Cassie saw, of all things, what looked like an arrow poking out from one of the women's bags.

Run.

Cassie jolted toward the first door she could find, the one leading to the bathrooms. She didn't understand why she was running, or whose voice it was in her head telling her to run, but she willed her legs to carry her away. Nothing from this day made any sense, from her burning necklace, to the creepy woman inside the closed shop, to the purple glare, to the two women now following her—with *weapons*.

She flung the door open and raced down the stairs, the cool metal railing providing her support. The door closed behind her, the pounding drumbeat fading out as a ringing shot through her ears. Her legs wobbled beneath her, threatening to give out at any second.

Approaching the bottom of the stairs, she frantically scanned the doors to find the women's bathroom, but as she heard footsteps approaching, she bolted through an unmarked door, locking it behind her.

She scanned her surroundings to make sure she was alone in what appeared to be a private bathroom, before hurrying over to the sink. She clutched the cold ceramic basin, the one thing keeping her from falling.

"It's not real, it's all in your head, it's not real . . ." she repeated to herself, her voice growing more desperate with each verse. Cassie wanted to believe it wasn't real with all her heart.

But a part of her knew that somehow, it was.

Cassie lifted her head to the mirror at last, unable to deny what was happening any longer. Her body convulsed, her heart dropping at the sight of what she'd already grasped in her mind, but didn't want to admit. A tear slid down her cheek.

This *other* stared back at her, again.

She now understood why the reflection in the shop window had appeared so strange, yet so familiar. Her own face glared back at her—yet it wasn't her at all. Her eyes were filled to the brim with mischief, glowing that same sharp violet. Her hair was streaked with shadows, all traces of the light silver she'd grown so fond of replaced with onyx. She wasn't herself.

A darkness crept around the person staring back at her. It reminded Cassie of the dead of night, of a certain type of misery she couldn't put her finger on—one that tore a shriek from her lips. And before she could even understand what she was doing, her fist collided with the mirror, shattering it into a million pieces around her.

Cassie couldn't hear anything aside from her own ragged breathing and the occasional drop of blood trickling down her hands, splattering onto the broken glass as the senses in her body faded.

The door of the bathroom shook as someone pulled at the handle. Cassie couldn't muster the energy to care. The room spinning around her made it hard to feel anything as the blend of alcohol and shock worked its way through her system. Her vision blurred. Her hearing dissolved as her limbs weakened. She could only shiver in response.

And then she fell, deeper and deeper into the obscurity, until it swallowed her whole.

CHAPTER 3

DÉPAYSEMENT

(N.) WHEN SOMEONE IS TAKEN OUT OF THEIR OWN
FAMILIAR WORLD INTO A NEW ONE

An awful taste coated Cassie's dry mouth.

The morning light filtered through her eyelids, but she refused to open them yet, her head already tight with pressure. The mere thought of moving upset her stomach. As her mind raced through the events of last night, attempting to piece together a blurry puzzle of memories, one worry became staggeringly clear.

She didn't remember coming home.

Her eyes snapped open, and she winced as she adjusted to the light and the continuous pounding in her brain. The bright white ceiling was the first thing she saw, detailed with elegant golden floral designs throughout the textured paint. It was a ceiling she had never seen before.

Cassie's fingers wandered across the bed. She didn't recognize the small, firm mattress beneath her. Her wavering touch drifted onto her body. She sighed in momentary relief as she felt the material of the dress Quinn had made her.

What happened to me? Where am I?

Her heart raced. With each blink, her vision became less blurry, but the sound of two voices froze her in place.

She wasn't alone.

"What do you think? Memory wiped?" a woman said. Her voice had a unique rasp, making each word sound callous.

Cassie turned her head to the side, trying to get a glimpse of them, but her eyes were met with their backs.

"There's no trace of Cassandra Smith in any Arena," the second one said. Her voice was sweeter and softer than the other's. But how did they know her full name?

"And you're positive she's one of us?"

One of them . . . ?

"She's the one from my vision. I'm sure of it."

"But the birthdate on the ID—a Gemini? And the Seekers and demons were after her too. Something's not right," the raspy one warned.

Demons? What the hell is happening?

She scanned the room, quickly noting its resemblance to an old-fashioned hospital. Rows upon rows of single beds were staged throughout the massive room, all with crisp white sheets and not a single speck of dust floating anywhere.

"What if it's a fake ID?"

"It's not. I know it's not. I saw that she was celebrating her birthday in my vision."

One of them sighed. "Well, then I'm surprised Diana hasn't ordered for her to be locked up yet."

At that, Cassie pushed herself upright, ignoring her shaking arms. Her throbbing head told her to lie back down and rest, but that was out of the question.

The two women whipped around, and Cassie's stomach dropped. They were the women from the club last night—the ones with the arrows. With a twist of panic, countless scenarios played through her mind: what had happened to her, who they were, and what they wanted with her.

"You . . . Where am I?" Cassie demanded. She jumped off the bed, her bare feet chilled by the cold marble flooring. She backed away from them until her body hit a wall.

"You're okay, you're safe," the shorter one with the soft voice assured her, her thin hands moving in a continuous motion as though trying to soothe Cassie at her approach. She had a long yet oval-shaped face, pale skin with yellow undertones, and sharp cheekbones. Her straight black hair stopped before her shoulders, and her dark eyes grew wary as she looked Cassie up and down.

Desperate and feeling trapped, Cassie looked around for anything she could defend herself with. A pair of black heels on the floor caught her eye—the ones Quinn had forced her to wear.

My shoes.

Cassie grabbed one of them, holding the stiletto like a weapon. "What's going on? Where am I? Tell me!" she demanded, her voice on the cusp of breaking as she threatened them like a crazy person. She was in dire need of the room to stop spinning, but at least she had a way to defend herself. She could fight them if she tried hard enough. At least, she hoped so.

The woman came closer to Cassie again, reaching out to take her makeshift weapon away from her. Cassie's grip tightened on it as she pushed herself off the wall. "Get away from me!"

The woman flinched, her face now filled with worry and fear. "You're okay, Cassandra. We found you unconscious on the bathroom floor of the club, and we wanted to help you."

A flood of memories rushed back into Cassie's mind: the woman in the reflection, the mirror, the purple glare, the necklace . . . She shivered as hot tears formed in her eyes.

What's happening to me?

"Where am I?" Cassie asked again, trying to mask the apparent tremble in her voice. It wasn't lost on her that they kept avoiding her questions. "And how do you know my name?" The words stuck in her mouth with each syllable. She needed water—and to get out.

The black-haired woman glanced over her shoulder at her friend, sighing as she turned to face Cassie again. "We found your wallet in your purse," she explained, her words slow. "I'm Nyssa. Nyssa Nakamura. It's nice to meet you." She smiled at Cassie—a cordial smile one would give when passing neighbors in the street, lips pressed together in a thin line, no teeth showing. A smile that wasn't a smile. "And that's Artemis." Nyssa nodded toward the olive-skinned woman sitting cross-legged on another bed, spinning a knife on her finger, eyes narrowed like an ill-tempered feline. Cassie's throat clenched at the sight of the weapon; the shoe she was feebly defending herself with was no match for a blade.

"Don't worry about her though," Nyssa added, whispering the next part: "She just acts tough."

"What happened to me last night?" Cassie pressed, ignoring the strange banter, and keeping one eye on the knife. She didn't know if they planned to use it on her or not, or if it was simply a scare tactic. It was working, but she couldn't let them know that.

Nyssa took a deep breath. "Something was after you. Something . . . dark. We knew you were in trouble, so we were trying to help you. *Are* trying to help you."

Cassie blinked. *Do they know about the purple glare, or the woman in my reflection?* She paused for a moment, trying to recall what she'd overheard of their conversation when she first awoke. "You said I'm one of you? What does that even mean?"

Nyssa rubbed the back of her neck. "It's very, um . . . complicated to explain."

Enough. "Look," Cassie said in a sharp tone that took her by surprise, "thank you for helping me, I appreciate it, but I should go back to my place now. My roommate's going to be worried." Spotting an open door, she stepped toward it.

Artemis flung herself off the bed and stood in front of the only exit. Her tongue glided over her teeth as she huffed through her nose. "You can't go back."

The warmth drained from Cassie's face. "Why not?" she croaked. Her thoughts ran wild, racing in every possible direction as she tried to figure out what to do. She glanced at the windows framing large treetops outside, and knew her chances of getting out that way didn't look good.

"Because your life is in danger, and frankly, we would rather you were *not* eaten by a demon right now," Artemis replied, without even a hint of sarcasm.

Cassie backed away, her heart racing and her palms dampening. They were crazy. They had to be.

"Artemis!" Nyssa snapped. "What happened to easing her into it?"

"We might as well rip off the Band-Aid." Artemis scowled, nodding toward Cassie. "There's no easy way to tell someone they have a target on their back." What she asked next echoed in Cassie's mind repeatedly: "You don't want to die, do you?"

A strange heat built in her bones, suffocating her, begging for a release, an escape. It was a flaming hot rage. *Darkness.* The energy inside of her needed out, and she was going to let it . . .

And then—

"Well, well. She's awake," a deep voice boomed.

CHAPTER 4

CRYPTADIA

(N.) THINGS TO BE KEPT HIDDEN OR SECRET

Cassie shot her eyes over to the strange man now leaning against the doorway, her breath catching at the sight of him. Each wild curl of his deep brown hair whisked around his face, framing his chiseled features in the morning light as a dark stubble crowded his cheeks. She froze as the darkness inside of her simmered, recoiled, and dug itself down deep within, as though it had seen light for the first time and been burned.

"Almost thought we lost you to alcohol poisoning," the man joked. His voice sounded low and rough, as though he had just woken up himself.

"Be nice," Nyssa scolded, folding her arms.

"I'm always nice," he retorted, running his hand through his hair. "I'm Hero." His eyes then lit up in what she could only assume was amusement. "I like your shoe."

Cassie peered down at the shoe in her hand and the red dress still clinging to her from the night before. But insecurity was the last thing on her mind as she lifted

37

her chin at him. "Are *you* going to tell me what's going on here? Or will there just be more death threats?" she demanded harshly. The longer she stayed here, the more her body and mind faltered with the possibilities of what was happening to her.

"Feisty. I love it. And Art, really? Again with the death threats?" Hero rebuked as lines formed above his brows, earning an eye roll from Artemis. "You'll have to excuse my sister. She's not a fan of anything, shall we say, new."

Siblings. Cassie drew the comparisons: the same tanned olive skin, the same dark hair, and full lips. Hero seemed less frightening than his sister, however.

"Well," Nyssa interrupted, training her eyes on Cassie, "I don't suppose you know much about Greek mythology?"

"Greek mythology?" Cassie scoffed. "How does that explain *anything?*" Her jaw locked, her teeth clenching in anger. All she knew about Greek mythology came from books she had read about fantasy adventures. Fiction. *Make-believe.*

She just wanted to go home.

Hero clicked his tongue, the sleeves of his red top bunching on the sides as he crossed his arms, his large muscles peeking through the fabric like mountains. "You honestly don't know anything about our world? I always liked a good mystery."

Cassie took a deep breath, feeling intoxicatingly innocent to their questions, and that infuriated her. *What world?* The darkness from before sizzled through her veins, reminding her of its presence.

Nyssa waved Hero off and tried to get Cassie to focus on her. "It's all true. All the gods and goddesses, all the monsters and stories," Nyssa said softly, with the quiet confidence that came with telling the truth—or at least, what she believed to be true. "It was never a myth."

Cassie looked away, unable to process whatever crap they were spewing. "That's great that you believe that," she said, "but I still fail to see how this relates to me."

Nyssa peered at her. "Have you noticed anything strange happening? Maybe another *you* trying to break through?"

Cassie's stomach coiled as she shot her eyes to Nyssa. "How do you know about that?" The memory flashed back into her mind: the *darkness* staring back at her in the mirror. It had terrified her more than anything else had in her entire life.

They know.

Nyssa smiled tightly. "It's one of the few things we know about Geminis. The rest of the information was forbidden to us."

"What is that? And why do you keep referring to me as one?" Cassie asked, her words coming fast; she was desperate for any kind of clarity. Better yet, an escape. Maybe she was being human trafficked, kidnapped by a cult, or was in a super lucid dream.

With her last bit of hope, she wondered whether they'd let her go if they finished whatever sick game they wanted to play on her. Regardless, she had to be smart about her next moves.

"You're a Zodiac, like us," Nyssa answered. "We're a race of demigods gifted with special powers. What power we have is dependent on when we're born. You were born within the time frame of a Gemini." She paused briefly. "We can die and grow old, as normal humans do, but we possess a power making us greater than the typical mortal. The twelve Immortals, the Greek gods, created us through the elements of the earth, the stars, and a piece of their own power, and those powers are passed down through our bloodlines."

Cassie exhaled roughly, shaking her head. This was worse than she thought. "You expect me to believe you have powers? Like, witchy-woo powers? And that I have them too?" She took a steadying breath, trying her best to calm herself. "Just please let me go. My friend will know I'm missing, and she'll be looking for me."

Artemis smirked mournfully. "Yeah, not gonna happen. We meant it when we said it's too dangerous out there for you right now."

Cassie's jaw clenched as she glanced to the side. *What the hell did I get myself into?*

"We all have different powers," Nyssa continued. "I'm a Virgo, so I can see the possibilities of the future, which is how we found you. A few days ago, I got visions of a girl with silver hair wearing a red dress—the one you have on. And she was in danger, just as you are."

Cassie's mouth slackened as she stood straighter, pointing at the three of them accusingly. "You were *stalking* me?" She ran her free hand through her hair, panic pulsing through her body. "How am I supposed to believe any of this? You're all insane!"

Nyssa counted on her fingers as she spoke. "It was your twenty-first birthday yesterday. You were wearing a necklace in the morning, a green one, and your friend made you that dress."

Were they watching me all this time? Planning this?

"Yeah, not helping the stalker thing," Cassie scoffed as she realized just how deeply in trouble she was. And if they truly believed what they were telling her . . . If they were that crazy, what else would they do to her? She didn't even have her phone to call the police. She had nothing but her shoes and the clothes on her back.

Hero chuckled in the corner, apparently enthralled by the situation. "I'm more than happy to show you my powers later too. I wouldn't want to break anything in here, though." His nose scrunched as he stared at Cassie, and for some reason she could hardly explain, she calmed down for a second. His broad and charming smile was almost enough for her to smile back. Almost.

"Hero's powers, well . . . The power of the zodiac sign Leo is strength. He's stronger than ten men—although he pretends it's twenty." Nyssa stifled a laugh. "And Artemis over there, she's a Sagittarius. Her powers are accuracy and fighting. She can master any weapon, and where she wants said weapon to go, it will. Never misses a target."

Artemis drew her dagger from a harness on her leg and shot it across the room. It landed right in the middle of a carved flower on the wall. She flicked her eyes across to Cassie, cocking her head as if to say, *"Is that good enough for you?"*

"So, you're great at darts. So is my dad, even after a few beers," Cassie responded, lifting her hands in the air, desperate to get them to stop and let her go already. "Well, I think I'd notice if I had any powers myself, and I don't."

"We don't fully receive our powers until we're around eight or ten, but the Gemini is more complex. And if you truly had no clue about us, or something hid you from it, it could explain why your powers haven't come yet. Or there's a blockage," Nyssa said, her mouth twisting to the side as though she were trying to figure it out herself—as though any of this had a logical explanation.

"Stop! Just stop," Cassie snapped. "Please, let me go home. I'm done with this game."

Hero pushed himself off of the door with his back, his face now a perfect sonnet of seriousness. "What do you remember from last night?"

Last night . . .

"I remember you two from the club," Cassie muttered in defeat, glancing between Artemis and Nyssa. "You were looking for someone. Looking for me, I guess." Her shoulders stiffened, but she willed her chin to lift. "I remember seeing this other person in my reflection in the mirror." Her brows furrowed as she spoke. "I saw myself in the mirror, but I was different. I wasn't *me*. The last thing I knew, I was breaking the glass—"

Cassie glanced at her hands. Flashes of the glass cuts covering them came flooding back. Her eyes widened as she examined herself. All tears in her flesh were gone, as though nothing had happened—exactly as the burns from her necklace had faded on her chest and finger.

Nothing.

"My hands . . . I could have sworn . . .Wait. How long have I been asleep? What did you do to me?" Cassie accused.

Hero held up his hands innocently. "Just the night."

"It's one of the perks of being a Zodiac," Nyssa said. "We heal fast—in most cases, anyway—and at least we know that part of your power has come through. Look, we can explain what happened last night. I know it must be so scary and confusing, but we just want to help."

Cassie could only stare at them. Her mind couldn't wrap itself around any of these possibilities. They were lying; they had to be. They had fixed her wounds somehow. They had stalked her, kidnapped her, and were now forcing her to participate in their messed-up fantasy.

Hero sighed, rubbing his forehead. "Come with me," he said as Cassie locked eyes with him. "I'll show you our world. And after I do, if you still don't trust us, if you want to leave, then we'll sort it out."

Artemis began to protest, but Hero held out his hand, silencing her.

Cassie clenched her teeth as she considered his proposition. She didn't trust that they'd keep their word about letting her leave if she wanted to, but getting out of this infirmary was her priority, and being shown around would probably increase her chances of escaping.

Just a tour. I can do that. I can find a way out.

"You can even bring your shoe, if you'd like," Hero said, the grin on his face widening.

She considered throwing the shoe at his head. The only thing stopping her was that it would lessen her chances of getting out of there, and that he would most likely just dodge it.

Cassie reluctantly put down the shoe and huffed. "Fine."

CHAPTER 5

TYRO

(N.) A BEGINNER IN LEARNING ANYTHING; A NOVICE

"I'm a Leo, in case you forgot," Hero said as he strode next to Cassie. His deep voice had an edge to it, the kind that could silence a whole room with a single word. "It means I have superior strength, the best leadership abilities, and obviously, amazingly good looks." He winked at her, then moved to get ahead of her, turning around to walk backward to carry on their conversation face-to-face. His wide shoulders blocked her view as they trekked the halls of what appeared to be a big, modernized castle.

Cassie rolled her eyes, tugging at the sleeves of the sweater Nyssa had given her. "Thanks for the recap," she said sarcastically, "but maybe you need to take a second look in the mirror." She almost wanted to chuckle at his mock-offended look, his mouth open wide as he clutched his chest, head leaning back as he laughed. In truth, he was possibly the most handsome man she had ever met. The faintest of freckles decorated his olive skin, mimicking constellations on a clear night. *Celestial.* His hand slipped through his dark mess of hair, his long fingers

43

coated with some sort of black powder—soot, perhaps. But, insane or not, his ego already seemed to know how attractive he was.

"Just show me what you have to show me so I can get out of here," Cassie muttered. She couldn't help but feel like a lone star in a sea of darkness, a total stranger in a make-believe world.

Hero gave her a faint smile, and she could have sworn she saw a flicker of disappointment in his eyes. "I will."

Their eyes locked together for a brief second while she stole another look at his perfect jawline.

"Something catch your eye?" he asked, breaking Cassie out of her trance.

Her cheeks flared with warmth, annoyed with herself, yet she still found it hard to look away. So, she raised her eyebrows instead. "Nothing worth noting."

Clearly entertained by her gaze, he smirked and said, "Well, then. To continue my riveting history lesson and tour of the Arena, Zodiacs exist all over the world, but we have seven main Arenas, such as this one here in New Orleans." He gestured around the large room filled with statues. The ceiling was painted like the night sky; her fingers ached to trace each star. The entirety of the place was comparable to heaven, brimming with golden art carved into pristine white walls, and the most elegant marble she'd ever seen adorned the floors. It was astronomical.

And oddly, a part of her felt called to it, as though it were like home.

Focus, Cassie, she rebuked herself. *Look for an exit.*

"Each Arena has an academy, kind of like a boarding school. We all study the basics wherever we're brought up, and when we're around fifteen or sixteen, we get to choose where we want to go. New Orleans is where you study to become a warrior. In Greece, you study the Immortals; in Italy, you study demons and the Underworld; Japan is poisons, potions, and so on. But the main purpose of the Arenas is to guard the seven gates of the Underworld," Hero continued, "as well as keep the balance between our world and that of mortals. Demons enjoy making a run for it more often than not."

Cassie stopped dead in her tracks. "You believe in an underworld?" She didn't know how much more of their mythology references she could take.

Hero opened a large door on their right, and Cassie, despite herself, peeked inside. *A library.* One larger than she could have ever dreamed of. Her heart tugged at the towering rows of books that seemed to carry on forever, and she yearned to discover each one.

He closed the door, and she snapped to, remembering once again her current mission of finding a way home.

They continued their tour, on to another hallway, to other doors. "The Underworld exists, yes, but not the way most people believe it to be. While most of the Immortals reside above in Olympus, Hades is the ruler of the Underworld. But it isn't a scary place, it's just where people go when they die," he said nonchalantly.

Hades. She had read about him once—the god of the Underworld, death personified.

Hero opened another door for her to see, introducing it as the common room. She found it hard to believe that between their kidnapping and elaborate stories, they found time to chill out in lush seating. On her left was an ornate bar, and a large pool table stood in the middle of the room. Swords and other weapons decorated the walls, as though half for looks, and half at the ready in case of a surprise attack . . . maybe by one of those *demons* they kept mentioning.

Where the hell am I?

She took one last scan of the room, glancing at the windows, but they had yet to drop down a level to make for an easier escape.

Moving back down *another* long hallway, Hero continued explaining, "Demons spawn out of Tartarus, the most treacherous region of the Underworld, where the worst creatures are kept in solitary confinement. But parts of their souls, the greatest evils inside, turn into these animalistic beasts that not even Hades can control. So, here we are, spending our lives protecting the world." Hero paused in front of a set of double doors. Cassie tilted her head back to see exactly where the tops of the doors ended; they almost reached the ceiling.

Hero opened the brass doorknobs to reveal a kitchen, replete with the smell of fresh bread and pastries and the sound of clanging pots filling the air. He strode inside and quickly passed Cassie a napkin filled with croissants, making her stomach growl.

She paused, biting her lip as she studied the food. *What if it's poisoned?*

Noticing her hesitation, Hero took a large bite out of one himself. "We're here to save you," he said, his words muffled, "not to poison you."

Cassie considered it for a moment, and against her better judgment, she began eating. The buttery flakes melted on her tongue, crunching delicately as she took another bite . . . and another. She let the food distract her mind from the tales of demons, Hades, and other creatures she had never even fathomed—couldn't fathom—existing.

Out of nowhere, an apple landed in Hero's hand. He yelled a thank-you to the chef, a heavier man in a white apron, covered in red splatters.

Is that blood, or just sauce?

Cassie gave a small awkward smile to the chef. Hero informed her that his name was Acastus, a Libra who preferred a skillet over a sword. But Acastus didn't return her smile. Instead, his face grew cold as he shifted back to his bubbling pot.

Cassie's shoulders tightened as his reaction reminded her exactly why she needed to escape this strange captivity. Her eyes wandered around the surrounding tables as Hero spoke with Acastus, looking for anything she could arm herself with. Her gaze snagged on a small knife next to some bits of cheese. She quickly grabbed it, hiding it in the middle pouch of her sweater.

"Ready to go?" Hero asked as he spun around, jerking his head toward the door. Cassie swallowed the knot in her throat and nodded. She let him lead, wanting to get away from the coldness of Acastus—and from her racing pulse as she gripped the knife's handle.

Hero led her down a few flights of marble stairs next. *Finally.* Her heart pounded at the opportunity to escape as they descended. He began to lead her through another room, but Cassie paused at a door that didn't look like the rest.

"What's in there?" she asked.

Hero glanced her up and down. "Garage."

An exit. A way out.

Cassie nodded slowly. This place was huge, but she could find that door again. She'd have to. Wanting to divert him from the plan she was conjuring, she asked, "So, you can choose your profession here?"

"We're all encouraged to fight," Hero answered as they began to walk again. Cassie tried to memorize everything around her as they went, half listening to him speak. "But if we don't want to," he continued, "or are unable to for whatever reason, we work in other areas around the Arena—cooking, cleaning, medical care, or even making our fighting attire."

"What are you, then?" she asked, but judging by his body, she already knew.

"A fighter." Hero smirked.

She looked up at him, hoping her next words were daring enough to make him topple. "And were you all taken captive, like me?"

Hero sucked in a breath. "No," he muttered, shaking his head. "We were born here, or in other Arenas around the world." He smiled tightly. "You're the first Zodiac to not know who they are."

Cassie bit the inside of her cheek. "A Gemini . . .What does that even mean?"

"It's your zodiac sign. I forget that mortals know nothing about it. There hasn't been one in around a hundred years, which is what makes you so interesting." He paused for a moment, his eyes flicking between hers, making her dizzy. "There was no trace of you anywhere, and suddenly Nyssa starts to get visions of you . . ." He trailed off, as though lost in a memory.

"A hundred years? Sure," Cassie scoffed.

"Granted," he said, ignoring her comment as they turned a corner, "we didn't know you were a Gemini until after we saved you. We just saw someone in trouble. A girl who was one of us, but didn't know it yet."

"Is that why you're keeping me here? Because I'm a Gemini?" Cassie asked, eyebrows raised.

"Well, as much as Geminis are rare, let's say. . ." He paused again. ". . . they're also dangerous." He took a final bite of the apple, tossing the core into a trash can.

Dangerous. Do these people really think I'm dangerous?

She thought back to the chef's stony response. Back to Artemis's cold demeanor, to Nyssa's padded words. Cassie felt a lump forming in the back of her throat as her hand grazed the handle of the knife in her pocket.

Above all, she didn't want to be in a position to be saved. She didn't want to be dangerous, to be feared. But maybe that could be an advantage in getting the hell out of here.

"If I'm so dangerous," she countered, "why humor me today with this tour? Why not just kill me right now?"

Hero froze, staring at her in absolute disbelief. "Because it wouldn't be right. Others may disagree, but I'm not killing someone innocent over a possibility of what they might become."

"And what might I become?" Cassie asked, defiant. She wondered how far they were going to take this game of theirs, and how much longer she'd have to play along.

"The Gemini has a dark side," Hero said as he continued walking. "More of a dark twin, I guess. It—"

Cassie gasped as the sharp clanking of swords sparked her attention away. Her fingers instinctively curled around her knife.

They came upon a circular room, filled with people fighting—training, she realized. Each movement appeared almost choreographed, swords swinging at the same time in opposite directions, blocking each other with perfection. A dance. Tall pillars supported the glass-domed ceiling, which cast light into every corner.

The sound of running water, like harsh rainfall on a cloudy day, and the smell of salt and musk filled the room. The source was a fountain at the room's center spouting turquoise water. The stone was covered in markings she had never seen before, the lines connecting gracefully with each other, like musical notes flowing into a melody. But these were symbols—runes, perhaps—ones she found herself wanting to write a sonnet about. *"A transparency forged in battle,"* she'd call it.

Cassie yelped as her attention was drawn to one of the fighters, a petite blonde woman who disappeared into a cloud of green smoke—only to reappear moments later behind her opponent, striking him in the back with her elbow. He fell with a grunt onto the mat beneath him.

Cassie couldn't believe her eyes. How had she done that?

Oh my god. It can't be possible . . .

Hero's voice rang in her ears as his body moved up behind hers. "She's a Taurus, so she can teleport. They can also create portals," he explained, his breath warm against her neck, but she focused on his words.

Teleportation. Holy fuck.

Droplets rose from the fountain, defying the rules of gravity, coagulating to create a larger mass. The liquid shot across the room, knocking the Taurus woman on her side. She gasped as she sat up, her whole body soaked, and disappeared into the ground in a flurry of emerald, this time not returning. The whole occurrence was outside of Cassie's entire understanding of the way the universe worked.

Another woman's arms lit up with flames, her skin cracking underneath, yet it seemed to cause her no pain. She shot a fireball at a girl, who blocked it with a shield she had created with her hand.

It's real.

CHAPTER 6

MONACHOPSIS

(N.) THE SUBTLE BUT PERSISTENT FEELING OF BEING
OUT OF PLACE

Cassie could only blink, taking in what was right in front of her eyes, something she could no longer deny. It was real, this entire world outside of her own, with demigods who possessed fantastical powers, and myths that were never really myths.

"Drones?" she asked, the logical side of her brain arguing back.

"Nope."

"I'm hallucinating, then."

"Again, nope."

"You—you've been telling the truth?" Cassie muttered her half-question, half-statement to herself. "This whole thing, everything that's been happening to me, is because of this world? And I'm one of you?"

Hero dipped his head. "Yes. I'm sorry you had to find out this way, but—"

50

"Stamos!" the Zodiac with the water ability yelled as he jogged toward them, interrupting their conversation. His cobalt-blue eyes flashed in great contrast to his dark skin, but then his eyes changed into a deep brown.

Hero lifted his chin. The two men met together with a complicated handshake she couldn't follow, ending with a hug and a pat on the back. They were around the same height, both towering over her.

"This the girl from last night?" the newcomer panted. Cassie detected a hint of a British accent, the words flowing out as though he were a real-life Mr. Darcy. He smiled at her. "Nice to see you awake." Beads of sweat dripped down his forehead, staining his gray shirt as his hands rested on his hips.

"This is her, alright," Hero said. "Cassie, meet Titus. He was on the mission with us to save you."

Cassie's mouth opened, but no words came out. How could she thank a guy for saving her from being eaten by a demon? The fact that demons even existed was still something she had to process, along with, well, everything else. Finally, because the silence between them was almost deafening, she muttered a simple, "Thank you."

Hero looked around before pulling Titus in closer. "You were too busy this morning to hear the brief, but . . ." His voice dropped to a whisper. *"She's a Gemini."*

Titus stepped back, his shoulders rising with the news. His face grew dark and cold, his nostrils flaring, his entire expression changing in a millisecond. *Fury.* "A Gemini!" he yelled. "What the fuck are you thinking, showing her off, parading her around? Don't you know what she's capable of?" he spat. "Not to mention, she's illegal!"

Her throat closed as she struggled to even breathe. Her body solidified into cement, unable to move, unable to speak.

Illegal . . . ?

The room spun around her, threatening to knock her free of the earth's axis.

"Keep your voice down," Hero growled at Titus.

"What if this is a game to her, playing the dumb, helpless girl, waiting for our rescue—and a welcoming invitation straight into our home?" Titus hissed.

Under his gaze, Cassie felt like an abomination.

"She didn't even know this world existed until today," Hero said, poking his index finger into Titus's chest, making him wobble back.

Cassie hadn't begun to understand what she was, what a Gemini truly was, or how this world had existed for so long in secret—and how she was somehow a part of it. Hero's words crystallized in her mind, frosting over like a cold day: "*As much as the Geminis are rare, let's say, they're also dangerous.*" But how could someone who didn't even know her be filled with so much hatred toward her? Her eyes stung with a mixture of anger and confusion as heat filled her cheeks. A force inside of her begged to be released. *Darkness.*

Her hands unclenched, and she could already feel where her fingernails had embedded into her palms. Cassie's jaw ached as her body loosened, pushing down the rage inside of her with each inhale. It wasn't her. *Is that the darkness? Is that why they fear me?*

Cassie backed away, blinded as her feet guided her before she turned in one swift movement. Still arguing, Hero and Titus didn't seem to notice as she slipped out of the door and back into the hallway.

She couldn't handle this. She didn't even know where she was going, but she had to leave.

Hearing Hero's frantic voice behind her, Cassie ducked into a small room with a few chairs and some art hanging on the walls, memories frozen in time, waiting to tell their stories.

Her escape plan could still work, even if she had no idea where she was, but her mind was in turmoil. The Zodiacs knew what was wrong with her, and they had shown her solid proof of their world. If she genuinely was dangerous—if they had told the truth about that too—would she be doing the right thing by running and hiding? Or should she stay, and fight to rid herself of the darkness inside of her—if that was even possible?

Her shoulders tightened as footsteps rushed up behind her.

Hero caught up with her within seconds. "I'm sorry about him," he said. "He's been through a lot, and it doesn't help that he's such a hothead—"

Cassie cut him off, turning on her heel to face him. "I don't need your excuses," she seethed. "What did he mean by 'illegal'? What aren't you telling me?" The words cut through her teeth like a saw on bricks.

He released a loud sigh, casting a sideways glance. "I was trying to tell you before we were interrupted. We don't know much about the Gemini. About you," he explained, his hand rubbing the back of his neck. "It's kind of a touchy subject, as you can tell. All I know for sure is that you have a dark side, and if that side comes out, terrible stuff could happen . . . hence the illegal part. But I promise we'll protect you."

The mirror, the woman in the reflection, the one that was me but wasn't . . . That was my dark side? And how bad can it be for them to make my entire existence illegal?

Cassie realized that if she escaped, it would be for her own selfish reasons. If who she was, if that evil hiding inside of her was as dangerous as everyone made it out to be, she couldn't just leave. At least, not for good . . .

Her shoulders slumped.

"Look," Hero said in an understanding tone, "you must be tired, and I'm sure we've overwhelmed you with enough information to last a lifetime." His lips disappeared into a fine line. "Why don't I show you to your room, so you can get some rest?"

Her head shot up. "My room?" She blinked in disbelief. *This is my life now, isn't it?*

"It's the one safe option right now. This place is hidden from anyone who isn't a Zodiac. We all live here, unless we have family houses, missions abroad, or have been excommunicated," he explained. "Our academy also has boarding houses on the grounds. But for now, the Arena is your home too. These walls will keep you safe—as will we."

She was shocked to feel like she believed him, this stranger she'd only met an hour or so ago, but everything else he'd said had been the truth thus far.

Hero cleared his throat, his expression growing uncomfortable. "Now that word has gotten out about you, there will be people looking for the Gemini—well, for you—everywhere. It might not be ideal, but I hope you choose to stay here, for your own safety and others'." His honest expression suggested that he grasped how much she would be expected to give up. "But, as I promised, if you wish to leave after knowing all of this, I can talk to someone and try to find a solution."

"I think I have to stay," she muttered. "I don't want this *other* person inside of me. I don't want to be dangerous."

Hero gazed at her as though he were truly sorry for her situation. But if everything they said were true—which she saw with her own eyes *was* true—the alternative was much, much darker.

Cassie didn't have a choice. She could leave, and be taken by demons or other creatures she didn't even want to consider, allowing her darkness to take over like it'd been trying to do all day. Or she could stay and become a Zodiac, or whatever the hell they wanted her to be, and fight to fix this curse within herself. But by staying, she would be abandoning everything. It meant no more Quinn, no more college, no more of her *life*. At least, not for the time being. She couldn't even bring herself to worry about what it would mean for her father.

Guilt built inside her—guilt for already falling in silent awe of this world, with how glorious and divine and ethereal this place appeared. She wanted to discover every corner of this so-called "Arena," learn all about what other creatures lived in the shadows, whatever powers she might have herself . . .

But above all, these strangers might know how to help her. They knew she wasn't going crazy—even if they had sounded crazy themselves at first. She pushed down the side of her that wanted to run and never look back.

Still, she knew she needed to do something about her life before all of this festered, and Cassie couldn't decide whether to trust Hero with that yet.

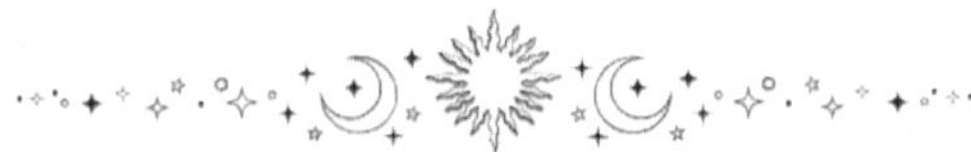

The halls seemed to go on forever. It was odd to her how such a vast and wonderful building could be kept from humans for this long. How no one knew about any of the Zodiacs astounded her to no end.

Maybe they have magic to hide it, but where is this place, anyway? It can't be in the city, can it? How far from home am I?

Hero stopped at a set of metal doors and pressed a button on the wall. Cassie's lips parted. The last thing she'd expected here was an elevator. They got in, and an awkward silence lingered as the elevator beeped through a few floors, finally pausing at the sixth floor. The doors opened on a circular vestibule with several long hallways sprouting out from it.

"We're down there," Hero said, tilting his head to the right.

"'We?'"

"Yeah. We room and work in teams, or groups of up to eleven. Nyssa, Artemis, Titus, Elijah, and I live in this quarter. You'll meet Eli soon. He's probably off doing something he shouldn't be." He chuckled to himself. "And now you'll be here too, in your own bedroom, of course." He led her down the corridor, stopping at the third door on the left. "We figured it would be best if you stayed with us for the time being, since we're the ones who found you and all."

Cassie paused, taking it in. "I guess it makes sense. I doubt that guy, Titus, will be pleased with that, though."

Hero shrugged. "He'll get over it. But don't let him get in your way. He's . . . well, you know."

Cassie nodded as if she did know, but in truth, she was an outsider peering in on the entire conversation, as though Hero was talking to anyone else—a friend who knew all of it, someone who could laugh along with him and make witty retorts. It was a feeling she knew all too well, and one she'd experienced many times in her life. Maybe one day she'd be able to join in on the joke, but for now, all she could do was stare at the door in front of her.

A meow sounded from inside the room, along with faint scratching against the doorframe. Hero opened the door, and a white cat squeezed through before sprawling itself across his feet. "Morning, Bones." Hero beamed, bending to stroke him. He peered up at Cassie. "This little one wandered in yesterday, not long before you did. I named him, but he seems to prefer this room over mine—the traitor."

The slim, white cat had piercing sapphire eyes, and Cassie could have sworn for a second there were galaxies in them. She crouched down to scratch Bones on the chin. "Well, at least there's someone else here as clueless as I am," she mused. A sad smile crept across her face.

"Big day, a bedroom and a cat," Hero joked, standing before offering her a hand.

Cassie stood, ignoring Hero's polite gesture, and investigated the room. It was larger than anything she had ever lived in before, and it didn't help that it looked like it belonged to someone else. The deep purple walls were carved with intricate detail, and a large bed rested in the middle of the room against the far wall, covered in pink and blue blankets. A circular rug filled most of the floor, the marble peeking out around the edges. An unlit fireplace sat opposite the bed, but the large television hanging above it was most out of place. It was as though she were standing in a mix between a castle and a hotel room, a fusion of past and present. It was truly luscious, filled with emotion, passion, and a sense of self. But it wasn't *her*.

A painting hung above the white headboard. Beautiful, dark colors danced across the canvas, in blues, blacks, and whites. A crescent moon lay on one side, with a young woman with her arms around a white wolf on the other. It felt protective, loving, and sad all at once. Cassie spotted the name *Hawthorne* scribbled at the bottom.

"This painting . . . A Zodiac did it?" she asked softly.

Hero's attention focused on the work of art. "The Hawthornes were one of the most prominent Zodiac lines. The man who painted this died decades ago, though."

Cassie studied the brushstrokes from afar, how violent yet delicate they were. "Was this his room?"

"No," Hero answered. "This room belonged to Josephine Reyes. I found an old diary of hers once. She spoke about the man who painted it. I think they were lovers." He cleared his throat. "Anyway, I assume he painted this for her. No one has ever had the heart to tear it down." He spoke as though he were saddened by it too. "She was the last permanent occupant of this room. She moved to the Hawthorne Manor in the late 1920s, I believe. They upgraded most of the room, but please feel free to redecorate however you want, or to remove any of her old belongings. It *is* yours now. For however long you'd like it to be."

Cassie took in more details of the room, trying to decide for herself if she would even want to put the effort into making it hers, or if she just wanted this to be a temporary home. She'd never been more conflicted, never felt the tug of two separate lives so deeply.

A gust of wind blew a white curtain through the open French doors that led outside. Cassie walked out onto a balcony, the smell of fresh-cut grass filling her nose, the view unlike anything she had seen before. If she could name this moment using one word, it would be *serendipity*—the beauty in finding something you weren't even looking for. The green stretched as far as she could see, marking the fact that they were definitely not anywhere near the city or anything she knew. Her chest hollowed as she realized she would have no chance of making it back to Quinn without help.

"Best part about this place," Hero mused, "are the views."

Cassie glanced back into the room at Hero squinting in the sun, holding out a glass of water. She walked back in and took the drink from him, the cool taste all she needed at the moment, her body being dehydrated with the whirlwind day she'd encountered after a night of drinking, along with the knowledge of powers and mythology and darkness she was still trying to wrap her head around.

A large white dresser that curved along the sides caught her attention next, her heart racing at the sight of the wide golden mirror hanging above it. Her footsteps were careful at first, hesitant—until her entire body became entrapped in her reflection. Her breath caught in her throat. Cassie saw the clearest picture yet of what she'd expected: her *dark side* stared back at her with a smile as sharp as a dagger. The violet eyes shone like wellsprings of power, seeping into her veins. Darkness danced around her, consuming her, taking her away deeper into the shadows.

Slipping.

It took all that Cassie had to pull herself out.

"I don't know if I'll ever get used to this," she uttered, her gaze fixing on a golden brush resting on the table instead.

Hero walked over to the mirror, peering around. "I've never seen anything like it before," he whispered.

"Yeah. It's creepy," she stated, swallowing the knot in her throat as she walked out of view.

Her hand went to the base of her neck, a habit of hers, touching the spot where her necklace used to hang. She hated it being gone, as though a piece of her were gone as well—seared off of her forever.

And then it clicked. *A chain reaction.*

"My necklace!" she gasped, turning around to face Hero. "I had this necklace my mother gave me before she died. I never took it off—but yesterday, it burned me."

"It *burned* you?" His brows knitted together.

Cassie nodded slowly. "Do you think it had anything to do with why I could only see this world yesterday and never before?"

Hero scratched his head, peering around the room. "It could be. It might be the source of a blocking spell from a witch? But I've never heard of it burning someone before. I'll look into it."

Cassie coughed, choking on her own spit. "Witches? As in, like, magical women casting spells?"

Hero's eyebrows lifted as he smiled. "Well, kind of. First of all, any gender can be a witch, and yep, all that casting spells and voodoo stuff. Zodiacs and witches have a long history of helping each other. If they need a creature killed, we do it. If we need some wards or a spell, they do it."

Witches. Another real supernatural force. If only Quinn were here, she'd love to know all about the witches and about the Zodiacs . . . about *her*. She had to get back to Quinn, at least to say goodbye and offer some sort of explanation.

Cassie found an opportunity and took it. "My necklace is back at my apartment," she said, trying to stop her voice from wavering, testing the waters.

"It can stay there for now. I can send someone to go get it when it's less dangerous," Hero said, his expression cool and casual. "Well, we have some food and water on the table, and the bathroom is through that door if you want to shower." He gestured to a closed door on the right of the dressing table. "And if you need anything else, I'm sure we can accommodate you. Take as much time as you need for yourself, and I'll come and check on you in a bit." He smiled sympathetically at her before reaching for the door handle.

Cassie knew this was her chance. "You said if I wanted an out, I could have one, right?" she asked as he was halfway out the door. She could see his muscles tense through the back of his shirt.

He turned toward her, his expression softer than she'd expected. "Yes. I did."

Even if she didn't want to admit it, she needed his help. If he refused, she'd find another way. It was risky, but it was worth it, and she knew if she was ever going to fix what was going on with her, she had to stay close to the Zodiacs. But she had to do this one thing first.

"I need to get out of here."

CHAPTER 7

THANTOPHOBIA

(N.) THE PHOBIA OF LOSING SOMEONE YOU LOVE

The seconds moved like raindrops hitting a windowpane.

Cassie watched as Hero's throat bobbed, his body stiffening as he shut the door behind him. The latch made a faint sound as it closed them together in the room.

"What do you mean, you need to get out of here?" he asked, his words remaining smooth. Yet his eyes flared, on guard—a true soldier.

It was no use lying to him, not when she needed him for this. She knew they were far away from the city center, and she barely knew New Orleans as it was.

"I'm not going for good, but I just want a day," she explained, pacing the room. With each step, a new worry came to mind, begging to be thrown out of her mouth. "When I woke up yesterday, all my problems revolved around switching colleges and lying to my dad about it. Now I'm a part of this secret world I know nothing about, and I'm supposed to leave everything behind?" She turned to face Hero, pleading for him to understand. "I see that your world truly exists now, and that I'm some dangerous part of it. But I moved here just weeks ago to be with my best friend and start my new life. How am I meant to live here? I need my own clothes, my own stuff." She stared down at Nyssa's sweater, and then she reached her fingers to her neck. "I need my necklace back. It was the last thing my mother ever gave me." She blinked away the tears threatening to fall. "I don't even have my phone to call and explain to anyone." She wanted to talk to her father, just to hear his voice. *Dad . . .* Her heart raced like a stampede of wild animals running through her. *What would he think of all this?*

Hero's fingers caught in his unruly hair, tugging at the ends. "We would never ask you to give it all up. And we won't hold you hostage if you truly want to go. We're just trying to keep you safe." He crossed his arms, leaning back on the door. "But we can get you a phone, and the closet is full of clothes. I'm sure Nyssa can pick out some more for you. And like I said, I can send one of the Zodiacs to get your personal belongings when it's safe to do so."

"You have a solution for everything!" she exclaimed, throwing her arms in the air. "And what about my roommate, Quinn?" Cassie had her mind set on getting out of here, to say goodbye and to get her stuff, whether Hero liked it or not. "She's been my best friend since I can remember. I *can't* just disappear," she huffed. It was too much—too big of an ask, too big of a sacrifice not to see her.

Hero glanced to the side. "If you wanted to leave for good, I would have planned something more elaborate. But leaving for a few hours is dangerous, especially with the demons on your trail," he said. Then he sighed. "As hard as it might be, Quinn is one of the people you *should* leave behind. You have to think about your safety *and* hers. Mortals don't belong in this world."

There was that word again: *dangerous.* But she would never put Quinn in any danger, and if it truly was that unsafe, wouldn't checking up on her be the better option, to make sure with her own eyes that she was okay?

"No," Cassie stated as plainly as she could, glaring at him with her mouth clenched.

His eyebrows disappeared under his curls as though no one had ever undermined him until now. "Excuse me?"

"I said no. She's not a *thing* I can toss aside. I'm going to see her." She'd see Quinn no matter what, even if she had to sneak out and walk for days. Quinn meant so much to her, and Cassie didn't even want to imagine leaving her behind—not when Hero kept throwing the word "dangerous" around like it was nothing.

Hero shook his head, rubbing his hand against his right eye. "I saved your life just last night, and now you want to go on a suicide mission?"

She crossed her arms. "If you want me to be a part of your weird fight club, these are the terms and conditions."

Hero let out a low grunt, his face scrunching in inner turmoil. "You won't even be able to tell her anything."

Cassie's eyes widened. "I know, and I won't. Just please, come with me. You gave me an out, and I'm not using it, but this is what I want instead." She had him on the cusp of agreeing; she wasn't backing down now.

He sighed loudly. "We'd have to be quick . . ."

Cassie felt the weight of this new world lifting off her as she regained control of an aspect of her life for the first time all day. She also smiled at him for the first time.

The corners of Hero's own mouth pulled up. "I'll get geared up, and we'll go. But tell no one about this," he warned, pointing his finger at her. Once she nodded, he turned, his muscled back rippling as he opened the door, and he glanced quickly from side to side before walking out.

Cassie exhaled deeply as she spun back around to face the room. She meant what she'd promised to Hero: she'd come back. If she was as dangerous as they all made her out to be, she had to.

Opening the wooden doors of the closet, she spotted fresh clothes folded on the shelves, not one item out of place or wrinkled—probably Nyssa's doing. But her attention caught on the other side, where older dresses hung on a rusted rod, and she noted the bursts of silver beads and jewels lining a short and sleeveless dress—a flapper dress. It appeared straight out of a novel she'd read repeatedly to satisfy a potent fascination with the roaring twenties. Cassie ran her fingers lightly over the endless beads . . .

Music faded in. The melody of a piano mixing with the blare of a trumpet consumed her, slowly, then all at once. Dancers rushed past her, laughing as they floated around in their partners' arms. The air was warm, filled with life and *fun*. She spun around, the dress she'd touched moments ago now on her own body, flowing off her as she marveled at the yellow glowing lights, the curtains draped around the room, the sounds of men yelling in triumph and women singing with glee.

Her eyes caught on a man. He was stunningly handsome, his hair a swooping softness of light auburn, his crooked smile shining at her, as though he had waited all his life to see her again.

Suddenly, coldness erupted inside of her. A shiver crawled up her spine, working its way to her teeth until they chattered. The music stopped, and the room emptied within seconds, everyone disappearing as though they had never been there at all—ghosts of a past she'd never lived. Her heart ached so deep that her hand flung to her chest, grasping as she gasped for breath. The pain of loss, of guilt stung her body. Venom seemed to course through her veins. She flinched.

Then it all went away. Cassie blinked herself back to reality, back to her own body, her own mind, her hand no longer touching the dress. Her eyes flicked to the painting Hero had told her about, trying to remember the name of the woman who had once lived in this room. It must have been her dress.

Cassie's fingers trembled. It was as though she had peered into another life, another time, into that woman's life. What she'd done, what she'd felt didn't seem possible. It couldn't be possible, right? Then again, everything that had happened in the past twenty-four hours had seemed unimaginable at first.

But she had to reset her mind to the task at hand: getting out of here so that she could see Quinn. She could deal with whatever had just happened to her at a later time, when she had the space to process it.

Pulling out some clothes from the closet, she came across a black leather top with cropped sleeves and a high neckline—one that was in her size. She slipped it on, along with a pair of dark cargo pants, and a pair of combat boots that miraculously fit.

What, did they take my measurements while I was asleep?

Shaking her head, she reached for the small knife still tucked in Nyssa's sweater, placing it in one of the side pockets of her pants just in case. Even if she didn't use it—and she certainly hoped she wouldn't have to—it still gave her a sense of control.

Cassie took one last glimpse in the mirror, slightly flinching at her dark side reflecting back at her. She had to return and figure out how to get rid of it for good.

Bones sat up from his nap on the bed, stretching out his body across the blanket, as though teasing her, telling her to stay inside and just rest.

She closed the door behind her.

CHAPTER 8

PARASTIN

(V.) TO PROTECT; TO KEEP SAFE

H ero spun a pair of keys on his finger as he led them down a flight of stairs, the air turning cooler and mustier with each step. "I told the others I ordered pizza. Hopefully, that'll divert them away from us and into the dining hall. *We'll* go to the garage," he explained. "I usually prefer motorcycles, but we're going to need something a little less conspicuous, so I stole the keys to Elijah's Jeep."

"You guys can order pizza here?" Cassie asked, her stomach grumbling. The croissants from that morning felt like a long time ago.

Hero paused, stopping mid-step. "That's what you took from that?"

Cassie frowned, a thought popping into her mind. "Quinn and I always order pizza and two milkshakes, one strawberry and one chocolate. It's a tradition we've had every Saturday since we were little." She smiled at the memory, but her sadness remained.

Will I ever see Quinn again after today?

Hero cleared his throat, eyebrows raising. "Again, that's what you took from that?"

Cassie huffed. "Well, I guess I assumed you'd keep this place a little more . . . hidden? Sounds like any delivery boy can just waltz in here."

"It *is* hidden. A powerful witch cast a spell on it to make it look like an abandoned office building. It confuses the mortals—but we tip them generously."

Witches, she remembered. She'd had a fascination with them when she was a child, a sense of familiarity, like an old friend. But back then, it was all fake—a bedtime story her mom would tell. At least now she had an explanation as to why no one knew about this place or the Zodiacs.

The stairs led them to the basement. Hero flipped a switch, and one by one, rows of lights flared to life, showcasing an expensive-looking line of vehicles and motorbikes. Duly impressed, Cassie walked down the line, her steps echoing off the walls as she admired the sleek SUVs and sports cars. Hero explained that the Zodiacs were *extremely* into their transportation methods—when they didn't use portals to get around, of course.

Obviously.

"How do you afford all of these?" Cassie marveled, her hand gliding over the glossy finish of a large motorcycle. She wondered what it would be like to ride one, the wind whipping through her hair, flirting with death at each turn . . .

Hero appeared beside her, gripping the handlebar. Cassie noticed a sword resting at his side, along with a selection of small daggers. She gulped. The knife she'd stolen seemed so *weak* compared to his weapons.

"When the Immortals created us, they also gifted us with an eternity of gold—a universal currency that can be converted at any time. Each Arena has a vault containing the gold, and we all get a monthly payment, like with any job." Hero spoke as though it were the most normal thing in the world, reminding her of just how clueless she remained—how she belonged, yet didn't, all at once.

She scoffed. "Oh, yeah, because all jobs have a vault with heaps of gold." Then another realization dawned on her: she might never have a career, or even finish her degree with this new life. Any ounce of normalcy, any hopes and dreams she'd had—*gone*. The thought made her sick.

"You know what I mean." Hero walked over to a bright red Jeep and climbed in, making the vehicle wobble. In stark contrast to the others, it was riddled with imperfections. "This is our ride for the day. Just never tell Elijah we did this, or he'll light my room on fire again."

"Your secret's safe with me," she muttered as she hopped in, still half-lost in the abyss of her mind. A room being set on fire was the least crazy thing she had heard all day.

The garage doors rolled up as the car's engine revved to life. Cassie squinted as light powered through the exit to the outside world, her heart pounding in her chest.

As they drove away, she peered out the window, taking in the view of the labyrinthine building they called the Arena for the first time. Nothing she'd seen before could compare. It looked like an old castle—historic and aged over the years, built with stone, and carved into shapes, patterns, and symbols of nobility or royalty. The structure was dressed in lush green vines of ivy and hanging plants spilling over the flat roof. Rounded walls flanked all sides of the building, and Cassie recognized one by its glass-domed rooftop: the training room. She now grasped just how much more of the Arena she had yet to explore. And as much as it terrified her, she also felt a quiver of excitement.

The ambrosial gardens went on for miles, it seemed, with tranquil ponds and gazebos dotting the surrounding forest. And then, in an instant, it all disappeared. Suddenly, Cassie was gazing at an old, run-down office building, the dull façade masking the castle's true identity. She sat back in her seat, completely awed.

"So, what drew you to New Orleans?" Hero asked as they entered the city—twenty minutes away from the Arena, she marked. It seemed wrong somehow now, the mundanity of driving, which had always been one of Cassie's favorite things to do before . . .

She cleared her throat. "I don't know exactly why, but I've always had a fascination with this place," she said, recalling the countless arguments she'd had with her dad about leaving California. "So, I applied to the university's summer program a few months ago. It seemed like fate when I was accepted and asked to carry out my final year here too, since my best friend moved to New Orleans after high school. And now, here *I* am, a few weeks in . . . and I have to leave her."

Just yesterday, she'd wanted a life here so bad that she'd lied to her father about it. But she couldn't go back and just continue that life as though nothing had happened. The person who wanted that life had changed the moment she was brought into the Zodiac's world and told that she was deadly enough to be feared by warriors with magical powers.

Hero sounded genuinely contrite as he said, "I'm sorry, Cassie. Truly. But you're making the right decision. It's not safe."

"I know. I just haven't figured out how to tell her that yet." Cassie sighed, leaning on the cold window. "Thank you, for coming with me."

Hero chuckled. "Well, it was either that, or watch you try and find a way out yourself."

Cassie's eyes widened in fake innocence, and Hero laughed even more. "Your poker face is terrible," he said. "I mean, did you really think you could make it all the way through a city you barely know, without any directions, water, or method of transportation? And not even a high heel to defend yourself with." He smirked knowingly at her.

She rolled her eyes, the sides of her lips curling slyly. *And the knife I stole . . .* "It was worth a shot," she said. But an odd feeling she couldn't quite place entered her as his words registered. He had known what she was going to do all along, yet he did nothing to stop it. He would have let her leave, or at least attempt to leave.

"What about you?" she asked after a long pause, wanting to draw the conversation elsewhere. "How long have you lived in New Orleans?"

Hero straightened himself in his seat. "Me? I've been here all my life. I've traveled to the other Arenas, and wherever they need me to go, but New Orleans has always been and always will be my home." His words had a weight to them—something *more* that he wasn't giving up.

Before she could ask him about it, the light blue townhouse Cassie had grown so fond of came into view. It was a bit run-down from the outside, with the chipped paint and the half-dead plants flopping out of their pots. She and Quinn had managed to fix the inside of their place by finding cheap furniture and decor online over the past few weeks. It wasn't anything much, but it was becoming home.

Cassie's stomach knotted as they parked on the street. Her heart sank; she knew this could be the last time she would ever be here again. But she vowed to make sure it wouldn't be the last time she'd ever see her friend again. She practiced what she would tell Quinn as she sat in the car, unable to move until she rehearsed it once more. *"My dad found out and is making me move back. I'll still be able to text and call, but I won't be able to visit for a while."* Her lies twisted themselves into spiderwebs, delicate and breakable, intricate and spiraled.

Cassie opened the door, a wave of heat washing over her. She and Hero crossed the street in silence, the uneven cobblestones making her ankles wobble.

The stairs were creaky and old, made of wood that must have been around even before the gods the Zodiacs spoke of. Each step she took was one closer to leaving the life she loved behind, and one closer to entering the great unknown.

Hero grabbed her by the arm, his touch soft like a warm blanket as he stopped her from reaching the door. "Mortals can't see our world, so our weapons and our powers are all hidden from their sight," he said, his hand now grazing over his sword and the string of daggers attached to his harness. "But even so, we should get in and out of here fast, in case any demons come sniffing for you."

Cassie nodded, biting her lip as she twisted the brass door handle to the right. Quinn always kept the door unlocked during the daytime. She said, *"An open home feels like home."* The latch clicked, sliding open, and the smell of her cinnamon candle filled her nose. For a second, Cassie let herself close her eyes and forget.

When she opened them again, she saw Quinn's hair bouncing from behind their gray couch as she whipped around. She jumped up and rushed toward Cassie, her socks slipping on the hardwood floor on the way over.

"Oh my god!" Quinn yelled as she enveloped Cassie in a hug. "I thought something had happened to you! Are you alright? Why didn't you come ho—" She stopped, peering around Cassie's shoulder, lifting her eyebrows as she gazed at Hero. "Well, now I see what kept you so busy!" she added, letting go and taking a step back. "And I guess I did have your phone after I took that photo . . . But I swear to God, you should have told me before you pranced off with some guy! I was just about to call the cops!"

Cassie shifted on her feet, avoiding eye contact with Hero as she cleared her throat. "No, it's not like that. He's a . . . friend, I guess."

Hero smiled, the picture of politeness as he dipped his head. He moved forward into the apartment, turning his body to the side to pass by them, his shoulders stiff.

"That's Hero," Cassie said as he picked through some books on the shelf, examining them. "I should have told you—I'm sorry. I got wasted, and his sister and her friend found me and took me to their place until I sobered up." The air burned in her lungs as she prepared herself, ignoring the way Quinn's eyes were widening already, her face paling as she stared at Hero. Cassie reminded herself that she couldn't see his weapons. "Listen, I have to tell you something, and it's not easy to say. My dad found ou—"

Cassie's voice was drowned out by the bay windows shattering into a million glittering fragments. Within seconds, her shoulder slammed onto the hard floor as her other arm wrapped around Quinn's body, holding her tight. Her head shot toward their broken windows, her stomach dropping at the three dark figures standing in their living room, cloaked in black material, their faces hidden and long swords at their sides.

Quinn's shriek filled her ears, and Cassie knew she'd messed up. The weight of her actions crashed down on her as fast as these *things* crashed through her living room. Hero had told her the demons looked animalistic, but these were more like people, a different threat.

And they all fixed their attention on her.

Hero threw himself between Cassie and the figures out of what she assumed was sheer protective instinct, his sword drawing out of his harness with a slight scraping sound. Three against one, but Cassie favored his odds, especially if she believed Nyssa's words about Hero's strength.

"Get out of here!" Hero yelled back at the girls while swinging his sword around, challenging their own long, thin blades. The iron weapons clashed together.

It wasn't safe anymore.

It never was.

Cassie scanned the room, her stomach twisting when she saw that the front door was blocked by one of those *things,* and she scrambled to her feet, pulling Quinn's shaking body along with her toward the kitchen and slamming the door shut. She tried her best to ignore the violent sounds coming from the living room. Each crash was like a dagger stabbing into her, a piece of her old life being ripped away.

Small slashes from the broken glass decorated Quinn's face, her eyes wide and vacant. Cassie couldn't stop the tears from streaming down her own cheeks. She wanted to tell Quinn how sorry she was, that this was all her fault, but the words wouldn't come out.

The gleaming kitchen knives caught her eye, reminding Cassie of the one hidden in her pocket. She grabbed it, as well as the larger one from the knife block. Hands shaking, she pointed them toward the door, ready to protect Quinn from her mistakes, ready to protect herself with everything she had.

The door crashed open, and a masked figure strode in.

Cassie glanced at Quinn, pressed against the wall, filled with terror. "Trust Hero," she said firmly to Quinn. Then she lunged forward, knives out, but the attacker's sword flashed out, slashing against the metal of her own feeble weapons. The knives clattered to the tiled floor.

The figure reached out for Cassie, gripping her throat. Her feet lifted from the floor, her entire body suspended in the air as she grappled with the hand crushing her airway, blocking each scream from escaping. Her body jolted as she scratched and kicked to no avail.

All the air was leaving her body, her legs losing their power. She couldn't breathe. She couldn't . . .

It can't end like this.

A sudden adrenaline rush had her kicking her legs up and into the cloaked figure's abdomen with all her might. They rolled to the floor, Cassie gaining the upper hand. She grabbed hold of the mask, ripping it off in one swift motion as the grip on her own neck loosened.

It was a girl.

Her red hair floated across her pale and freckled face, her vibrant green eyes staring into Cassie's. Desperate and crying, she couldn't have been more than a teenager. Each moment this girl lived clearly pained her, as though she hated who she was.

Instinct took over Cassie's body as her muscles loosened. She couldn't fight a child.

But the girl's eyes suddenly flooded with onyx, and she pushed Cassie off her and back against the wall. She grabbed Cassie by the locks of her hair, pulling her upwards, taking full advantage of her empathy. She'd tricked her.

Pain lanced through every crevice of Cassie's body as her head hit the kitchen table. Her eyelids fell heavily, the noise of the fight fading away.

CHAPTER 9

KADOTA

(V.) TO DISAPPEAR, VANISH; TO BE LOST

There were too many of them.

They kept coming through the windows, rolling inside to fight him faster than he could kill or injure them. Hero had lost track of Cassie and Quinn; all he could do was hope they were safe.

The Seekers piled on one by one, Hero's muscles burning as he fought them off. Two more charged at him, and a third walked up to him menacingly, sliding a sword out of the leather sheath on its hip. The cold metal brushed against the thin skin of his throat as he tilted his head back, clenching his jaw.

A scream sounded from somewhere in the apartment.

Cassie.

A spark of power surged through his body, filling his very being. His veins pulsed as he flung the Seekers off him. Hero walked over to where his sword lay, flicking it upward with his foot, and then he plunged the weapon into a Seeker, watching as it vanished from beneath him. A dagger flew at him, and he leaned back, catching it by the handle in mid-air. He sprinted across the room, slashing the weapon across his attacker's neck, blood spurting out onto the floor as the body and all remnants of it dissolved. And with it, several of the others disappeared too. Hero's brows furrowed.

Did they give up? Or did they complete their mission?

With one Seeker left, Hero narrowed his eyes, the fire burning through him. The Seeker took its chance, throwing itself at Hero and taking them both to the ground. But he gripped the dagger tight, shoving it into the Seeker's heart. The weight heavy on his chest, he shoved the lifeless body off of himself, watching it disappear to the same fate as its companions.

Heaving in a fury, Hero got up and scanned for any more movement. Yet the fury became fear as he realized the silver-haired girl was nowhere to be seen. The room spun as he darted from corner to corner. Frantically, he burst through every door around him.

Hero found Quinn curled in a ball on the kitchen floor, her face tucked underneath her folded arms, her entire body shaking. The table had been turned upside down, and trickles of blood decorated the tiles, along with a knife . . . one that came from the Arena's kitchen, one decorated with golden swirls on its white handle. *Clever girl.*

Hero bent his knees, placing his hands on Quinn's arms, careful with his touch. She flinched, her head shooting up while her body convulsed. Her eyes were as red and bloodshot as they were wide and confused. She held a different knife in her hand, raising it before she stopped, hopefully recognizing who he was. Hero looked her over, confirming that she didn't have any serious wounds.

"Quinn, I need you to focus. What happened to Cassie? Can you tell me?" He tried his best to speak calmly, though his mind whirled at the possibilities of Cassie's fate.

"They . . . they took her," Quinn breathed, her voice shaking with each word. "I don't know where. We need to call the cops." Her words came out faster and faster. "Those . . . those things in the dark capes, their eyes were pitch black. And then they just vanished!"

Hero stepped back as Quinn pushed herself off the ground. Panic filled him. "You saw them?"

"Of course I saw them! They destroyed my living room!"

His mouth went dry. *It isn't possible, is it?*

"You've been bonded to Cassie," Hero muttered. There could be no other explanation as to how Quinn could see the Seekers. She couldn't be *another* Zodiac. "Normal humans can't see them—not for what they truly are."

Quinn exhaled, the muscles under her jaw flinching. "What the *hell* does that mean?"

"It means you need to come with me." Hero knew the consequences of taking a mortal back to the Arena, but he had no other choice. "It's not safe for you here anymore. Those *things,*" he said, gesturing around the room, flashes of the Seekers tumbling through the window still fresh in his mind, "can and *will* come back. We need to get out of here."

"No," she objected. "First, tell me what happened to Cassie."

Hero balled his hands into fists. They were wasting too much time. "There are bad people after Cassie, and my friends and I are trying to help her. I just messed up big time by bringing her here. So, please, do what I say, and I'll tell you everything once we're in a safe place." The words rushed out of his mouth. "I need to get a few of Cassie's things, but we can't come back here, not for a while. You need to pack some stuff as well, okay? Try and keep it light."

Quinn blinked at him before standing and turning around to disappear into her room as though she were on autopilot. He heard her rummaging around and the sound of a bag being opened.

Hero swore under his breath as his mind ran through the next possible steps. He would have to call in and ask for a favor—get Kalix to come by to help Quinn and Cassie disappear for a bit, and to gather the rest of their belongings. Kalix might not be welcome in the Arena anymore, but he was still Hero's go-to person for these sorts of things.

Hero cursed himself. He should have known better than to let Cassie lead him blindly into what she wanted. He'd had no reason to do what he did, refuting all his warrior training.

While waiting for Quinn, he walked into what he guessed was Cassie's room. It was clear she'd moved in only a few weeks ago, with books stacked high on the floor and boxes still crowding the corners. Hero spotted a duffel bag out of the corner of his eye, grabbed it, and threw it on the bed. He opened it and tossed in anything he deemed essential.

A green glimmer on her vanity table caught his eye. Hero picked up the necklace by its golden chain, carefully touching it to the palm of his hand to see if it would burn him too. But he felt nothing. He pocketed the necklace and made his way back into the living room with the bag, his boots crackling on the shattered glass.

Quinn stood outside her door with an overstuffed bag at her feet, looking around at the mess, lost in defeat.

Hero squared with her. "Look, I know you don't know me, but I need you to trust me. Can you do that?"

Quinn nodded slowly. "Where are you taking me?"

He lifted their bags over his shoulders, opening the door for Quinn as they walked out without so much as a glance behind them. "To my home. To Cassie's new home."

CHAPTER 10

PARADOXICAL

(ADJ.) THE OPPOSITE OF WHAT YOU EXPECT

The leather of the steering wheel dug into his palms as he squeezed tighter, his knuckles turning white. Hero glanced over at Quinn, who seemed to be watching every turn he made, studying the pattern of the roads.

She had been bonded. Quinn could see their world in all its depth and horror. It was rare—rare enough that he had merely heard tales and whispers about it, but had never seen it for himself. Until now.

He could sense Quinn's eyes shifting to him, searing into his skin. Her voice broke through the heavy silence they had suffered through for the past fifteen minutes. "So, your name's Hero? Bit pretentious, don't you think?"

Hero sighed. "I think it says a lot about the expectations my parents had of me when I was born." He hated his name, even more so in situations like these, when he was the furthest away from being a true hero. When he had failed his mission. *Lost* his mission. Lost *her.* He knew there would be hell to pay once

78

the rest of the Zodiacs figured out what had happened, never mind his own self-torture. His shoulders tightened.

"Are they going to kill Cassie?" Quinn's voice squeaked through the thoughts whirling in his head.

It was the one question he refused to ask himself. *She can't die. She won't die*, he reasoned in his mind. Cassie must've been part of a greater reason for the Seekers to come out of hiding. If they wanted her, they probably wanted her alive—or wanted her dark side alive, at least. Why else would they take her instead of killing her outright in the kitchen?

"No. She's too valuable to kill right now," he stated, reassuring himself as much as he was Quinn. A game of Russian roulette was being played with Cassie's life, and Hero did not want to lose.

She swallowed, her shoulders slumping. "Who took her? What do they want with her? And why aren't we trying to find her?" Her haunting questions came fast.

"They're called Seekers. They're humans possessed by dark souls. I'm not exactly sure what they want with her," he said, not wanting to spill the whole truth about Cassie's condition just yet. "And I don't know where she is. I need to go back to my place to find out." He forced himself to think with his head instead of his heart, to think logically about how best to find her, even though every part of him wanted to tear through the city looking for her.

"What are you? A warlock or a vampire or something?" She eyed him sideways.

How much should I tell this mortal? She already saw the Seekers . . .

"Oh, come on," Quinn cajoled. "I'm not stupid. No one carries around a sword like that, and I saw you fighting. It wasn't natural."

Hero cleared his throat. "Vampires don't exist—that's just a tale higher demons tell to cover their massacres. But no, I'm not a warlock either. I'm . . . a demigod. You know, you're taking this a lot better than Cassie did." It wasn't lost on him that Quinn seemed as though she already knew about this world, or at least she had an inkling.

Quinn's eyes widened. "A demigod? Like Egyptian stuff, or Greek? Norse?"

Hero raised a brow. "Greek."

"Oh." She shifted to the side. "Do you have any . . . *abilities*?"

Hero knew Quinn must be in shock. Her questions came out as though nothing had happened, but the words trembled with a heavier weight. He leaned his head back against the seat and said, "I'm strong. Way stronger than any mortal."

"I'd want to be able to fly," Quinn mumbled, gazing out the window.

"Flying isn't one of our abilities. Tauruses can teleport, and Libras can make things move with their minds, but that's about it."

She frowned. "Right. Of course."

The conversation died as Hero turned onto the familiar drive of his home, the New Orleans Arena. Talking with Quinn was more than he could handle, and each sentence was a waste of time. His focus remained on one thing: his mission. Cassie.

"What is this place?" Quinn straightened in her seat, reaching for her bag. She rummaged around in it, pulling out a can of pepper spray.

Hero sighed. "It's my home. And you can put that down—I'm not a threat to you or Cassie." He was more worried about her being able to see the Arena than her trying to harm him. It was complex magic to break, even with their bond.

He pulled into the garage, their headlights being the only source of light before the sensors lit the room.

"This is how I get murdered: following a random dude into a castle-like building I've never seen before. It never works out in the horror movies," Quinn said as she crossed her arms.

Hero stepped out of the car and opened the door for her. "You're not going to die. But if you don't hurry, Cassie might," he added hurriedly, trying to remind her of what was at stake.

He grabbed their bags and led her up the stairs. "Stay behind me," he ordered, pressing the elevator button several times, needing it to come faster than it did.

The doors opened. *All clear.* Hero stood in front of her, shielding her with his body in case anyone saw them. The elevator beeped as they passed several floors. The doors opened again, this time on a familiar hallway Hero had called home since he was twelve.

Quinn glanced around, mouth wide open, taking in all the glory this place had to offer. "But how does no one know about this place?" Her hands glided across the marble walls as they walked down the silent hall.

"It involves a witch and a lot of voodoo." He opened one of the doors a few steps down—the one across from his room. "This is where Cassie is staying, so I think it'd be best if you did too. Be quiet, and don't let anyone see you. I'll be back in a few hours."

"How can I see all of this? I mean, whatever all this is," Quinn asked, gesturing around as she walked into Cassie's room.

"It can happen when a Zodiac creates a bond with a mortal; then they begin to see our world. It's rare, but it's one of the many reasons why we're banned from associating ourselves in any way with mortals." He cringed as the words left his mouth, but it was the truth. Nothing good ever came out of a mortal knowing about their world. The last time that happened, it had ended in bloodshed for all.

Quinn still grimaced. "And Cassie is one of you?"

"She didn't know it until this morning, but yes." Hero chucked the bags on the floor by the dressing table.

Quinn sat on the edge of Cassie's bed, biting at her nails. "Why is she in so much trouble?"

Hero sighed. "The powers she possesses have the possibility of being danger-ous, so some people want her gone, and others want to use her for their own selfish reasons."

"What do *you* want to do with her?" Quinn narrowed her eyes.

Hero stared at her, full of certainty. "I want to save her." He couldn't fathom why he cared so much about Cassie, painting the lurking feeling in his gut as ded-ication to his mission. But that's not why he was saving her. She had something more to her, something that wanted to survive, something greater. And that was worth it all.

Quinn's shoulders slumped in what Hero assumed was exhaustion. "Then find her. Please," she responded, her voice cracking.

"I will. It's what I'm good at," Hero replied, shooting her a quick, reassuring smile before disappearing out the door.

But there was something else he was good at: losing her.

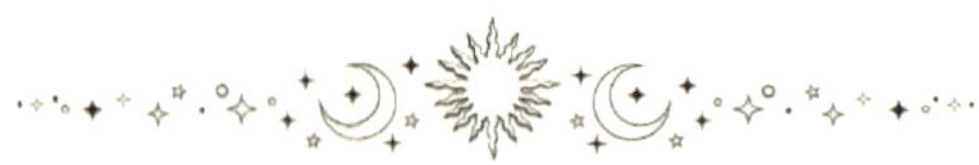

He dreaded the voices he heard inside the mission room, but swung the door open regardless, the urgency of the matter throbbing through his blood. He ignored the stares of his team. "Cassie's gone," he announced, striding over to the desk covered in monitors.

Artemis huffed. "What do you mean, 'gone'?"

Hero ground his teeth together, fighting against the words he had to speak. "We snuck out, and the Seekers found us."

"You *lost* her?" His sister's voice raised, her hands slamming on the table as she stood. "We spent all night trying to save her after Nyssa's visions, and you lost her already?" Her words softened. "Do you not remember what happened the last time you snuck out?"

Her words hit him like a punch in the gut, but he knew he deserved it.

"Did you think we wouldn't notice you took her?" Titus said, jerking his chin at him.

Elijah pulled a face. "What were you guys doing, anyway? Sightseeing?"

"Let me explain before you guys freak out, okay?" Hero pleaded, and then he told them what had happened. "In the end, there were so many Seekers, I couldn't even see them all. They took her."

"For Olympus's sake, Hero, what the hell were you thinking?" Artemis scolded, sounding just like their mother.

"I know I messed up. I know," he said through gritted teeth, his fists clenching. "We have to find her, and I need you guys' help."

"And what about the other girl? The friend you mentioned?" Nyssa demanded.

Hero knew he couldn't tell them about the mortal yet. It was against their laws, for one, and he didn't want to spring any more surprises on his friends. That one could wait. "She's fine. I took her somewhere safe."

As Titus rose from his seat, Hero's stomach rose into his throat. The room quieted. But then Titus said, "What's the plan?"

Relief washed over Hero. No matter what they disagreed on or fought about, Titus was always there for him in the end. "First, we have to find out where they've taken her." He had no idea where the Seekers could be, or where they might have taken Cassie. What they knew about the Seekers was limited.

Nyssa glanced at the ground. "You need me to find her, don't you?" A slight sadness ran through her words.

"I'm sorry, Nys. I wish there were another way." Hero's whole body ached with the pain he knew he would cause her. Nyssa struggled with her powers more than anyone else. They hadn't yet found the reason why it pained her whenever a vision came her way, and he hated himself for putting her through this.

"There was another way: not losing the Gemini on the first day," Elijah snapped.

Hero nodded in silence. He deserved their grief and his best friend's rage.

"Not now, guys." Nyssa looked between them, shaking her head. "Do you have anything of hers? I'll need to channel her." Her voice was soft and trembled with the preface of pain, making Hero's heart tighten even more.

He dug through his pockets, pulling out Cassie's necklace. The emerald dangled in the air as a beacon of hope. "Here, this is hers." He passed the necklace to Nyssa, placing it in the palm of her hand.

She smiled at him as she closed her hand around the jewelry, the gem disappearing from his sight beneath her dainty fingers.

Hero winced as Elijah gripped his forearm, his fingers burning the skin. Elijah's eyes turned a molten gold, stinging with an anger that rarely came out to fight. "Don't take her help for granted," he muttered to Hero, his hand heating even more. "Your mistake is costing her."

Hero tensed, but he didn't move away from the burn. Guilt tied a noose around his neck and seemed to tighten with each passing moment. Elijah and Titus were his best friends, his brothers in every way except blood. And to let them down like this . . .

Elijah then took Nyssa's free hand in his as he knelt in front of her, all heat removed from his body, no harm coming to her.

Nyssa's eyelids fluttered like the wings of a butterfly, and her breathing shallowed. The gem glowed green in her hand as she sucked in air through her mouth, her eyebrows bunched together. Beads of sweat rolled down her forehead. Then she withered in pain.

Hero wanted to be sick all over the floor at the sight, but he clenched his fist, digging his fingernails into his skin to stop himself from punching the wall. This would forever haunt him, adding to the stain already consuming his soul.

The moment flowed between seconds and hours, everyone watching her torment, watching her try to grasp at what little she could.

Nyssa's eyes shot open, shining a rich emerald as they darted through the room, searching. Her knuckles whitened as her grip on the jewel tightened, the lightbulb in the lamp next to them bursting in response.

With a final groan, Nyssa released the necklace from her hand, her shoulders slumping as she collapsed into Elijah's open arms.

He planted kisses on her hair, rubbing her arm. "You did so great, darling."

Hero reached to the floor to pick up Cassie's necklace. Taking another look at Nyssa, he felt a mix of shame and appreciation coursing through his veins.

Nyssa took a moment to catch her breath before rasping weakly, "I saw lights, fake little horses, a Ferris wheel . . ."

Hero's shoulders loosened as she spoke. She'd found a lead, and now he—*they*—could find Cassie.

"Got what you need?" Elijah asked Hero harshly, clinging onto Nyssa as though she could slip away at any moment.

Hero leaned down, rubbing Nyssa's balmy arm. "I'm sorry, Nys. Thank you," he whispered, his eyes flooding with a sincere apology before he rose to his feet and commandeered a nearby computer. Sliding his hand across the screen, he lifted it into the air as it turned into a hologram, the blue lights reflecting off his body. He swiped through the database as fast as he could, scanning for any location that might fit Nyssa's description.

Artemis appeared beside him, her arms crossed. His sister could hold a grudge forever if she wanted to, and him sneaking out and losing the same person they had risked their lives for just last night would be high on her list. "What do you need me to do?"

"I need you to get our weapons ready, but be sneaky about it." Hero glanced at her. "No one can know we're going on this mission."

Her brows lifted. "Why ask me and not Titus? He's the better sleight of hand."

Hero glanced over his shoulder at his friend. "I need his eyes on something else. And are you saying you can't even sneak a few weapons for us?" He knew the challenge would work on her.

She snorted a laugh. "I grew up stealing your stuff. I think I can do a few swords." Her voice then turned quiet. "How do we even fight the Seekers? Last night I saw more of them than I ever have in my entire life."

Hero raked his hand through his hair. "We know they don't like fire, and once they're injured, they don't tend to come back. Let's kill the ones we can and hurt the rest enough so that they disappear." He swallowed the knot forming in his throat. They had to go into battle with an enemy too large to defeat, because of him—an enemy he'd hated for years. The same enemy that'd taken so much from him already.

Artemis turned on her feet as though she thought the same, leaving the room without so much as a word.

Titus approached him then, eyes filled with pity, making Hero tense. "Don't beat yourself up over what happened. You were trying to help her." His gaze flickered to the tiles under his feet. "I know how it feels, but it's still early. We'll find her."

Hero nodded at Titus and passed him a quick smile. It had always been the three of them together: Hero, Elijah, and Titus. But today, a shift had come, rumbling them at their core in the form of a woman. He'd find a way to fix it, to get them back on track.

Hero studied the screens in front of him. A series of buildings stood tall around them as he walked through the holographic city, trying to find any hint of what Nyssa had spoken of. He exhaled hard through his nose, racking his brain for answers.

"LaLaurie Mansion?" Hero questioned, zooming in on the large and dark building. Even the picture of the mansion caused shivers to snake up his spine, and although he didn't believe in ghosts, something *awful* haunted the place.

"No, that would be too obvious. The few reports on them say they prefer run-down, out-of-town abandoned places, not smack-dab in the city center," Titus said. Then he snapped his fingers. "I know where they are."

The team gathered around the desk. Hero flicked the screen in the air with his fingers once more, causing it to zoom in on his find. Jazzland, an abandoned amusement park, radiated around them, a broken Ferris wheel floating in the distance, along with a merry-go-round replete with little horses.

"Suit up and get ready," Hero ordered. "I'll meet you all downstairs."

His team filtered out of the room, but he lingered, swiping his fingers upwards as the map of the park materialized. Multiple entranceways, various hiding spots, and so much destruction. Hero bit the inside of his cheek at how massive the place appeared, and at how royally screwed he was.

He whipped around at the sound of running footsteps, his hands balling into fists, his senses on high alert.

Artemis raced through the corridor toward him.

Shit.

"Hero!" Her words rushed out. "I went into Cassie's room to get this dagger I left under her bed in case she turned dark and, you know, we needed to stab her, and I found a—"

Hero shoved his hand against her mouth, silencing her before anyone else could hear. "Be quiet!" he hissed. "That's Cassie's friend, okay? She was there when the attack happened. She's been bonded, and the Seekers could have caught her scent. I couldn't just leave her." He lifted his hand as he gave his sister a look of *"If you speak, I'll hurt you."*

Artemis scowled at him. "There hasn't been a mortal in the Arena in decades! They're all going to freak, especially Mom!" she whispered harshly.

He stared at his younger sister. "Mom doesn't have to know. . . not yet."

"This is such a big risk, you dumb ass! What if the Seekers tracked you back here? Dear Hades, we're going to be excommunicated like Kalix! In one day, we've brought a Gemini *and* a mortal here," she said in a frenzy.

Hero put his hands on her shoulders. "Nothing will happen to us. I'll talk to Mom when she gets back, but please keep this a secret for now. I've messed up enough as it is."

Artemis lifted her chin at him and loosed a sigh. "Fine. But she'd better be worth it, that's all I'm saying."

"The mortal, or Cassie?" Hero smirked, poking his elbow into her side.

Artemis frowned as she glanced up. "Both. Let's go."

CHAPTER II

ERIPIO

(V.) TO TAKE AWAY, RESCUE

At first, it sounded like a clock ticking in her ear. It awoke Cassie from her deep sleep with each swing of the pendulum, her consciousness seeping through. She opened her heavy eyelids, but only darkness awaited her.

Both her heart and her head pounded. Some sort of material covered her eyes. She didn't know where she was, who had her, or what was going to happen—again. Her breath came out in short puffs as she jolted her body, only for her to discover that she was restrained.

She was sitting; she knew that much. On something firm and hard. Her wrists were bound behind her back, and her ankles to the legs of what she assumed was a chair, the rough, brittle material rubbing hard against her skin with each movement.

Cassie's stomach crawled into her throat, begging to be released as a shriek left her lips, echoing across her unknown location. She wanted to cry and scream for help, but a part of her knew it would be no use.

88

She was trapped.

The cloth wrapped around her eyes was ripped off in one swift motion, and the realization that she wasn't alone rushed in like a tidal wave. She blinked rapidly, trying to adjust to the lights around her so she could see who was there. The candles in the room cast shadows across the abyss of darkness as a string of icy dread passed its way through her veins, slithering like a snake.

Her eyes slowly made out dozens of figures surrounding her. Cassie's throat closed as she tried to move again, desperate to loosen her bindings. She couldn't . . . she couldn't breathe. She had to get out. This couldn't be happening.

No, no, no . . .

She glanced down and realized it wasn't a clock that had woken her from her sleep. A puddle of red pooled at her feet, dripping loudly from a wound above her eyes. If she were *human*, she might have been dead by now. Instead, she felt her cells slowly stitch back together as it healed—just as Nyssa claimed it would.

Her breath hitched as the figures standing in front of her moved. Large black cloaks covered their bodies. Only the outline of their hoods could be seen within the shadows covering them, masking their true identities. But she knew what lay underneath: human faces. Trapped souls. Just like that girl in her kitchen.

Sharp whispers filled her ears, sounding everywhere and nowhere all at once.

"Let me go!" she yelled as she tried to move again. The chair squeaked against the floor, making her wince.

There has to be another way . . . Please. I can't . . . I can't . . .

Breath tickled her neck, sending shivers down her spine as she yelped.

"How fascinating," a man said into her ear, causing her to flinch. "We haven't seen a Gemini in so long." His words hissed out of his mouth as though his tongue dripped with venom.

Cassie tried to stop her body from trembling, but the terror only increased at his words.

His laugh rippled into her other ear like sandpaper, making her skin crawl and shudder. "It's a shame your dark side isn't here to play. We wanted to meet her."

Cassie struggled against the chair, cursing herself for not listening to Hero, for pestering him so much to go and see Quinn while knowing how much danger she could put them all in.

Quinn . . .

She hadn't even begun to think about what had happened to Quinn. Or Hero. The last time she saw him, he was being attacked by a horde of these beings, and Quinn was huddled in a corner. *Is she here?* Her stomach wanted to jump out of her throat again, but to survive this, she had to control her emotions. Letting herself focus on a different emotion other than fear and despair, she chose the one screaming at her the loudest: *rage.*

"I don't know what you're talking about," Cassie spat. She balled her hands into fists as her body pulsed with anger. "Why am I here? What do you want from me?" she demanded. *Keep them talking.* She had to trick them, anger them, lie to them—whatever it took to escape.

The cloaked man drew a dark finger down her face, his sharp claw like a nail traveling along her jaw, making her shrivel in disgust. "We had to make sure it was you," he said before he leaned down, his voice louder than a whisper. "Queen's orders."

Queen?

His footsteps sounded on the wooden floorboards as he stepped in front of her, drawing his hood back. "We were robbed of our chance last night, thanks to your Zodiac friends."

Her mouth went dry as she saw his face for the first time. He was the exact opposite of his malicious voice. The man had big bushy eyebrows, thin lips, and small wrinkles surrounding his mouth. But his eyes were a deep, bottomless abyss; not one bit of light reflected from them.

The creature before her was more than a man, and more than a demon.

Her mind flashed back to the girl in her kitchen, the one who had taken her. How her face cried out against her actions, yet something darker took over her. Something evil, without a soul.

Cassie's back straightened as she willed herself to stare at him. She pitied their hosts, but pity wasn't enough this time. She wouldn't be fooled by their human faces again.

Focus on the anger. See past them, Cassie.

A darkness flooded up inside of her, reminding her that she could rely on not only herself, but also her *other*. It seemed tempting, to let her dark side out, to see what exactly it would do . . . but so much unknown lurked in that area. How would she unleash it? Would she be able to rein it back in? Would it *kill* them?

And isn't that what her new captives wanted? To *"meet her dark side?"*

Dangerous. That was what she was, and she didn't want it. She'd have to do this herself, as herself, not wanting to risk anything else. She mentally pushed the darkness away, deep inside.

Cassie readjusted her body as much as she could, her wrists burning against the rope. "And what does your *queen* want with me?" she demanded.

The man sneered. He stepped behind her once more, dragging his nails across her neck, causing goosebumps to ripple across her skin in response. "That will become clear with time," he said, his cold, wet lips pressing against her ear as her muscles tightened. "But for now, we want to know what the Zodiacs are planning. We know the war is coming."

She tilted away in disgust and looked up, her heart fluttering at what she saw. They were in a tent—a big-top one like she'd seen once at a circus. A beacon of hope shot through her. A tent meant no doors, and no doors meant no locks, and no locks meant a way out.

"A war?" Cassie questioned.

"The War of Gods. You must know about this." His tone scolded her.

She shook her head. "The War of Gods . . . Hmm. Doesn't ring a bell." Cassie rubbed her skin against the rope, cringing at the burning sensation. But then she remembered that it didn't matter: she'd heal.

I'll heal. That's how I'll get out.

She moved her hand again, slower this time. If she could get the rope loose enough to slip off one hand . . .

"See, I think you're lying," the demon man hissed. "Tell us what we want to know about the Immortal gods, and you won't suffer."

"Let me go, and *you* won't suffer," she spat back, her grin growing as the man wiped his face in outrage. If he got angry enough, maybe he would show her what weapons he had on him—ones that she could take from him.

His face twisted, his eyes widening. "Then tell us what you know about the Gemini."

She stiffened at the name. Of course they knew who she was; that was why they had taken her. But what would they do to her because of it? "I'm the Gemini," she said. Warm blood trickled from her rope burns now—but her hand was squeezing out ever so slowly. "What are you?"

"That's not your concern right now," he growled, baring his teeth. "What did the Zodiacs tell you about the Gemini?"

"We didn't get that far," she muttered, trying to mask her pain. "Why do you even want to know?"

He rolled his eyes. "You Zodiacs are so deceitful, just like the Immortals. There hasn't been a Gemini allowed to exist in centuries, and suddenly you pop up—the perfect little weapon for our side of the war."

They wanted to use her as a *weapon.* The thought chilled her to the very bone, but she used that to channel her strength.

"Your friends burned us last night because of you," he snarled, continuing whatever rant he was on now, rolling up his sleeve to show Cassie his charred and pulsating skin. And as much as it disgusted her, she smiled. *Fire—a weakness.* "S omeone has to pay for this, and because you've been such a bitch, not answering our questions . . . We're not allowed to kill you, but our queen never said anything about causing a little bit of pain." He cackled as he drew out a thin blade.

A weapon. You fool.

"And you," he continued, "you have such pretty skin . . ."

Cassie's arm seized in pain as he grabbed her, the chair screeching against the floor in resistance to the rope. He gripped her face, holding the blade against her cheeks. The cool metal flirted with the thin line between pain and safety. She repressed a shudder, staring him dead in the eye, and he drew the sharp edge down her face. Wincing in agony, her teeth clenched.

The blood trickled down as he made another slice. He moved the blade to her neck, pressing the tip of it into her, causing a small spurt of blood to exit. The pain pinched her nerves as she finally released a scream, the tears in her eyes falling freely.

Her captor's eyes widened as a large grin crossed his face; he was enjoying her torture entirely too much. It hurt more than anything she'd ever experienced, but it would heal.

It doesn't matter. Fight through the pain.

He had confessed it himself: he couldn't kill her, only hurt her. The question of why loomed over her as she pieced together the clues they let slip out. *She, the queen. They have a leader.* But the more he focused on her face, the less he focused on her hands—and through the pain, she set herself free, the rope no longer restricting her.

Cassie slammed her head forward, crashing into the demon man's skull. She shrieked at the pounding pain in her own skull, but she shot her hands out, grabbing the blade from him with the few seconds of surprise she had on her side. The chair was still roped to her feet, but at least now she could stand—and she had the weapon.

The man hissed as he rubbed his head, black veins running through his face as he heaved in front of her.

Cassie held the dagger toward him, her posture straightening, challenging him, because he had no idea what she was capable of. She hadn't even known it herself until this very moment. The rest of the demon people began to close in on her, and though the dagger was beginning to feel feeble in her hand, she lifted her chin at them.

Shadows flickered in the distance.

With the way the demon man whipped his head around at the noise, Cassie sensed something else had entered the fight—something not even her captors knew of. Her heart raced, but she took the moment of distraction to cut her feet loose, dropping into a crouch and sawing the blade on the last bit of rope containing her.

She blew a breath of relief. *Freedom.* But then, the sound of swords unsheathing in unison filled the tent. Cassie's eyes darted around, trying to get a glimpse of what was happening and any sign of an exit, but she couldn't see much.

She couldn't be trapped again. She couldn't be tortured again. She needed more leverage.

Cassie hooked her arm around her distracted attacker, pulling his back toward her as the blade now rested on his neck. "Back away, or I'll kill him right now!" she yelled into the darkness. She had no idea if it would work, her stomach sinking like a ship as dread wrapped itself around her hands, making her hold the blade tighter to his neck.

One of the cloaked figures surrounding her fell, grasping at his side where a sword had impaled him. Then another one, and another, creating a gap in their fortress of bodies.

A large figure emerged from the darkness, the candles shining enough light on his face for Cassie to see who it was. She laughed shakily as her shoulders slumped, losing her stiff posture.

Hero.

CHAPTER 12

FÉROCE

(ADJ.) FEROCIOUS; WILD

Hero's sword spun in the air, dripping with blood. A sly smile took over his face as he looked at her, and she couldn't help but feel proud of herself.

"You ruined my rescue party," he said as he approached them, his weapon now ready for the man she held hostage, eyes lit in mischief.

The rest of the cloaked figures were fighting what Cassie assumed were other Zodiacs that came with Hero, and she felt entirely relieved by that fact.

"You Zodiacs and your big entrances," the demon man said through gritted teeth. "We'll make sure we torture you before we kill you and your friends."

Cassie strengthened her grip on him as he seethed at Hero. She kicked her leg into the back of his knee, and he fell. Without a second thought, as though it was in her nature, she stabbed the demon man's neck deeply, and his writhing figure dissolved into thin air, leaving only a trail of smoke. For a moment, his death felt good on her hands, but then her mind cleared.

Did I just kill someone? No . . . Wait—what did I just do?

95

Her hand shook as the candles around the tent went out one by one, plunging everyone into obscurity. Cassie tightened whatever hold she had on herself, on that *other* side, worrying she had let it slip too much.

She had just become a murderer.

A scream sounded from one end of the tent. Cassie felt like she was blindfolded again, only able to hear the body blows and screeches around the tent.

The heat from another's body came up behind her, making her flinch at the touch. She opened her mouth to yell for help before a calloused hand collided with her lips, stopping her. Cassie swung her knife around indiscriminately, making contact.

Whoever it was inhaled sharply. "It's me. I've got you," a deep but familiar voice strained.

Her body slackened in relief at Hero's voice. He grunted and placed the bloodied dagger back into her hands.

"Are you okay? Did they hurt you?" he questioned quickly.

"I'm fine," Cassie said breathlessly as she rubbed the back of her hand across her healed cheek, trying to forget the pain of the demon man's knife slicing her skin. "But did I hurt *you*?"

She'd killed someone, and then she'd stabbed Hero. *What's wrong with me?*

"I'm fine too," Hero reassured her. "Nice aim, though. I gotta get back to the fight; be careful." His heat left her in seconds, leaving behind a chill that she didn't like.

Cassie's eyes adjusted to the darkness while she focused on her other senses, trying to forget what she'd just done, who she was becoming.

A fiery ball soared through the air, touching the side of the tent, igniting it. Cassie could now make out the scene unfolding around her. They were all there: Nyssa, Artemis, a blond guy she hadn't met yet, and even Titus. They fought the cloaked figures one by one, their swords clanging and scraping, killing dispassionately as though it were a sport.

Sweat dripped down Cassie's neck, her lungs beginning to burn with each breath.

Fire—their weakness.

One of the cloaked figures ran past her, engulfed in flames. The lanky blond Zodiac sent a fireball from out of his hand toward the demon man, causing him to disappear in smoke. Hand still outstretched, he turned his head and smiled at Cassie.

"I don't believe we've met. I'm Elijah," he announced as he approached her, bowing with a flick of his hand.

"I'm Cassie. Watch out!" she yelled as she fell to the side, taking Elijah with her as they dodged a wrathful demon *thing*. She still couldn't figure out what they were—something possessed and evil.

"Lady, I'm taken, and at least buy me a drink first," Elijah snickered before he ran off, flicking his fingers alight with crimson flames.

Nyssa had wrapped her thighs around the head of the demon who'd attacked them, toppling him to the ground. Whipping out her sword from the scabbard on her back, she plunged it into the man's back.

Cassie then spied Titus as he leveled his hand to the ground, the earth below him shaking. A pipe burst out of the floor, water shooting out everywhere. The sheer pressure flung several of the demon people back, their bodies lying motionless on the floor.

Despite the Zodiacs' efforts, dozens of cloaked figures remained, seeming to disappear and reappear within seconds, as though they couldn't die. She knew Hero and his team, as skilled as they seemed, couldn't keep this up forever. If they didn't act fast, they wouldn't make it out of here alive.

Hero sliced his way through the demon people, every move effortless, watching in amusement as they disappeared into the ground.

"Hero!" she yelled over to him, coughing from the thickening smoke.

Within moments, as though her call had beckoned him like a siren, Hero raced toward her, butchering any stray figure interrupting his path.

"We need to get out of here—we don't have much longer with the flames. Can Titus push the demons back with water, and Elijah light them on fire? I'll find our way out!" He needed to trust her—and fast.

To her surprise, he nodded, cupping his hands around his mouth before yelling, "Alleyway! Last night! Same protocol!"

Cassie's eyes darted around the flames, looking for an escape. Finally, she spotted a clearing—no figures, no fire.

There you are.

Cassie glanced back, the blood draining from her face as she witnessed the man who'd tormented her—the one she thought she'd killed—creeping up behind Hero, sword gleaming. She didn't have time to think as she shoved Hero to the side with all her might, angling the knife in her hands into the demon man's torso. He growled, but then Hero swiped his sword and slashed him across the chest, and within seconds his body dissolved again into a cloud of black smoke around them.

Cassie looked at the blood-coated dagger in her shaking hands. It was as if her body had acted without her mind once again, as though it were instinct to kill these things, even as her consciousness barked against it. She wanted to be sick, but reminded herself it was Hero or them. She had to—*right?*

Did we really kill him this time?

A devilish smirk crawled across Hero's face.

The sound of the fight came rushing back in as she found Artemis loading her bow next to her. "You two done?" Artemis yelled as her arrows flew. She then lunged forward, gripping a demon by their hair, their mask dropping off onto the floor as she drew her knee into their face repeatedly.

It didn't take long for the smoke to start sucking all the oxygen away. Cassie forced herself to worry more about her plan than her ambient guilt over her newfound violent actions. They had to get out as soon as possible—or they wouldn't at all.

Hero's face turned serious as he gazed around at the fire, wiping away the sweat dripping from his forehead. "Get out of here. You need to get to safety. That's the mission."

Cassie protested. The Seekers couldn't hurt her, *badly*—they needed her alive—but they *could* hurt Hero and his friends. They'd threatened that much already. She wasn't about to let anyone die on her account. "I go when you go. I'm one of you now, remember?"

"It's your death wish," Artemis muttered, drawing an arrow out of her quiver, and aiming at another demon man.

Hero looked at Cassie, nodding at her as a vote of confidence before charging back into the battle.

Cassie tightened her grip on the dagger. *You got this.*

She ran over to the clearing she had spied, and sliced the tent's material with her blade. The cool air hit her skin, and she replenished her lungs before rejoining the fight.

Fire soared through the air; over half of the tent was covered in flames. Several pipes lifted from under the ground, the water forming into one big wave as it pushed the demons back, drowning them as the others burned.

But in seconds, all traces of them vanished into the ground.

My plan worked. It actually worked!

The Zodiacs ran toward the exit, Hero holding the flap of the burning tent open for them as they stumbled out, coughing violently as fresh air entered their lungs once more.

A few recovering breaths later, Cassie could see where they were for the first time. Rusted roller coasters and rides surrounded them, covered in graffiti and decay.

She looked over her shoulder and was about to ask why the demons had chosen this place to keep her when Titus's body lifted into the air, a sword impaling his side. A badly burned girl heaved in glory behind him, her face on full display as her eyes seeped deeper into the darkness. It was the same one who'd kidnapped Cassie in her kitchen—the one with the red hair.

In less than a second, the demon's head slid off her body in a clean cut, decapitated. Cassie nearly toppled over at the sight, her hand clasping around her mouth to stop herself from screaming or throwing up, unable to stomach the gore of what had just happened to that girl.

Nyssa stood behind the beheaded demon, the long handle of the sword gripped in both her hands as her knees bent. Blood dripped as the girl's body soon followed her head to the ground, disappearing into the same inky smoke.

Placing a hand around her neck, Cassie tried to steady herself from what she had just witnessed, which she was sure would haunt her for many nights to come. How could anyone live with that? How could Nyssa live with that?

Hero ran to Titus, catching him as he fell. Titus clutched his side, blood flowing around the sword still trapped in his body.

"Hold on," Hero instructed as he gripped the sword by its handle, pulling it from his friend's abdomen in one swift movement. Titus's body lifted, his back arching as a grunt escaped his mouth. Cassie could only blink as she witnessed the blood traveling back into his wound, the stab mark sealing shut around it. Their ability to heal was like no other, and it was what had saved her life back there.

Hero examined his friend's skin, brushing his finger over the scar that was already beginning to fade as well.

"I'm fine, I'm fine. Just a scratch," Titus snapped, pushing his hand away.

"Okay," Hero said, raising his brows. "Come on. We need to move before any of them come back. Now."

Cassie dropped the dagger, wanting to leave it behind, and took off running with the rest of them, following their lead to safety. But she didn't know how to feel—relief over finally being safe, fear over whatever had attacked her, panic over how violent she'd acted in the tent, and grief for the girl Nyssa had decapitated. She was among those who killed as if it were nothing, and as much as it scared her, it also made her feel oddly protected.

With the amusement park well behind them, they slowed to a stop. Cassie held her side as it cramped in pain, the adrenaline leaving her system. Then another emotion flooded in—tremendous guilt.

She cleared her throat, gaining the attention of the group. "I'm so sorry, Titus. And to all of you. I never meant to put you guys in danger." Glancing at the ground, she watched as a stray piece of ash flowed across the gravel.

"That's the second time we've had to save you, Gemini. Try not to make it a habit, would you?" Titus's accent carried thick in the air as he pulled his shirt over his dark brown torso. From his pocket, he took out some keys and walked over to a large black SUV.

Cassie shut her eyes for a moment, accepting the hit.

"I think Titus almost enjoys putting himself in situations where he knows he's going to get hurt," Nyssa whispered, nudging her in the side and trying to lighten the mood. She walked off humming—as though she hadn't just sliced the head off a teenager only moments ago.

"Come on, let's go," Hero bellowed to the group, who all started walking to the car. But Hero's pointed look told Cassie to hang back. "Are you sure you're okay?" he asked once they were alone, scanning her face.

She knew she must have had an obscene amount of blood on her, but larger worries consumed her mind. "I'm so sorry for putting you in the middle. And for accidentally stabbing you back there." She swallowed. "Is Quinn okay?"

"She's fine," he assured her, his thumb gliding over her face to brush off some dried blood.

Cassie's breath hitched. The blood flaked off her skin like the ash from the tent, drifting into nothingness.

"She's back at the Arena," Hero continued, "and we'll probably need to talk about the fact that she's been bonded to you, which means she can see our world for what it is." He nodded as her eyes widened. "But don't worry about me. I'm just proud of how badass you were in there, fighting off the Seekers all by yourself."

Cassie breathed out. "Seekers? That's what they're called?" The cloaked figures had an identity at last.

"I should have warned you before. I'm sorry." He rocked on his heels, his eyes fluttering down. "They're not human anymore. They're possessed. We don't come into contact with them often either."

"Did we kill the one in there? That man?" she asked, remembering the pained face of her attacker as she plunged his own dagger into him.

"No, we didn't kill *it*," he assured her, and a weight lifted off her shoulders. "We just injured it enough for it to stay gone."

She *wasn't* a murderer. Her knees buckled with relief, even though she now understood what they were.

"Hey," Hero said, his tone causing her to look at him. "What you did back there was incredibly brave. The Seekers aren't something to feel sorry for, but I get why it takes a toll to kill one. I try to think of it as releasing the human from the demon inside."

Cassie's heart lightened slightly at his words. She hadn't killed him—*it*—but if she had, she'd try her best to think about it that way. And maybe if she encountered another one, maybe she could release them from themselves . . . maybe.

"This doesn't make us even for saving your life—twice—by the way," Hero said, holding up two fingers while grinning.

"You're welcome," she said with a chuckle, relieved to know that she could at least still smile in the face of this taxing day.

"Come on, demon slayer. Let's get you back." Hero smirked before walking to the car, where the rest of the Zodiacs waited, opening the door for her.

CHAPTER 13

RAISON D'ÊTRE

(N.) A REASON FOR EXISTING

In the back seat with Hero, Cassie rested her head against the foggy car window. Every time she breathed, it created a mark on the window, and she traced her fingers around it in return. Ever since she was a child, focusing on her breathing had steadied her, made her feel more in control. She found herself needing that control back more and more.

The sun's warm light floated up, marking a full day since she'd begun this new life. She'd fallen asleep in one world and awoken in another. Cassie shivered at both the thought and the brisk early morning finding its way into the moving car.

Hero must have noticed, as he peeled off his leather jacket and placed it around her shoulders. She thanked him with a nod.

Cassie was still coming to terms with her place among the Zodiacs, let alone the mere existence of them, but something inside her had changed back in the tent. A strength she hadn't even known was there, exploding inside of her. Although that

103

strength came with a stroke of darkness, she'd try her best to manage it—to defeat it, she supposed.

A dull silence permeated the vehicle, aside from the occasional giggle from Elijah and Nyssa in the middle row. Titus sometimes checked on them in the rearview mirror from the driver's seat, while Artemis sat in the passenger seat, toying with her knife, spinning it around on the tip of her finger.

"They said a war was coming?" Cassie croaked out, loud enough for Hero to hear. Her voice was hoarser than she'd expected.

"The War of Gods," Hero whispered, looking out his window.

She inhaled sharply. The Seeker's words echoed in her mind. "What's going to happen?"

Hero shook his head. "I don't know for sure yet; we've only heard bits and pieces from Olympus. We just know that it's coming—and it's not going to be pretty."

Cassie swallowed hard. "Is that why you're helping me? Because the darkness I possess could be used for it?" She had to know what was so important about her, why the Seekers wanted her, and why the Zodiacs had made her their mission. Did they want to use her as a weapon too? She had a darkness inside her, yes, but what could it do?

"No, no, of course not." Hero faced her. "The night we found you, it was because Nyssa didn't have just a vision, but also *a feeling*. That you are a beacon of hope. Of light, not darkness. And that we can help guide you there."

Light. Cassie wanted to believe that so badly—that she could be light, and not this darkness that seemed to solely define her over the past day.

"Of course," Hero continued, "when the time comes, maybe you could help us fight in the war. But that's not why I, or anyone in this car, is doing this. I see a girl who didn't ask for this life, but who has taken it in stride." His voice had a certain roughness to it, like gravel and smoke mixed with whiskey. But his words stayed soft, like silk and daisies.

Cassie played with the zipper of her jacket. "I don't know how you expect me to help with a war?" She didn't even know if she wanted to help these strangers. Would this be their price for helping her with her dark side? What use would she be in battle among the Zodiacs anyway? "I'm not like you," she muttered. "You all have these amazing powers and have trained all your life . . ."

"I'm sure you'll get your full powers soon. We don't know the full extent of power the Gemini has, but I can train you in the meantime. I'll whip you into shape—and considering how you fought back there, it won't take long."

Her shoulders loosened at Hero's words. "They have a queen, you know. The Seekers," Cassie said.

His eyebrows raised in surprise. "I'll add it to the mission report. Well done for catching it."

Cassie glanced up; Hero was staring right at her, and in that moment, she swore his brown eyes could make anyone tremble at their knees. He gazed at her as no one ever had before—as though she were worth saving. "What's the war even about?" she asked, trying not to focus on how that made her feel.

"What else would a bunch of old Immortals fight over?" Elijah exclaimed, turning his head to address her, his green eyes wide. "Power, control, domination." He propped himself up on the seat to face them. ". . . Sorry, I was eavesdropping."

Hero chuckled, then got serious. "There's been a divide between the Immortals for decades now. A few are content with residing in Olympus and staying out of mortal affairs, such as Athena and Apollo. But others—Zeus and Poseidon, to name a couple—they want more. They want free rein over the earth while killing anyone in their path. So, they're declaring war on each other."

"They don't sound much better than humans," Cassie muttered.

"Maybe not." Hero ran a hand through his hair. "But they have a hell of a lot more power and can cause serious damage and death."

Elijah smiled sadly. "Some of the Immortals think they're owed something because of who they are. But we're obviously on Athena and Apollo's side in the war. We'd like to avoid all the death and pain Poseidon and Zeus wanna bring about."

"Can the war be stopped?" Cassie asked. A war meant carnage for both humans and Zodiacs.

Hero shook his head. "I don't think so. At least, I wouldn't even know where to start with stopping it. We can only try to avoid as many casualties as possible."

The thought made her skin crawl, but as Titus turned the car into the entrance of the Arena, she couldn't help but take in the absolute beauty of the building. The sun seemed more prominent in the sky then, casting an orange glow across the white marble. And for a moment, she forgot about the war, about her darkness.

"It's been a long day," Hero sighed, noting Cassie's drooping eyelids. "Tomorrow's going to be another hard day. Rest for now, but Artemis will come by later to prepare you."

Her shoulders tensed. "Prepare me for what?"

"Meeting Diana, the Archon of the Arena. But don't worry, we'll be with you every step of the way," Hero assured her.

Their surroundings went dark as they pulled into the garage, and Cassie had a strange sense of being *home*.

"Oh, and don't fall asleep yet. There's someone waiting for you." Hero smiled as he hopped out of the car, holding his hand out for her.

Cassie jumped down with his help, the excitement of seeing Quinn jolting her awake.

She followed the team into their quarters, not going fast enough for her liking, searching each face and corner on their way, looking for her best friend.

"She's in there." Hero nodded toward her new room, and Cassie couldn't wait another moment. She flung the door open wide, and Quinn's kind and beautiful face poked out from the bathroom, causing a wave of relief to wash over her.

"Oh my god, you're okay!" Cassie cried as she ran to embrace her. She tucked her head into Quinn's shoulder, the sudden weight of her day crashing down on her. It had all been so much, but so worth it for this very moment.

"I was so worried about you," Quinn sobbed, her body shaking against Cassie's, making her cry even harder. "Come on," she cooed as they parted, swallowing harshly as she took in her face, no doubt caked with the battle she'd just faced. "Let's get you cleaned up."

Cassie's friend placed her hand on her back, guiding her toward the bathroom. A shower was exactly what she needed right now. She glanced back at Hero, who was leaning against the doorframe, and gave her a small smile before he walked away.

CHAPTER 14

MOED

(N.) BEING STRONG AND CONFIDENT IN THE FACE OF INTIMIDATION

Cassie's eyes ached from the afternoon light as she touched her chest. She'd only slept a few hours, with her mind flashing back to the red-haired girl's head sliding off her body, to the knife she had plunged into both the neck and stomach of that Seeker.

"I think the necklace my mom gave me has something to do with it," Cassie mumbled to Quinn, wondering if she would ever get it back.

"You think your mom knew about them?" Quinn readjusted herself from where she sat cross-legged on the bed, pulling down the sleeves of her pajamas.

"I don't know. Maybe?" Cassie shrugged. "Whatever it was, it stopped me from being able to see them, or what they do. It all happened once I took it off. Well, it burned me first."

And those burns disappeared, thanks to my now magical healing abilities.

"I just think it's cool. You're like a superhero now," Quinn joked, always able to inject humor into any situation.

Cassie huffed, placing her head in her hands. "I'm more like the superhero intern everyone's trying to save."

Quinn snorted. "I mean, is it that horrible having a bunch of hot people running to rescue you all the time?"

The side of Cassie's lips curled, but the joke didn't make her feel much better. Placing her hand on Quinn's, she said, "This is a lot bigger than any of us know. I don't think we can go home, at least, not for a while." She paused and shook her head. "I'm so sorry for dragging you into this. All I wanted to do was say goodbye, and I wound up messing up your entire life." Cassie couldn't stop the culpability churning inside over dragging her friend into this chaos, but a small, horrible part of her was glad to have Quinn along for this journey, to help her through it. She didn't know if she could do it alone with a bunch of strangers.

"What matters is that we keep you safe," Quinn said, holding Cassie's hand tight and grinning. "And it's kind of cool, being the only 'mortal' allowed here."

Cassie wanted to smile along with her friend, but the situation felt too heavy. "There's a war coming," she confessed. "One that the Zodiacs are fighting in, and I think it could affect all of us. Humans too." She took a deep breath and waited for Quinn's reaction, but it didn't come. "I still don't understand how you can see all of this, and how you're so . . . fine with everything."

Quinn laughed, but an uneasiness rested in her eyes. "I don't know either, but I guess it just kind of feels normal? In the least normal way possible, if that makes sense. I always had a tingle that something more was out there, waiting to be discovered, and I felt a part of it somehow." Her shoulders slackened. "It's so crazy, how you knew nothi—"

A deep bellow echoed through the hallway—one Cassie recognized. She placed a single finger on her lips for Quinn to stay silent.

"I'm not letting *anything* happen to her," she could hear Hero say. A weird feeling brewed in her stomach at the sound of his words. Cassie gestured for

Quinn to stay hidden in her room while she snuck out to the hall, trying to hear more.

"Well, you certainly did when you lost her to the Seekers," an older woman's voice cut like a knife as Cassie tiptoed to the outside of Hero's door. "We'll just have to see what Calypso has to say at the Oracle. Apollo will speak to her and instruct us on what to do with her."

"She's innocent!" Hero spat out. "We can't just throw her to the wolves if Calypso doesn't give her a positive outco—"

The woman cut him off. "We'll decide what fate she deserves *after*."

Hero's door suddenly opened wide, and a woman walked out. She stared down at Cassie with an intense gaze, and her voice held a hint of anger as she spoke. "The Gemini, I presume."

Cassie just blinked between the woman and Hero. The woman reminded her of her old principal in high school; both robbed her of the ability to speak.

"Artemis, prepare Cassandra for the trial," the woman ordered as Artemis appeared from behind Hero, holding a gray garment bag in her arms. "And put the *mortal* in the room I had prepared for her, would you?" she scolded, looking at them knowingly with blatant displeasure.

She knows about Quinn? And gave her a room?

Hero only passed Cassie a small, thin-lipped smile before following the woman down the long and narrow corridor.

Cassie glanced over at Artemis, whose icy eyes were closed off. She gulped. "So, she's the head of the Arena—Diana? She seems—"

"The Archon, not head," Artemis corrected. Cassie couldn't help but notice the bitterness in her voice as she said, "And scary? Yeah, that's Mother Dearest."

"She's your mom? And Hero's?"

Artemis rolled her eyes. "That's how it works, yeah."

"Did Hero tell her about Quinn?" Cassie asked, nervous about what could happen to her friend. Hero had said that mortals shouldn't know about Zodiacs, and with herself already being "illegal" and dangerous to them, she could only hope they had good intentions when it came to her friend.

"My mom can sniff out mortals a mile away, but to be honest, she reacted a lot better than either of us anticipated." Artemis shrugged a shoulder.

"What's the Oracle?" Cassie asked, her mind trying to catch up with yet more information about this life.

"You like your questions, don't you?" Artemis shot at her. She drew a breath and said, more calmly this time, "The Oracle's kind of like our courthouse. It's named after an old prophet. We use it as a place for big discussions, to make or dismiss laws, and to hear new prophecies." She then walked into Cassie's room like nothing had happened, as though her mom berating her was second nature.

Artemis paused mid-step when she spotted Quinn, who stood upright by the bedpost like a mannequin. "Um, so," she continued, pulling her gaze from Quinn and back to Cassie, "we have to present your case to our council and prophet, who will speak to the Immortal Apollo and see whether you'll kill us all or not."

Cassie's eyebrows shot up, her heart pounding against her ribcage. "You don't sugarcoat anything, do you?" She couldn't help but also feel a chip on her shoulder at Artemis's reaction to Quinn, a protectiveness surging through her.

"Why would I do that?" Artemis said as she hung the garment bag she had in her arms on its golden hanger on the door of the closet. "One of our seamstresses picked out a dress for you for the Oracle. You'll have to wear it today. It's over the top, I know, but that's how things work around here." She unzipped the bag, revealing a long, flowy white dress, detailed with white lace sleeves and bodice. Cassie's eyes drifted to the bottom of the dress. A dark ash seemed to coat the material—the white fading into a darkness, as though it were stained.

A cruel joke, perhaps?

"Wow," Quinn commented, reaching out to touch the fabric. Artemis recoiled at the closeness, making Quinn step back toward the bed. Cassie shot daggers at Artemis, who stared at her as if she couldn't care less.

Quinn smacked her lips awkwardly before pulling a bag out from under the bed. She rummaged around before taking out a pair of black heels with a silver pattern and holding them out for Cassie to take, now beaming.

To her surprise, Artemis nodded in approval. "Change into this, and then you can fix your hair and face."

Cassie reached to hold out a piece of her hair, frowning as she examined the knots decorating it. She walked into the bathroom connected to her room and closed the door behind her. She'd never had an ensuite bathroom before, but having her own space was peaceful and private.

A purring sounded, as though reminding her that she was, in fact, not alone. Glancing down at Bones lying casually on the bathmat, licking his paws, she smiled.

Slipping her pajamas off, she let the plaid material pool on the floor before kicking it to the side. Cassie held the dress up, spinning the hanger around to see it from all angles. She sighed and undid the zipper.

Stepping into the dress, she pulled it over her body as the curves of her hips fitted into it. She slipped her arms into the lacy sleeves, the dark-to-light material now covering most of her pale skin. Cassie walked over to the mirror above the white basin, the dress flowing between her knees as she flipped her hair over her shoulder, staring at her reflection—into the vibrant purple eyes that glared back at her, the onyx hair falling past her shoulders, and into the pure wickedness that entrapped her.

Cassie wondered when she'd be able to see herself again and not this "dark side." And this dress was a reminder of that same darkness threatening to spill into her soul at any moment, staining her as it had done the material.

It's just a dress, Cassie. Stop overreacting.

She straightened her back, biting the inside of her cheek. Instead of peering away this time, she stared her dark side down in the mirror, holding up her middle finger as a smile pressed against her teeth. She didn't want to be fearful of herself anymore.

Zipping up the rest of the dress and slipping into Quinn's heels, Cassie took one last glance in the mirror. It was a beautiful dress, despite the face staring back at her. She took a deep breath.

Back in the bedroom, Quinn was telling some joke, making Artemis swing her head back in laughter—something Cassie had never thought she'd see from the tough and guarded Zodiac. In fact, this was the first time she had seen Artemis smile. She'd been an entirely different woman moments ago, but Quinn always had that effect on people. And maybe Artemis's initial reaction was not from disgust, but from something else . . .

Their laughter faded once they noticed her. Cassie knew the glint in Quinn's eyes, the one she had when she found someone attractive and seamlessly and successfully flirted. She made a mental note to ask Quinn all about it later.

Artemis stiffened like a kid caught doing something they shouldn't. She then pulled out the vanity chair, gesturing for Cassie to sit.

Cassie picked up a hairbrush she had laid out earlier from the bag of things Hero had packed, and she sat. The sound of the bristles working through the tangles echoed in her ears.

"Were you born with silver hair, or did you dye it?" Artemis asked, her arms crossed as she watched.

"Born with it—not sure where it came from, though. My mom had light blonde hair, so maybe her?" A memory of her mother popped into her mind, her locks twirling in the wind as they drove with the windows open. She smiled at the memory, then tucked it away, willing herself back to reality.

Artemis's attention was now on Quinn, who was rummaging through the closet. "But I'm guessing the bit of red in your hair isn't natural."

"Not unless you call a drunk fashion student trying to make a statement by dyeing a strip of her hair red *natural*, no." Quinn laughed. "It's better than the time Cassie tried to dye her hair blue. It turned green. She wore a hat for weeks."

Cassie couldn't help but grin as she loosely braided her hair to the side. "Yeah, that was pretty bad."

"I've never dyed my hair before," Artemis muttered as she ran her fingers through her own loosely curled brown hair.

Quinn beamed at her. "That'll change soon enough, with us in your life."

Artemis glanced between the two of them, a smirk lurking on her face. "Quinn," she said, as though her name sounded foreign, "we've arranged a room for you, the one right next to this one. You'll stay as long as you need to, or until we deem it safe enough for you to go back to the mortals. You're welcome to get set up in there whenever you want."

The corners of Quinn's mouth tugged. "Yeah. I'd like that."

"Then it's settled." Artemis pulled her shoulders back. "Come on. I'll show you your room while Cassie finishes getting ready."

Cassie tentatively watched as her friend left the room, not knowing how to feel. Quinn did have the summer off, and she'd told her family she was going to spend it with Cassie anyway. Crossing her fingers, she hoped she'd get out of this Gemini mess by the end of summer so Quinn could go back to her normal life. So that they both could.

But hope only goes so far . . .

She reached down to grab a small makeup bag and placed it on the table in front of her, pulling out different products and tubes. Cassie lifted her chin, finding herself compelled to look in the mirror, knowing what awaited her—but the longer she stared at it, the more she felt herself slipping. A voice whispered to her, one she wasn't sure was herself or not: *I am not afraid of you.*

Cassie tilted her head, and with it, her dark side did the same. She moved her hand up, her fingertips grazing the mirror, touching it through the glass. A popping sound echoed in her ear, then another, and another . . . The mirror cracked underneath her fingers, moving faster as the lines moved to the walls, until the entire room was overcome with veins of darkness.

Her pulse raced as she stood. She wanted to scream, to yell for help, but she froze as the light appeared stolen from the sky, cascading around her in twilight. The wind picked up outside, and a lightning bolt made her jump.

Cassie ran to the door, trying to pry it open, but she was locked in, trapped in this hellish room. Another thunderclap ended with a spark of purple light, and a figure appeared.

Her dark side stood in front of her, a smile slashed across its—*their*—face.

All the breath left Cassie's body as her eyes drifted down to her dark side's hand, to the bloodied blade resting in her fist. The door to her room swung open, revealing a pile of bodies.

Her knees began to buckle, her throat tightening.

Her dad. Quinn. Hero. Artemis. Nyssa. Countless other faceless people—all dead.

What did you do? Cassie thought, the words unable to leave her mouth.

That same voice whispered back, *You mean, what did* we *do?*

"Quinn's getting settled," someone else said, sounding far yet near all at once.

Cassie flinched at the words, and within a heartbeat, the world around her returned to normal. Her eyes shot down to the chair she sat on, as though none of what she'd experienced was real—as though it were a just dream.

Or a premonition.

Artemis stood by the doorframe, eyebrows knitted together. Her lips parted to say something.

"Has a mortal ever been to the Arena before?" Cassie asked before Artemis could speak, before she could question what had just happened to her. She wanted to lock it up deep inside and never tell another soul. She also thought back to what had happened to her yesterday, when she touched that dress and felt transported into a different time and place. Was this the same thing?

One emotion weighed on her the most: *fear.*

Artemis's eyes narrowed before she said, "Zodiacs aren't allowed to associate with mortals. It was banned after an uprising long before we were even born." She crossed her arms. "But it's also part of our job to protect the mortals, so we'll bend the rules for her, for a while."

Cassie took a deep breath, shutting her eyes. "I just want her to be safe and away from wars and evil gods and demons." *From me.*

"I know," Artemis sighed, a rare sadness washing over her. "Look, a little advice: In the Oracle, don't let them see you waver. Be strong in front of them, even if you don't feel it on the inside. A prophet will come and tell you your fate, but both Hero and I will be there as a part of the council. We can help sway the votes in your favor."

"Thank you," Cassie whispered, ignoring how her body was now covered with goosebumps.

"And wear the red lipstick. It's more daring," Artemis said with a smirk, reminding Cassie of Hero.

Cassie smiled graciously and applied the red lipstick. Artemis was right. It painted a picture of boldness, of the *badass* Hero claimed her to be.

Her memory flashed to Hero's face, the life drained from his golden skin.

"You ready?" Artemis asked, shaking her free from her nightmare.

She couldn't turn back now. Even if she was the illegal and dangerous Gemini, she also had a hell of a lot of fight to give. She had to. She could never let herself become what she had just seen.

"As I'll ever be."

CHAPTER 15

SORTIGER

(ADJ.) DELIVERING PROPHECIES OF THE FUTURE;
HAVING THE QUALITIES OF BEING ORACULAR

Fate. What a funny thing. A dangerous thing.

Life splattered itself across souls like water on ink-touched paper, and Cassie cursed herself for believing in such a thing as fate, as though the universe aligned every meeting, every relationship, and every death perfectly to its needs and desires.

Cassie stood awaiting her own fate—whatever that may be and whoever would decide it—and all she could do was hope that her dark side wasn't destined to unleash itself, harming those she loved. There could be no worse fate than that. She shivered at what her dark side had shown her: the potential of eternal rest cast on everyone she cared for, by her own hand.

Her thoughts fell deeper and deeper into an abyss she could not crawl out of. She dug her way through the ground, in the mud, for an escape—the freedom to have her life turned back to a day when she didn't know this world existed, or to a future where she took no part in it.

Yet the other side of her soul tugged. A glimmer of hope shone through the cracks, another half of a life that could be exhilarating—a life that wasn't lived in a small bedroom, rotting away at an office job filled with mindless scrolling, losing herself with each passing moment.

But what if this is it? What if this is how I die? All because of a prophecy and a vote from people I didn't even know existed two days ago?

She stared at the large doors blocking her from the room holding that prophecy, and willed herself to breathe.

This is it. This is now. I am here.

The doors opened, each pulled by two tall men, both dressed in black suits spun through with lavish gold embroidery, decorating them as though they were an ornament, and perhaps that was an indication of the room to come: lavish, brilliant, and terrifying. Cassie held her head high as she walked through the doors, authoring herself to look confident, as Artemis had told her to be.

The doors closed behind her with a boom, her dress flowing at the force of the wind behind her. She swallowed any fear or anxiety, tucking it deep into her soul. As for the hairs rising on her skin, standing to applaud her fate, she willfully ignored them.

The room was large and circular, decorated with the finest gold and marble. Ancient crumbling paintings of what Cassie assumed were the twelve Immortals covered the ceiling. She paused on one face, recognizing him as though it were a distant memory. The man appeared golden, his light blond hair cascading to his shoulders as light shone out from behind him.

The murmurs of the Zodiacs filled the room. Cassie released a small breath of relief as she found Hero; his unruly hair and kind eyes were a true blessing in the moment. Hero and Artemis flanked Diana at a table, along with several other Zodiacs who must have been the council Artemis had mentioned.

Hero's nod was gentle, his slight smile a reminder of his promise to be there for her.

Diana, however, stood tall, her cold stare making Cassie shiver. Her raw power hushed the room into silence, with her hair drawn back into a tight bun and sharp makeup on her aging face—not too much, but not too little. Her navy dress was fitted to her curved shape, almost like what she'd seen people wear to a business meeting. And maybe that's what this was: business.

Diana took a seat, and the other Zodiacs on the council followed suit. She rested her intertwined hands on the table, directing Cassie to sit with the bowing of her head.

Cassie made her way to the singular throne-like golden chair opposite Diana. She smoothed the front of her dress as she sat, raising her gaze to stare Diana in the eyes.

Don't let them see you waver. Be strong, even if you don't feel it inside.

Diana stood again, scanning the crowd of people standing behind Cassie, and spoke. "We are gathered here to discuss the finding of the new Gemini. I understand her presence here comes as a shock, but rest assured, we will soon reach a fair conclusion." Diana's voice remained clear and composed, like a trained politician, as she continued her speech. "Should the prophecy reveal a positive outcome, we must do all that is in our power to protect her."

Positive outcome. What happens with a negative outcome? Will I be discarded? Thrown out of this world? Will I hurt anyone? . . . Kill anyone?

"Cassandra, for your knowledge, I will now read out the Gemini Law," Diana said, clearing her throat. "The act of the Gemini Law ensures, after years of dark Geminis bringing terror, death, and destruction to Zodiacs and mortals alike, that extreme measures will be taken should another Gemini be at risk of being born. September will be the month of abstinence among the Zodiacs, and labor shall be induced early for anyone expecting a child within the Gemini time frame. And in rare, worst-case scenarios . . ."

Cassie wanted to wilt down into the ground at what the silence implied. Was being a Gemini so bad that they'd go to such measures to ensure no Gemini would live? She scanned the endless faces that were judging her fate, waiting to see if she should be granted life or not. As she flicked her eyes up to meet Hero's, he swallowed visibly, as though confirming the monstrosity, though he himself had mentioned yesterday that he was against killing her or any Gemini—something others clearly were not.

Diana's words cut through her like a blade. "Since there's no law or writing that states how we should handle your specific case, we will hear from the prophet Calypso to learn what may lie in your future."

Cassie turned at the sound of the doors reopening, straining to make out a face on the hooded figure walking in. The white silk cloak rippled off the newcomer's body, as though transformed into liquid. The woman's rich blonde locks flowed to her thighs, blending with the shining material of her dress. Cassie found herself entranced by the sheer beauty of this glorious being. Each feature of the woman's face held its own prominence on her pale skin, and even from this distance, she smelled like daisies and storms. Cassie could almost taste the divinity wafting off of her.

Calypso stepped closer to her. Cassie straightened her back and lifted her neck, trying not to seem small, despite her awestruck gaze. She wanted to write millions of poems and sonnets and stories about the prophet.

Calypso's hands reached toward Cassie's forehead, placing her dainty fingers on each temple. A spark traveled through Cassie's body, as though connecting her to the prophet with each flicker. Calypso lifted her head toward the skies, her eyes glowing a sharp white, and soon after, Cassie's own head shot back, her vision fading to blankness. She floated through the sky, clouds surrounding her as the air danced around her skin, weightless and free.

In the distance, Cassie could make out a figure walking toward her: a man, wrapped in golden clothes, holding a wooden bow in one hand as feathery arrows poked out from behind his back. His shining blond locks cascaded around his chiseled face. She recognized him from the paintings on the ceiling.

Apollo.

"Hello, Cassandra," he called, his voice deep and powerful. "It's nice to see you again."

Again?

The light behind him shone like the sun. She lifted her arm to her eyes, shielding herself from the blinding radiance.

Apollo continued, "When the stars meet the tides, and darkness rises over the sea, you shall be reborn in the moonlight. That will be your power. Keep your friends close, for they will keep you warm, and in turn, they will keep you alive."

The words tumbled around in her mind like a hurricane as she tried to register what he meant.

"You mustn't tell anyone about our encounter," Apollo said. "Keep it our secret, for now. All will be revealed in time. I wouldn't want to ruin the surprise."

What surprise? She wanted to know more, she wanted to speak, but before the words could leave her mouth, something pulled her away.

The world fit itself back into pieces before her.

She was back, sitting on the golden chair, in the golden room, looking at the golden prophet.

"She is one of the Divine Prophecies," Calypso said, speaking for the first time, her voice sounding close and afar all at once.

Gasps echoed across the Oracle, ringing in Cassie's ears.

"The Divine Prophecies hold multiple strands of reality, each one as possible as the next. I see her on two paths, one of light and one of darkness. The path of light will aid her in becoming a guiding force for us in the war. With her, what is broken shall be bound. All twelve must be together in the end."

Cassie sucked in a breath as Calypso continued, "However, the path of darkness will lead to the demise and misery of us all. It is different from anything I have encountered before. The Gemini may be the last hope remaining for the

Zodiac and human race alike, but if she should fail, grave tragedy will befall the world." Calypso paused as everyone remained silent. Cassie could only hear her heart beating in her chest. "Given all this, Apollo wishes for the Gemini to stay protected."

Cassie's mind overflowed like the tide rolling in, waves crashing on every riddle and thought and memory she had.

The war. I could help them win the war. I could prevent everyone from being enslaved and tortured—or worse. But how? What could I possibly do to help them? I don't want to go to war. And if I turn dark . . .

Her worries didn't disappear the way she thought they would after her fate was revealed. Instead, they grabbed onto her, dragging her down into the shadows. She was stuck in a life she didn't know how to escape from, and in a war she might have to fight in, regardless of whether she wanted to or not.

Calypso disappeared into thin air in front of her.

Diana's expression remained unchanged. "The council will now take its vote."

Cassie's eyes shifted as everyone whispered among themselves, shaking or nodding their heads, her entire future in their hands. She spotted Titus and Elijah together in the crowd, their mouths unmoving as their eyes trained on Hero.

Hero rose from his seat, muttering words in Diana's ear.

The Archon cleared her throat. "The council has voted, five to two. With the prophecy revealed, we must conform to Apollo's wishes. The Gemini will remain protected in this and every Arena. She is our hope for the war, and we will guide her toward her victory against darkness."

A crest of relief broke over Cassie. But then the murmurs began, voices growing louder and louder from each corner of the room.

"Protect her? Are you insane?" a copper-haired woman's sharp words cut through the uproar.

"It's not safe while she's here," another Zodiac in the crowd yelled. "Not to mention, she brought a *mortal* into the Arena!"

"That was me!" Hero exclaimed, his body drawing taller before Diana threw her arm across him, dragging him back into his seat.

"The mortal has been bonded. There was no choice in the matter. We will deal with her accordingly," Diana stated.

Deal with Quinn? What will they do to her?

"Did you not listen to the prophecy? Do you not care about the war?" Hero snapped back at the Zodiac.

"Have you forgotten what happened with the last Gemini? How many lives did he take? Over two thousand, if I remember correctly," a Zodiac man at the table called out.

"The last Gemini attack happened a century ago. This time will be different," Hero responded.

Cassie darted her eyes around to focus on who spoke the loudest, her breath quickening. *Two thousand lives* . . . The heaviness of another's murders came crashing down on her at once. The token of the Gemini sign weighed heavily with so much blood already, and she didn't want to add a single drop to it.

The copperhead Zodiac shot back, "She's a Gemini, Stamos. We can't risk it. She could kill us all. I say we kill her first."

They want to kill me even now? Cassie drew her shoulders in—as though that could protect her from the violent inclinations of those around her.

But Diana's voice quieted all who spoke. "We are not *killing* her. She has not provoked a single drop of bloodshed, and we don't know if she ever will. Both the council and Calypso have spoken. The Gemini will remain unharmed, and we shall do everything in our power, within reason, to provide her with a favorable outcome. I'll make sure of it myself. I promise you all."

After a moment of silence, a Zodiac from the crowd called out, "And what if she turns?"

Nothing had changed for them after the prophecy. They still feared her. She couldn't stop her body from trembling, but she needed to fight, to win. She couldn't let this darkness out; she couldn't be the murderer, the bringer of de-struction they were talking about. She had to be the light. She *had* to.

Diana stood abruptly. "We will have measures set in place for such a tragedy. We will not let history repeat itself, but we must try to save the Gemini. It will be a long battle, but it is one we have to fight. After all, if we want peace, we have to prepare for war."

Those words echoed in Cassie's mind: *"If we want peace, we have to prepare for war."*

Diana's tone silenced the enraged crowd in seconds. "We shall heed Apollo's warning, but we shall take his encouragement more. This meeting is adjourned." She remained in place, her gaze keeping the Zodiacs in line. They filed out of the room at her order, not one of them meeting her eyes.

Minutes after the room had cleared around her and she was entirely alone, Cassie pushed herself off the chair, the weight of her trial heavy on her chest. Tears rolled down her face as she dropped to the ground, utterly and fully consumed by how much her life had changed. While she wanted to fight—to live—it also terrified her. She didn't want to lose herself. She couldn't stand the idea of hurting anyone or watching anyone get hurt. She could be a savior in their war if she defeated this darkness. But that war was coming, and she might be there on the front lines—where death lurked, waiting to pounce.

"Hey, hey, hey." Hero was suddenly at her side, comforting her, making her flinch at the contact. "You're okay." His hand fell to her shoulder, rubbing it with his thumb. "You did it. The outcome was good. You're going to be okay."

But Cassie couldn't stop the questions from churning in her mind. "If you knew I was this dangerous," she said, "if your kind would have rather me dead, then why save me?"

Hero looked down briefly. "I've never agreed with the Gemini Law, with anyone being forced by law to give up their right to choose," he said. "But when I found you, a small part of me hoped this may be a chance to change the way others think as well."

Although her heart softened at Hero's words, she shook her head. "Why give me an out? Why give me a choice when you knew all this?"

"Because you *always* deserved one—even if it was a shitty one. Stay here and fight, or leave and risk it all." Hero sighed, moving his hand to tuck away a piece of her hair.

"But Diana? How would any of the Zodiacs be okay with me leaving?"

"They wouldn't have been," Hero said, and Cassie's heart skipped a beat. "But I would have gotten you out of here if that's what you wanted. Even if I had to hide you somewhere. And when the time came, if the darkness were too much, I would have handled that myself."

Cassie looked at him, unsure of what to say next. Hero would have put himself on the chopping block just to give her that option—even if it meant having to kill her himself if the darkness took over . . .

She narrowed her eyes at him. "Hold up. You would have hunted me down and killed me?"

"Well," he fumbled a bit, "it's not as if I'd *want* to, of course. But if you were about to become a killing machine, I would do anything to protect those around me."

Cassie couldn't help but admire that about him, how he would literally do anything for those in his life, and that even included her—even if it was a bit twisted.

The premonition that her dark side had shown her flashed in her mind, and she knew if it ever came to that point, she'd plunge a dagger into her own heart. Hero would protect them, but Cassie wanted to believe she'd never let it get far enough for him to need to.

"What happens if I turn dark here, though? If all our efforts fail, and it takes over for good?" Cassie asked, needing to know they had a plan to stop her . . . just in case.

"First of all," Hero said, "our efforts won't fail. Let's try and think happy thoughts about that." He smiled widely. "But we have stuff in the Arena we can use to dampen your powers, certain . . . restraints, for lack of a better word. Though it would only last a few weeks at best before our bodies could heal from the magic. It's complicated." His expression tightened.

"Why not just use that on me now?"

Hero's eyebrows raised. "Do you want us to?"

Cassie considered it for a beat, then shook her head. No, she didn't want to give up, or be a prisoner in shackles for the rest of her life. She didn't want to be *dampened*. What would that mean for the war? For everyone she loved?

"No. I don't," she said after realizing she hadn't replied out loud. "Not unless *she* comes out and you have to."

"That's why, then. We'll only use them if push comes to shove, okay?" He stared at her until she nodded. "But I'm sorry you had to go through this trial. You've taken this much better than I would have." His lips thinned. "Come on, let's get out of here. Anywhere in the Arena you want to go?"

"Just my room for now," she said, her eyes drooping with exhaustion.

Hero wrapped his arm under hers and lifted her back to her feet. "I've got you," he whispered, his voice reaching out like a hand to hold through the mist of her thoughts.

And she believed him.

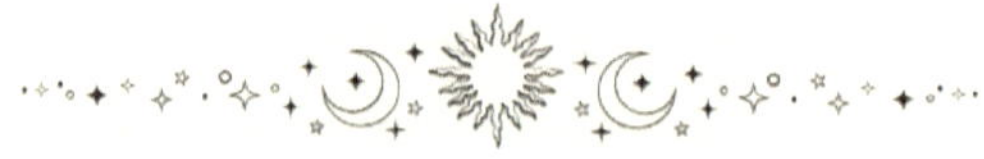

After Hero walked Cassie back to her room, he found himself outside his mother's office. He took a deep breath before knocking.

The door opened within seconds, his mother's composed face coming into view. She invited him in with a tick of her head, and once they were inside, she finally spoke. "Is everything alright?"

He cleared his throat. "I wanted to thank you for sticking up for Cassie. I knew she had more in her; I knew it from the moment I saw her." The corners of his mouth lifted as he spoke. The prophecy had had a better outcome than he could have imagined, and he still couldn't ignore that something in him had changed around her. A small fire was ignited within him.

"As Calypso said," Diana responded, "she is a beacon of hope, and that's what our people need right now. Even if we don't know how she will help us win the war yet, she is a necessity for it." Diana cleared her throat and clucked her tongue as she walked over to her desk. Hero followed behind her.

"I see the way you look at the girl," she continued, turning back to him. "Hero, my boy, the Gemini could be our weapon in the war, but the odds are not in her favor. There has only been one light Gemini—*ever*—so don't give her more hope than she deserves. Do you understand me?"

A quick flash of rage erupted in him. "She's not a *weapon*, and she shouldn't be treated as one!" The words tasted bitter in his mouth, the anger rising at what little hope his mother had, even after Calypso's prophecy. His gratitude for her a minute ago left without saying goodbye.

"There is another prophecy I learned about many years ago," Diana muttered after a heartbeat of silence, gazing into the distance. "Shortly after your second birthday, Apollo came to visit me. He told me of a Leo and a Gemini fated to be together, two lines meeting at a time in life when they needed each other the most. I thought it was nonsense—there hasn't been a Gemini in *years*—but then news broke of Cassie's sudden appearance." She paused, her eyes darkening. "Apollo warned me the Gemini would be the ruin of the Leo. Of *you*."

Hero froze as he struggled to process his mother's words. *Cassie and I . . . fated to be together? And Cassie would be my ruin?* He couldn't breathe. This couldn't be possible. She was lying. She had to be. But why would she lie about this?

"You feel a connection between the two of you, yes?" his mother continued. "A divine connection you can't explain, but whenever you're around her, you're captivated by her. As though you would do anything for her?"

The world swam before him, his chest heavy and his heart aching with the newfound prophecy. He couldn't deny that he was drawn to her, but he'd only known her for two days, and he'd passed it off as him being protective of her.

Is this all an elaborate plan from the Immortals? Is how I feel for her even true? Do I even feel anything?

He knew his silence gave his mother all the answers she needed.

She placed a cold hand on his cheek, rubbing her thumb against his skin. "I already see the change happening within you. You let her stay in your team's quarters, giving her a chance instead of putting her in a cell as I'd suggested. And know I'm only allowing it now because of what Calypso said. But speaking out for her at the trial—had I not stopped you—could have spelled the end of everything we have worked for: you taking over the title as Archon of this Arena." She paused briefly. "She could destroy it all."

He clenched his fists. "Have I changed, or do you just not like the fact that I'm my own person enough that I'll question orders *and* your commands?"

"Enough!" Diana's voice echoed off the walls. "I've already lost your father and your brother. I will not lose you too, especially not to some girl. The sole reason she's still alive is because it's the best hope for our people, for the war. But she is not the best for you."

Hero's teeth clenched together. "Prophecies can change."

Diana shook her head. "Rarely do they alter. She is beautiful, but she is not worth your future—or your life."

VERIDICAL

(ADJ.) TRUTHFUL; VERACIOUS

Alone in her room, Cassie twisted her hand behind her back to reach her zipper, desperate to get the dress off her body. The material pooled to the ground around her feet, and she sunk too, the cold wall stinging her bare back as she hugged her knees.

The words from Calypso echoed through her mind, tearing any sense she had away from her. Any ability to be herself—gone.

"Two fates: light and dark.

Grave tragedy will return.

Loss. Death. Destruction. Misery."

And whatever the hell Apollo's riddle meant. *"Reborn in the moonlight"?*

A war brewed in the skies, one that could destroy everything and everyone she loved if they lost. If *she* lost. If she turned dark, she would be the cause of all their deaths. The thought overwhelmed her to no end.

She didn't know how long she sat there. When she next looked up, the sky was painted a deep amber gradient. Her eyes stung, puffy and swollen from tears.

Cassie pushed herself off the ground, shivering at her nearly nude state. She searched through her clothes, picking out a pair of leggings and her blue sweatshirt. The logo of her old university in Malibu stared back at her as she imagined the lighthouse blinking at her, taunting her. Her dad still believed she was there, lying on a beach, a half-day drive away from home. *Safe.*

But now she knew that no one was safe.

At least she had time, she supposed. She was a wild and strange beacon of hope for the Zodiacs—and for the "mortals"—but she didn't know how to help either of them.

Cassie reached for her phone, charging on the nightstand of her bed. A single text from her father popped up on the screen.

Hey, kiddo. How was your birthday? All okay?

Her fingers tapped against the side of her phone. She wanted to tell him about the Zodiacs, about her new life, but she couldn't risk dragging one more person into this mess. *My mess.* Especially after what had happened to Quinn.

Had the best time, thanks, Dad. I'll call you in a few days.

Cassie sat cross-legged on her bed, playing with the strings of her sweatshirt. Her chest tightened, as though no release would ever take the pressure away. Too much had happened, and there was too much yet to come. There was no way out anymore, for anyone.

She was the Gemini. The girl of two paths, two choices, two souls.

Uncertain shuffling sounded outside her door, and as curiosity got the best of her, Cassie pushed herself off the bed and swung her door open.

Hero jumped back, his eyes wide. Quickly composing himself, he crossed his arms.

"Are you okay?" Cassie asked, her voice soft. She could tell something was troubling him right away. Something was off about him, distant.

Hero nodded in silence, his eyes glued to the ground. His curls were wet, making them seem darker than usual, like midnight, and drips of water threatened to fall down his tanned face. He seemed so different, standing there in a white shirt and gray sweatpants, leaning against the door—not one morsel of the demigod warrior she knew him to be.

"Thank you for taking care of Quinn," Cassie said, careful of her words. "It means the world to me. And for what you said at the Oracle. For believing in me."

"I've got something for you." Hero's voice rang through her ears after what seemed like an eternity of stillness. Cassie lifted her head in anticipation.

He dangled her necklace off one of his fingers.

Cassie exhaled in relief as it gleamed in the air. She couldn't help the wide smile that spread across her face as another piece of her old life was restored. She hadn't thought she'd ever see her necklace again; she'd thought it was lost with her other life.

"Hero, thank you," she gasped as he handed it to her, careful not to touch the actual gem. She placed it on her vanity. "I don't know how to repay you."

Hero shrugged. "No big deal, just a necklace."

"Not only for that," she said, turning back to face him. "For being one of the few people here who doesn't treat me like I'm this ticking time bomb." Her shoulders dropped. "You saw how they all acted in the Oracle. They're scared of me." In the short time she'd been here, Hero had been a guiding hand, a light within the darkness.

"They just think they should be because it's what we've been told our whole lives. But they aren't, not really." His eyes flicked up, meeting hers. The shimmering hues she'd seen dancing between his irises earlier had dulled.

But why? What changed?

Cassie's stomach twisted. "Are you? Ever scared of me, I mean."

Hero shook his head as he closed the door behind them. "My dad taught me when I was young that you have to judge people individually, not based on how others perceive them. You have to make your own conclusions; it's the only way to lead." He paused. "I know there's strength and bravery and *good* in you. You've been thrown into a world you know nothing about, but you've shown your resilience, even if it pains you." The sides of his lips curled as he gazed at her so deep, she found herself wanting to drown in the pool of umber. "So, am I afraid of you? A little bit. You're a fighter. I mean, hell, when I first met you, you were waving a shoe around as a weapon." He laughed. "You practically saved yourself from the Seekers on your first day here. You're tough. That's a blatant fact. But am I afraid you're going to turn evil and kill us all? No. I'm not."

She felt she could breathe again as the words left his mouth. That reassurance grounded her, steadying her whirling mind. "Thank you." Cassie smiled. "For your honesty."

Hero gestured to the necklace on the table. "You said you were only able to see the Zodiac world once you took that thing off, right?" Cassie nodded before he continued. "I want to try something," he said, picking up the necklace. He then took her hand, holding her palm upward. "Can I?"

Cassie gulped but nodded once more. He lowered the gem to her skin, and it pierced her the same way it had on her birthday. She gasped, and Hero pulled it off the moment she did.

"Shit. I'm sorry," Hero muttered as he put the necklace back down on the table. "You alright? How badly does it hurt?"

Cassie shook her head. "It's fine, it's . . . it's already healing." *My body is healing itself.* "I think it's going to take me a while to get used to that." She frowned. "Wait—but it didn't burn you? Why just me?"

"You sound disappointed that your freaky necklace didn't hurt me."

Cassie rolled her eyes.

"I don't know why it has no effect on me," he said. "Someone gave you this necklace for a reason, but I think someone else might have made it so you could no longer use it. I had a suspicion that would be the case when you first mentioned it burning you, but I wanted to make sure." Hero paused as he stepped closer to her, making her breath catch in her throat. "It would have given you a better choice if you could have gone back to the way life was, where it protected you from our world and the Seekers . . . before you knew all of this, rather than just choosing between life and death."

Her heart pounded at his words. "Even after everything that was said in the Oracle, you're still looking for ways I can get out of here?"

Hero's face tightened. "I had this idea when the Seekers first took you, and I wanted you to know, even if it didn't work. There's still a possibility we could find a strong enough witch to recreate whatever magic is in this necklace." His gaze settled on the floor, dashing around as though searching for more possibilities.

"I . . . I can't," Cassie stuttered. "I don't want to someday be hunted by you. I don't want to die, or to cower and hide until I finally succumb to that *darkness*. And how can I stand by and put myself back in hiding when I know there's a war coming, when I know the gods plan on destroying everything to get their way? If there's a chance I could help, no matter how small, I have to do it." She surprised herself with her own words, her own certainty that she had to help, that she *could* help.

Something glimmered in Hero's eyes. "You're pretty amazing, you know that?"

The edges of Cassie's mouth twitched. But something else he'd said rang in her ears: *"Someone gave you the necklace for a reason."* She walked to her bed and sat on the soft edge. "My mom gave me the necklace when I was a little kid, right before she passed away. She told me to never take it off, that if I wore it, she'd always be with me." Cassie touched the part of her neck where her necklace used to lie. *Is Mom part of all this?* "She died when I was eight, although it feels like yesterday," she began, unable to stop herself. "After that, my place in the world kind of just . . . fell apart." She glanced up at Hero, who tilted his head, urging her to continue.

"It was my fault," Cassie mumbled, blinking the tears away. "We were supposed to stay home while my dad was away on business, but I begged her to take me to the movies. On the way there, a drunk driver came out of nowhere and smashed right into us. I woke up in the hospital with a broken arm, and never saw her again." She avoided his eyes as she finished, the heat rising to her cheeks. She hated oversharing, most of all about this. "Sorry for dumping all this on you. I don't know what came over me," she said, playing with the sleeve of her sweatshirt, fixating on how the fabric rippled under her fingers.

Hero sat on the bed beside her, the heat from his body both far and near. "Actually, I understand," he confessed, a deep ache in his words. "When I was around eleven, I snuck out of the Arena. My dad and my older brother, Jason, went on a mission late one night, but I wasn't allowed to go. I was too young, and it was too dangerous. But I went anyway." Hero's face scrunched as he spoke. "I followed them until they got to the docks. They started talking to someone I didn't know, so I hid behind a couple of crates. But I tripped, and one of the crates fell, and they spotted me. The person they were with got mad, and Seekers appeared out of nowhere. It was the first time I'd ever seen them." He shook his head, and his words trembled. "I remember my dad yelling at me to go, and Jason running toward me, but swords came out from behind him, slashing his back. My dad went in to kill them, but when he turned around . . ." Hero grew quiet, pausing for a moment. "There were too many of them. Their wounds were too deep. They both bled out on the street in front of me."

Cassie's eyes stung as Hero recounted his story. He understood her, in the darkest of ways. He had mourned the same as she had.

"It took them hours to find us. I was curled up on my dad's dead body," he croaked out as Cassie wrapped her arms around him. She didn't know what made her do such a thing, but something felt natural about it. She nuzzled her face into his neck as his warm body tensed.

"I'm so sorry, Hero," Cassie said, struggling to swallow the pain they shared. She knew how it felt. She recognized his grief, making it a thousand times harder to keep herself composed.

"I was young, and Artemis even younger. It's just something that happened." His shoulder lifted, knocking Cassie's head off him. She stiffened at his sudden movements, watching as he stood and drew himself away from her, her insides shrinking.

"But one day, I'll avenge them," he said, jaw flexing. "I'll kill every last Seeker if I have to, and the flip side of the coin of you being attacked by them was that I got to learn more about the Seekers than I ever had before."

"That they have a queen?" Cassie asked, hushed.

"That, and their weaknesses." Hero ran a hand through his hair. "Looks like we're both kind of messed up." He forced a laugh, his signature smirk popping out as he cleared his throat.

But Cassie knew the truth. Yes, people died all the time—some sudden, and some over a long period of time. At the end of the day, everyone was going to die, and every inhale brought them closer to death. It was inevitable. But none of it could ever stop grief, or guilt.

"I had nightmares as a kid," Cassie confessed. "Ones where I was back in the car with my mom, riding along, then it would all happen again. It was like I was in—"

"Hell?" He cut her off, eyeing her knowingly. "I had them too. The one thing that helped me was doing something—"

"Creative?" Cassie asked, finishing his sentence this time.

"Yeah. How'd you know?"

"I guess I see a lot of myself in you." She peered up at him, drawing her knees in tight. "I turned to writing and reading. I liked the way I could transport myself into another world and forget who I was for a while. Plus, I noticed your fingers are always covered in charcoal."

Hero's chuckle was light and airy. "I guess drawing, to me, is like your reading. The moment the charcoal hits the page, I'm not myself anymore. It's my therapy."

"If you ever need to talk about it, I'm here. I get it." She found herself unable to meet his eyes, however, biting the inside of her cheek. "Losing a loved one is hard, but you don't have to go through it alone."

"I think it's why I want to win this war so badly. I don't think I can lose anyone else," Hero said, his lips pressing into a tight line.

"I don't want to lose anyone else either," Cassie muttered. "I'll do all I can to help. I couldn't live with myself if I didn't."

He came closer to her, bending down before her. He lifted her chin in his hand, their eyes meeting. "I know you will. But—"

Cassie placed her hand in his, her breath catching as she awaited his words. But he withdrew his hand, as though he'd realized his actions and wanted to take it back.

"I should get going. I'm sorry," Hero said, shaking his head.

Her stomach twisted as she watched him leave her room in a rush. He seemed different with her, though she'd only known him for two days, she reminded herself. Maybe it was the shock of opening up to a person in such a raw way. Or perhaps he'd lied, and *was* scared of her failing, terrified of her becoming the darkness and killing everyone he'd ever loved.

Cassie squeezed her eyes shut at the worries clouding her mind, needing them to fade away and for the light to return. She grabbed a book out of her bag, a story about the roles of judgment, of a woman being shamed for being different, for doing something wrong, when she herself was the true victim of others' assumptions.

There was a fine line between light and dark, good and evil, strong and weak. Cassie had yet to find out which one she'd fall into. She would fight for as long and as hard as she could. But fate, prophecies—those were sealed futures that would not change. She was a girl comprised of two. How could anyone trust her?

CHAPTER 17

AESTHETE

(ADJ.) SOMEONE WITH DEEP SENSITIVITY TO THE
BEAUTY OF ART OR NATURE

The charcoal snapped in Hero's hands as he pressed down on the paper.

He always loved the way the black lines contrasted with the white of a page. It had been a home to him. Not one with four walls and a roof, but an escape into comfort, a place where he could be himself, allowing the darkest parts of him to show, with no fear of judgment. Nothing in his life was colorful, after all. It was death, slaughters, training, and orders.

But this time, it didn't feel right. He glanced at the floor, where a pile of crumpled paper lay like mountains of failures.

His conversation with Cassie yesterday repeated in his mind, mixing with his mother's words of the prophecy. *How could she be the ruin of me?*

He hadn't spoken about his father's and brother's deaths to anyone besides family before. The rest of the Zodiacs had all learned about it in their own ways, through gossip or from the formal publication of their deaths. His mother being Archon meant having his life on display, but never once had the words tumbled out of his mouth to another.

A shift had happened inside him—a vulnerability he didn't *want* to shy away from. It was strange, letting Cassie in, especially after being told the prophecy. Maybe it meant the prophecy was coming true.

The undeniable truth banged in his chest. He was drawn to her. She'd opened the most concealed parts of herself to him, and he had done the same.

His mind drifted to the way Cassie smiled up at him, her singular dimple popping out. The way the light caught her eye, the plump of her lips . . . A pull deep inside of him wanted to learn the colors in her soul, no matter how bright or dark. To learn the way she tasted, the way she felt, what she'd look like sprawled out on his bed . . .

Hero shook his head, desperate for those images to leave his mind. He was being stupid—lustful, even. He was a soldier, and Cassie was his mission. He would look out for her, train her, protect her, but he couldn't think of her as any more than a *friend*. A strictly platonic friend. With zero benefits. He willed himself not to.

A knock sounded at his door as Elijah peeked around it. "Hey." One of his oldest friends flashed a smile, his kind voice filling the room. "Just wanted to check on you after the trial. Things got pretty intense."

Hero nodded, glancing at the ground. "Yeah, they did. But I'm happy with the outcome, even if some won't agree with it."

"People like Titus?" Elijah asked, frowning as he leaned against the door frame. "Give him time. We fight, disagree, bicker, but at the end of the day, we'll always be there for each other."

Hero chuckled, a small smile tugging at his lips. "Did Nyssa bribe you into saying that?"

"Nope." Elijah grinned crookedly, his white teeth flashing. "That pure poetry came from the brain of yours truly. It's a fun place up here." He pointed to his head.

"I'm sure it is." Hero sighed and set down his charcoal. "I don't know what his problem is. It's like he's completely closed off from me, because of her." He paused. "Because I believe in her."

"This whole thing brings up memories of his sister," Elijah said softly. "He doesn't want to lose anyone else right now. Not with the war coming."

"Neither do I," Hero argued back. "Did he speak to you?" He felt a pang of jealousy in his chest. It was always the three of them, and rarely did one go without the other, whether it be missions, talks, or drinks at Psyche's bar. And then came the guilt of not realizing that his friend was struggling so much.

Elijah shrugged. "A little."

He clenched his jaw. "Do me a favor and tell him Lukas is coming to the Arena soon," Hero said. Titus deserved a heads-up. "I've asked him to come help with Cassie."

Elijah's eyes widened at the mention of Titus's ex. Hero knew that Titus and Lukas hadn't seen each other in a while, not since . . .

Elijah nodded. "I'll let him know."

"And what about you, Eli?" Hero's eyebrows raised. "How do *you* feel about Cassie?"

Elijah leaned against one of the posts on Hero's bed, his golden hair glistening in the sun streaming through his window. "I guess I know what it's like to be thought of as the 'dangerous' one. I mean, when was the last time my dads visited me? After I accidentally burned their house down . . ." Elijah's face stilled with the memory, shivering. "This team—our team—is the only family I have, the only ones who've accepted me, flames and all. And if winning the war means I get to keep you guys, then I don't care about the other risks. Plus, Cassie's nice. I like her."

"You'll never lose us," Hero assured him. He knew this was another reason he had to keep his distance from Cassie. Elijah had already lost his other family, and Titus had lost his sister, and it had destroyed them both. He didn't want to be another loss or death on his friends' shoulders.

Hero rubbed his face, sure to be leaving smudges around his jaw. "I don't think my mom will ever trust Cassie. She's just letting her stay because she could help us in the war."

"Did you expect anything less from Diana?" Elijah asked, flopping onto the bed.

"I guess not." He exhaled through his nose. "But Cassie's strong—we've all seen it. And she wants to help. If there was ever a Gemini who could stop from turning, it's her. It's gotta be her. She's different . . ." And brave, and strong, and beautiful . . . and all he'd ever wanted in a woman wrapped in a red bow of his potential death. He cursed himself.

Elijah eyed him knowingly. "Maybe Titus isn't the only one who should give Cassie a chance."

"No," Hero muttered. "There's too many risks."

Elijah remained quiet for a moment before saying the last thing Hero expected to hear from him: "Some people are worth risking it all for."

As the sun approached its descent, the final shadows of the day stretching long across the uneven pavement, Hero made his way down the street. His scabbard rested against his waist, his hand loosely gripping the hilt of his sword, fingers tapping against it in a faint pattern as he tried to clear his mind. Tried to forget Elijah's words.

"Some people are worth risking it all for."

Mortals passed him by, oblivious to the weight pressing against his chest, the mission he was on. Some staggered, already softened by alcohol, others clutching shopping bags in their hands, their eyes wide with wonder as they took in the magic of the city. The wail of a trumpet threaded through the air, and Hero allowed himself the pleasure of a smile, even if for a fleeting moment. Noticing the way the golden light bathed the surrounding four-story Creole townhouses in a final kiss before sinking into the deep indigo of night, he felt a sense of appreciation flow through him. This was his place in the world, an honor bestowed upon him at birth, and one he would carry to his grave. It was his purpose to keep these mortals blind to the horrors lurking in the shadows, to ensure that they never had to know the things that stalked them, craving their blood.

The music swelled, winding through the streets like a living thing. He followed it. A lone performer stood beneath a lamppost, his trumpet crying out a melody that sent a shiver down Hero's spine. It was raw, aching. The sound of a city that never stopped breathing, never stopped fighting, even in the thick of the darkness.

It reminded him of Cassie.

Hero slowed, listening, letting the moment settle into his bones, engraving the sound into his memory. He allowed himself a rare stillness, the kind of peace that came before a battle, before a storm.

The song reached its crescendo, then the last note of the trumpet faded into silence. The gathered crowd erupted into applause.

Hero didn't want to linger too long. Digging into his wallet, he pulled out everything he had, and dropped the bills into the musician's open case. The man caught his eye, giving him a slow, astonished nod of gratitude. Hero returned it before turning away.

His boots scraped against the cracked pavement, the uneven cobblestones worn smooth from years of careless footsteps, of stories that had been lived and forgotten over the ages. His pace, however, was measured. Controlled.

A woman's voice, low, sultry, and inviting, called down from a balcony above, her silhouette framed by the soft glow of string lights. Hero paid her no mind. Not tonight. Tonight, he wasn't a man in search of pleasure.

Tonight, he was hunting.

Five demons had appeared on the Arena's radar an hour ago, sighted near the Museum of Art, heading toward mid-city. He'd been alone in the mission room when the report came in, and a hunt like this was exactly what he needed. The distraction, the clarity . . . Something to focus on that wasn't her.

Cassie.

He huffed out a quiet laugh, shaking his head. That prophecy was the most ridiculous thing he'd ever heard. Maybe his mother had only said it to toy with him, to manipulate him into keeping his distance from her. Maybe it was his punishment for allowing Cassie onto his team, for putting his name and reputation on the line to protect her. But he only did those things because it was the right thing to do, not because he felt any which way about her. Gods, he barely knew the girl.

Sure, she was gorgeous. Feisty. Brave. He admired that. She was one of the most beautiful woman he'd ever laid eyes upon, so of course he was attracted to her. Anyone would be. She was also a mystery, and possibly dangerous. And that intrigued him . . . But feelings? No. He couldn't afford the luxury of catching feelings. Not even a little crush. Not in his line of work. He had seen love destroy people. He had watched it unravel destinies, crack open souls, watched it ruin plans for the future in one simple flick of a sword. He had witnessed its carnage firsthand, from the Zodiacs to his own mother. He had sworn long ago never to fall victim to it.

Of course, he *cared.* He cared for his mother, his sister, his team—his friends, who were as much his family as those who shared his blood. But love? That was different. That was something he'd never allowed himself. He'd had flings to satiate his needs over the years, of course, from his time in the Academy to now, but no one had ever seemed worth the risk. No one had ever seemed worth the darkness of love and loss. Of grief.

And Cassie wouldn't be any exception. Not to his attraction for her, and certainly not to his heart. She never could be. Even if there was the slightest chance that the prophecy was real, even if fate had already woven their threads together, he wouldn't let it take hold. He wouldn't let her become a weakness, a vulnerability. And his mind was only on her so intensely because of his mother's words. But his job was to protect her. Nothing else.

He paused, homing in with his senses. The city felt alive around him, a thrum of music and chatter, neon signs buzzing like insects against the silky night. But beneath it all, Hero heard something else . . . something that didn't belong. He followed it. The Zodiacs had devices to track demons, but tonight, he wanted to do it the old-fashioned way—to stalk them, to find them himself, to really revel in the game of it all.

A low, guttural hiss followed a sharp clicking, like talons scraping against concrete. A flicker of movement, just ahead, past the towering brick buildings that funneled the night like a tunnel. Hero's grip on his sword tightened.

Found you.

He slipped into the narrow alleyway, cloaked in shadows.

Five demons skulked through the alley, their grotesque forms twisting beneath the flickering streetlights. Their flesh was layered with thick, jagged scales, their elongated limbs tipped with curved black talons. Their jaws stretched too wide, splitting at unnatural angles to reveal rows of serrated teeth dripping with saliva.

Rolling his shoulders back, Hero drew his sword in one smooth motion. "Say hello to Hades for me," he said, announcing his presence. The element of surprise didn't matter to him. He wanted the challenge, the fight.

Their heads snapped toward him in unison, a loud growl echoing through the small space. The largest of the group took a step forward, baring its teeth, its hollowed-out eyes gleaming like fire. Recognition flickered in those pits of crimson. They knew who he was. *What* he was.

Good. He smirked. *That'll make it more fun.*

"Ready?" he prompted. Then he moved. Fast. Brutal. Precise.

The first demon lunged at him, claws slicing through the air. Hero dodged, twisting his body just enough for the attack to miss. In the same breath, he swung his blade upward, cutting through its ribs. A sickening hiss tore through the demon's throat as green ichor splattered across the alley walls. It staggered backward before disintegrating into a column of black smoke.

Four left.

The second and third came at him together, flanking him from either side. Hero ducked beneath the swipe of one's claws, slamming his elbow into its throat before driving his blade straight through its chest. The demon let out a gurgling snarl before vanishing into smoke.

Pain flared hot along his bicep as he let out a cry. The third demon had managed to rake its talons across his arm. Hero gritted his teeth and gripped the creature by the throat, his fingers digging into the thick, scaly flesh. His sword hit the ground as he reached his other hand to the base of the demon's neck, and *tore.* The ripping of flesh and bone and muscle made his stomach clench, but it was done quickly with his inhuman strength. Its body and head crumpled into nothing.

Two left.

He launched forward, picking up his blade as it flashed under the glow of a street lamp. The fourth possibly fought the hardest, clawed hands swiping for his throat. Hero ducked, drove his blade through its ribs, twisted, and ripped it free.

Four down, one to go.

The last one ran.

Coward.

Hero sighed, rolling his neck before taking off after it. The demon weaved through the streets, darting past the unaware mortals. Hero followed, steady and relentless.

It made it three blocks before he caught it. A sharp turn into another alley—a dead end. The demon whirled to face him, snarling. With a final, decisive thrust,

Hero buried his sword deep in the demon's chest. It screamed, body writhing before it collapsed into smoke at his feet.

Silence.

Hero exhaled slowly before wiping off and sheathing his blade. The city around him remained unchanged, unaware. The music still played. The mortals still laughed, still stumbled through the night without a clue.

His job was done.

And yet, as he turned back toward the street, his mind wasn't on the hunt, on the mission completed. It was still on her. *Cassie.* The prophecy. The impossible truth that had lodged itself in his fate. He swore under his breath. If he was smart, he'd keep his distance.

But fate always had a cruel sense of humor.

CHAPTER 18

AGATHOKAKOLOGICAL

(ADJ.) COMPRISED OF BOTH GOOD AND EVIL

Cassie sipped her coffee from where she sat on a couch in the common room. She chose the one by the large windows so she could watch the storm outside, the rainfall filling her ears with a certain kind of serenity.

She used to love sitting on the porch of her family home on a summer day, watching the downpour from the safety of cover. She loved the way the heat combatted the new coolness, and the fresh smell of rain.

She hadn't been outside the Arena since the Seeker attack. The furthest she'd gone was a walk around the gardens with Quinn, Nyssa, and Elijah. They'd stopped off by one of the three lakes, dipping their toes in the water, laughing about nonsense. Cassie wondered when—or if—she'd ever see the real world again.

At least Quinn seemed to fit in here more than Cassie could have hoped. A few days in, she found Quinn coming out of the seamstress room with a tape measure around her neck, having secured a job for herself through mere conversation.

146

Making clothes had always been Quinn's dream, and she guessed making battle attire was better than nothing.

Hero popped around the corner, drawing Cassie's attention away as he patted his hand on the doorframe. "Meeting in the comms room. Lukas Garcia will be here any moment."

Her breath caught as she saw Hero standing there. She hadn't seen him since they'd spoken a few days before, their conversation leaving her longing for more. "Okay," she replied, getting up from her seat. He stiffened as she walked closer to him, before taking a step back.

Brushing off his coolness, she followed him through the doors and into the comms room.

"You're late," Titus remarked from a far corner of the room, his arms crossed. Cassie straightened at his tone, marking two people being cold with her today. At least with Titus, she was used to it.

"Relax," Nyssa jeered from her spot on the couch, so tangled up with Elijah that it was hard to tell where one of them ended and the other began. "Lukas isn't even here yet." Nyssa began to hum a melody as Elijah rubbed his fingers up and down her arm. Cassie glanced away from the couple, a tinge jealous of their love. With her fate on the line, it was hard to even fathom if she'd ever find that before her time ran out, or if anyone would even want her with the darkness hidden inside her.

Artemis met Cassie's gaze from where she flipped her knife in and out of its casing. "Where's Quinn?"

"She's at work," Cassie answered coyly. "She's helping out the seamstress."

Artemis cocked her head to the side, her brows furrowing. And after a long moment, she said, "That's good. I'm glad."

"Anyway," Hero began, dragging them away from their conversation, "I've asked all of you here today so we can work on helping Cassie fight her dark side as a team. We could all do with more information on her predicament. We can't tell you much about being a Gemini," he said, his eyes meeting Cassie's, "seeing as it was mostly wiped from our history books. But Lukas can."

"Shocker." Elijah sniggered. "Trying to cover up great tragedies in history to save face."

Hero cleared his throat. "He should be teleporting in any minute now."

As if on cue, a spark of green sputtered in the air. Cassie squinted at the light, shielding her face. She could just about make out a man walking out of the emerald portal before it closed behind him.

Teleportation—he must be a Taurus.

He was on the scrawny side, his black shirt too big for his figure, but his black jeans were a bit too tight. His short hair hung like curtains off his head, bits stuck together from wax as though he had planned every effortless piece. His coffee-colored eyes swirled like Cassie's favorite espresso from the diner she and her father always went to.

"Lukas!" Elijah shouted, jumping off the couch and embracing the newcomer. "It's been years, buddy."

Lukas pulled Nyssa in for a side hug next, and then Hero for a handshake and a pat on the shoulder.

Artemis's eyes widened as she grabbed one of Lukas's tanned arms in her hands, examining his tattoos. "Sick tattoos. I'm jealous," she pouted.

Cassie's attention caught on the black tattoos covering his arms from his wrists to up under his shirt, ranging from flowers to animals to waves crashing against rocks. He looked rougher than the rest of them, she noted—less pristine, more worn. She hadn't seen many tattoos on the Zodiacs yet, aside from the occasional swirl poking out from covered skin. She wondered if Hero had any, or if she'd ever see one on him, if they ever became vulnerable enough with each other to search their bodies for any marks, crevices, and pleasure . . .

Cassie stepped back, shocked at herself for the new desires tormenting her mind. She hoped no one else noticed she'd drifted elsewhere for a moment—to a place of forbidden want.

"Perks of not having a prestigious family, like some of you guys." Lukas smiled before tugging on his sleeves.

"Nice to see you, Lukas," Titus said after a beat of silence, his strained voice filling the room. His face dulled with a certain type of sadness.

Lukas shifted on his feet, dipping his head in acknowledgment.

Hero broke the awkwardness consuming the room. "I trust all at the Naples Arena has been well?" he asked, gesturing for Lukas to sit on one of the large, comfy chairs or couches before seating himself next to Cassie on the couch.

"Yeah, pretty standard. Business as usual," Lukas replied, sitting in the corner. Cassie couldn't help but notice an Italian accent peeking through on the occasional word. "This must be Cassandra," he stated, staring at her. "Or Cassie, sorry. It's nice to meet you." He ran his hand through his chestnut hair, giving her a half smile.

"You too." Cassie smiled warmly back. "So, how do you know so much about the Gemini?" she asked. The rest of the Zodiacs in the Arena only gave her halfhearted answers to her questions, and most tried to avoid the topic altogether, as though it were too dark to even speak about.

"My great-great-grandfather's brother was the last known Gemini. He got through the cracks of the law, like you did. But he died in 1927, and with him over two thousand people." Lukas paused as if to mourn the loss. "Stories of him were passed down through generations, but he was a good man; he was just cursed to become dark." He locked eyes with Cassie, a glimmer of hope shining in them. "It's a shame others see Geminis as inherently evil. I see you as a chance to break the cycle."

Cassie smiled again, almost blushing this time. "Did he live here? Or in a different Arena?"

"Yes, he did. I guess New Orleans is the hot spot for Geminis. He was born and killed here." Lukas rushed to say something else once Cassie's face fell. "But that's not to say it will happen to you, of course," he added, rubbing the back of his neck. "May I ask what stage you're at? What . . . symptoms do you have?"

"I . . . I don't know." Cassie peered down, playing with the hem of her sweater. "It began a week ago, on my birthday. I have this necklace that Hero believes a witch cast a spell on to stop me from seeing this world, but one morning it burned me, and that's when this all started to happen, and then they found me." She looked up at the Zodiacs.

"What exactly happened?" Lukas pressed, leaning forward.

"I kept seeing this *other* me in the mirror, or in any reflection of myself. It hasn't gone away since." Cassie grimaced. She tried to avoid mirrors at each turn now. "When I stare at her too long, it's like I'm slipping into someone else, like my mind is changing. But it hasn't taken over yet." The premonition, the vision her dark side had shown her the day of her trial, was as far as it had gone, but she had yet to mutter a word about it out loud.

"You're further than I thought," Lukas said, his tone somber.

Hero rested his forearms on his steady knees as he stared at Lukas. "What can we do?"

"The Gemini has always been equal parts good and evil," Lukas explained. "But in the end, only one side will remain. And for every other Gemini aside from the first one, that fate has been dark. We have to push her dark side away for as long as possible, until we can get a cure of sorts. But it might be too dangerous to find."

"What is it?" Artemis asked, sitting up from her slouched position. Her ears had clearly pricked up the moment the word "dangerous" left his mouth.

Cassie, however, had a different reaction: her gut shriveled. She hated that word, that possibility of what she could become.

"Apollo fashioned a way to help the Gemini, since it was his gift to the Zodiacs that became tarnished." Lukas frowned. "He made an Elixir out of the blood of a Gemini, and with the help of the Twin Cup, the Gemini could split their dark side and light side into two separate identities, giving both sides a fighting chance, mentally and physically. Without the Cup, the dark side will torment Cassie until she submits. It would take over, leaving nothing left of the Cassie you know."

Icy dread made its way through her at the thought. But there was hope—*a cure.* Cassie knew in an instant that nothing could stop her from finding the Elixir and Cup. She would not submit. She'd rather die than lose herself or anyone else.

"One of the Sacred Cups? Where is it?" Hero pressed, as if reading her mind.

"And if it exists, why hasn't it been used before?" Nyssa asked.

"Maybe it doesn't exist," Elijah said, eyes wide as though he'd uncovered a conspiracy theory.

Lukas chuckled. "No, it exists. But before it could ever be used, Poseidon stole it. He hid it, and no one has ever been able to find it."

Hero shook his head. "If this would help the Gemini, why would the Immortals hide it?"

Lukas sighed, leaning back. "When the War of Gods began to fester long ago, a few of the gods—Poseidon and Zeus, to be exact—thought a Gemini, or all twelve Zodiacs together, could *complicate* things. They wanted the Arenas to keep their ban on Geminis and let us all assume there was no solution."

Hero placed a gentle hand on Cassie's back, the heat from his fingers burning into her skin, stopping her whirling mind, grounding her. But in seconds, he removed his touch, and Cassie was left to merely grasp at that feeling of calm.

"So, we have to figure out where it is before Cassie goes crazy and kills us all," Elijah quipped. "Easy enough."

Cassie flinched, but then said, "I need to know. What are my powers?" *Is there more to my burden than the darkness?*

Lukas's posture became fixed as his eyes flashed with excitement. "You're a hybrid, essentially. Your powers are muted right now, since they're split between both you and your dark side. But once that side is defeated, with or without the Cup and Elixir, your duality doesn't just disappear." He beamed. "You'd be able to shape-shift."

"Shape-shift?" Cassie repeated, her eyebrows lifting. "Into what?"

"Anything you'd like," Lukas said, "from animals to looking like any of us." He gestured around the room, and Cassie followed, studying the Zodiacs around her. "When the War of Gods comes, you could even appear to be one of them, or something so insignificant that they wouldn't even notice you. You could be a spy. That's how I believe a Gemini could help win the war, anyway."

"Lethal." Hero smirked. "I like it."

A spy. A master of deceit. Of lies. It seemed almost too perfect. All she needed to do was to get to that point. Easier said than done. Cassie bit the inside of her cheek, saying what was on everyone's mind. "Who knows if I'll even make it until then?"

"You will," Hero stated. She knew that he needed her to get through this war. She knew what they—all the Zodiacs and mortals alike—stood to lose if she didn't.

Cassie's voice squeaked through her next question. "Why just the Gemini sign, though? All the other Zodiacs seem to be okay with their powers." She shot Nyssa an apologetic smile after the words exited her mouth. No one understood why Nyssa's powers pained her, but it had nothing to do with her sign, Virgo. Only *her.*

Lukas exhaled sharply. "When all the Immortals went about creating their respective Zodiac signs, Apollo was attacked by demons. We don't know why they chose Apollo, or the Gemini; it's just what happened."

"Demons are assholes; that's what happened," Artemis said through gritted teeth.

"A darkness was instilled within the Gemini," Lukas continued, "from the first Gemini ever. And that darkness passed down to everyone cursed to be born in the time frame of the Gemini. So, you see why you pose such a risk . . . and why someone went to such great lengths to hide you." His voice softened. "Probably your parents."

"I think my mother could have been a Zodiac, but she died years ago." Cassie glanced at Hero, who stared back at her with sadness in his eyes. "I barely remember anything about her." She didn't want to mention her father. She knew he couldn't have been involved; in fact, he couldn't have led a *more* mortal life. And she couldn't risk dragging him into this.

Titus exhaled, slumping back in his chair. "Seekers or Demons most likely killed her. Picked up her Zodiac scent and hunted her."

"Titus!" Hero hissed, his body heaving with fury at the comment.

"It's okay," Cassie said, though tears pricked at her eyes at the thought. She moved her face away from the room's gaze. "How long do I have?"

Lukas peered at her through his dark eyelashes. "Maybe a few months? Maybe more?"

"What's the game plan, then?" Titus asked, rubbing his palms together. He shot an apologetic look at Hero.

"First, we need to find out where the gods hid the Elixir and the Cup." Lukas glanced around the room, his eyes lingering for a moment on Titus. "It might take time, and some good old-fashioned digging, but with all of us working together, we'll find it."

"And what about Cassie's mind? Her dark side?" Artemis questioned.

"I've asked Lukas to train you." Hero turned to face Cassie. "In strengthening your mental shields. Hopefully, he can teach you how to use your shields to keep your dark side locked up—literally. As part of our training as Zodiacs, we learn to place a sort of protection in our minds. It helps us against all kinds of threats, like keeping Seekers from possessing us. The training will be helpful in more ways than one."

"Keeping your guard up so that your dark side can't even be seen in a reflection is the goal," Lukas confirmed, nodding at Cassie. "But it won't last forever. The split will happen soon, no matter how many shields you put up, but it'll give us a chance to find the Elixir and the Cup."

She would try anything if it meant not seeing her darker half every time she looked in the mirror. Cassie only prayed it would work.

CHAPTER 19

NOETIC

(ADJ.) OF, ASSOCIATED WITH, OR REQUIRING THE USE
F THE MIND

Their library was pristine—three stories high of bookcase after bookcase, complete with rolling ladders reaching to the top. Faint markings on the wood peeking through the white paint caught her eye. If they weren't trying to find information about the mass murderer trying to break loose inside of her, Cassie would have loved to discover every inch of this place. They had everything, from the classics to books she had never even heard of before, in languages she didn't know.

We're not in Kansas anymore, Toto.

"There's some more back there," Nyssa called out, pointing around the corner of the library.

Cassie nodded, heading toward a new row of books. She and the others had decided the library was the best place to start their search for information about the Elixir and the Cup and had each taken up a section to search. She scanned

154

the shelves, looking for anything that stood out. Something drew her to a red leather-bound book with the inscription *Castor and Pollux.* She ran her finger down its spine. As she pulled it off the shelf, an array of dust came with it, making her sneeze, but when she opened the book, the smell of earthy age filled her nose, a smile now tugging at her lips.

She flicked through the pages of the heavy book, scanning for anything related to her situation. Her attention caught on an illustration of two men: Castor and Pollux, the twin sons of Zeus and Leda, gods of horsemanship and protectors of travelers. *The Geminis.*

Turning on her heels, Cassie walked back to the Zodiacs, eager to devour the story.

Hero turned his attention toward her as she neared, only for a heartbeat before absorbing himself back in a holographic screen. Cassie watched as his brows furrowed deep as he scrolled, causing rivers to form on the skin between them. The information in their database moved at a dizzying pace before him.

Hero remained distant with her, and Cassie didn't know if she had said or done something wrong, or if he was just preoccupied with the burden of trying to save them all—of trying not to lose anyone else. Either way, every time she looked at him, a stabbing pain shot through her chest, one that made her want to run toward him and never look back. It was confusing, to say the least.

Cassie huffed as she plopped herself on a large leather chair, draping her legs across the arm and leaning her head over the other side, staring at her upside-down friend. She had to get the thoughts of Hero out of her mind, crumble them like a piece of paper and throw them in the trash.

Quinn peered up from the book she was reading about gods, shooting Cassie a wink. "Anything?" she asked. Her hair was pulled back, her dark and coiled curls bunched together on top of her head, the streak of red visible. She looked so casual, so in place with her off-white loungewear set, sitting with legs crossed, as though she had always belonged here.

Cassie shook her head before glancing back at the book in her lap, opening it once more. *Castor and Pollux, immortalized by Zeus when Pollux pleaded with him to bring his brother back to life after he died in battle. They spent the rest of their days half on earth and half amongst the stars, and the Gemini constellation honors them and can still be seen by sailors at night, guiding them with luck.*

The original Geminis, before the Zodiacs had even existed, the inspiration for herself and every other Gemini . . . and yet nothing about the Elixir or the Cup. Nothing about the Zodiacs, a dark side, or the darkness wrapping around her soul. Cassie slammed the book shut.

"Jeez. This dude is terrifying," Quinn uttered, holding up her own book and showing it around the room.

Cassie swung her legs, positioning her body upright to see what Quinn was referencing to more clearly. A drawing of a creature rising from flames and piles of dead bodies covered the page, making her shiver.

"That's Phobos. The god of fear," Artemis explained, lifting her head for a better look.

Quinn huffed as she turned the book back around. "I didn't think you guys had anything to be afraid of."

"I dunno. Elijah's afraid of water," Nyssa teased, plonking a kiss on his cheek.

Eli narrowed his eyes at Nyssa playfully, making Cassie chuckle.

"There's nothing to be scared of in the water. It's the most peaceful place to be. Except for narwhals. Narwhals are weird," Titus remarked, staring blankly into the distance and rubbing the back of his neck.

Elijah choked on his spit. "That's a new one."

"They have a horn like a unicorn. It's freaky," Titus defended himself. "I never knew they existed until I left England. Terrified the shit out of me."

"How long did you live in England for?" Cassie asked, swallowing her own fear of having an actual conversation with Titus for the first time.

Titus blinked before he said, "Six years. My family relocated there to tear down a demon drug operation in London. But the accent won't seem to go away."

"It's a cool accent," Cassie muttered, looking him in the eye, trying not to push too far or pull too much.

Titus held her gaze before nodding a *thanks*. It was probably the furthest she would get in being accepted by him, but she'd take it. Although she and Titus didn't get along by any means, Cassie could appreciate his attractive features. His dark brown, almost black skin, those dark eyes that occasionally flashed the most vibrant blue, the soft yet distinguished features of his face . . . Perhaps if he weren't a demon hunter, he would have been a model.

"I'm afraid of the dark," Nyssa added. Cassie wanted to gift Nyssa with a thousand bottles of wine for dragging the conversation away from her awkward interaction with Titus.

"Well, it's a good thing your boyfriend is a human torch, then," Artemis said, grinning. She then tilted her head to Hero. "Future Archon?"

Cassie's head shot up at that comment. *Is Hero going to take over for Diana?* What he'd said about how New Orleans would always be his home made more sense now. She could see him as a leader—a great one too.

"Alright, alright." Hero smirked, holding his hands up. "I'm afraid of being forgotten," he said, his voice softening as Cassie's heart ached. Although she had only known him for a short time, she knew she could never forget him—never forget the golden gleam that sometimes shone in his eyes, the fierceness of his heart, the stars shining in his soul. "I don't want to die one day, and no one remembers me."

The room was silent for a moment before Artemis scowled. "That's the most Leo thing you could have ever said."

Hero bellowed with laughter at his sister's comment. "What about you, Miss Arrow Girl?" He stared at Artemis, wagging his eyebrows. "What made you sleep with a nightlight until the age of twelve?"

Artemis's face fell. "If I tell you, I'd have to kill you," she said through gritted teeth.

Hero pushed his hair back, trying not to laugh. He stepped away from Artemis, his eyes narrowing on Quinn. "Alright, what about you? What scares you?"

Quinn twisted in her seat, thinking a moment before speaking. "Before I knew you all existed, I was afraid of heights. But now I hate those Seeker things more. They're terrifying, like demonic parasites." Her face scrunched as she spoke, rubbing her arm.

Nyssa smiled at her. "Well, you're safe from those as long as you stay near the Arena." Cassie's heart warmed at the conversation flowing around her, one that seemed truly family-like. She couldn't help but listen to every word, chuckle at every joke and jab.

"Garcia?" Elijah asked, his eyes wild and wide, finding the next target in the game.

Lukas tensed, straightening his back. "I guess I have a fear of losing people I love. But there's not many of those around anymore." He passed a side eye at Titus, who in turn glanced away.

Awkwardness filled the room. *Definitely more to that story,* Cassie noted. She'd have to remember to ask someone to clue her in later.

"And last but not least," Elijah announced anyway, grinning wide, "Cassandra Smith, what is *your* fear?"

Her heartbeat accelerated, banging against her ribs. Cassie knew her fear like the back of her hand, but she didn't know if she was ready to admit it. She could lie, spew some typical fear about spiders or sharks, but how could she when they had been so vulnerable with her? They'd put their lives on the line for her, fought for her, and were now helping her. The least she could do was be honest with them.

"My fear is being the cause of pain and death," Cassie mumbled, digging her nail into the leather chair. "And I'm reminded of the fact that my fear could very well come true every day."

The stillness flooded back, along with a snake of dread from her words.

Elijah was the first to speak, his tone now serious. "And we'll all be here to make sure it doesn't happen, as a team."

They consider me a part of their team? The side of Cassie's mouth lifted as she considered it. A team. Friends. A home. She'd had a crack in her heart for years, and maybe the people around her could be the glue.

But that only gave her more to lose.

"In fact . . ." Elijah's eyes widened as he double-checked the book in his hand, placing it on a table. "I think I found something! Right here." He pressed his fingers against a page as they all gathered around. "Since the twelve Immortals can't be on land for more than twenty-four hours a year and they can't bring anything that belongs on earth back with them either, it says the Immortals use the nymphs as their missionaries on earth."

The Immortal gods could only come back for a single day on earth a year? Cassie didn't know if that knowledge made her feel better, or more on edge.

"You think the nymphs are hiding it?" Hero asked. Elijah nodded in response.

Cassie scoured the page, which was full of illustrations of women covered with leaves and flowers dancing near lakes, trees, even mountains. *Nymphs,* the page read. *The female divinities exist throughout all nature. The Nereids are found in the sea, the Naiads are found in rivers, the Meliae are found by mountain ash trees . . .*

"There's a colony of river Nymphs nearby, in Jean Lafitte National Park. I'll set up a mission request to go visit them," Hero said, collecting the book in his hands.

"When can we go see them?" Cassie asked, wanting to jump up and down with excitement at the chance of finding a possible cure.

"When you're ready," Hero assured her as he touched her arm, then removed his hand quickly.

Cassie tried to ignore the stabbing pain in her chest at the continuously confusing interactions she had with him, and the embarrassment she felt whenever she let herself be vulnerable around him or thought more of him, only for him to recoil at her touch.

Hero cleared his throat. "Nymphs are tricky creatures and could use your mind and body as a weakness. Once Lukas says your mental shields are ready, and once we've gotten some fight training in, we'll go."

Titus's eyebrows shot up. "You're going to *train* her? With weapons? Are you joking?"

Hero lifted his head, challenging. "She needs to be strong, both mentally and physically, if she's going to defeat her dark side."

"No way. Train her brain, her mind—I don't care," Titus said as he clenched his fists. "But she's not fighting. You can't put a weapon into the Gemini's hand and expect us all to be okay with it!"

"You want her to be defenseless?" Hero's voice boomed through the room, his face turning red. "She's one of *us*, not just a Gemini, and we can't leave her unprotected against the Seekers or demons."

"I'm just trying to protect *us*—the job you should be doing!" Titus spat, pointing at him.

Hero ran his hand through his hair, scoffing. "If the Seekers take her again—or worse, kill her—then we lose everything. Protecting Cassie *is* protecting us."

"I . . . Let's just focus on my mind for now," Cassie said quickly, asserting her opinion on the matter. In seconds, all eyes fell on her. As Hero said, she was one of them . . . but she didn't want to take the chance that being trained would put them, her new friends, in more danger. At least, not until she had a handle on her mental shields. "We don't even know if I'll manage that yet."

Hero clenched his jaw, his arms crossing. "Fine. If Cassie does well in her mental training, and if Lukas deems it safe enough, I'll train her. If you want to, of course." Hero shot her a glance. "But no one on my team can afford not to fight. That's you too, Cass."

And even though Hero affirming she was part of their team warmed her heart, Cassie couldn't help but feel as though she had also disappointed him by not wanting to train. Or maybe it scared him, her being unprotected. If the Seekers took her again, wanting her dark side to come out, what would happen if they succeeded? It terrified her too, because what would happen if her premonition—if what her dark side had shown her—came true, and she killed all of them? If she truly lost herself?

She risked killing them either way, it seemed. Now, it was a mere coin toss as to which path she would take.

CHAPTER 20

ELEUTHEROMANIA

(N.) AN INTENSE AND IRRESISTIBLE DESIRE FOR
REEDOM

The room hummed with an unnatural stillness. Cassie stood in the center, arms crossed tightly, her muscles tense as she took in her surroundings. Mirrors. Everywhere. They lined the walls, stretching from floor to ceiling, their surfaces fogged slightly with age. The dim light from the overhead sconces cast flickering reflections of hundreds of her dark side, stretching in every direction. The air was cold like steel, sharp like something—or *someone*—waiting to strike.

Exhaling slowly, she resisted the urge to rub at the goosebumps forming along her limbs.

A few feet away, Lukas stood with his arms folded, watching her like he was gauging her reaction. "What's wrong?" he asked, though his tone said he already knew the answer.

Cassie scowled, shifting her weight. "I'm just not the biggest fan of mirrors at the moment."

He chuckled loosely. "That's something you don't hear around the Arena often."

She shot him a glare. "Well, I'm sorry I'm not your normal *demigod*." The last word came out more like a bite, feeling wrong on her tongue. Even though everyone here told her she was a demigod, right now, she felt like the furthest thing from it.

Lukas stretched his arms above his head before cracking his knuckles. "Exactly. You're *not* a normal demigod. And that's why I have faith that you'll be able to do this."

Cassie exhaled, forcing the tension from her shoulders. She *had* to do this. It wasn't as if she had much of a choice, anyway. If she didn't, if she failed, her dark side would keep clawing its way to the surface, waiting for the moment she lost control.

He gestured to the floor. "Take a seat."

Cassie settled onto the cool stone, crossing her legs. The chill from the floor seeped into her skin, grounding her. But the mirrors still surrounded her. Even with her gaze focused straight ahead, she could feel them. Pressing in. Multiplying.

The thought of entering her own mind—walking into it like a room she could simply step into—both astounded and terrified Cassie.

Lukas circled her slowly, his movements measured, his steps almost silent. "Close your eyes," he instructed.

Her hands rested on her thighs as she drew in a slow, deep breath, then gently closed her eyes. She exhaled. The world around her blinked out until there was nothing but darkness. She waited. The seconds stretched into the silence. She tapped her fingers on her leg impatiently. Cassie frowned. "I don't think it's working." She cracked one eye open, only to find Lukas glaring at her, unimpressed.

"Eyes shut," he said flatly.

Cassie sighed dramatically, but complied, her lashes pressing together again.

"What?" Lukas mused. "Don't tell me you're one of those people who think Rome was built in a day?"

She scoffed. "It's just . . . not what I was expecting."

"Mental shields take years for Zodiacs to perfect," Lukas said. "What we're trying to do? Building a prison in your mind, something strong enough to contain your dark side? It's not going to happen overnight."

Cassie clenched her jaw as her fingers curled against her knees. "How am I meant to start if I don't even know what I'm doing?"

A sharp whoosh of air sounded, and suddenly, Lukas's voice came from behind her. "Good question."

Cassie stiffened. "Teleportation must be nice," she muttered, a feeling of jealousy rising in her. *Why do Geminis have to be the only sign cursed with this?* "Much better than an evil twin."

At her words, something inside her stirred. A faint, icy pressure brushed against the edges of her mind, like cold fingers skating across her consciousness, testing the surface, searching for cracks.

Or perhaps a blessing, a voice seemed to whisper.

Cassie swallowed, willing the sensation away.

"Let's try this," Lukas said, still behind her. "Tell me about your dark side. Tell me what it looks like, what it feels like. Try and visualize her in your mind, rather than just in the mirror."

Cassie hesitated. She knew exactly what that darkness looked like, what it felt like. She just hated to admit it. "It looks exactly like me," she said.

Lukas's tone remained steady. "Details."

A lump formed in her throat. She squeezed her eyes shut tighter, forcing the image into focus. "Jet-black raven hair," she murmured. "Piercing violet eyes—too bright, too sharp. Like something unnatural." A pulse of cold coiled inside her chest. Cassie kept going. "There's ... a darkness in them. You can *feel* it when you look into them. It's soul-sucking. Like it's reaching into you, trying to take something. Like it's trying to pull you under." Her breath came out shorter.

"And it's smiling," she whispered. But that smile . . . It wasn't friendly. It wasn't kind. It was a promise of death worn across its face.

Lukas paused for a moment. "Good," he said, his tone portraying a calm Cassie didn't fully believe. "Keep going. Dive deeper. Feel her completely."

At that, a door inside her mind clicked open. Cassie's pulse spiked. Suddenly, she *could* see the darkness, she could see it within her mind. There it was, standing in front of her. The air in the room shifted, growing as cold as death. And then she *felt* it. But not just in her mind. Not in the visualization Lukas wanted her to hold. She felt it like it was real—and it was ready to pounce, to take over.

Cassie gasped. Her hands pressed into the floor to steady herself. No! *No, no, no* . . . She tried to pull back, to slam the door shut, but it was already too late.

She snapped her eyes open.

The room hadn't changed. The mirrors still lined the walls. But in the one directly in front of her, her dark side moved, leaning in closer, smiling at her in a slow, predatory way. Cassie's pulse spiked as she pushed herself back, shaking in fear. Her dark side wasn't just a reflection, but a *thing* that had a mind of its own. And it was latching onto her.

Cassie had given it a gateway, and the second it opened, her dark side launched.

Lukas's stance shifted, his fingers twitching slightly like he was about to do something. He moved, stepping between her and the mirror. Cassie exhaled sharply as his body blocked her vision of her dark side, obscuring it like an eclipse. She felt the darkness slip away from her, fading back into a locked door in her mind, somewhere for safekeeping. For *later*.

Lukas watched her carefully. "You felt it, didn't you?"

She wiped her clammy palms on her leggings. "That was more than *feeling* it."

Lukas sighed, rubbing his jaw. "Your dark side's stronger than I thought."

Cassie's stomach dropped.

He met her gaze. "But so are you."

Hours had passed, or maybe days. Cassie wasn't sure anymore. The only measure of time was the dull, throbbing ache behind her eyes, the sweat clinging to her skin, the way exhaustion dragged at her limbs, but refused to let her rest. Every muscle burned, her body teetering on the edge of defeat, yet she remained in the battle of her own mind.

Across from her, Lukas sat motionless, as still and composed as he had been when they'd started. He hadn't shown the slightest hint of impatience. He simply watched her, studying her like a puzzle waiting to be solved.

She clenched her fists, her nails digging into her palms, grounding herself in the sting. Her mind felt chaotic and raw. She had been trying for hours—trying and *failing*—to craft something within the space of her thoughts, *without* letting her dark side take over. An object, a sword, *anything*. But no matter how hard she fought, no matter how much she pushed, it was *still* there. A shadow at the edge of her consciousness, lurking just beneath the surface, waiting for her to fail.

Which was why this mattered more than ever. If her dark side could take control with just a little falter in Cassie, she had to trap her, and soon.

Her dark side's voice slithered through her thoughts, sharp as a blade. *This is pathetic.*

Cassie flinched, her eyes slamming shut. She was in the void again—the one she had built within herself. The cold, endless, suffocating blackness where her dark side lived. And across from her, reclining like she had all the time in the world, sat her evil twin, no longer tied to a mirror, or a reflection.

Her twin was *alive. Real.* At least, in Cassie's mind, it was.

It looked exactly like her. Same pale skin. Same full lips. Same nose, same soft cheekbones. Yet its hair was ink black, curling down its back like a sheet of darkness, its eyes gleaming with a haunting shade of violet, still shooting a look of amusement. Leaning forward, it rested its chin on its hand, smirking. *You really think you can keep me out?*

Cassie gritted her teeth, ignoring the way her chest tightened, forcing herself to hold her ground. She'd been here before. She'd fought this battle before, and she refused to lose. Inhaling sharply, she pushed with everything she had. The space around her shuddered, and finally, *finally*, something formed in her hands. She looked down, heart thrumming.

A dagger. Small, simple, but solid—*real*. She had made it. But as soon as it had appeared, the dagger flickered, disappearing back into the darkness.

Her twin laughed, a sharp cackle that spurred anger through Cassie's veins. It tilted its head, black hair cascading over one shoulder. *A dagger? Cute. What were you going to do with it? Stab your own mind?*

Cassie ignored it. Hope sprung alive in her chest as she focused on creating, a new idea forming. Another object flickered into existence—a chain, thick and iron, curling like a snake in the void.

For the first time, her dark side's expression faltered.

Cassie exhaled, pouring more energy into it, making it stronger, heavier, unbreakable. She gasped, her muscles cramping, her heart racing, but she pushed through until her legs gave out.

Her knees crashed against the floor as the chain clanked against it too, but it didn't disappear like the dagger. No . . . it stayed.

Her dark side let out a low, mocking hum. *You think that's enough?*

Cassie clenched her jaw, a smile snaking its way onto her face. *I think it's a start,* she spoke back into her mind.

Her dark side rose, walking closer to Cassie. *Maybe,* it said. *But you know as well as I do . . . nothing will hold me forever. We'll be together, one day.*

Cassie's stomach twisted, because it was right. The darkness had always been there. It always would be. The best Cassie could do was keep it caged. But she wouldn't let it in. Not tonight. Not ever.

"No," she whispered. Exhaling sharply, Cassie pulled herself back to reality, opening her eyes. Her body jolted, her muscles seizing as she was yanked back into the room.

Lukas shot up from his seat, watching her, his gaze unreadable.

She let out a shaky breath, her body drenched in sweat, her fingers still curled like they were holding the dagger that no longer existed.

Lukas raised an eyebrow. "Well?"

Cassie swallowed, her heart still pounding. She had done it. She had created something. And for the first time, she truly believed in herself. She met Lukas's gaze, her hands still trembling, and nodded.

Lukas's lips curled into a proud smile. "Again."

And the training continued.

Five days.

Cassie curled her fists. She'd been in this room for five whole days, only leaving at night and for meals—failing at each turn. She had to train here until she could no longer see her dark side in the mirror, until she had control over herself again.

But it still stared back at her in her reflection, laughing at her miserable attempts to lock it up.

Lukas stepped around her like a schoolteacher trying to get a student to do their work. "Come on, Cassie. You can do this."

"I . . . I can't," she muttered, her jaw clenching. Her mind felt exhausted. The more she stared at her dark side, the deeper it sank its claws into her, dragging her further into the darkness and away from her own self. Her fingernails embedded into the wood of the chair she sat on.

"Picture it in your mind. Again," Lukas said, his words both encouraging and strict.

She knew the longer her dark side was free, the more her true identity would slip.

Slamming her eyes shut, Cassie envisioned the room she had crafted to perfection over the past few days. It was pitch black, the obscurity stretching across eternity.

She walked closer as her dark side watched her; a wicked grin stretched across its face. Cassie's own face scrunched as she willed her mind to picture a cage around her dark side. The ground shook below her, the steel bars beginning to form as a sharp pain shot through her body.

Devilish laughter echoed through the room.

You think you're strong enough to do this? her dark side sneered at her. *You're pathetic. Weak. And everyone knows it. That's why Mom never told you about the Zodiacs.*

Shut. Up, Cassie shot back.

You know Hero's only helping you because you can win the war. You're nothing more than a weapon to him, a tool. He doesn't care about you. He pities you.

Cassie's knees buckled as she fell to the ground, the steel bars of the cage falling with her, disappearing into the void.

She couldn't be in this room for a second longer. She couldn't take the raw anxiety of not being able to fight her darkness and dooming each person she'd ever loved to an unimaginable future.

Get out of my head!

No, her dark side snarled.

Cassie hated the vulnerability she had in here, the way her thoughts weren't even her own, and neither was her mind, body, or soul. Anger swelled inside of her as she lifted her hands, conceptualizing the mental cage once again.

Four silver beams shot from the floor.

You know it won't work.

I said, shut up!

Her memory flashed to her father's face. If she failed, what would it mean for him? Would the gods destroy the world and her dad along with it? Would he be made into a slave for them, be forced to bow down to their wants and needs until the day he died? Would she kill him herself?

What about Quinn? And the Zodiacs? Hero, Artemis, Nyssa, Elijah, Lukas . . . even Titus, *dammit.* She cared about all of them, whether she wanted to admit it or not. And she would do all that was in her power to succeed. For herself. For them.

Cassie visualized every last molecule of strength floating out of her and into this cage, the bars rattling and forming, piecing together into a prison. *Almost.*

She cried out, unleashing the last bit of herself she had to offer.

Until she had nothing left.

Cassie's breaths drew deep as she stared at the ground. Her mind felt like fog on an early autumn morning, seeping into each crevice, unable to conceive a thought, let alone enough strength to even rise. She had failed again. She wasn't even sure if she could go through this one more time. It was too much.

Did you make this all for me? That's cute.

Cassie whipped her head up.

The cage. It was built.

She chuckled, pushing herself from the ground, ignoring how her legs wobbled and barked for her to stay down. She'd done it. And her dark side had hell to pay.

I'm not leaving until you're locked in there—for good.

You can't trap me forever, you know.

I can try.

Actually, I think that cage of yours would suit you better. Maybe I'll *do the trapping.*

Cassie lunged at her, taking her dark side down by the shoulders.

Her dark side pushed up, hooking her leg around Cassie's, and throwing them across the floor. They struggled together, her dark side's face taunting her. Cassie's mind spiked in pain as the dagger formed in her hand.

Cassie plunged the dagger deep into its stomach, and her dark side wailed with agony.

With every last piece of her, Cassie threw her dark side back into the cage, her ears ringing with its shrieks as she pushed it more and more.

The door slammed shut, catching it in the trap—right where Cassie wanted it. A key fashioned in her hand next, a shining purple one with two heads opposing each other. Her own consciousness's sense of humor, it seemed.

Cassie slotted the key into the keyhole of the cage and locked it.

I'll see you in the Underworld.

Her dark side's fingers curled around the bars. *You can't get rid of me. I'll always be here . . . waiting. You'll need me sooner or later.*

Cassie fumbled with the key in her hands as she took one last look at her dark side. Pocketing the key, she only smiled. She hadn't thought she'd be able to, but she'd trapped it.

"It's done, Cassie." Lukas's voice echoed in her mind, excitement lacing his words.

Cassie fluttered her eyes open back to reality, the room she'd created in her mind gone. Lukas stood in front of her, a smile curving on his lips. He slid to the side, the large mirror now in full view.

Cassie breathed out shakily, her body slumping in the chair. She had done it; she was herself again. No sign of her dark side in sight. Staring at her true self in the mirror for the first time in weeks, she could hardly tear her eyes away, her smile widening while tears streaked down her face in juxtaposition.

"How do you feel?" Lukas asked, pushing back strands of hair from his tanned face as he leaned forward.

She felt strong—protected. As though she had a true grip on her dark side now, and she told him that.

"Heightened emotions might trigger your shields to unravel," he said, tearing her away from admiring her true reflection for the first time since her birthday. "So, just keep an eye on it, but it should be okay for now."

"I understand," Cassie said. "I'll do all I can to keep my dark side in there."

And whenever she felt it slipping, she could close her eyes and check on her cage. It bought her time. It bought her a chance.

Now she had to figure out if she was ready to put a weapon in her hand.

CHAPTER 21

SELCOUTH

(ADJ.) UNFAMILIAR, RARE, STRANGE, YET MARVELOUS

Cassie stared at her reflection in the lake, her calves numb. She'd sat on them for hours, staring and staring, waiting for it to change.

It never did.

Her silver hair drifted in the warm wind, wisping around her face, her gray eyes glimmering. Unmistakably *her*. She was giving herself time to figure out if she should train or not, even if every fiber in her body yelled at her to fight. But how could she train when she knew her dark side could be watching at every turn, learning alongside her?

The Zodiacs—well, most of them—welcomed her in with open arms, accepting her as their friend, and as part of their team. She remained hesitant with what all that meant, but she knew how it made her feel, and it was a weightlessness she'd never experienced before—as though she had a place among them, and it was *right*. But with that came the crushing weight of making sure nothing happened to them—that *she* didn't happen to them.

173

Cassie shut her eyes, finding her way back to the room—to the cage—as she had done almost every hour since her training. Her dark side was still in there, locked up, rattling her nails across the steel bars.

Come to keep me company? Plenty of space in here, it taunted.

I'd rather drown.

Cassie opened her eyes again, a momentary relief shining on her. She had to learn to trust herself, to stop herself from having to check on a consistent basis. But when she'd try to refrain, to tell herself that her dark side was still locked up, it crushed her chest, wrapping its slithering anxiety around her until she suffocated.

"See anything cool in there?" a voice so uniquely raspy sounded from behind her, tearing her from her thoughts.

Cassie turned her head, resting her chin on her shoulder as she smiled weakly at Artemis. "Just myself."

Artemis sat on the grass beside her, tugging her knees in tight. "Good."

"Where have you guys been?" Cassie asked, shielding herself from the sun as she stared at Artemis's face. Her freckles were more prominent in the daylight, her loose brown curls hanging down her back.

"Mission downtown." Artemis shrugged. "Couple of demons were spotted lurking around a bar. We cleaned it up in no time. Zero casualties," she said matter-of-factly.

Cassie nodded, dragging her eyes off Artemis and back toward the lake. She had chosen the smallest of the three lakes at the Arena, but the most beautiful. Lilies surrounded the water, along with grass long enough to hide in if she wanted to, and the gazebo behind her was equipped with a romance novel she'd left in case she needed to wish her thoughts away. She could also see the academy boarding houses and schooling areas, separated from the main Arena, and luckily, it didn't seem like the kids stayed for the summer. The last thing she'd want was children running around when she could turn dark at any moment. Another reason to fight—and another reason not to.

"Have you decided on training yet?" Artemis pried.

Cassie played with the loose thread on her shorts. "Have you come to talk me out of it?"

Artemis scoffed. "On the contrary. I think it's vital that you train. You'd be stupid not to."

There it is.

Cassie huffed. "Always the words of wisdom."

"I know Hero told you about our dad and brother, Jason," Artemis said after a few moments of silence. Cassie's heart tightened at the mention of it. "I was nine when it happened, so I don't remember them all too well, but I still feel the pain in my heart because of it. I also know the guilt that weighs on Hero's shoulders for their deaths, even though I never blamed him for it." Artemis pulled handfuls of grass out of the ground as though she could pull the pain out of her with them. "But even after all that guilt, after the torture he's put himself through all these years, he found peace in fighting. Just as I did."

The words rang in Cassie's mind as she tried to make sense of them. She didn't understand how a physical activity could ease her mind; no, it had always been reading or writing. But ultimately, those vices couldn't help her current situation, no matter how much she wanted them to. And if Hero could turn to both fighting and art, could she do the same?

Even so, how could she reasonably risk turning on all of them with the added expertise on how to fight?

Artemis must have sensed her thinking and said, "It might seem like we're a bunch of heartless killers, or at least you might think I am." She breathed out a sharp laugh. "But there's a reason why. And maybe learning to fight will help you keep hold of the darkness in your mind and help ground you more. So that you can find your calm in the storm."

The calm. She craved calm. "And if I fail and turn dark? Then she—*it*—knows how to fight," Cassie argued back. A part of her hoped that Artemis had an adept enough answer to convince her otherwise.

"When we *do* succeed at finding the Elixir and the Cup, do you want to be defenseless in a fight against your dark side, or would you prefer to at least know how to wield a sword?"

Cassie knew she was right, and that was what her heart was telling her to do. But her mind still argued back, reminding her of the risks she faced by training, and the risks she faced by not. It was a constant cycle of *yes* and *no*. So, she threw another wall Artemis's way. "I don't think a sword is my thing, anyway."

A feline grin crept across Artemis's face. "Come on. Follow me," she insisted, pushing herself off the grass.

Back in the fighting room at the Arena, Artemis nodded toward the entrance to one of their armories. "I chose a bow and arrow, Hero chose his sword, and so on. Now that it's safe to do so," she said, pointing at Cassie's head, "it's your turn."

The room they entered was nothing Cassie could have even fathomed in her dreams. Lights lit up whole shelves and cases stocked with weapons, ranging from large swords to small throwing stars.

Cassie's father had never let them have any kind of guns or weapons in the house, too worried that there'd be an accident, or she'd get hurt. And now here she was, a demigod, fighting off demons, Seekers, and her own *dark side*.

"How would I even know which one to choose?" Cassie asked, scouring all the possibilities in front of her.

Artemis flipped her usual knife out of her pocket, spinning it around. "Go with your heart. Let the weapon choose you."

Cassie let her hand drift across the wall of sharp objects, careful not to touch the edges. She stopped at two daggers mounted on the wall in a cross. Their handles and casings were decorated in gold, and each had a different jeweling to it. One was black, and the other white.

"Dual daggers. Bold choice," Artemis remarked. "Both daggers are equally deadly. Double the power and double the danger."

Cassie picked the daggers up by their hilts. They were lighter than she'd expected them to be, the blades thinner than the ones Hero fought with. They fit in her palms with ease, as if they were made for her.

"Are you right- or left-handed?" Artemis asked, running her finger across the top of her knife.

"I'm ambidextrous," Cassie mumbled, fixated on *her* daggers.

"These really are the best weapons for you, then. They're yours." Artemis pulled out a drawer filled with a smaller assortment of weapons, along with a harness Cassie could keep them in.

She smiled at Artemis, nodding in approval. Although Cassie had never once imagined she'd be learning how to fight with daggers—or any kind of weapon, for that matter—something about these felt . . . *right*. "You know, I still don't understand why you don't just use guns," she said.

Artemis cocked her head. "Guns don't work on demons. Their skin is too hard. The cyclopes forge our weapons, which allows us to use them on threats of the supernatural kind."

Artemis began explaining about how she had always wanted to see them work in the Naples Arena, and as alarming as it was that cyclopes were real, Cassie couldn't quell her excitement for when she could train with Hero. It seemed perfect, as though she had made the honorable decision, flipped the right side of the coin.

Fate.

Right on time, Hero knocked on the door. "You ready for your first training session, demon slayer?"

Cassie blinked and looked between the two siblings. "You guys planned this, didn't you?"

"We had to get you to fight somehow," Artemis said while smirking, just like her brother.

CHAPTER 22

AEIPATHY

(N.) AN ENDURING AND CONSUMING PASSION

A hum cut through the air as Hero whipped his sword around. His baggy tank top showed off each chiseled Greek muscle on his body, his tanned olive skin glistening in the rays of the sun from the glass dome above them. His brown hair was matted to his face with sweat, but he was still as frustratingly handsome as ever. Cassie wanted to slap him—in a friendly way—for making her heart flutter.

"Show-off," she muttered.

Hero chuckled and patted his sword against Cassie's inner thigh, soft and careful to the point that it felt like a tickle. "Keep your feet more separated. You'll have better balance." He circled her, his breath contending with the back of her neck, causing an army of shivers to charge up her spine.

Cassie had done no more than a few kickboxing lessons when she was a teenager, but she was ready to learn. She had made her decision. Her arms burned from keeping her daggers lifted, but she carried on, needing to prove herself. And

179

whether that was to the Zodiacs, to Diana, to Hero, to Titus, to her dark side, or even just to herself—or possibly all of them—she couldn't back down now.

"We don't have years on our side to train you the way the rest of us were," Hero said, rolling his shoulders. "We have to go right into the hard stuff. Try and keep your balance, remember to breathe, and always stretch after our sessions. Got it?"

Cassie nodded. Although she loved her life as a mortal—that her mom had granted her that life and saved her, no doubt—a part of her wondered what her life would have been like if she had grown up in this Arena. If she weren't a Gemini, of course. Would she and Hero be . . . friends? Or maybe more? Would her mother still be alive? Would she still have met Quinn somehow, some way?

"Ready to go again?" Hero asked, ridding her of her thoughts, distracting her with his trademark smirk.

"As I'll ever be," she grunted, arms wavering in pain and anticipation at the same time.

He took a swing at her. She struggled to block it, her dagger nipping the top of his sword as she stumbled to the side of the mat. *So much for my balance.*

Hero took a step back, spinning his sword around. *Cocky bastard.* "Keep your arms up. Use your daggers to block yourself from an attack," he instructed. "You're going to have to put your all into this, Cass. You can't shape-shift yet, so you have no advantage here."

She did as she was told, tightening her hold on the daggers.

Their moves mimicked poetry in her mind. Cassie would push forward, adding more words to their page, and Hero would move backward, washing them away. He blocked her, one . . . two . . . three times. Her muscles screamed at her to stop, and her hands opened on demand. The daggers clunked to the floor in front of her, along with her pride.

"You gotta get some muscle on you. You chose two daggers as your weapons, remember?" He breathed a laugh through his nose, a sore attempt to lighten the mood.

Cassie wiped away the beads of sweat making their way down her forehead. "Don't remind me."

His expression turned to sympathy. "Come on. It's okay. It's your first try. You're a Zodiac, remember? You were made for this, and fighting will come easier to you for it. Your muscles will build faster, and you'll heal faster. You'll adapt."

Cassie nodded, taking in his words. *I'm made for this. I'm a Zodiac. I'm one of them.*

She ignored the daggers resting on the ground and planted her legs, holding her fists in front of her instead.

Hero's eyebrows lifted, amusement dancing in his eyes as they lit in golden flames. He threw his sword down in return.

Cassie took her first punch.

Hero caught her fist and flipped her around, holding his arm against her neck with her back against his chest. She tried to wriggle free, but he was too strong. Cassie shot her elbow back into his side, but he just held onto her tighter.

"You need to work on your defense," he muttered into her ear.

His touch felt strange, yet euphoric. She didn't understand the way her chest tightened, or the way her breath caught in her throat. Yes, he *was* devastatingly handsome, but he was just her friend—a friend she thought about from time to time in ways she shouldn't.

His hold on her loosened as she turned around, her mouth drying at how close she was to his face. "Your eyes . . ." she mumbled, trying to distract herself from his body inches away from hers. "They glow when you fight. Why?"

Hero tilted his head to the side. "That's our connection to the elements. They're a part of the Zodiacs, and a part of our powers. Yours will glow as well, probably after you split."

Cassie glanced at the marble pattern on the floor. "When I see her . . . well, the other me in the mirror . . . its eyes are purple."

Hero threaded his hand through his hair. "Your element is air, as are the signs Libra and Aquarius. Fire signs are gold, earth signs are green, and water signs are blue. When we use our powers, our eyes shine their respective colors."

"Can I see?" Cassie asked, dizzying herself from switching between each of his eyes, mesmerized by the way his pupils grew as he stared at her.

Hero closed his eyes, his muscles tensing, and when he opened them again, a wildfire had erupted inside.

She reached to touch his face with the tips of her fingers, as though she were hypnotized by the flames. Cassie's mind waved through a staggering peace as her gaze slipped down to his glistening lips, studying the way they curved, like mountains she couldn't wait to climb.

Hero backed away, swallowing roughly as he avoided her gaze. "Let's go again. With weapons this time." His voice sounded distant, but the words still registered in her mind as she stepped away too, her heart pounding.

Cassie picked up her daggers again, swinging herself around into position as her jaw clenched. *Now* she wanted to fight. The anger she had for letting herself want Hero for even a moment filled her body, because she knew he'd never want her back. Why would he? She was the Gemini, a ticking time bomb. She hated that part of herself with every fiber of her being. That darkness lurked around her life, around her soul, waiting for a moment of weakness to pounce.

Cassie slashed forward, not taking the time to memorize his fighting style, and swung with all her emotions at once. She wanted to show her darkness that she was not weak. She was not to be messed with, and she would keep that side of herself in the cage, locked away for as long as possible.

Find your calm in the storm.

Hero stumbled back, shocked at her harshness, but continued blocking each of her assaults.

The weapons clanged together as Cassie grunted with each push. Each time she slashed down, another word floated in her mind. *Death. Destruction. Gemini.* It was all the same.

Find your calm, Cassie. Find it.

Her foot caught on her other ankle, one of her daggers slipping across her arm, slicing her skin as she tumbled to the mat below.

Hero appeared next to her in seconds, gripping her face in his hands. She stared at him blankly, but then his attention went to her arm.

"It's not healing," he said, concern lacing his words.

Although the pain dulled, the warmth of her blood dripping down her arm made her wound clear. She found herself unable to care.

Hero took her arm in his hands to further inspect it. "The healing process can get stuck sometimes, if we're too in our heads, or in shock, or if the wound is too bad to come back from." He sucked in a deep breath. "All your mental training might have taken a toll."

"I just got carried away," she said, her voice and mind off in the distance, her words monotone.

"Yeah, I could tell," he muttered, grabbing a spare towel off the rack on the wall. "What were you thinking about?" He sat next to her with his legs crossed, pushing the fabric against her arm to stop the bleeding.

She shrugged. "I wasn't really thinking. I was just mad, I guess."

Hero nodded slowly. "Anything in particular? Anything I've done?"

She couldn't tell him she was mad at herself for wanting him, and for being so *tired* of this other inside of her, pounding on the cage to be let out. She couldn't, because what she needed most in her life was friends who believed in her, so she had to push down whatever she felt deep inside, holding it in, just for her.

Cassie shook her head.

"I have some herbs in my room that might help clear your mind a bit, ease you enough so that your body can heal. I used them a lot after my dad and brother died, and still do from time to time," Hero offered, his eyebrows high as he waited for her decision.

It was the first time Cassie had been in Hero's room, despite it being opposite to hers. Sketchbooks and pencils were scattered across all surfaces. Swords hung on the wall, and a punching bag hung in the corner of his dark room. The walls were painted black to match most of his furniture; the only pop of "color" came from his bedding and the matching gray rug set half under his bed. Windows soared from the floor to the ceiling, the outside light trailing in a line across the floor through the heavy curtains.

It was like peering into Hero's mind. It felt strange and comfortable all at once, but at the end of the day, it was just a room with a bed . . . *his* bed.

Hero searched through drawers for the herbs as Cassie sat on the edge of his bed, still holding the towel against her wound to avoid dripping on his duvet.

He held up a wooden box in triumph. "Here, this should help." He walked back over, the mattress dipping as he sat beside her. Cassie could smell lavender and something else as he opened the box, revealing a small vial of liquid.

"It's a mix of kava, chamomile, and lavender. A few drops of this will ease you in seconds," he assured. "It works best when consumed orally. Can I?" he asked.

Considering it for a moment, she tilted her neck back and opened her mouth. Hero placed the bottle above her, and two cool drops dripped down her throat.

As she put her head back down, her eyes widened at how the wound had already begun to fade.

She couldn't deny how gentle Hero always was with her, an unsuspecting guardian angel of sorts. For a moment, it was as if they had known each other their whole lives, or were long-lost friends from another life. Something felt complete—*serene*—when she was around him, and that same thing inside her *ached* when they weren't.

But then her mind flashed to all the moments he'd backed away from her. How he left her room so abruptly after their soul-baring talk. How he always removed his touch or always looked away from her first.

As she tried to ignore her thoughts and Hero's body heat while he put the vial away, a pile of loose papers and a sketchbook lying on his bedside table caught her attention.

"May I?" she asked, her fingers toying with the cover.

Hero looked up from the now closed box, his brows furrowing as he spotted her hand. "Uh, sure. Go for it." His gaze burned into her as she began to flip through the pages. He stood and walked back to the other side of the room, leaning against the fireplace mantel, as if he had to be as far away as he could from what lay in the book. "My dad was always proud of my art," he said after a moment. "He said I was blessed by the muses."

His dad was right. The sketchbook was full of creatures and demons, all incredibly detailed. She flipped through until a different drawing caught her eye, one made with charcoal—of her. Her eyes were drawn closed, at peace. She was being carried, her hair dangling from her face as another's arms wrapped around her body, holding her.

She remembered Hero's fingers from the first time they had met—the way they were coated in charcoal.

Her eyes found his from across the room, and they were filled with truth. He must've carried her like this on the night of her birthday, when he'd saved her from the demon and Seekers. He had carried her into this world, and then he drew the memory, immortalizing her on the page. No large stroke of darkness, no harsh lines.

The door from his balcony pattered against its frame, enough to draw her attention away. She pushed herself off his bed and made her way over to the glass panels, ignoring the butterflies rising in her stomach at his drawing.

Hero met her there, opening the door wide for her arrival so Cassie could stare out into the gardens.

"I'll never grow bored of this view."

Hero shoved his hands into his pockets. "I've probably been taking it for granted."

Cassie stayed glued to the gardens reaching each corner. It was another world. "It's easy to do. Taking things for granted, I mean." She paused. "I want to learn to appreciate things more, especially knowing that there's a chance I won't be here next year. This view is a start." The side of Cassie's mouth lifted, a mix of sadness and appreciation washing over her.

"You're welcome to come here anytime you want. The door's always open."

She turned around to face him. His curled hair whipped around his ears, his stubble shorter than usual. "You're a great artist, you know."

"I just draw what catches my eye," Hero whispered, staring at her so deeply.

And just like that, she found herself falling into him like quicksand, with no way out. Cassie swayed toward him, no longer able to deny the pull she felt between them. She pined for it—her calm in the storm.

Hero cleared his throat, moving a step away from her, *again,* as though he'd read her mind and didn't like what he saw. "You should get your rest. I'll check on you tomorrow."

His words stabbed her in the heart. Just when she'd thought maybe he felt the pull too . . . But it seemed it was all one-sided, all in her mind. She didn't know why she kept trying when it was so obviously clear he wanted nothing to do with her. Why did her brain stop working the moment she was around him? Tears that only brought on further embarrassment pricked at her eyes before she excused herself, running out of his room.

The storm came back with a roar.

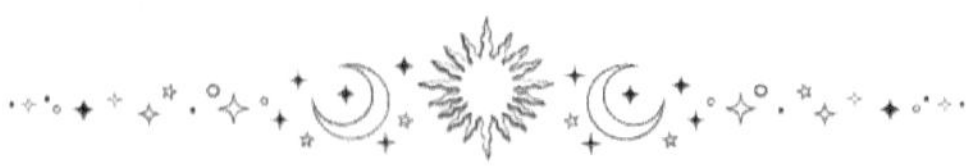

Hero swore under his breath as Cassie left his room, the disappointment and the sadness blatant on her face.

He didn't want to push her away. He didn't want any of this. All he wanted was her. And maybe he was being a coward, putting his fear of the prophecy before his desires, but he knew he had to do it. She could be the ruin of him, and maybe everyone around him.

Clenching his jaw, Hero knew he had to do a better job at keeping his space from her, for his sake and hers. He couldn't play with her feelings. He couldn't be selfish. He would continue training her, much to Titus's annoyance, but he'd have to be more careful.

He had to keep his distance, to be her friend, her mentor, and only that, no matter how wrong it felt. And ignoring that feeling, he picked up a book on the laws issued from the eighteen hundreds to the nineteen hundreds for the Zodiacs, furthering his knowledge to become the future Archon. Diana was right, in a way: he could be sacrificing his future because of Cassie. He hadn't been as focused on his studies, on his community.

Being Archon was a dream he'd had since he was a kid, when he saw his mother making a positive change in the Arena, with how she could influence others through respect, education, and pure leadership. He wanted to be able to do the same.

But perhaps, like his mother, being Archon would mean sacrificing other parts of himself. Sacrificing his own happiness, his relationships with his family . . . his heart.

It was that which caused him to slam the book shut and pick up his charcoal instead.

CHAPTER 23

VERENDUS

(ADJ.) TO BE FEARED, WORTHY OF REVERENCE;
GIVING AN IMPRESSION OF AGED GOODNESS AND b
ENEVOLENCE

The overhead fluorescent lights buzzed softly, casting long shadows over racks of gleaming weights. The Arena's gym was quieter at this hour, most of the other Zodiacs having gone to bed or on late-night patrols, leaving just the distant rhythmic clang of metal and the low hum of a song playing from the old speaker mounted in the corner.

Hero preferred it this way. The solitude. The focus. No distractions. At least before he *hesitantly* agreed to a weight training session with Cassie, after Artemis had commented on her lack of muscles. Now, as Cassie lay on the bench press beneath him, struggling through the last of her reps, he wondered how he'd been stupid enough to think this was a good idea. He'd sworn to keep his distance, yet here he was, right back with her. He exhausted himself.

Her arms trembled as she pushed the bar up, her breath coming in short, sharp exhales. She was stubborn; he'd give her that. Even when she was close to failing, she refused to let him step in.

"That's it," Hero murmured, standing just behind the bench, his hands hovering beneath the bar, but not touching it. He'd learned his lesson the last time he tried to help. "One more."

Her jaw clenched as she forced the weight up, her muscles taut with exertion. The moment she racked the bar, she let out a big breath and dropped her head back against the bench. "That was heavier than last time."

Hero smirked, tossing her a towel. "Yeah. I added ten pounds."

Cassie shot upright, her sweat-dampened hair falling into her face. "You *what*?"

He shrugged, trying to contain his laughter. "I thought you said you could handle it?"

Her glare could have cut through stone. "Maybe warn me next time before you try to *kill* me?"

Hero chuckled, watching as she wiped the sweat from her forehead, the towel trailing along her throat, her collarbone. He *should* look away. He should focus on loading the next set of weights, on literally *anything* else. But he didn't. He shook his head, exhaling slowly before turning toward the weight rack. "Come on. Deadlifts."

Cassie groaned. "I hate you."

He huffed. "You wanna get stronger or not?"

She sighed dramatically, but stood, following him over. He loaded the bar, adjusting the weights carefully.

"Feet shoulder width apart," he instructed, stepping in close behind her. His voice was even, but he could already feel the heat radiating off her skin. "Engage your core. Keep your back straight."

She stiffened at his proximity, and for a second, Hero almost stepped away . . . *almost*. But then she exhaled and shifted her stance, rolling her shoulders, adjusting her grip. She was listening to him, trusting him.

Hero's hand rested briefly on her hip, adjusting her positioning. His fingers skimmed the bare skin where her tank top had ridden up, and the contact sent a sharp, unexpected spark up his arm. He tensed.

Cassie didn't react—at least, she tried not to. But he could tell by the slight hitch in her breath, the way her fingers clenched tighter around the bar, that she'd felt it too.

Fuck.

"Good," he murmured, forcing his voice to stay level.

She bent at the hips, her muscles flexing as she pulled the bar up. Her form was strong, her movements fluid. He should be proud. He should be focused on her progress, on making her stronger, faster, deadlier. Instead, his mind kept wandering to how close she was, how her scent—warm, sweet, something like honey and sweat—curled in the air between them.

She racked the bar after a few reps and turned to him, triumph shining in her eyes. "Didn't think I could do it, huh?"

Hero smirked. "I knew you could. Just had to push you a little."

Cassie took a slow step toward him, tilting her head, a bead of sweat trailing down the curve of her throat. Too close. "And what if I pushed back?" she whispered.

The mood shifted. The teasing, the fire, the tension . . . it all crackled between them, thick enough to drown in. Hero clenched his fists, fighting the urge to reach for her. To close the distance between them. To drag his knuckles along the dip of her spine, press his mouth to the corner of hers, taste the salt on her skin...

He needed to shut this down. Now.

He took a step back, putting space between them. "I'd have to put more weight on the bar."

Cassie gave a small smile, before she turned away. "Maybe I *should* try more weight, then." She headed toward the weight plate tree.

Hero exhaled, dragging a hand through his hair. *This is a bad idea. A really bad idea.* But he followed her anyway.

Cassie reached for one of the tens, her fingers just brushing the cold iron of the plate when her foot caught on the edge of the metal leg. She twisted back in an attempt to stabilize herself, her body colliding with his.

Hero's instincts kicked in before he could think. His hands gripped her waist, but the feel of her body made him stumble, sending them both down. His back hit the mat with a dull, resounding thud, and in the next breath, she was on top of him.

His mind stopped functioning.

Cassie's body sprawled against his, the curve of her waist pressed against his calloused hands, her thighs framing his hips. She was breathless, her chest rising and falling quickly. For a single, excruciating moment, neither of them dared to move.

Hero's heart pounded, too fast, too loud; he was afraid she would hear it. But she felt so good against him, in his grip. His fingers tensed before he could stop himself, tightening around her, his thumbs brushing the bare skin where her shirt had ridden up. She felt *right*, like she belonged there, as if she were always meant to be there, and for a second, he allowed himself to believe that he could hold her for just a little bit longer, and pretend it wasn't a mistake.

Then she lifted her head, and his control *snapped*.

Her gray eyes were wide, searching his, her lips parting as if she was about to say something, but had forgotten what it was. And gods, *that* was a mistake, because now he was staring at her mouth—soft, flushed, close. So fucking close to his. He could kiss her. Just once. Just to see what it would be like, if she'd taste as good as she smelled, if she'd want it just as badly as he did.

It would be a colossal mistake.

And yet, Hero's body betrayed his mind yet again. She moved, just barely, and the shift of her weight, the way her body moved right up against *him*, the friction making him want to thrust his hips up for more...

Her fingers curled around his forearm, small but deliberate. It was a silent question. A dare.

Hero clenched his jaw, inhaling sharply through his nose. This was dangerous. He had to stop this before it went any further, before he did something reckless, something irreversible. He couldn't kiss her, because he couldn't hurt her. He couldn't abide by his wants or needs, because he knew they couldn't go any further, and he didn't want to lead her on.

He could hurt, but not her.

Without a word, he let her go.

The warmth of her body disappeared almost instantly as she pushed herself up and off of him, turning away from him. Her absence was the coldest, and most jarring thing he'd ever experienced.

Hero stayed where he was on the floor, staring at the ceiling. He had to get himself under control. If she ever looked at him like that again, if she ever *touched* him like that again? He didn't know if he'd have the strength to let her go next time.

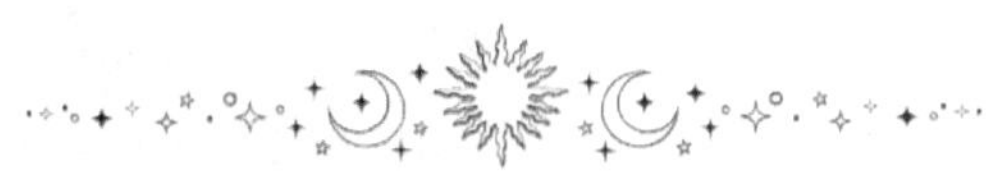

It had been quiet all week.

Cassie spun herself in her chair, the mission room circling around her as she yawned. She should've been more thankful for the time off, but her heavy eyes were a constant reminder of her sleepless nights, tossing and turning in her bed, waiting for the day they could go see the nymphs. Waiting for the day she could get this darkness out of her.

The Zodiacs had invited her and Quinn to see what they did for work, and so far, all they had done was sift through surveillance footage with a few other teams she'd seen around the Arena. All available and able teams had to do rotational shifts for missions as part of their duty. Sometimes it would be nonstop, and other times there would be no demons to slay, no monsters to catch.

Most of the Zodiacs avoided her, passing her the occasional awkward smile when they ran into each other, but she'd learned to be okay with it. At least she had her friends—even if her muscles and mind ached from the near-daily training she had. Artemis, Hero, and Lukas all took turns, teaching her different skills and moves. She was stronger than ever, but Cassie still felt so weak compared to the rest of them. The more she trained, though, the less she found herself needing to check on her dark side. But the calm she desired still only appeared around Hero, so the fighting would have to do for now.

She watched as Hero stood at one of the holographic screens, one hand propped on his hip, the other sifting through imaging. As though he could sense her staring, he moved his head to the side and smiled faintly at her. Cassie tried to ignore the flutter in her stomach at the small gesture and visualized herself pushing down the heat rising to her cheeks. They hadn't spoken about what had happened in his room, or while weight training the other day. By her count, he'd turned her down twice. Had walked away from her—twice.

Maybe it *was* her. Maybe he'd lied the day he said he wasn't frightened of her. Maybe it was all an act, and she just imagined the connection between the two of them to distract her from the darkness inside her.

The sound of cosmic laughing shook her from the depths of her worries. Quinn was joking along with Elijah, and even Artemis had a smile on her face. It warmed Cassie's heart to see her friend so joyful and bonding with the Zodiacs so well.

Lukas and Titus stayed on opposite sides of the room, and Cassie wondered if either of them knew how often they stared at each other without the other one knowing. It was clear they had an unresolved history, but neither of them wanted to admit it out loud or solve any of it.

"There's been a demon sighting on Oak Street. Who wants it?" one of the Zodiacs shouted, a brown-skinned man Cassie couldn't remember the name of. So many Zodiacs portaled in and out on a regular basis. Some even had houses outside the Arena: the older ones who had survived long enough to retire and those with small children.

Screens with what appeared to be security footage of a street with a demon crawling around it filled each monitor. Cassie gulped. It looked more vicious than they'd described to her. The scales . . . the claws . . .

Elijah swung his arm around Nyssa's shoulders, ruffling his shaggy blonde hair as his big goofy smile popped out. "We can do it!" he called out. "Cassie *needs* to see this firsthand."

Cassie's palms went damp with terror as she scanned the faces of the team. She wasn't sure she was ready to fight a demon yet. She didn't even know how to kill one.

"What?" Elijah shrugged as the rest of the team stared at him with their eyebrows up. "It'll be fun. And Cassie should have field training; we can't leave her cooped up in here forever." His chin lifted toward her.

Hero clicked his tongue, rubbing his hands together. "Never thought I would be saying this, but Eli makes a good point." He squinted closer at one of the screens before turning back to Cassie. "It's just one demon. You wanna go with us?"

"I don't know how much help I'll be." She breathed out a troubled laugh. A part of her wanted to jump with the exhilaration of leaving the Arena for the first time since the Seeker attack, but the other part of her wanted to hide under the covers.

"Don't worry, you won't be alone," Hero said with a smile that disappeared as fast as it came. He cleared his throat. "Plus, if you get through this, we'll know you're ready to go see the nymphs."

Taking a moment to consider it, Cassie finally nodded. "Okay. Let's do it." She then glanced at Quinn, who stared back, blinking. "Are you going to be okay staying here by yourself?"

"I can stay with her," Artemis announced, her eyes widening at her own quick words. "I mean, I have loads of work to do around here anyway." She waved an arm in the air. "Logging the new weapon shipments and all. You guys will be fine without me." Artemis raised her chin, silently challenging anyone to say differently.

Hero smirked as he crossed his arms. "Yeah, I'm sure we'll be fine without our best fighter."

"Well, it might give you guys a nice challenge for once," Artemis shot back, poking Hero in the side with her elbow.

He huffed in laughter. "Okay, fine. Artemis and Quinn, stay here. As for the rest of us, meet downstairs in ten, ready to go." Hero walked over to Cassie next. "Come on. I'll take you on a motorcycle ride."

Ravens soared in her stomach as she thought about her arms wrapped around his torso. She sighed as she followed him.

It's going to be really hard just being friends.

Cassie threw her leg over the side of Hero's motorcycle and pulled her helmet off, the rush of exhilaration gliding through her like a stone skipping over water. In fear, she'd clung to Hero tighter than she would care to admit, but she loved the way her hair drifted in the wind, even if her heart still pumped at the speed.

Titus, Lukas, Elijah, and Nyssa jumped out of the red Jeep.

"Let's go kill a demon," Cassie said, her voice wavering as her feet itched with anticipation. The summer heat shimmered around her, and sweat dripped from her forehead as she ran a hand through her wind-matted hair. *This is it. My first mission.* She had to admit that she loved the way it sounded, and how her newly toned muscles pulsated. She was really one of them.

Hero chuckled, whipping out his phone from his pocket. "We like to think of it like a game. Whoever kills the most each month wins. It should be just around this corner," he said, glancing at the map on his screen. Cassie peered over his arm, seeing a singular red dot blinking in the alleyway up and to their right.

Her gaze then caught on the street ahead of her. *Oak Street.* Creole buildings surrounded them as college kids roamed around, heading in and out of cafes, restaurants, and bars. In another life, she would have been one of them. Perhaps she'd be in one of those metal chairs, drinking coffee and reading a book. But that wasn't her life anymore. Now, she was here to fight demons. It seemed crazy how much her life had changed in such a short time.

"Nervous?" Nyssa asked, walking beside her.

Yes. Cassie shook her head, ignoring the thunderstorm brewing in her stomach. "How could I be when I have you guys?"

Lukas smiled at her. "Just keep your shields up, and you'll be fine."

Cassie nodded back at him.

"It's probably a newbie demon anyway." Elijah grinned. "Perfect for your first mission."

Titus merely huffed.

Frantic beeping sounded from Hero's phone, more red dots pinging all down the alleyway. Shaking her nerves off, Cassie followed the others as they rushed around the corner, their conversation over in seconds.

Her mouth went dry at the sight of dozens of demons slithering over the walls, hissing at them. The rest of the team armed themselves as Cassie watched with her mouth agape.

Cassie's hands flung to her daggers, her heart pounding in her chest. This was way more than she was ready for.

Hero clearly thought the same. "Cassie. Run. Now," he demanded, whipping out his own sword, his now golden eyes never leaving the demons.

Cassie's feet stayed planted as one of the creatures flung itself at Nyssa. Nyssa spun around, her katana slicing its scaly form in half. Another went for Lukas, screeching in his face, but Lukas killed it easily, his sword sliding into the demon's abdomen like it was butter.

Cassie felt as though the cement had swallowed her whole. But she held the daggers the way Hero had taught her to and waited. *I can do this.*

A demon made its way through the group, bloodied and bruised, yet it staggered tall in front of her. Cassie swiped at it and pierced it, but that didn't seem to matter in the slightest to the demon. It slashed its claws at her, tearing at the skin on her forearm as she yelled out in agony. One of her daggers clinked against the cobblestones, far out of her reach.

A sword shot through the neck of the demon, splattering its viscous green blood on her face. Her knees wanted to buckle beneath her at the stench and the feel of it on her skin, but her lips pressed tight as her fingers curled in a swirl of anger and shame at being unable to kill the demon like the rest of them.

The sword exited, and the demon's body fell to the ground. Hero stood behind it. "I *said* get out of here," he ordered, rougher than before.

A demon raced past her and out onto the road, using their distraction as an opportunity to get free.

"I got this one!" Cassie yelled with adrenaline powering her, one dagger remaining, already turning toward the exit of the alleyway. She knew she'd have a better time asking for forgiveness than permission to go off on her own during her first mission. And technically, she did get out of there, as Hero asked. But she wanted—no, needed—to prove herself.

She bolted down the street, disregarding Hero's protests, the hard concrete stinging her knees. Turning onto a new street, she followed the beast as far as she could, ignoring the shock, ignoring the blood drying on her skin. Her arms were almost done healing themselves.

A parking lot came into her view as she willed her body to run the rest of the way there, her side cramping in pain. The demon prowled around the cars, but it hadn't spotted her yet. She had the upper hand. Cassie skidded around a large yellow van, her chest heaving in and out as her body slid to the ground. She closed her eyes, trying to conjure a plan.

The heat from the sun disappeared, replaced with something else. Cassie's eyes shot open, now staring right into the glowing red eyes of the demon.

Shit.

CHAPTER 24

UITWAAIEN

(V.) TO WALK IN THE WIND

Her heart drummed in her ears, racing faster with each second. The metal of the car burned her skin from the heat. Her blood rose, fear coursing through her body, her dark side begging to be released. She had to focus. She couldn't change now. If she did, it would be out of weakness.

And that wasn't her.

Cassie held onto her last dagger, but the demon swung at her first, slashing her arm and face with its claws. The wounds stung as her dagger rattled to the ground. The demon moved closer, kicking the weapon away with its claws and further from her grasp.

Her warm blood poured down her skin, and she caught a glimpse of her sliced cheek in the car's reflection as she recoiled from the attack.

The beast heaved before her, inching closer and closer. Cassie pushed her back further against the car she hid behind, her shoes grinding against the gravel and dirt, trying to escape the inevitable. She just needed her dagger . . .

The demon's back arched as a longsword exited through its abdomen.

Cassie rolled her body over as she reached for her dagger, gripping it as a last hope. She pushed herself off the ground in one swift motion, and, as she'd witnessed Hero doing minutes ago, plunged the weapon straight into the demon's neck. She watched as it choked on its own blood before falling limp to the ground, disappearing into a cloud of smoke moments later, exactly as the Seekers had.

"You okay?" a deep voice boomed as she breathed heavily, her dagger now soaked in green gunk. Her eyes flicked up to meet a strange man.

"I think so," Cassie mumbled. She held out her injured arm; almost all the skin had healed. She hoped it did the same on her face.

"You must be the Gemini," he ventured, intrigued. His narrow eyes flashed from a dark brown to a vivid purple.

"And you're another Zodiac?" she asked him, her shoulders loosening as the dagger fell from her hands in exhaustion, clattering to the ground below.

"Yep. An Aquarius." He wiped his sword off and plunged it into a harness on his back. Then, he lifted his hands to the sky as a strong gust of wind sifted through the parking lot. Cassie's silver hair flew in a small tornado as she gasped at his powers in amazement. *An Aquarius. Weather control.*

The wind slowed as the world went back to normal.

The man picked up her fallen dagger, wiping it off on his jeans before passing it back to her. "Don't worry. You get used to the blood, and the demons, and whatnot."

Cassie nodded, but she wasn't sure if she would ever get used to killing. While it was much easier than when she thought she'd killed that Seeker in the tent, she knew that taking the life from someone, or *something*, would always take a toll on her. Although, she credited that to being brought up as a mortal. *Sort of.*

"Who are you again?" she questioned. For a moment, she hoped they hadn't already met and that she'd just forgotten him in the sea of Zodiacs she'd met recently.

"I'm Rane. I'm from the Mount Osore Arena in Japan, but once I heard about you, I had to see if the hype about the beautiful Gemini was true." He winked at her as heat rose to her face. "I stayed in New Orleans as a teenager, and I have some family here, so two birds with one stone, as they say."

She tried to smile at him, her gut still queasy from the killing as she attempted to figure him out. Something about him caught her interest, something different from the rest of the Zodiacs she'd met so far.

The sound of running footsteps distracted her from her thoughts as Hero, Elijah, and Nyssa rounded the corner.

Hero ran over to them, pausing for a second when he saw Rane, but his gaze shifted back to her. "Are you okay? Did the demon get you?" His hands lifted toward her face, but he dropped them before he could touch her.

"I'm okay, don't worry," Cassie replied, her voice shaking as she tried to ignore his usual hesitant gestures. "Rane stabbed it, then I killed it."

"Your first mission kill," Hero said proudly. "Need I say I'm impressed?"

Her cheeks flushed at his praise. She'd killed a demon, even though it was gross, and a part of her never wanted to do it again. But she did it. It felt like an initiation almost.

"Oh my gods!" Nyssa rushed past, shoving Hero out of her way, and flung herself into Rane's arms. She pushed herself back before swatting him on the chest. "Where the hell have you been? No one's heard from you in months!"

"I know. I'm sorry. I just needed time after Baba passed," he replied, rubbing the back of his neck. His eyes flashed a sudden vulnerability that was gone as quickly as it had come.

With the way Nyssa frowned, Cassie wondered if she'd lost the same person Rane had.

"Well, I'm glad you're back now." Nyssa turned around to the group. "Cassie, this is my cousin, Rane!" she announced, slinging her arm around his waist and giving him another tight squeeze.

Cassie could now see a resemblance. They had the same flattened nose, plump lips, and pale skin tone. Even their hair was similar, the black stopping at their shoulders, although Rane's had a less silky texture, and didn't fall as straight as his cousin's did.

Elijah made his way through, throwing his arms up for a hug. "Hey, buddy!" he quipped, pulling Rane in. "Great to see you again." He patted him on the back before drawing away. "What are you doing here?"

Rane smiled soft as a cloud. "I wanted to check in on Nyssa. Hana was worried when she heard about a Gemini appearing out of the blue, and I was curious." Rane winked at Cassie again as the heat surged to her face. "I was just out on a walk when I saw the demon running down the street."

Hero cleared his throat.

"Hero, nice to see you again, bud." Rane extended his hand for a shake. "Been forever."

Hero met his hand with his own, along with a curt nod. "You too."

"Where's Titus and Lukas?" Cassie asked, looking around for the two missing team members.

"They portaled back to the Arena," Hero explained. "A Seeker was spotted lurking around there. Artemis reported it, but it seemed to have gone away by itself."

Cassie sighed in relief, knowing Artemis could look out for Quinn, as would their wards.

"Well, then," Rane exclaimed, clapping his hands. "Anyone want some food? I'm craving some beignets."

The chill from the air conditioner was a welcome feeling compared to the sweltering heat outside, as was the smell of the fried food wafting through the restaurant.

Cassie couldn't comprehend how they could sit in the middle of an everyday restaurant, with all their weapons, yet no one paid the slightest bit of attention to them. She wondered how many times she could have passed a Zodiac in her life without even realizing it. Touching her chest where her necklace used to hang, she sighed. Although she missed the reminder of her mother, she was beginning not to miss being hidden from the Zodiac's world. *Her* world.

"So, how do you two know each other?" she asked Hero and Rane after a few minutes of silence while everyone ate their food.

Rane looked up enthusiastically. "We went to the academy together. Hero and I were in the same year," he boasted, staring right at Hero, who picked at his burger. "So," Rane continued, diverting his attention back to Cassie, "are you coming to the party at the end of the week?"

"I didn't know there was a party," Cassie said, looking around at her friends.

"Oh! I totally forgot to tell you," Nyssa squealed. "Every year at the end of May, we have a party celebrating the goddess Maia. We've pushed it back a bit because of your arrival, but you have to come!"

Cassie's eyebrows lifted. "Goddess Maia?"

"Yeah, she symbolizes the month of rebirth and new beginnings. Pretty cool chick," Elijah explained, reaching for a fry off Nyssa's plate before she swatted him away.

"You can't miss it." Rane placed his hand on hers, his gentle touch shooting electricity through her. "Come on. I'll even be your date."

Cassie glanced at Hero, whose jaw locked as he stared at the ground. She didn't know what reaction she wanted from him, but it wasn't that.

"I'd be happy to." She smiled back at Rane.

Elijah turned in his seat to face Nyssa. "I know we haven't known each other long," he began, picking up her hand. "Just nine years. But will you go to the dance with me?"

Nyssa gasped as her eyes widened. "I thought you'd never ask!" She flung her arms around him while laughing.

Cassie found herself giggling alongside them, but Hero remained silent.

"I'm gonna go settle the bill, then we can head back," Hero mumbled as he stood.

Her eyes flew to his hands, balled into fists, and her shoulders slumped, the pit in her stomach growing. Hero had been playing a hot-and-cold game with her for weeks, and now he acted upset? Maybe it was the anxiety of watching her run off after a demon, or maybe he just didn't like Rane. Whatever it was, she didn't care for it.

A sudden shrilling sound of agony broke into her thoughts, and her eyes flew to Nyssa. A long, painful wail screeched from her lips, and her hands gripped her hair, as though to stop her mind from exploding. Elijah's face paled as he dropped before her, hands on her legs.

Chest tightening at the sight, Cassie stood, desperate to help. She had never seen Nyssa having a vision before. It made her want to be sick. The lights above her flickered and popped, mimicking the sound of bones breaking. Cassie flinched at the sound. She took in the diner, noticing how everyone else carried on eating, not seeing or hearing Nyssa's tortuous screams, as though nothing were happening at all.

Finally, silence fell.

Cassie shot her attention back to Nyssa, who had tears falling from her face onto Elijah's green shirt.

Having hurried back at her episode, Hero bent down beside her. "Nys, are you okay? What did you see?"

Nyssa's eyes traveled to them, her breathing quickening. "We have to go back to the Arena. Now."

CHAPTER 25

APPETENCE

(N.) AN EAGER DESIRE, AN INSTINCTIVE INCLINATION; AN ATTRACTION OR A NATURAL BOND

Cassie ran to Quinn's room, flinging the door open. Still nothing. She had called and texted her friend countless times, but she hadn't heard back, and the worry built in her with each passing moment.

Nyssa had had a vision of Quinn possessed by a Seeker, standing over Artemis's bleeding body. *If something happened . . . No.* Cassie couldn't think about the possibility. Not yet.

"Guys!" Elijah's voice sounded in the distance. "Found 'em! In the kitchen!"

Cassie sprinted as fast as she could, and she could hear Hero joining in behind her. They hadn't muttered a word to each other since the diner, but she didn't let herself go there. She had to focus on finding Quinn.

"Quinn!" Cassie yelled as she threw the kitchen doors open, her eyes falling on her friend. "Are you okay?"

Quinn cocked an eyebrow from where she sat with Artemis, a spoon of chocolate ice cream in her hand. "We're fine. Why?"

Cassie's shoulders loosened, her heartbeat slowing. Both Quinn and Artemis were okay, safe and together.

"Nyssa had a vision of Quinn being attacked by Seekers," Hero announced, his voice ragged. "And then standing over you, Artemis. Killing you."

Artemis crossed her legs before smirking at Quinn. "It's cute that you think she could kill me. I gave her a quick training session; this girl could barely hold a stick. Hence the consolatory ice cream."

Cassie glanced at the half-eaten carton of chocolate ice cream on the metal table.

"I even have the bruises to prove it," Quinn laughed, rubbing her own thigh. Cassie noted how Artemis's gaze traveled to Quinn's leg and lingered for a moment too long.

"Dear Hades, I hate running," Eli breathed out as he, Rane, and Nyssa burst into the kitchen. "See, I told you. They're fine."

Nyssa shook her head, biting her lip. "But the alarms? Titus and Lukas left to come back because of a breach. What happened?"

Artemis shrugged. "False alarm. Probably just a drill. Titus and his ex-lover boy are double-checking the grounds to make sure as we speak."

Quinn's face fell as she looked around the group. "Are your visions set in stone, Nyssa?" she asked, her words wary.

Nyssa frowned. "Not always. Our visions are based on possibilities, different paths to be taken, guiding us through fragments of what could happen should we intervene or not. But the vision I had . . ." Her face scrunched, as though reliving the pain of what had happened. "It felt so real. Like it was the only outcome."

Hero scratched his stubble. "Nys, when did your vision feel like it would happen?"

Her shoulders slumped. "It was happening then and there, but also far away. I don't know. It was all jumbled up."

The side of Hero's mouth pulled. "I checked on the wards. They're secure. And I scoured the security footage. It showed a Seeker and some demons getting close to the Arena, and then turning back. No one got in, though."

"Lucky for us," Rane said.

Artemis scanned Rane, lifting her chin. "And when did *you* get back?"

"Today," Rane countered. "I came all the way here just for you."

Cassie's eyebrows lifted as she waited for whatever snarky comment Artemis would shoot back. But Artemis smiled widely and threw her arms around him. "It's nice to see you again, but don't you dare get into as much trouble as you did last time!"

Rane laughed. "Well, if you see Professor Alan, give me a heads up." His chuckle died down, but the grin on his face remained. "But no, your brother and his team ran into some trouble on their mission, and I was just in the right place at the right time." He winked at Cassie once more. She wondered if he had a weird twitch, but she also couldn't deny that she enjoyed the attention.

Hero, on the other hand, rolled his eyes. "Well, until we can get a clearer idea of what happened, Quinn," he said, turning toward her, "try not to take a step out of this Arena. This is the safest place for you."

"I won't leave," Quinn assured them. "If there's even a slight chance something could happen, that I could hurt you," she turned to Artemis, her expression solemn, "I'm staying right here."

Elijah swung his arm around Nyssa's shoulders. "Let's get some rest."

As she and Elijah walked out, Nyssa took one last glimpse into the room. Cassie could see her uncertainty, and she shared Nyssa's wariness.

Cassie would have to do a better job of ensuring nothing harmed Quinn. Quinn couldn't build mental shields as the Zodiacs could, so the Arena's wards would have to do for now.

Rane dipped his head as he left, and soon after, Hero followed. Cassie looked back at Quinn, who was laughing along with Artemis again. Trying to push down the fear she felt, she smiled at her. Quinn would be safe here, with Artemis.

"Hero, wait!" Cassie then yelled out, rushing after him as he disappeared down the hall. She needed to know what was wrong, utterly done with this weird game that was playing out between them.

Hero paused but didn't turn. "I'll see you at training tomorrow," he muttered as he continued to walk away, his fists clenched.

Cassie exhaled roughly, frustrated that he wouldn't even talk to her.

She didn't know how much longer she could pine over someone who wanted nothing to do with her.

The following day, a soft knock sounded at her door.

"Come in," Cassie said, pulling her damp hair into a bun. She'd taken three showers since their mission yesterday, needing to wash off every bit of the demon, and of the anxiety riding her about Quinn, and about Hero.

She glanced over as her door opened, and Rane's kind face popped through. "Hey." He smiled widely before entering the room. "Hottest day of the year. Thought you might enjoy this." He held a large glass of lemonade. The cold drink against her palm felt nothing short of euphoric.

"Thank you," she said, taking her first sip. "To what do I owe this pleasure?"

"I wondered if you wanted some company," he said. "Nyssa and Elijah are bickering about something, and Hero and the rest of them went off somewhere, so I thought we could band together as outsiders?"

Cassie chuckled, although not a true laugh. She didn't consider herself an outsider anymore, but maybe she was wrong. "Did something happen between you and Hero back at the academy? He seemed . . . off yesterday." She gestured for them to go outside to her balcony, where two white chairs and a small table stood. Her white dress flowed in the wind as she took her spot, setting her drink on the table.

"I don't think his reaction had to do with me," Rane explained as he sat, leaning back on the seat as the sun hit his face. "I just don't think he's used to competition for those he likes."

Although Hero liking her was a lie, Cassie couldn't help but feel amused by his comments. "And you deem yourself competition?" she asked, her brows rising.

Rane chuckled. "I guess you'll have to decide that. Anyway, I didn't come here to talk about Hero. I wanted to talk about you." He gave her a small smile. "I know it must be difficult being a Gemini with our laws. How are you holding up?"

Cassie sighed. "It's been okay. I guess I have an insane prophecy to thank for an easier experience than what normal Geminis go through. But it's still scary. The possibility of what I could be . . ." She paused for a heartbeat, remembering the image her dark side had shown her of her friend's and families' bodies piled up—because of her. She shuddered. "But I train almost every day to avoid it."

Rane stared at her, his lips parting. Somehow his features looked even sharper this way. "You're really impressive."

Impressive. She grinned. "So, what really brought you to the Arena?" Cassie pried, leaning her head to one side as she studied him. "It couldn't just be curiosity."

Rane's face fell, his smile fading and his eyes darkening. "My best friend . . ." he began, voice somber. "She fell pregnant, and the baby wasn't due until July, but she went into early labor. A few months later, she came back alone, claiming that they took her baby and that she never saw him again." He paused, swallowing what appeared to be anger and sadness mixed together.

Cassie tried her hardest to remain composed as she heard Rane's story, but the words staggered through her like jagged knives: sharp, relentless, and unforgiving.

"So, when the gossip started to travel about the first Gemini allowed to live in years, and the possibility of her helping us win the war, I had to meet you," he continued, pushing his raven hair behind his ear. "To see with my own eyes that there can be a better future, and that there's hope that other women won't be forced to go through what my friend did."

Anger swirled around her. She'd thought their laws were horrid when she'd first heard them, but hearing an actual story, firsthand, of how it had affected a woman, for having a child with the same zodiac sign as her . . . it not only made her blood boil, but the lack of choice around it all devastated her.

"I despise these laws," she said through gritted teeth. "It makes me sick to my stomach. I hope one day I can influence change."

"I hope so too. When I saw you, dagger in hand, with pure fierceness irradiating through you . . . I was amazed. At both how resilient you were . . ." He paused, glancing up at her. "And at how utterly beautiful you are."

Her face warming, she said, "Thank you. You're not too bad yourself." She winked back, watching how his chiseled face blushed.

Rane laughed breathlessly. "Any compliment from you means the world." There was a buzzing sound, and he dug into his pocket, pulling out his phone. He sighed. "And as much as it pains me to leave, Nyssa just asked me to go to lunch with her."

A small part of her wished that he'd stay; she enjoyed his company more than she'd like to admit.

Standing, Rane said, "But meet me in the gardens tomorrow for a walk? I'll show you my favorite spot."

Cassie couldn't help the grin on her face. "Of course."

ECCEDENTESIAST

(N.) SOMEONE WHO ONLY PRETENDS TO SMILE

The Arena was eerily quiet tonight. Cassie walked slowly through its endless corridors, letting her fingers graze the cold stone walls, wanting to learn the history beneath them. There was so much *unknown* history here—to her, at least.

She should be training, should be doing something *useful* instead of wandering like some lost soul. But the others had gone on a mission without her, and Quinn had been snoring by the time she passed her room. She had nowhere to be, and no one to turn to. So, she walked.

It still felt strange. This place, this life, this new reality she had been thrust into. She had spent her whole life hiding, thinking she was normal, thinking she was safe. Now, she was standing in the heart of the very world that had outlawed her existence, surrounded by people who wouldn't have hesitated to put a sword through her as a newborn.

A dark presence curled inside her, in a way that almost felt comforting for a moment, an understanding, a sorrow that lived within both her and that darkness. Cassie clenched her fists, exhaling slowly. *No.* She would not feel sorry for this entity inside of her that threatened everything she held dear. She closed her eyes, checking her mental shields, and threw some energy at it, further solidifying them before continuing on her walk.

Cassie walked through the training hall next, her shoes scuffing against the marble flooring, the familiar scent of sweat and steel still lingering in the space from a recent session. She'd spent countless hours here, had been knocked down on her ass more times than she could count, and she had been forced to unlearn everything she thought she knew about herself. Every moment in this Arena had been a battle—a battle against her body, her mind, and the darkness clawing to break through. She had fought for every inch of control she now had, and even that seemed limited at times.

Just then, voices drifted from an adjoining hallway, low and hushed, but sharp enough for her to hear.

"I don't care what the council says. That *thing* shouldn't be here." Male. Rough and irritated.

Cassie stilled, pressing her back against the cool stone, her breath caught somewhere between her ribs as she tucked her hair back, straining to listen more closely. She knew without a doubt that she was the subject of their conversation.

"I know. But Apollo said that she could be some sort of savior," another voice muttered. Another male, but with less bite.

A scoff followed, cold and sharp. "He's a typical god. He doesn't have to live with her, doesn't have to share a space with her like we do. I mean, you've seen her fight, right? You've seen what she is." Cassie's pulse hammered in her ears, her fingers curling at her sides. "I wonder how long they expect us to act as though she's normal," he continued, voice quieter now, but edged with something raw. Not just disdain, but *fear.* "She's an abomination."

"I know," the second Zodiac said. "But what are we supposed to do? She's under Diana's protection. If we so much as—"

"I don't care about the Archon!" he interrupted, his tone seeping rage. "And I don't care what Apollo and Calypso have to say either. The fact is, she shouldn't exist. Why is *she* an exception to a law we've had for centuries?"

Cassie's stomach twisted. She knew some of the Zodiacs around here didn't like her, but it was still tough to hear that they'd prefer her dead.

"You think the council was wrong in their decision?"

"I think the council is playing with fire," he muttered. "And when she finally snaps, they're going to act shocked, like they didn't see it coming. And we'll be the ones left to clean up the blood—if it isn't ours that's shed first."

The silence that followed his words suffocated her. No matter how much she trained, no matter how hard she fought, no matter how much she proved herself, there would always be people out there who would never trust her.

"Come," the second one said. "We shouldn't talk like this out in the open."

Cassie held her breath as footsteps sounded, waiting until they drifted out of earshot, before she let it go. She wiped at her cheeks, damp with tears that had fallen at some point, and tried her best to keep her composure. She shouldn't care what they thought.

But she did.

And deep down, she wondered if they were right. Geminis had been banned for centuries, so why *was* she the exception? What had she done to deserve that? But within the same breath, she had never asked to be here. She had never asked to be a Gemini, to have this burden.

Her hands clenched into fists at her sides, her nails pressing hard into her palms. They didn't know what it was like to fight for control every single day. They didn't know what it had taken just to stay standing, what she had sacrificed to be here.

They had no idea how much she feared herself.

She exhaled slowly, forcing the weight in her chest to loosen, forcing the thoughts to quiet. She wouldn't give them the satisfaction of doubting herself. She would not let their words become the truth. She'd prove them wrong.

Cassie exhaled sharply and turned away, pushing through another set of doors, deeper into the Arena, until she ended up in a small gym Hero had shown her once, the one away from the main training hall, in case she ever wanted to train alone, away from prying eyes. She hadn't realized how much she'd need it until now. She sent a silent *thank you* to him.

It was empty, dimly lit, the only sounds being the distant hum of the air vents and a steady drip of water somewhere in the distance. She walked over to the rack of dumbbells and picked one up. Not too heavy, not too light. Hero would probably tell her to go heavier. *"You wanna get stronger or not?"* Cassie rolled her eyes at the thought of him, but her lips twitched into something dangerously close to a smile.

And then, her mind betrayed her, her thoughts drifting to the way his shirt had ridden up when he lifted weights, revealing that sharp, perfect cut of muscle that disappeared beneath the waistband of his pants. The way her mouth had gone dry, the way her stomach had twisted in a way she wasn't prepared for. The thought of his hands—rough, strong, and calloused from years of combat—on her skin. Touching her. Tracing down her spine. Holding her against him . . .

Heat rushed to her face.

Okay, nope. Absolutely not.

This was just biology. A stupid reaction to an *absurdly attractive* warrior who just happened to be very large and very shirtless most of the time. That was it.

Stephen was the only guy she'd ever been with. And sex with him was fine, nice. But it wasn't like in the books, like in the movies. Not the kind of thing that left a mark on your soul, that made you crave someone like they were air, as though you couldn't get enough of each other.

But *this*? The way Hero made her feel when he so much as looked at her? It was dangerous. Because it wasn't just sex she imagined. It wasn't just the way his body would feel against hers, the way his mouth might taste, the way he might sound when he—

She stopped that thought *immediately.*

No, worse than that, worse than the physical want, was the other thing. The softness. The way she caught herself thinking about his hands holding hers, instead of just on her. About his lips brushing against her forehead. About what he would look like in the mornings, sleepy and tousled, his voice still rough with sleep.

And that? That was a problem.

Sex was simple, easy. This was *not*.

Her chest tightened. Cassie set the dumbbell down with a *clank* and dragged a hand through her hair. Hero would never see her that way. Why should he? He was a warrior, a legend. He was made for this world, for this life. She was an anomaly. A mistake. A walking threat.

No one wanted to love the girl with a dark side. Hero least of all.

She let out a slow breath, forcing the thoughts away, shoving them into the deepest part of herself, where all her other unwanted feelings lived. And then she picked up the weights again, and she kept going until her muscles gave out.

Artemis cleared her throat, the sound echoing through the training room. "As I was saying, studying *The Art of War* will teach you to be ready for your opponent, even if there's a chance they won't show."

Cassie guided her daggers into a cross formation. Artemis and Hero had told her she needed to practice fighting with her mind distracted. If she entered a fight with the Seekers again, she would have to fight them while making sure her shields remained, so that they couldn't possess her.

"You're dropping your right elbow," Hero muttered.

"Want to show me what's right, then?" Cassie countered. She dropped her elbow even lower on purpose.

"Just watch me and do what I do," he pleaded. "Please, Cassie."

"*The Art of War* also talks about how you need to make informed decisions. Don't trust your gut; trust your mind." Artemis continued speaking as she flipped her knife into the air once more, catching it by the handle.

"Easier said than done," Cassie said under her breath, slashing her hands down again. And again, she dropped her elbow. Maybe she was being stubborn, or it was a form of payback for Hero ignoring her so much, but she just wanted some kind of reaction from him.

Hero's jaw clenched. "Here," he said, walking over to her. He placed two fingers on the nape of her forearm, pushing it upward. "Keep it like this. You want your left arm to hold higher so you don't slice your right hand."

Cassie held her breath, acutely aware of how close Hero was—the closest he'd been in weeks.

And with the way Hero's muscles tensed, Cassie knew he realized it too. Yet he lingered, his calloused fingers grazing her skin, his breathing falling unsteadily.

He backed away. "Lesson's over."

Cassie watched him and Artemis leave, unable to keep the disappointment from her face. With a sigh, she closed her eyes and focused on her breathing. She found her momentary tranquility with Hero, but she needed to find another way. Training helped, making her stronger, more in control. But her heart still raced, her hands still growing sweaty when she refrained from checking her mental locks. A sign, perhaps, that she *should* check them. She gave in to the need.

Back here, in the dark room, she shivered. She wrapped her arms around herself. It had never been cold in here before. But there her dark side sat—*it* sat. Locked in the cage, its teeth chattering as it stared at her, black hair wet and stuck to its face.

It spoke first. *What happened to you?*

What do you mean?

There's been a change in the weather. A warmth replaced with ice.

Cassie knew what it was. *Hero's being distant with me. Avoiding me.*

Let me take charge. I'll fix it.

Liar.

I could say the same to you, Cassandra.

Cassie shot her eyes open, flexing her fingers from where they had found their way into fists, crescent moons crowding her palms. When she was around Hero, she discovered not only an ease, but also a warmth, a light in the dark.

But now it had vanished.

Cassie exhaled as she waited for Rane in the library. She'd arrived early to spend a few moments alone with the books, grateful that no other Zodiac had come in today.

Rane had taken her on a walk across the grounds yesterday, showing her a beautiful area where all the trees formed a perfect circle. The sun gleamed through the leaves, casting a chessboard of shadows and light on the ground. She'd told him how much she wanted to travel, and her fears of never being able to—her fears of her life being stolen away by her dark side.

The door opened, disrupting her thoughts. *Rane.*

"All okay?" he asked, scanning her.

Cassie faked a wide grin. "Of course. I was just lost in a daydream."

Rane smiled as he walked over. "Good. I wanted to show you a book I found, one I think you'll enjoy," he mused, leaning beside her, brushing his lips against her ear.

Cassie turned, her face inches from his. "You couldn't have just brought it to me?

"Well, then you wouldn't have had the full experience." Rane's dark eyes twinkled. "Follow me."

She couldn't help but be entertained—excited even—by Rane. It helped that he was handsome, his kind and caring personality shining through, not to mention the lean muscles she could see through his tight red shirt.

Cassie followed him to a section of old books bound in black leather with silver engravings. Rane pulled one out, a half circle of moons decorating the cover, with the word Nyx written in large letters. "Have you ever heard of Nyx?" Rane asked, opening the book wide.

Cassie shook her head.

"Nyx is the goddess of the night. Even the Immortal Zeus is terrified of her." Rane chuckled before handing the book to her.

Cassie took it and scanned the pages. A depiction of a stunning woman illustrated on one page stopped her in her tracks. She was dressed in all black, her inky hair waving in the dead of night. But her eyes . . . her eyes shone like moons and stars and ice.

The daughter of Chaos, able to bring sleep or death to mortals, her abilities are used for both good and evil. Pictured as a villain due to her obscure nature, she is merely the goddess of night, not of darkness, nor of death.

Rane cleared his throat. "I wanted to remind you that your darkness can be a strength, and that I see both the light and beauty in it. By being a shape-shifter, you could be such an advantage to us in the war, but your resilience is even more so." Rane stepped closer to her. "I know what it's like to lose someone, and it's a pain I'll never get over. But it eases knowing you're here, fighting for us all. And hopefully, we don't have to lose anyone else."

He brushed the hair from her face, his fingers lingering on her cheek. Cassie's lips parted as she stared into the midnight pool of his eyes. Her heart pulled like a current. A part of her wanted to get lost in him. He found beauty in her, in her dark side. He had not shied away from her, or *it*.

Rane frowned at her. "I'm sorry."

Cassie raised her eyebrows. "For what?"

"That you have to go through this," Rane said softly, his face leaning closer to hers. Cassie glanced at his lips, moving toward him, yet her heart tugged her back.

"Too soon?" Rane chuckled airily as Cassie closed the book.

"Now *I'm* sorry," Cassie confessed, posture slumping. "I'm just a bit of a mess right now." *In more ways than one.*

"It's okay," Rane said, placing his hand on hers. "All we have is time." He smiled at her, so sincere, so vulnerable.

The door behind her opened, and through it came the other half of her. Hero paused as he saw her, his sight shifting between the two of them, to where Rane lingered too close to her, standing in front of her still.

"Hero," Cassie muttered, looking into his gorgeously pained eyes.

"Cass." He dipped his head, and in seconds, he left without a single acknowledgment of how he felt. His face remained stone cold, no emotions for her to grasp at, to give her any hope for her own feelings for him.

Cassie knew she was holding out for a distant dream, a fate that would never happen, because how could he feel the same as she did?

Rane cleared his throat, and his jaw clenched. "Hero may be an old friend of mine," he said, his tone a warning, "but I know what he's like, and he's a hard man to be with. He has too many demons."

But that's what Cassie adored about Hero. They both had their demons, and they were one and the same.

"I should go." Cassie stood, feeling feverish, overwhelmed by herself. "I told Quinn I'd help her think of an excuse as to why she's not going to see her family soon," she lied as she put the book back in its place.

"Do you still want me to come by your room at seven tomorrow night for the ball?" Rane asked, his hand gently going to her wrist to stop her.

Cassie bit her lip as she glanced at him. Shadows in the form of her guilt wrapped around her shoulders, entrapping her. "I can't wait," she replied, feigning a smile before she turned around and left.

CHAPTER 27

MAMIHLAPINATAPAI

(N.) A LOOK BETWEEN TWO PEOPLE THAT SUGGESTS AN UNSPOKEN SHARED DESIRE

Hero slammed the door behind him. He despised the nausea building in him from watching Rane parade Cassie around the Arena the last few days. Rane was his friend—well, more of an acquaintance now, he guessed—but he knew from the moment he saw them together that Rane had different intentions than being just friends with Cassie. Rane had always had a knack for wanting what Hero wanted, after all.

It seared his eyes red with anger.

He dragged his punching bag out into the room, then strapped his boxing gloves on. He hit it as hard as he could, over and over again.

No matter how hard he tried to stay away from her, he couldn't. Every cell in his body wanted to be near her. The weeks they'd spent training together were the best of his life, even when he tried to keep his distance.

He had never believed himself to be a jealous man, but since Cassie had entered his life, everything he thought he knew was turned upside down.

Am I too late? Did I ruin things beyond repair with her?

His internal struggle tore him to pieces—and he destroyed things too easily.

The door swung open, his sister's voice sounding through the room. "Hero! What the hell are you doing?"

He turned around to see her gawking at him. Looking down at himself, he saw blood dripping down his arm; his rage had masked the pain.

He slammed his hands onto the punching bag, leaning his forehead on it in defeat.

"Hero," she said, her words soft and padded, "let me help."

Hero shook his head. "You won't understand."

"What I understand," she paused, taking his covered hand in hers, "is that you're afraid of how you feel about Cassie. You're afraid to let yourself be vulnerable for once in your life. You're too afraid that once you let your guard down, someone will love you back. You're afraid you'll ruin it—ruin her."

"It's the other way around!" he yelled, yanking his hand out of hers. "She'll ruin *me*."

Artemis huffed. "What are you talking about? Are you worried about your future as Archon if you're with her or something?"

He staggered, his body swaying. "The prophecy. . ."

The prophecy that will damn me, that will ruin me if I follow my heart.

"I don't get it," Artemis said. "The prophecy was positive. They think she has a chance."

"Not that one," he muttered, pacing the room. "There's another one Mom told me about afterward. We're fated to be together." He slammed his fists on the ledge of his fireplace, dust falling out from under it.

"Okay. . . but isn't that a good thing?"

"There's more." He took a deep breath. "As much as we're supposed to be together, she's also supposed to be the ruin of me. My *destruction*." Artemis fell silent at his words, as he assumed she would. "So, you see why I'm having a bit of a problem with this. Should I gamble everything I've worked for, along with my actual life, to be with this one girl?"

Silence.

"Does Cassie know about the prophecy?"

Hero shook his head.

"Isn't this whole thing we're doing—training her, building her shields, having faith in her—so we can save her from whatever prophecies may be?" She sighed. "No matter the outcome, I think you should follow your heart, wherever that may lead. Life's too short not to."

Hero exhaled deeply, his entire chest deflating. He hadn't realized just how excruciating it'd been to keep this information to himself. He didn't feel as though he could even tell Titus, terrified that it may spur his distaste for her even more, and Elijah wouldn't have been able to keep the secret for long.

"You think I should let her ruin me?"

"No," Artemis scowled. "But you're ruining yourself already by not being with her. And I'm really done with all the sexual tension cramming its way into the training sessions with her," she joked. "If your heart is screaming at you to go be with her, then be with her. The Hero I know would never back down from a fight. You always find a way, so find a way to break this stupid prophecy too."

Hearing the truth in his sister's words, Hero's stomach dropped. He looked down at his bloodied hands, the evidence right in front of him. *Could there really be a way to break it? And does it even really matter, if I'm damned either way?*

A flicker of hope pulsed through him.

He wanted Cassie—so undeniably so, that he decided right then and there. He had to show Cassie his true feelings, fight for her alongside Rane, and pray to the gods she would choose him. Hopefully he wasn't too late.

"What about you, Art?" he asked finally. The Velcro scratched him as he ripped his gloves off and threw them to the floor.

She crossed her arms, her eyes narrowing at him. "What do you mean?"

Hero couldn't help the smirk on his face. "I see the way you look at Quinn. She's mortal, need I remind you."

Artemis scoffed. "I don't know what you're talking about. She's just a friend," she claimed, her voice softening as she sat on his bed, pulling out their dad's old knife to toy with.

"It wouldn't matter to me if you did like her," Hero said, stepping closer to her. He knew his sister liked both men and women, but their laws were strict when it came to mortals. "Just be careful. You could be excommunicated over her. I can't do this without you."

Artemis frowned. "You never will. Besides, nothing's happened with her. I promise."

Hero sat on the edge of the bed with Artemis, pulling her closer. "Thank you, for always being there for me."

She grinned at him. "What are little sisters for?"

Hero shrugged. "For annoying the hell out of me, and occasionally giving okay advice." Artemis flung a pillow at him, hitting him in the face.

He laughed, properly, for the first time in . . . Well, he couldn't remember how long. Now he had to clean up his messes, and he knew exactly what to do, and who to ask for help.

Cassie's shoulders relaxed as she closed the door to her room. Hero hadn't shown up for today's practice; only Artemis had. She wondered why it caused her heart to tighten, to make her mind drift to the possibilities of where he could be, who he was with . . .

But today was the ball, and she was Rane's date.

She sighed. When she was around Hero, everything else seemed to melt away, dripping off her like mud in the shower. But when she was with Rane . . . it felt like something new, something different that made her feel on the edge of her seat. And at times, it was a cool winter's chill, a blanket wrapped in snow.

Cassie shook her head, annoyed at herself. She *felt* a certain way about Hero; that was a fact. But he didn't want her. And she couldn't let Rane be a second option either. He deserved better.

For now, she didn't know what *she* wanted.

A small chirp tore her from the chaos in her heart.

Cassie looked down to see a ball of white fur slinking around her ankles, demanding her attention. She smiled, bending to scoop Bones into her arms, and the cat purred as it nuzzled further into her neck. Bones then jumped out of her embrace and onto the bed, drawing Cassie's attention to a white box, perfectly wrapped with a gray bow. Spotting a small card tucked underneath the ribbons, she flipped it over. One letter written in gold graced the white paper: *H*. Her breath caught, and a smile crept over her face, one she couldn't stop.

Paper rustled underneath as she pulled the cardboard top off. She lifted the heavy material, revealing a flood of silky green fabric, the emerald beading dancing across the bodice.

Hero had sent her a gown made for a queen. And in her favorite color, too.

But why?

Her initial excitement gave way to anger. One minute he was hot; the next cold. She had no idea what this dress was supposed to mean, especially when he'd done so well at keeping his distance from her. She also couldn't help but notice he'd only done this after someone else had paid attention to her.

Still, she glided her hand down the luxurious fabric.

It would be rude not to wear the dress, she repeated to herself as she showered, curled her hair, and put the dress on.

The silky material floated down her body, hugging her curves, her silver hair contrasting with it in the best way. She spun herself around, adoring what her reflection showed her.

A soft knock sounded at her door. Rane stood there, his long black hair tucked behind his ears, a black suit framing his tall body.

"Wow," he proclaimed, mouth gaping. "You look stunning." He stepped closer to her. "It's not a tradition here, but I wanted to get you this," he said, holding out a box with a corsage made up of three small orange roses bunched together inside.

Maybe she was being stupid for not giving Rane a full chance, for caring too much about Hero, the man who had never shown a genuine interest in her other than occasional flirting. Rane was handsome, sweet, and perfect. And he'd been an amazing friend to her in such a short time.

Rane placed the box on the vanity, glancing at her through the mirror with a soft look. He spun back around and carefully placed the corsage on her wrist.

"Ready?" he asked. He held out his hand, and she took it, admiring the flowers wrapped around her. Yet Cassie couldn't help but notice how the color clashed terribly with her dress.

Ignoring the ache in her heart for Hero, she followed Rane toward the muted music flowing through the halls.

The ballroom doors opened at their arrival, ushered by a man and a woman in white uniforms traced in golden patterns, buttons, and ties as Cassie entered for the first time. It was large and elegant and washed in a sea of warmth. The sound of violins filled the air, each string tuned to perfection, feeding her senses with love.

People around them waltzed in pairs, holding onto each other as if they could slip away in a moment's time. Champagne poured into glasses stacked high by young waiters in penguin coats, and laughter and chattering sounded from where others huddled in circles, murmuring about everything and nothing.

Elijah sat at a table nearby, his eyes on Nyssa, who was making her way to the orchestra. Cassie could hardly blame him. They had a special kind of love. She could see that as much as they loved each other, they were also each other's best friends. Cassie wondered if she would ever find that— if she would ever have the time to.

"Dance with me?" Rane asked.

Cassie nodded and let herself be taken by him. He held her as though she were silk, and although her chest roared in excitement as he gazed at her, it wasn't enough.

Her eyes wandered around the room, searching for *him.*

An elegant voice, like honey and ash, flooded her ears. Everyone's attention went to the stage.

"Half of me is all of you,
Everything I love and more,
Pieces of me live in you,
And in your soul, I soar."

"I had no idea Nyssa had such a beautiful voice," Cassie beamed, still half entranced by the lyrics of the song. She glanced over at Rane, who squeezed her waist softly.

"She got it from our grandma. They used to sing together all the time." Rane swallowed hard as his eyes coated with gloss. "This song is about a woman whose lover dies in her arms. She's so saddened by his death, she tears her heart in two, so that they can both live with it."

Cassie craved a love as strong as the one Nyssa sang about—one that would make her want to tear her own heart in two. But that wasn't what she felt for Rane. It wasn't what she'd felt for Stephen either. They were an almost: almost perfect, almost what she wanted.

Almost, but not quite.

The dance changed, the tempo slowing, and before she could blink, she found herself in the arms of another. All the dancers had switched partners. She glanced up, meeting the golden-brown eyes she dreamed about.

CHAPTER 28

PSYCHOMACHY

(N.) A CONFLICT BETWEEN THE BODY AND THE SOUL

"It's a different world here, isn't it?" Hero mused. "Nice dress, by the way." He smirked at her, and his grip on her waist tightened, easing that calm into her.

"I guess I have you to thank for that." She smiled back at him, trying to be polite and to push down any feelings she might have—even if dancing with him felt like the most natural thing in the world. Like *home*.

"What's going on between you and Rane?" he whispered in her ear.

Cassie shook her head, glancing to where Rane danced with another. "Why? Is someone jealous?"

"Me? Never." He pulled an offended face. "I just wanted to check in."

Cassie swallowed the knot building in her throat. "He's a friend."

Hero's expression fell, but he recovered so quickly that she almost didn't catch it. "Are *we* friends?"

230

"What else would we be? Enemies?" she asked, earning a loud chuckle from him.

He leaned closer to her, his voice low. "I want to be more than friends."

Cassie's breath hitched. *What?*

He pulled her along with the music, and she went willingly, utterly consumed by him, dancing and flowing across the room like poetry. She thought back to their first training session, how then they were fighting each other, and now they had melded into one.

Cassie shook her head. "What does that even mean, Hero?"

His movements slowed as he stared at her, all his emotions floating to the surface at once. "I'm sorry. For how I've been acting the past few weeks. But I'm done hiding my feelings for you."

Cassie's heart could have fluttered out of her chest at that very moment. Yet something else stirred deep within her, something upsetting, fragile. She shook her head, staring down at how their feet moved together in perfect unison. "I . . . I—"

"You what?" He inched closer to her, hope and doubt warring in his eyes.

The heat swelled to her face as she dug her nails into the seams of his jacket. "How can I trust you after you pushed me away so many times?" she questioned, desperately hoping he wasn't lying to her or to himself, that he wasn't toying with her.

"I'm so sorry I did that, Cass. But I care about you, way more than you might think. There's just so much more you don't know about. Things about me." He paused, his eyes sad. "About us."

She huffed but didn't let go of him. "And what don't I know?"

Before he could answer, the dance changed yet again, this time erupting into a crescendo, the music fast and wild, and another pulled her away.

The world outside came flooding back, crashing down on her like a violent sea. Rane held her again, gliding her across the room. She finally mustered the strength to look into his dark eyes.

"I don't mind having to fight for your attention, but don't play me, please," he whispered in her ear before the music came to a stop.

Rane picked up a glass from the waiter passing by, handing it to Cassie. "To the month of rebirth and new beginnings."

Cassie downed the cool liquid. "I'm sorry. I need a minute," she mumbled, passing her empty glass back to him and walking to the other side of the room.

Her emotions swirled around her, consuming her on all sides. She needed some time to herself, to breathe, to think about what Hero said. Did he truly want more from her? Did he genuinely feel the way he said he did, all this time? But then why did he push her away?

None of his actions made sense to her. They only made her angry.

She couldn't deny the way she ached for Hero, but she also couldn't help but be furious that he only paid attention to her the moment someone else came into her life.

Cassie pulled her hair up off her neck, allowing a rush of air to cool her down. She needed to gain some of her common sense back.

A waiter passed by with another tray of champagne, and she eagerly reached for a glass. The bubbles burst on her tongue and tickled her throat. Cassie held her drink to her lips to take another sip of the cool liquid. But she froze as something caught her eye—something dark. She tilted her head in confusion, drawing back her drink and examining her hands. Her veins were growing darker and darker with each passing second. She fixated on them, her vision and hearing blurring.

The black veins flowed through her skin, taking over her body. She hardly noticed the champagne flute slipping from her fingers and shattering across the floor.

Heart drumming in her ears, she stared at the crowd around her. They all looked at her, doubling over in laughter at what a disgrace she was to them.

No. This can't be happening.

A scream rippled through the room as their laughs turned to fear. She glanced shakily at the ground, catching her reflection in the spilled pool of champagne on the floor. A devilish grin smiled back at her as her long silver hair stained itself stark black. She shut her eyes, desperate to find her dark side and throw her back in the cage, but something blocked her. She couldn't access anything in her mind. It was *gone*.

Her eyes opened again as her body reacted on instinct, running away from the crowd.

Stop. Please, stop! she silently begged.

She turned a corner, stopping at the third door on the left. Her room. Swinging it open, she ran to the mirror, needing to see for herself.

Her body fell in on itself in horror. Her face distorted, morphing into someone else, something else.

Her eyes flashed the familiar deep purple, signaling the final change.

And just like that, she wanted to kill.

CHAPTER 29

SCIAMACHY

(N.) A BATTLE AGAINST IMAGINARY ENEMIES; FIGHTING YOUR SHADOW

Hero's blood boiled every time he looked at Rane—his stupid, smug face, the way he had Cassie wrapped around his finger within a week. But he couldn't blame her. He'd pushed her right into Rane's open arms.

Their dance didn't go as he had expected. He'd confused her too much, and he only had himself to blame. He'd taken too long to admit how he felt, and then he told her too suddenly.

Give her time. Give her space.

He vowed to himself that he would be there for her, to help her defeat her dark side, and devote himself to her over and over again. And if, in the end, her heart chose him, then no matter what the damned prophecy said, he would let her ruin him over and over again. After all, he was ruined either way.

"Looks like you need one of these." Artemis appeared next to him, handing him a glass of champagne.

"How'd you know?" Hero replied, taking the glass hungrily.

His attention caught on his mother, who stood with her head held high, staring him down with anger. His mouth went dry. He shouldn't have danced with Cassie in front of everyone, especially in front of Diana. But he had no choice; his feet followed his heart. And he wouldn't stop it. Not anymore.

Artemis's voice chimed him back into focus. "You both deserve to be happy, one way or another."

"Do you think she'd be happy with Rane?"

She sighed. "I'm not going to answer that. She'll figure it out, like you did." Artemis passed him one more smile before she walked back to Quinn.

He grabbed another glass of champagne from a waiter and gulped it down. Then his phone vibrated in his pocket. Pulling it out, he saw the screen flash with *her* name.

Hey. Meet me in my room?

His heart pounded so rough in his chest he could have sworn it bruised his ribcage. He knew what he wanted, and it was Cassie. She was all that consumed his mind. He devoured another drink for confidence before rushing out of the ballroom.

Hero found his way to her bedroom; the sound of her giggling through the door warmed his heart. The handle's cool touch on his sweaty hands steadied him as he twisted it open. His face fell as he saw the sprawl of silver hair on Cassie's bed—and someone else on top of her.

Fury dug deep in his bones as Cassie tilted back in pleasure, wrapping her legs around no other than Rane. Her eyes met his from across the room, smirking before she busied herself again with Rane, kissing him ravenously.

Tears threatened to roll down his cheeks, his heart cramping. He had messed this up beyond repair.

He slammed the door shut, sliding his back down the wall as the sounds of moaning came from her room. Hero gripped his hair, trying not to hear it.

It should have been him in there. He knew it; his sister knew it; the whole damned Arena knew it.

He wasn't worthy of her. He never would be.

I'm a failure. I don't deserve her. I fucked up too much. She'll never want me. Why would she?

His thoughts threatened to consume him, until the next thing he knew, he was drenched.

Hero shot up, his clothes sticking to his body, his hair matted to his face, the sound of music blaring back into his ears. "What the hell?" he shouted, seeing Titus standing there with a guilty look. Hero shook his head, looking around at the ballroom he now stood in too. "How did I get here?"

"Sorry, mate. Had to get you out of the trance. I need some help around here." Titus gestured around to all the Zodiacs erupting in screams and laughter and chaos. They weren't in their right minds, as though they saw something else.

"You were here the whole time. You walked about halfway across the room before collapsing into a ball, rocking yourself back and forth, muttering nonsense about the moon having feelings," Titus explained, cocking his head.

Hero's shoulders loosened as he exhaled deeply. He pulled out his phone again. No text from Cassie—not one trace. She wasn't in there with Rane. He hadn't lost her yet. "What's going on?" he asked, focusing on the matter at hand.

Titus shrugged his shoulders. "I don't know. Everyone's acting like they've been drugged, running around like a bunch of drunk toddlers."

Hero filtered through the room, trying to locate members of his team first. They needed help to get everyone out of their trances; the two of them weren't enough for over a hundred Zodiacs losing their minds.

He found Artemis first, huddled in the corner while gripping her knife. His heart leaped as he sprinted over to her. "Artemis, you okay?" he pressed, her face cold in his hands. He peered over his shoulder at Titus, who had already formed a ball of water. Unceremoniously, he dropped it over her.

"Shit!" Artemis spluttered, standing. "You better have a good reason for doing that, Titus," she gritted through her teeth. Her eyes then widened as she took in the scenes around them.

Lukas and Quinn ran toward them, sweat dripping from their foreheads. "Elijah," Lukas panted, hands on his knees, "just chased us from the bathrooms all the way here."

As if on command, Elijah bounced through the room, his hair on fire without a care in the world. He spotted Lukas, a wicked smile appearing on his face as he sprinted toward them. "Is it hot in here, or is it just me?" he asked, winking at them.

Quinn gasped, pulling a towel from off the bar and swatting him with it to try to get the flames to go out. "Elijah, you're literally on fire! Stop it!"

Titus huffed as he cupped his two hands together, creating a ball of water in between them. His fingers swirled as the liquid formed before he pushed it toward Elijah, soaking him.

"Dude! This is a new suit!" Elijah yelled, using his hands to wipe the material down, spraying water droplets around them. He froze as he looked around, suddenly seeing all the mayhem unfolding before him. "Um, guys, what's happening?"

There had to be a way to get everyone back to sanity, water being the key.

"They're all drugged for some reas—" Lukas began to explain before Nyssa ran past them, screaming like a banshee.

Elijah nodded his understanding, a frown forming on his face. "I'm gonna go deal with that. Be right back!" he blurted, sprinting after her.

The chaos was never-ending. Half of the Zodiacs who attended the ball remained in the room, meaning some had already dispersed throughout the Arena. It was too large an area to cover with just Titus and any other Pisces they could find to shake out of their trance.

We need water, and a lot of it.

"The sprinklers! We need to set them off," Hero ordered, eyes wide.

"I'll go find the controls," Artemis said before running out of the room.

"I think it had something to do with the champagne and Scorpio poison. I wasn't drinking it, nor was Titus, and Quinn wasn't affected," Lukas noted.

Hero's face scrunched. Scorpios had a unique ability to create poison from any liquid, and when consumed by other Zodiacs, the effects were unstable—deathly, if they had too much. Water, luckily, could help erase them.

"Someone did this on purpose," Hero seethed. "We need to find Cassie."

Abruptly, droplets of water rained down on them as the fire alarm blared, the entire ballroom, and hopefully the entire Arena, now drenched in water. Zodiacs around him snapped back to reality, the murmurs of confusion beginning.

"I saw Cassie run to her room," Quinn rushed, picking her wet hair off her face. "Find her. We'll help here."

"Hero, wait!" Titus yelled as Hero turned to look at him, his brows high. Titus paused for a moment before shaking his head. "Never mind. Go."

Hero sprinted toward their quarters, his legs moving faster than they ever had. Slowing as he reached Cassie's door, he inhaled sharply, the images of Rane on top of her stabbing his mind, but he willed them to vanish, and pushed Cassie's door open.

Nothing.

Her room swirled in the darkness of the night, her bed untouched. No one had been in here.

Goosebumps traveled up his arms, his skin crawling as a deathly scream sounded from across the hall—his room.

CANTRIP

(N.) A MISCHIEVOUS OR PLAYFUL ACT; A TRICK

Hero tried to open his door, but it was jammed shut. He slammed himself against it, breaking the wood around its hinges easily.

Empty.

The scream sounded again from his balcony, the one place the sprinklers couldn't reach. He ran to it without a thought.

Hero's heart stopped at the sight of Cassie, tiptoeing across the ledge, six floors up, the wind threatening to pull her straight off as she danced delicately with death.

Rane flinched at the sound of Hero barging out onto the balcony before his attention went back to Cassie. "Please, get down from there," Rane pleaded, his hands wide, like he was trying to catch her. "Hero, man, you gotta help me!" he yelled out to him.

"I didn't mean to. I'm so sorry. I killed all those people," Cassie sobbed, leaning further over the edge. The wind became harsher, as though trying to push her off.

"No, you didn't," Rane insisted, his voice deep. "You've been hallucinating this whole time, Cassie."

Hero raced over to her, his body catching up with his mind. If she died—if even one small cut appeared on her skin, and he wasn't there to catch her—he'd never forgive himself. "Cass, come to me. It's all okay," he said, holding his hand out for her to grab.

He had to think of something to knock her out of her trance . . .

"Rane!" Hero yelled over at him through the harsh wind, remembering that Rane was an Aquarius. Ignoring the slight irony, he said, "You have to make it rain; the water stops it!"

Within seconds, Rane glanced up at the sky, conjuring rainfall.

Cassie's hands lifted, palms upwards, collecting the water. She glanced down—and her body jolted, her ankles giving way as she fell.

Right into Hero's open arms.

Hero carried Cassie over into the room, thankful the sprinklers were now off, and set her down as her body shook from the sudden wetness. He exhaled so deeply as he gazed at her, safe and sound in front of him, that it felt like he had no more oxygen left. "It was all a hallucination. You're okay," he assured as she peered worriedly into his large mirror, blinking as though she expected to see someone else. Hero wondered what she'd experienced. Whatever it was, it wasn't good.

"Is everyone okay? What happened?" she asked, eyes wide.

Hero nodded, wrapping a towel around her shaking body. But the words seemed to escape him at her questions. Yes, they were okay. But she almost hadn't been. If he'd showed up just moments later . . . His jaw clenched.

"We were poisoned," Hero said, his gaze drifting to Rane, who still stood outside in the downpour, his head hanging. He felt a pang of guilt, for vying for the woman they both wanted, but right now, all that mattered was her. "Anything you thought you saw, or did, it was fake," he assured Cassie, rubbing his hands up and down her arms.

A knock sounded at the door as the rest of his soaked team joined them. "Everything okay? We heard yelling," Nyssaasked, her eyes drifting from Hero to Cassie.

"We're fine," Hero said, looking down at Cassie's shivering form once more.

"Rane, where were you? I couldn't find you." Nyssa rushed to her cousin's side as he returned to the room.

Rane shook his head, his face sour. "I've been drugged with Scorpio poison before," he said somberly. Hero remembered Rane telling him the story, when he had been drugged at a party, as they had been tonight. He had been beaten up, and all his belongings were stolen. "When I started to feel the effects, I jumped into the shower, praying it would go away. Then I saw Cassie."

"We need to find who was responsible for this attack," Artemis said through gritted teeth. "It could have been done to try and get rid of Cassie."

Hero's throat tightened at the idea of someone orchestrating this to hurt or kill her.

"I agree," Rane snarled, his eyes shooting to Titus.

Titus's eyebrows flung upward at Rane's unspoken accusation.

Hero looked between the two men. "Wait—you think *Titus* did this?"

"I'm sorry, but it makes the most sense," Rane said, crossing his arms over his soaked tux. "I overheard him talking about how much he hated her. We all know he doesn't want her here."

Hero's heart sank. Titus had spoken those words, but he would never put Cassie in harm's way. He couldn't, right? Hero glanced at Elijah, who already stared right back at him, a silent conversation flowing between them.

Titus scoffed. "Why the hell would I poison everyone? I spent the night running around taking care of all of you!"

Silence answered in return.

Hero recalled how Titus had stopped him when he was going to find Cassie, how he'd told him to wait. He staggered back.

"You don't seriously believe this, do you?" Titus asked his team, his chest heaving.

Rane stepped closer to Cassie, standing next to her as though guarding her from Titus.

Nyssa picked at her lip as she quietly said, "Titus and Lukas were the only Zodiacs not affected." Her words were met with even more silence; they all seemed too shocked to answer as the possibility took root in their minds.

This can't be happening. Not Titus. This is wrong. Hero refused to believe it, every fiber of his being going against the accusations. His friend might not have favored Cassie, but he knew the losses Hero had faced in life already, and he wouldn't put him through more . . . would he?

Lukas remained quiet in the corner, his eyes glossed over.

"I didn't do this," Titus pleaded, as though the words pained him to say. "You have to believe me! I would never poison any one of you!"

"Guys, come on," Hero addressed the group. "You can't seriously believe this? And Rane, I get where you're coming from, but Titus wouldn't have done this."

"What about the Scorpios in the Arena?" Elijah asked, crossing his arms. "It's their poison, right?"

"Titus's mom is a Scorpio," Artemis muttered.

Titus shot air through his nose. "Is this really what you think of me?" He turned to the rest of the group, staring at each one of them. "Is that what you all think of me?" A muscle in his jaw ticked. "Well, I'd rather rot in the dungeon than be around people who don't trust me not to do anything this stupid."

Diana walked into the room, looking at the mess of Zodiacs before her. "What's going on here?" she demanded.

Everyone's attention shifted to Titus, and Hero failed to do any different.

Diana inhaled sharply. "Titus, was this your doing?"

Hero's stomach turned. He refused to believe it unless the words came out of Titus's mouth himself.

But Titus clamped his jaw shut and raised his chin, not saying a thing.

Diana looked him deep in his eyes before turning to speak to Hero, to give him an order he had no choice but to follow. "Secure him in one of the cells while we arrange a date for his trial."

Hero wanted to collapse at his friend's betrayal and his mother's command, even if a part of him couldn't believe it. He placed a hand on Titus's shoulder, but Titus only jerked his body away from Hero's touch. They both walked out of the room in silence toward the holding cell, Hero's mind spinning with all the different possibilities and outcomes, all coming to one conclusion.

And it hurt beyond repair.

CHAPTER 31

METANOIA

(N.) THE JOURNEY OF CHANGING ONE'S MIND, HEART,
SELF, OR WAY OF LIFE

The water from the shower dripped down Cassie's body, washing away all of the afflictions from the night before. The heat burned her skin, and as much as she wanted to shy away from the pain, she remained. It meant she was alive. She was here, breathing, existing—herself and no one else.

Last night, she'd been shown a glimpse of what could happen should her dark side break through. Even though none of it had been real, thankfully, she still remembered her entire hallucination. She had killed—and she'd enjoyed it. The premonition had come true. She had sliced Hero's throat, smiling down at him as he choked on his own blood. Then Quinn. Then her father.

It was so clear in her mind, so fresh.

She needed now more than ever to find that Elixir and Cup. She'd rather die than let anything happen to those she loved, as shown last night.

Cassie was still trying to piece together the events of how she had ended up on Hero's balcony, but based on the few bits she could make out, she didn't think she wanted to know. Instead, she studied the detailed white ceiling above her shower, letting her mind drift across the waves of paint, conjuring fictional tales of the mermaids who swam through them and the sailors who got lost, only wanting to find their way back home.

She flinched as a knock sounded on her door. Turning off the water, she stepped out into the foggy bathroom, wrapping a towel around her before peeking out from behind the bathroom door.

"Hey," Hero said, his eyes wide as he looked at her. "Just wanted to check and see how you're holding up after last night?"

"As good as I could've hoped, I guess." Cassie shrugged.

"I want to be more than friends." His words echoed in her mind, but she was too tired, too emotionally taxed to think about it now, or the swirl of emotions it had stirred up in her: anger, confusion, happiness.

Most of all, she felt stupid for spending so much time and energy on her feelings for Hero and Rane rather than what mattered the most. She'd lost sight of her goal.

He gave her a weak smile. "Keep reminding yourself that it was just a hallucination. That's what I keep telling myself, anyway."

"I know. I've checked my shields about a hundred times since last night. It just felt so *real*," she mumbled, turning back into her bathroom to put on her bathrobe. As Hero had promised, all of her and Quinn's stuff from their apartment had been brought to the Arena a few days ago. There'd been no reports on the Seekers for a week, and the Zodiacs assumed they had gone back into hiding . . . for now.

Cassie pulled her hair into a bun, letting a few wisps of hair frame her face. "I honestly thought my dark side had escaped."

"That's what Scorpio poison can do," Hero said through the cracked door. "They usually use it to take down corrupt nymphs or demons, or even to tame a chimera, but it's illegal to use it that way on Zodiacs . . ." Hero's voice trailed off.

The fact that Titus had broken their laws to try and kill her upset her more than she could articulate. Just as she was beginning to feel a part of the team, beginning to feel like their friend, one of them had done something like this. But she honestly didn't know if she could blame Titus or not. It had reminded her of what was at stake and what she stood to lose, and most importantly, how deadly and fearful this darkness inside of her really was.

She exited her bathroom, scanning him. Something more sparkled in his eyes, something trembling between desire and hesitation. *I want to be more than friends.*

"Hero, about Titus," she asked, careful not to overstep. "Are you okay?"

"Yeah, I'm fine," he said casually, as though she had asked him how going to the grocery store went. "He confessed to it on our way to the holding cell, so we'll deal with it according to the law. His trial is next week."

Cassie smiled sadly at him. He clearly didn't want to speak more about Titus; maybe *not* dealing with it was how he dealt with it.

Hero clapped his hands, abruptly changing the subject. "Now. Don't you want to go see the nymphs?"

Cassie's head snapped up. *Yes. Please. A million times, yes!* "You think I'm ready for the nymphs?"

"After last night, I think you need a bit of hope. And yes, you're ready." He walked over to her windows, pulling the curtains open to let in the sunlight. Cassie's eyes squinted in response. They still ached from the flood of tears she'd shed after they all went to bed. She hoped he wouldn't notice.

"Come on," he said, the sad look on his face making it clear that he did. "I made some waffles. They're not the best, but they're in the dining hall. And be quick, Elijah's already made a dent in them." Hero chuckled as he made his way to the door, then paused. "Oh, and no matter how much Eli begs you to let him come with us, don't. Last time he saw the nymphs, he set a fire during one of their weddings."

At that, he sauntered out of the room, leaving Cassie alone with the anticipation of going to see the nymphs and getting one step closer to never letting what she had seen last night come true.

For that, she'd do anything.

She needed this to go as smoothly as possible, and she didn't want to make this day about Hero and Rane when it held crucial steps to finding the Elixir and the Cup.

The leaves crunched beneath their feet as they trudged through the forest, the trees around them reaching to the sky, decorating the world with flashes of earthy green.

Cassie couldn't help but find irony in going on a mission with the two men her heart was divided between, even if one side tugged stronger—*much* stronger.

Just stay focused on the mission.

She needed this to go as smoothly as possible, and she didn't want to make this day about Hero and Rane when it held crucial steps to finding the Elixir and the Cup.

"Do nymphs just hang out in the forest for anyone to find?" Cassie asked.

Hero held a branch out of the way, letting her pass in front of him. "The nymphs live in our world, but on a different plane, like the Immortals do. You have to know where to find them first," he explained. He let the branch go before Ranecould pass.

Rane huffed, catching the timber moments before it hit him in the face. "And luckily, I'm the best spotter of nymph portals."

Cassie glanced over her shoulder at him, shooting him a small smile.

"The elements—water, earth, fire, and air—all hold magical properties," Hero continued, crouching to dig his hand through the dirt before letting it fall back through his open fingers. "When the Immortals made the first Zodiacs, they used the elements to enhance our powers and healing abilities, and to help hide us from the mortals by making us appear like normal humans. The elements can even take the effects of our powers away, like with the Scorpio poison last night, or they can amplify them. Like with Elijah's fire and Titu—" Hero stopped himself, shook his head, then stood, wiping the remains of the dirt on his pants. "And they help the nymphs hide from mortals."

Aside from those who are bonded, like Quinn, Cassie added mentally. She also didn't miss Hero's near mention of Titus, and her heart hurt for him.

"But what if a human came across the portal by accident?" Cassie asked, running her hand along the bark of a tree.

"It's incredibly rare, but it has happened. Usually because of some clumsy mortal tripping and falling in," Rane said, moving in front of them to lead the way.

Cassie's eyebrows lifted. "What happens then?" A part of her was worried about the answer, unsure of just how deadly the nymphs were.

"Usually, a potion to make them forget," Rane replied over his shoulder, as though it were no big deal.

Hero smirked. "Or a good bang on the head should do it. They'd think it was just a weird hallucination."

"Ugh, don't mention hallucinations," Cassie groaned, her head still throbbing with the memories of last night.

Rane cleared his throat. "We're getting close."

A stiff awkwardness filled the air, but Cassie was determined not to let it ruin the day. "Are the nymphs immortal?" she asked Rane.

"Not really. If you kill them, they'll die, but they hardly age and can live for thousands of years. Oh, and don't take anything they say literally. Their lifespan isn't the only thing they care to exaggerate." Rane pointed to a clearing in the trees. "There, that's it."

Cassie peered closer, trying to understand how he could tell, and that's when she saw it: the slight glimmer between worlds. She noted the way the trees didn't rustle, how the colors of nature brightened and shone, the swirls of golden glitter reflecting the sun. It hummed, luring her forward. She approached it cautiously.

The line between the two realities faded as Cassie stepped farther into the portal. The sound of women giggling filled her ears, and her vision became blurry. When the world came back into focus, it wasn't her world at all. The ground was covered with thousands of violet and yellow flowers—daffodils and lavender. The entirety of the space smelled sweet, like an apple pie waiting to be eaten, and the sun shone into a clearing in the forest, urging her to explore. She glanced over her shoulder to see Hero and Rane's reaction—but they weren't there.

Her chest tightened, panic building inside her. Darting her eyes around, Cassie grew frantic as she realized she was alone.

Leaves rustled beside her, and she jolted away from the sound. She whipped around as she heard more rustling on the other side of her. "Hero! Rane!" Cassie yelled out, feeling her heart racing.

The rustling, now paired with whispers, answered, saying her name repeatedly. "*Cassandra. Cassandra. Cassandra . . .*"

"Who's there?" she demanded, her voice wavering.

"*Cassandra . . .*"

Women appeared suddenly from behind the bushes and trees. They wore dresses that barely covered their beautiful bodies, the light material flowing in a gust of wind. Flowers decorated their hair and faces, just as they did the trees, making them look otherworldly.

Nymphs.

"Where are my friends?" she demanded, refusing to let them see her falter.

"They'll join us soon," one of them said, stepping closer to her. "We wanted a moment alone with the Gemini."

Cassie's palms dampened. "Why?"

A different nymph spoke, her voice silky sweet. "We wanted to see for ourselves. To make sure you have remained pure, and that the darkness has not yet broken through. You will not be able to meet our queens before we do this."

"Ouch!" Cassie yelped as her hand flew to her head.

A nymph appeared next to her, a younger one, holding a strand of her silver hair.

Another flash of pain came from her other hand as she clenched her teeth. She looked down to find an even younger girl slicing her palm with a knife and collecting a few drops of blood into a small glass bottle. Then, the nymphs added the strand of her hair to the bottle, swirling it together. They held the glass up for inspection, watching the concoction as it transformed. Cassie's breath hitched as she saw the contents glowing a perfect mixture of light and dark.

"How peculiar," an older nymph said, and the others hummed in agreement.

Hero and Rane appeared next to her then, as though they'd been standing there the whole time. She gasped as her hand flew to her chest.

"Are you okay?" Hero said, looking her over worriedly.

"I'm fine." She glanced at the nymphs, giving them a nod of thanks for letting her friends go. "Are you?"

Hero nodded, warily eyeing the nymphs surrounding them.

Rane brushed himself off in response before walking toward the nymphs, stopping far enough away to keep a respectful distance.

More nymphs appeared from the river, the water dripping off their long hair and bodies, their hands clenching wooden spears. They knelt as the earth trembled beneath their feet. Then, the ground opened before them as three thrones rose, and in a flash, three women appeared sitting on them.

"Our queens have arrived," a nymph with brassy hair announced. "Cia of the Rivers, Volna of the Lakes, and Ivy of the Springs."

Cia's shimmering blonde hair flowed to the ground, her face soft and rosy. Volna's red hair curled wildly around the freckles sprinkled on her skin. Ivy's hair fell dark and short, her face tattooed with golden leaves and flowers. The three queens sat regally on their thrones, their faces cold and guarded as they stared down at the trio.

"Your Majesties," Hero said, his deep voice echoing through the forest. Hero and Rane bowed, one hand behind their backs. Cassie panicked, her knees bending as she attempted to curtsy. Hero chuckled beside her, and she slapped her hand onto his chest.

"Her beauty lies unmatched," Volna said, her chin lifting toward Cassie.

Hero's eyebrows shot up. "Yeah, well, so does her stubbornness."

Ivy's hands wrapped around the armrests of her throne. "And to what do we owe the pleasure of a visit from the Zodiacs?"

Hero took a step forward. "We seek the Gemini Elixir and the Twin Cup. We believe you know their whereabouts."

"We know only about the location of the Elixir," Cia answered. "Another source was entrusted with the Twin Cup."

Cassie's stomach dropped. If the nymphs didn't have the Cup, who did? Her mind spun with possibilities and anxiety.

"But why would we want to help you, Gemini?" Cia asked dispassionately.

Rane bowed his head, stepping up beside Hero as he spoke. "Because the prophecy says she can help us win the War of Gods. We believe her shape-shifting abilities could be vital against Poseidon and his army."

"While it is our wish to stop Zeus and Poseidon, we do not want to take part in unleashing a dark Gemini on the world," Volna said.

Rane tried to take another step, but the nymphs lifted their spears at him, warning him not to come any closer. "Without the Elixir, the war might as well be lost," he huffed. He glanced over his shoulder at Cassie, but her thoughts were racing too quickly for her to pay him much notice.

The Cup's location was still a mystery, and it would take even longer for them to find it now. How much more time did she have before her dark side took over? Was it long enough to find the Cup? Another challenge for her to face. But she had to at least get the Elixir, and the sooner, the better. At least with that, she'd be one step closer to defeating her dark side.

"Our help will come at a price."

Cassie lifted her chin and pushed her shoulders back. "I'll do whatever it takes."

She watched as the queens stood and walked down to her, the ground shifting to form stairs with each step they took.

"We need three things," they spoke in unison. "Your heart, your mind, and your soul."

CHAPTER 32

KENSHŌ

(N.) THE ZEN EXPERIENCE OF ENLIGHTENMENT, WHEN
ONE'S OWN NATURE IS SEEN FOR WHAT IT TRULY IS

A string of dread went down her spine, wrapping around it like a snake.

Cassie reached for her daggers, pulling them out, ready to fight. *Did they trick me? Are they trying to kill me before the darkness unleashes?*

"We have no desire to harm you, young Zodiac," Volna said, as though she could hear Cassie's thoughts. Her red hair bounced as she nodded once—a silent order for Cassie to lower her weapons.

Cassie gulped and did so before looking back at Hero and Rane, whose swords were also out, nodding at them to follow suit. Hero's jaw tightened, but he followed her order, swinging his sword back into his scabbard. Rane begrudgingly did as well.

"We will put you in a trance," Cia explained as the queens formed a line before them. "Each of us will test you with a different journey. The first will be the mind test, where we will examine you through memories. The second will be the soul test, where you will have a choice to make. The last will be the heart, where your deepest desire will be shown."

Ivy stepped forward to touch Cassie's cheek. She wanted to flinch at the contact, but forced herself to remain still. "Not everyone who goes through this comes out alive. It will be your choice." Her voice was soft, but the words held weight.

A tornado of butterflies swirled within her, but she had to do this, no matter the consequences.

"I'll do your tests," she said, walking toward the nymph queens. "But you should consider rephrasing your initial demands."

Volna floated her hand over the ground as a fury of roots rose from the soil, forming into a bed. "Lie down," she commanded. The nymph queen flicked her hand toward a nearby stream, and within moments, the water lifted into a long rectangular shape, appearing as a full-length mirror. "The Narcissus mirror," she explained, "so that we're able to see your trials and monitor your progress."

Cassie's mouth went dry. They'd all see her. Whatever happened in there, Hero and Rane would see it all.

"It'll be fine," Hero reassured her. "You make the rules."

Her body cascaded with goosebumps as she glanced back at him, trying not to lose herself in the way his eyes shone perfectly in the light.

She ignored the prickling on her back as she lay down, her hair mingling with the leafy vines. Her eyes fluttered shut. She could do this. No matter how harsh their tests would be, they could unlock the first half of her freedom.

Come and get me.

Volna's hands reached her temples, her fingers soft and cold. A sharp pressure flooded into Cassie, as though someone was crushing her—killing her. She screamed, her body squirming. Her eyes shot open, wanting to tell them to stop, to tell them it hurt too much, but then her view of the world faded into nothingness.

She couldn't breathe. The unnerving sense of being alone enveloped her. She screamed again, falling for an eternity, never coming up for air.

Water surrounded her.

Cassie pushed herself up—or what she thought was up—through a dark vastness, but she found no escape. She couldn't even tell which way to go. Every direction pulled at her.

Hero's words echoed in her mind: *"You make the rules."*

She stopped fighting the current, letting herself be taken by the harsh water. Her eyes closed, and she inhaled deeply.

A sweet melody flowed into her ears as someone sang along off-key.

When Cassie opened her eyes again, her vision filled with light. She was sitting in something moving. *A car.* Her silver hair floated through the open window, swirling around her face. She glanced down at the yellow sundress she wore, her hands grazing over the white leather seat. It had been so long since she had been in this car.

Her head lifted to see a woman smiling back at her in the rearview mirror.

"M-mom?" she mumbled, tears pricking her eyes.

She looked exactly like her photos, her wild blonde hair tied up, her lips painted in her signature red lipstick, her kind blue eyes sparkling in the sun. Cassie's memories of her mom had blurred with age, so she kept as many photographs of her around as possible, but it wasn't the same. Nothing could ever be the same as this.

"Yes, darlin'?" her mom said, her voice sounding just as Cassie imagined it did each night before she fell asleep. Vera patted her hand on the steering wheel along with the song playing on the radio.

Cassie's lip wobbled as she stared at her mother, trying to keep this memory alive, trying to soak up every last bit of this gift.

"Mom, I miss you so much," she said, her eyes stinging. "I wish you could see me, be with me."

Her mom looked back at her, her brows scrunching together. "I'm with you right now. I always will be. In here," she said, pointing to her heart.

Cassie's body flew forward with the force of a sudden impact, only stopped by the seat belt as shattered glass sliced her skin. Her vision blanked, and then pieced together again, turning and spinning like a washing machine.

The car slid for what seemed like an eternity, and then it stopped. Cassie coughed, trying to understand what had happened. She found herself upside down, her hands extending to the roof of the car to try and stabilize herself. She couldn't hear anything; her ears were ringing. She shot her eyes up.

Her mom hung from her seat, her hands limp across the windshield, her seat belt keeping her body from falling. Blood stained every surface, splattered across the car, across her body.

"Mom!" Cassie screamed out, and it felt as though her entire soul came out with her voice. Her hands reached up to free herself from her seatbelt so she could help her mom, but she was stuck.

This couldn't be happening again. *Please, no.* She ignored the tears rushing down her face as she reached out, trying to catch her. "Mom, please . . ." she pleaded, her voice breaking. *Please.* "Wake up! Don't do this to me!" Her voice cracked as she sobbed.

Hero's voice sounded in the distance. "What the hell are you doing to her?! Stop it now!" she could hear him yell, and she felt his hand slip into hers even though she couldn't see him, holding her as she broke in another world. His words echoed in her mind again: *"You make the rules."*

She studied her mom one last time through teary eyes before they closed, her heart breaking into a million pieces.

The pressure in her head disappeared, but for only a moment. Cassie felt numb, and she could only hope she'd passed the first trial. She couldn't take any more memories, any more torture. It would break her.

She opened her eyes.

Cassie blinked at her new surroundings, at the room she was now in. A singular ray of light cascaded down into the middle of the ruins she stood in. She spun around. It seemed to be a circular space, with pillars surrounding it—and then it clicked. It was the Oracle at the Arena, only if something had destroyed it and left it to decay for thousands of years.

The floor began to shake and crack as concrete fell from around her. She yelped, falling hard onto her side. Within seconds, the movement stopped, and Cassie found herself still on the ground—but everything within a few feet of her was gone, replaced by empty air. She was trapped on a pillar of rock.

Cassie peered to where water now flowed below her, watching as steam floated off it, bubbles bursting and sputtering. The heat of the boiling liquid snapped at her skin. One misstep, and she would be dead.

"Help!" a voice shouted from a distance. The Oracle shifted, growing as though making room for a new reality.

Cassie crouched low, stabilizing herself as much as she could as the rocks around her rumbled.

"Cassie!" the familiar voice shouted again from a distance.

She turned at the sound. Quinn stood on a nearby tower of rock quaking in the vastness of the boiling water spurting around her. Then, the stone began to tumble and fall . . .

"You have to jump over here!" Cassie yelled, moving her body to the edge of the rock as carefully as she could.

With the last bit of might she had in her, Quinn leaped.

Cassie caught her by the arm, her body pulled flat on the rough surface as she put everything she had into holding onto Quinn. She threw her other hand down, gripping her tight.

A voice sounded in her head. *Let her go. Save yourself.*

"What? No!" Cassie said back, her eyes wide.

"Help!" Quinn called out, her hands beginning to slip from Cassie's.

You're more valuable than her. You can save us. We can be together, as sisters. You don't need her.

"Stop!" Cassie yelled, wincing as she felt a sharp pain in her head. The cage in her mind rattled, her dark side's eyes gleaming viciously.

Cassie shot her eyes back open. *No,* she snapped back at her dark side. *I will never be you. I'll never let you win.*

She tightened her grip on Quinn, and with every last bit of strength inside her, pulled her up to safety.

A wooden bridge appeared beside them, barely held together by pathetic frayed ropes, leading them to a shining bright light that must mean freedom from this torture.

"It'll only hold one of us!" Quinn yelled as the rope frayed and popped.

Cassie looked to the side. A roar of cheers came from the table the council had sat around during her trial, now filled with faceless bodies egging her on. Her eye caught on one in the middle, with two glowing purple orbs in place of eyes and stark black hair drifting down her shoulders. *My dark side.* It chanted for her to choose herself. She didn't give it a second thought.

"You go. I'll be right behind you," Cassie reassured Quinn, though she knew only one of them would survive this.

Quinn stepped onto the planks of wood as the bridge wobbled in the air, gripping onto the sides for dear life. She was a few feet ahead when the ropes snapped, the bridge falling out from underneath her.

"Quinn!" Cassie screeched, throwing herself to the rock as she looked down for a sign of life.

Quinn grasped tightly onto the rope, her body dangling off the side of the rocky cliff. She pulled herself up, bit by bit, until Cassie could see her hand gripping the gravel, safe.

The ground shook beneath Cassie as she accepted her fate. She refused to lose anyone else, the image of her mom's lifeless body flashing back into her mind as a tear rolled down her cheek.

She sunk deeper and deeper, the air around her getting hotter by the second until she emerged into the heat. It burned like nothing she had ever experienced, and she wasn't even sure if the sounds coming out of her were screams or not as her skin melted off her bones.

Still, she died knowing that Quinn was safe, that she hadn't succumbed to the darkness.

The world went black.

Abruptly, the pressure released, and she opened her eyes again, awash in a flood of relief. Back in the forest with the nymphs, the weight lifted from her chest. The tests were done. She shot upright, looking around breathlessly. The three queens stood by the bed, but she couldn't see anyone else. All the other nymphs, Rane and Hero . . . gone.

Her pulse raced. "Where are my friends? What have you done with them now?" Jumping up, she reached for her daggers, but her harness had also vanished.

The queens stepped away from their line, revealing Hero and Rane trapped in a wall of vines. Cassie could just about make out their faces, the leaves growing quickly around them. They were choking, barely hanging onto life.

Cassie ran to them, desperately pulling at the vines with her hands.

"Your heart can only pick one in order to save them both," Cia announced.

She turned back around, facing the queens. The words repeated in her brain once more: *"You make the rules."*

"No," she snarled. "I choose myself. Let them go, and take me instead."

They shook their mighty heads. "Not an option here, Cassandra. Choose."

Cassie peered back at the two men, her chest tightening. She had to face the question she longed to push aside. She had to make her decision. Her mind told her this had to be another trick, another test.

So, she let her heart decide.

"Hero," she muttered. "I choose Hero. Now save them."

The vines on their bodies unraveled, progressively revealing the helpless men more and more before they fell on the ground, knees buckling as they coughed and sputtered, their hands going to their throats.

Cassie knelt next to Hero, her arms wrapping around him as she tried to hold him up. She glanced at Rane, who sat on his knees, expressionless. Her stomach shrunk.

"I did your tests. Now take me back," she demanded.

The men next to her vanished into the wind.

Cassie opened her eyes. Her hands pricked with splinters as she threw herself off of the bed, reaching for her harness, and pulling out one of her daggers. "Is this real?" she demanded, her chest heaving.

"Cassie! Are you okay?" Hero questioned, running to her. "It's real, it's real," he assured her, pulling her body into his.

Cassie's breathing slowed as she melted into Hero's calm embrace. *They're alive. I'm alive.*

"Congratulations on surviving the tests. Not many do," Cia intoned, bowing her head in tribute.

Cassie stepped away from Hero's embrace, the anger rising in her bones. "What did you do to me?" she demanded.

"Your mind was tested when you showed us your darkest memories. Your soul was tested when you chose to sacrifice yourself instead of your friend. Your heart was tested when you chose one over the other," Volna said, gesturing to the men beside her. "I apologize for the harshness of the tests. Sometimes memories can be the worst kind of torture."

Cassie shook her head, staring at the ground. "The first memory I had, in the water, I don't remember it happening." The second memory of her mom, however . . . That was sealed in her mind forever, and she didn't think it would ever go away. Especially not now.

Ivy's back straightened in her seat. "Memories are strange. Sometimes we remember things before they even happen."

"What the hell is that supposed to mean?" Cassie spat.

The three queens considered each other before Volna spoke. "It means you have passed our tests. You've chosen light over dark, repeatedly, even when tempted. Your heart is pure, and for that, we will tell you the location of the Elixir. It is located on a small island in Greece, Anthemoessa. It is guarded by our sisters, the Nereids, or as you might call them, mermaids."

Mermaids, Cassie thought. A fairytale creature from the books she'd read as a child, fascinated by the tales of their tails. And now they held the key to her salvation.

"They were once kind and beautiful," Volna said, "but over time, they've grown vicious and cold, as their ruler Poseidon has. He is a cruel and monstrous god, one who'll make you believe that not all demons reside in the Underworld. If he learns one word of your plan, or what we have told you, it will not end well—for any of us. Everything you do from here on out must remain a secret. Only trust those who you believe can be trusted."

"We promise not to speak of it." Cassie knew she could never put these women in harm's way, regardless of what they'd just put her through. But it had gotten her answers, and that was worth everything.

Within a split second, the nymphs disappeared, as though a veil had lifted around them. Cassie was left with the location of the first half of her freedom, as well as the threats of what could happen should the wrong person find out.

She finally mustered enough strength to look behind her at Hero and Rane, the guilt of the last trial consuming her.

Catching Rane's eyes, she opened her mouth to speak, to explain why she'd made the choice she did. She didn't want to hurt either of them; Rane had been so kind to her. Even though she felt something for him, it would have been worse to choose him when she knew her heart belonged to someone else—to Hero.

But before she could speak, Rane spun around on his heel, leaving without a word.

"Rane, wait!" Cassie yelled, reaching out to him as he walked away. She didn't know how to make things right with him. Worst of all, what if he wouldn't let her? She didn't want to lose him as a friend, even if she fully understood that was more than likely to happen.

Rane froze in his tracks, and after a heartbeat, he turned to face her. "It's okay, Cassie." And with a tone that sent a pang of shame through her chest, he said, "I'm glad I know how you feel. I'll see you back at the Arena." In seconds, he disappeared into the forest.

Cassie's face scrunched as she tried not to cry. She didn't want to hurt anyone.

"Hey," Hero said softly, walking closer to her. "You okay? I'm so sorry you had to go through that." She knew he was referencing what she had told him weeks ago, about the nightmares they'd both had reliving the event of their parent's deaths. She shivered at the memory of the trial and of seeing her mom again—a blessing and a curse.

"I'm okay." She shrugged, not wanting to remember it any longer. "How do we keep this a secret from everyone? From the gods?"

"I'm not sure." He shook his head, and panic and perhaps something else flashed in his eyes. "I'll tell Diana and our team. We can trust them, but all the other Zodiacs will be kept in the dark. We just can't let anyone know what we're doing." He ran his knuckles across his stubble.

"Small price to pay," Cassie mumbled, covering her face with her hands. "I can't believe you guys saw all of it. Especially the last trial."

"I mean, it made sense that you chose me. I saved your life a few times, so you metaphorically saved mine," Hero said as he smirked. She loosened in relief at how he didn't press on her feelings for him, thankful he knew her well enough to know she'd only feel more embarrassed.

"Come on, Cass." He slung his arm around her shoulder, tugging her in close. "Let's go home."

She glanced to the side, to the man she did choose, and that guilt building inside of her was swept away, replaced with a different feeling. She didn't regret choosing Hero—not for one second.

"I want to be more than friends," he had said to her. And now she had her reply. *Me too.*

CHAPTER 33

ERLEBNISSE

(N.) THE EXPERIENCES, POSITIVE OR NEGATIVE, THAT
WE FEEL MOST DEEPLY, AND THROUGH WHICH WE t
RULY LIVE

The creases of the duvet imprinted on Cassie's face, carving lines into her skin. She'd spent her entire day in bed, wishing it would swallow her whole.

Within two days, she had been drugged, almost fallen off a balcony to her death, and had her desire for Hero revealed, paining Rane in the process. Her mind had been manipulated into believing she was in a car crash and witnessing her mother's death again . . . She missed her mom so much.

And her dad. It was one thing spending the summer apart, but now she had no idea when she'd ever see him again—or *if* she'd ever see him again. The seriousness of her condition became more apparent with each passing day.

A heaviness weighed on her chest. *My time here is limited. I have to keep fighting.*

264

She turned her head to the side; the fresh air was a welcome sensation after planting her face in her pillow for so long. Cassie narrowed her eyes as the evening sun blared red through her windows, blinking to adjust. The sun glistened and gleamed in the sky, turning her room to gold—her new favorite color. The dust danced through the beams of light shining through her window as she adored how such small, insignificant things could look so beautiful without even trying. But no matter the beauty, everything on this earth was small and insignificant—at least, according to the Immortals.

The Immortals. Big, eternal beings, and all they did was fight and argue with each other. She had always wondered, in a world full of death and hate, that if there was a higher being, why wouldn't they intervene to make the world a better place? But now she understood: they were selfish, arrogant, and evil, just like people. They caused wars that could kill millions, all for their own gains, no longer caring about the lives of others.

Closing her eyes, Cassie arrived back in her inner room, her dark side still locked in the cage. But this time it wasn't shivering. It wasn't wet.

I like what you've done to the place, it snarled, rolling its eyes.

Cassie found golden flowers stemming from around the cage, decorating it. She reached out to feel one, its molten touch almost . . . calming.

I chose Hero.

Interesting.

Cassie opened her eyes.

A familiar face popped into her vision, her black ringlets bouncing as her head crooked to the side.

"Quinn?"

"I can hear your brain overthinking from Artemis's room. I came to kindly ask you to tell it to shut up."

"If I could tell it to shut up, don't you think I would have already?" she groaned, turning over in her bed.

Her body lifted with a grunt as Quinn flung herself over top of her and laid right in front of her face. "Well, I have the perfect remedy for a troubled mind like yours," Quinn replied. She became golden in the sunlight, her green eyes shining bright, her curls highlighted in the gleams, as if diamonds ran through her hair.

Cassie sat up excitedly like a little kid on Christmas morning. "Movie night?" she asked, trying to contain a squeal. They'd always order a large pizza, with extra mushrooms, and two milkshakes. She got chocolate, and Quinn always got strawberry.

Quinn dug into her bag, pulling out several bars of chocolate, and of course, a bottle of wine. "Movie night," she affirmed, looking proud of herself. "We both need a night away from all that crap, so no Zodiacs allowed. Just you and me, girl." She shifted on the bed, getting comfy. "I already told Hero to leave us alone, or at least to try for one night. I know it's going to be hard on him, and he's probably sitting outside your door right now, moping around," Quinn joked, reaching for the remote.

"I'm not sure about that," Cassie sighed, her head leaning backward as she stared at the ceiling.

"What's going on between you two?"

"I don't know," Cassie said. "I thought all he wanted was to be friends, but at the ball he told me he wanted more."

Quinn's eyes widened, her mouth gaping. "Tell me everything!"

"The nymphs made me choose yesterday, between him and Rane," Cassie revealed, playing with the side of her duvet. "And I chose Hero."

Quinn raised her eyebrows. "And how do you feel about that?"

A smile crept onto Cassie's face. "We have this . . . connection . . . one I can't ignore. And my heart goes to him. I just. . ." Her smile dropped as her fear set in. "I'm afraid he's going to change his mind again. Or that he's just doing this because he's jealous of Rane."

"See, this is why I date girls," Quinn stated while scrolling through the channels on the television. "Men are too much drama."

"Speaking of," Cassie asked, changing the subject, "what's going on with you and Artemis?"

"Nothing." She frowned. "I don't even know if she likes me the same way, and it's not as if she could date me if she wanted to. Apparently, you guys have a law against dating *my kind*," Quinn mumbled. She grabbed the white wine, flicked the cap off, and muttered "Cheers" before taking a sip right out of the bottle.

"It's a stupid law. Especially when it comes to you," Cassie said, looking at Quinn meaningfully.

Quinn huffed and threw the remote at her.

Cassie clicked through the options on the screen, deciding for them. *Romeo and Juliet* seemed fitting for their current situations, and she found nothing wrong with staring at DiCaprio for a couple of hours. Quinn rolled her eyes at her, but she pressed play anyway.

Two knocks came on the door as the movie began. "I got it," Quinn groaned, voice filled with annoyance. She walked over and opened the door. "Huh," she muttered, sticking her head further out into the hall, looking both ways.

"Who is it?" Cassie questioned.

"Aaaah!" she screamed, making Cassie jump. Quinn bent down, picking something up, and as she turned around, Cassie could see a pizza box and two milkshakes in her hands. "Did you order this?" Quinn questioned, walking back to the bed.

"No, I didn't. How—" Cassie paused as Quinn took a bite of the pizza, mozzarella hanging from her mouth like spiderwebs. "I told Hero on my first day here. I didn't even think he was listening to me ramble." She gazed at her hands, picking at the loose bit of skin by her nail, but she still couldn't help the smile drifting onto her face.

"Told you," Quinn muffled out in between chews. "Wonder boy—well, *man*—is in love."

The kitchen seemed even darker than the halls as she and Quinn entered it, on a mission to find more alcohol for their movie night.

Cassie's eyes adjusted to the darkness, enough to make out a bar cart near the back. "Bingo," she muttered, pointing to it.

Quinn gasped as she rushed toward it, examining each bottle on the shelf. She handed a bottle of red wine to Cassie and started to grab another bottle of liquor herself when a stream of light flashed inside, strobing around the room.

Cassie shot down, her knees cracking as they bent, dragging Quinn with her by the arm. An older Zodiac walked in, the chef she'd seen on her first day here, looking around for them.

A giggle popped out of Quinn's mouth as she flung her hand over it.

"Hey!" the chef yelled, spotting their location.

Cassie took Quinn's hand, pulling her along while gripping the bottle in the other. They sprinted toward the exit, narrowly avoiding the chef running after them.

"Stop!" he yelled.

"This way," a voice hissed from the darkness, followed by a flicker of light—a flame. Elijah and Nyssa stared at them, clearly amused, their eyes finding the bottle with ease. Elijah sniggered before turning around and taking off. "Come on, follow us!" he shouted back at them.

With no other choice, they followed them up a staircase Cassie had never noticed before, the chef fading into the distance.

"Only a few special people know about this place," Nyssa said. "We made it while we were studying in the academy." She opened a glass door at the top, the cool fresh air of the night rushing against Cassie's body.

Cassie looked around at the sight in front of her. The rooftop was covered in overgrown plants and flowers. She could also see the outline of couches and seats decorating the middle. Elijah flicked his fingers, and rows of candles lit in an instant.

A secret hiding place.

Quinn hiccupped behind her.

Elijah snatched the bottle from Cassie's hand. "Nice. Good find." He threw his body onto the couch, his head on the armrest as his lanky legs sprawled out. Nyssa cleared her throat, looking at him with eyebrows raised. He lifted his legs so she could sit next to him, then plonked his limbs back onto her lap. "I can't believe you stole this and ran from Acastus. He's so going to spit in your dinner now."

The cork popped.

Nyssa took a swig of the wine. "Ignore his empty threats. What were the river nymphs like? I've never seen one outside of a nightclub or some sort of celebration before."

Cassie's eyes widened as she and Quinn each took a seat on one of the cushioned chairs. "Those things party?" She couldn't imagine the delicate yet scary nymphs dancing the night away. That would require them to let loose.

Nyssa hummed in affirmation. "They're notorious for it. Echo's club—the one we found you in on your birthday—is owned by them. As are several others around the world. You just saw one side of them."

Echo's club. Had she passed a nymph that night?

"They're divinities, warriors, and alcoholics all in one." Elijah grinned wide. "They make for great company when they're not in their world."

Nyssa toyed with the ends of her short black hair. "So? What were they like?"

"They were different, I guess, than what I imagined. They looked normal, except for the pointy ears and clothes made from leaves."

"Well, we have the location of the Elixir now. That's what matters, right?" Quinn asked, shooting a smile at Cassie.

"Yeah. It's definitely a start." Cassie glanced at the clear night sky and watched the stars glisten. One fell from the sky, shooting across the darkness.

Elijah stood from his seat, running toward the ledge of the roof. "Quick!" he shouted. "Make a wish!"

"You guys believe in that kind of stuff?" Quinn asked, eyes wide.

Nyssa smiled. "Gotta believe in something."

"I wish I could live forever!" Elijah shouted from the terrace, floating his arms forward as if he were Rose and the wind was his Jack. He raced back to Nyssa, kissing her with about as much passion as anyone could ever dream about. She giggled into his mouth, her laugh as sweet as rain.

It made Cassie's heart ache. She loved the fact that they had found something so pure, but she wanted it for herself too. *With Hero.* Cassie wanted the love she found in the books and in the movies. It was clear to her now that that kind of love existed. She could see it right in front of her, with her friends. Cassie didn't want a love filled with sun and stillness; she wanted one that would withstand the worst weather. A love that could be tested in the most extreme ways, yet still persevere.

A knock sounded at the glass door. "I thought you guys might be up here. Nyssa," Rane's soft voice said, "I have Hana on the phone. She wants to speak to you. She said it's something important about your mom." Rane's eyes found Cassie's, and guilt threatened to consume her again. He looked away in a moment's passing, and back toward his cousin.

"That's my sister," Nyssa explained, standing. "I'll be right back."

Elijah caught her hand, his face serious. "Be safe," he said.

Nyssa furrowed her brows at him before she walked out the door, Rane closing it behind them.

"I didn't know she had a sister," Cassie said, trying to ignore the unease building in her stomach. She hoped her friendship with Rane hadn't been destroyed by her actions.

"Yeah, they don't talk much. Well, she hasn't talked much to any of her family since they moved her here." Elijah shrugged, taking another sip of wine.

Cassie leaned her head to the side. "They moved her here? Without them?"

Eli made an expression that seemed to say, *I know, right?* He sighed. "She doesn't like to talk about it much, but it's about the pain she has with her powers. I don't think her family knew how to handle it."

"That's still not right," Quinn huffed, "just casting someone away like that."

Another knock sounded at the door, and Quinn threw her head back against the wicker chair. "Ugh," she groaned. "Can't we be left alone to drink and talk about our feelings?"

Hero cleared his throat, making Quinn whip around to face him. She threw her arms out in joy. "Hero!" she yelled, jumping up to go hug him while slurring her words. "I thought you were the party police. Come join us!"

Cassie watched as Hero smiled, though it didn't reach his eyes.

Her stomach dropped.

"Something happened," he said. "Poseidon knows our plan."

CHAPTER 34

ZEMBLANITY

(N.) THE INEVITABLE DISCOVERY OF WHAT WE WOULD
RATHER NOT KNOW; THE OPPOSITE OF SERENDIPITY

Cassie tapped her fingers on her arm as she leaned against a wall in the mission room, awaiting Diana's arrival. Her entire team had been summoned, with only Nyssa and Rane missing, presumably still speaking with her sister.

Cassie's heart raced with every second.

How did Poseidon find out already? What did he do? Is anyone dead?

She held her breath as Diana entered the room, dressed in a black pantsuit, her hair pushed back off her tanned face into a high bun. Several guards followed behind her.

Diana cleared her throat, pausing for a moment, and Cassie knew whatever news she bore would cut deep. "Poseidon was here on land," she said, the usual ice blatant in her voice. "He attacked a restaurant full of people this morning. Their bodies were found mere hours ago."

272

Cassie's face slackened, her shoulders following suit. A knot formed in her throat, her knees threatening to buckle. *No, no, no, no, no . . .*

"Oh my gods," Elijah muttered, eyes wide and blinking.

Hero peered at Cassie, worry flashing on his face before he spoke. "Only our team, the Archon, and a few trusted members of the council knew about our plan to steal the Elixir. We have a mole."

Someone betrayed us again—someone I know. Her body numbed at the thought.

"We'll set up rigorous questioning and tests to see who leaked this information," Diana said. "Luckily for our alliance with the nymphs, their involvement was left out of all reports. They remain untouched by Poseidon."

"At least whoever played us had some sense of morals," Artemis snarked, her fingers curling around the knife she always had on hand.

Cassie's throat tightened. More must've happened for them all to gather this late at night. She glanced at the faces in the room, unable to believe anyone here could have betrayed her—betrayed them all.

Diana's eyes met hers. "The mission you were planning to get the Elixir can no longer happen. It is too risky with Poseidon knowing, and I cannot in good conscience allow it."

Cassie's mouth gaped as her stomach fell. All she wanted to do was curl up in a ball and wish this were some cruel joke. All they had worked for was for nothing. They didn't even know where the Cup was, and without the Elixir, she knew she couldn't rid herself of her dark side. It was lost to the wind, to the waves, and to the fires below. Her fists curled. What had happened at the restaurant was beyond sickening, but it wouldn't stop there. This was just the beginning of Poseidon's plans for the mortals—for all of them—and now she had no idea how to help, how to prevent it.

The cage rattled in her mind, her dark side begging to be released, to *feel* this for her, so she did not have to. And a part of Cassie wanted to let it.

"One other thing . . ." Diana paused, glancing at her. Cassie steeled herself, not knowing how much more she could take. "The diner they attacked—it was in your hometown," Diana said, sadness apparent in her expression as Cassie's heart stopped in her chest.

My dad. No . . . Please don't be dead . . . Please. Tears welled up in her eyes as she took a step back.

Diana's hand flicked up, and a blue holographic screen appeared in front of them. "It's called Jessie's; do you recognize it?" A picture of the diner appeared on the screen, a sight Cassie knew all too well. At each word Diana spoke, a part of Cassie drifted, farther into a darkness she did not wish to turn to light.

"Me and my dad used to go there every weekend; we live right around the corner," she breathed out. "Is . . . is he . . .?" *Please,* she prayed to whoever listened—to the stars, to Apollo, to the elements. *Please let him be okay.*

Hero shook his head, catching Cassie's attention as he spoke. "Your dad wasn't one of the deceased," he said, and tears drifted down her cheeks in relief. "But what it does mean is that this message was directed at you," Hero continued. "We might be able to see what Poseidon's next move is, if any. Nys, are you able to—wait, where's Nyssa?" Hero asked, glancing around the room.

"Rane wanted to talk to her and Hana," Elijah said, cocking his head to the side. "Something about her mom."

Hero's face fell. "Eli, go find her," he ordered.

Elijah's eyes widened. "You don't think . . ." But before he could finish, he sprinted out of the room.

Hero rubbed the back of his neck, his body becoming restless.

"What's going on?" Cassie asked, pulling him to the side. Her cheeks were warm from her tears, but an anger sizzled deep inside of her. And whatever troubled Hero, she knew it had to be serious, something else he was keeping from telling her about. Something *more.*

She had to find out who had betrayed them. And Hero seemed to know. If he was hiding something from her, especially about this . . . Her hands clenched into fists.

Hero shuffled on his feet, frowning. "What do you mean?"

Cassie stared him down. "You've been acting off since the party. Something happened that night, with you and Titus. He poisoned us and tried to kill me, yet you seem oddly fine about it." She paused for a moment. Things were wrong, different. But Cassie realized the look in his eyes, the lies dancing between them. And she knew. "If it even *was* him."

Hero glanced at her. The answer was clearer to her than ever. Titus hadn't poisoned her. He didn't try to kill her. But then, who did? And why was Hero covering it up?

The door slammed open, and Elijah ran through with Nyssa's limp body in his arms, her arms and legs flowing from his hands. "Someone get the doctor! I found her unconscious in her room. I don't know what happened." He placed her body on a metal table as Artemis shoved the remaining items off in one swift movement.

Cassie's stomach dropped at the sight, her eyes going to Hero—but she couldn't find him. "Where did Hero go?" Cassie asked, but no one else seemed to notice that he'd disappeared.

She glanced back at her friend lying on the table, her heart begging the universe for her to be okay.

Nyssa's body stirred in small movements on the table, Elijah offering her terms of endearment to try and wake her. "Come on, darling. Please."

Her eyes blinked open slowly, and she gripped Elijah's hand. "Eli," she mumbled, her head turning from side to side. "Something's wrong."

"What happened? Are you okay?" he rushed out, searching her face and patting her hair down.

"My visions. They're gone. My mind is just dark," she sobbed, her voice trembling with each word. Tears streamed off the side of her face, and Cassie couldn't bring herself to look any longer, or she would join in her cries.

Fear struck inside of her. Someone was strong enough to take Nyssa's powers away. Someone close to them had done this, and if they did it to Nyssa, who was next? What more would they do?

And yet, another side of her found a weird sense of relief knowing this could happen. Maybe they didn't need the Elixir; maybe whoever did this could take her own powers away.

The doctor rushed in, followed by several nurses, and began to examine Nyssa. Silence, interrupted with a few murmurs, filled the room as they waited to see what had happened to her, and if there was any way to help her.

The doctor turned around, her voice somber. "Her healing seems intact," she said, pricking Nyssa's finger with a needle. The blood dripping sucked back inside of her in moments, the skin repairing itself. "This isn't the first Virgo we've seen tonight. Every single one of them seems to have had this happen. Something is blocking the rest of their powers. I can't sense it, not fully. As though it's muted."

Cassie breathed out. Why would someone drain the Virgos' powers? Unless they didn't want anyone seeing what was coming their way . . .

"Is she going to be okay?" Elijah asked, his face pale. He leaned toward Nyssa, guiding some hair off her wet cheeks. She tried to smile at him before her head lolled, and she passed into slumber once more.

The doctor nodded. "She needs to rest. We'll take her to the infirmary with the others to run more tests, then we can help her to her room. I'm sorry."

More nurses appeared with a gurney, carrying Nyssa's body from one surface to the other, and in moments they left.

Elijah ground his teeth, slamming his hands on a nearby desk, and Cassie flinched at the sudden noise. "I'm going to murder somebody," he said through gritted teeth.

But as Elijah looked up at the monitors, his eyes widened. "We need to get to the prison. Now."

CHAPTER 35

COZEN

(V.) TO TRICK OR DECEIVE

Hero crept around the entrance of the dungeon, his back against the wall as he peeked over, locating his target. It had gone too far—first with the party and Cassie, then Poseidon, and now Nyssa. His fists clenched, and all he wanted was for him to pay.

Rane strutted down the darkened stone hallway toward the cells, the lights on the walls enhancing his face, beaming with the pretense that he'd gotten away with it.

Titus was the perfect victim; he'd give Rane that. Titus had a motive: to protect his friends, and to protect his family from another loss after his sister, Serena, went missing. And it helped that Titus didn't care for Cassie. But the one thing Rane-hadn't bet on was Hero knowing his best friend better than anyone. While he could be an asshole at times, he knew he would never harm Cassie.

Hero had suspected it the minute Rane had accused his friend of poisoning the whole Arena. He and Elijah had tracked Rane, keeping a close eye on him to

278

monitor him and confirm their suspicions. Nyssa was an unexpected turn. Hero hadn't anticipated that he'd do anything to hurt his own cousin. But he also hadn't suspected Rane of working with Poseidon—a beyond stupid assumption on his part.

But when Hero saw Rane on the security feed moving toward the guardroom, he knew he had to end it. He didn't know what Rane had planned next with Titus. All he knew was that he wouldn't let him get away with it. And if it weren't for the laws, Rane would pay for it with his life. But Hero could settle for years spent in the dungeon. *Decades.*

Rane dug his hand into his pocket, reaching for the keys to the cells. Before he could pull them out, Hero launched at him, throwing his body against the stone wall, ignoring how both it and Rane's bones cracked.

Hero pressed his arm against Rane's neck, cutting off his air.

"Stamos," Rane croaked. "What are you doing here?"

"Bad move, making one of my best friends out to be the bad guy," Hero spat, applying even more pressure to his neck.

Rane tried to shove Hero off him with all his might, his jaw clenching. "You figured it out?"

Hero shook his head, huffing. "I've known since the moment you set foot in *my* Arena. Those mortals died because of you." Hero let him go only to take a swing at him, his fist landing right in his face.

Rane blinked rapidly, his face scrunching from the blow. "I didn't know Poseidon would take it that far," Rane muttered, his voice strained as regret flashed in his eyes. "But that was out of my control. I'm not the villain of this story."

Hero's nostrils flared as his chest heaved, the anger rising in his body, consuming him. Everything bad that had happened was because of Rane. Cassie almost dying. Nyssa's powers being taken away. Them being drugged. Titus being locked in the dungeon. Pain drove each punch he threw at Rane—the pain of his friends, his family . . . his . . . Cassie.

Hero hit him again . . . and again . . . and again. But it didn't seem to be enough. He grabbed at Rane's shirt, holding him upright against the wall. "Why did you do it? Why string Cassie along? Why hurt Nyssa?"

"How could you so blatantly forget the past, Stamos?" Rane spat blood, which dripped down Hero's face. "The Gemini is dangerous, no matter what hope you have for her."

"She's different!" Hero yelled, pushing him so hard that he could hear his collarbones crack beneath his hands. Rane yelped in pain.

"Cassie . . . She's strong and brilliant . . . but she has to go," Rane sputtered in between coughs. "I didn't *want* to kill her. I don't want to kill anybody! I tried to take her powers, like I did Nyssa's, the night I poisoned everyone, but it didn't work. I had no other choice but to try and get her to finish the job herself—but of course, you came to the rescue." He grimaced. "Poseidon and Zeus want her gone, Stamos."

But Hero had no remorse, even if Rane carried guilt. "What about the war? You've fucked us all over."

"I just want what was promised to me by the Immortals. I want my freedom," Rane muttered. "Poseidon said if they win the war, we get to be free. No more risking and devoting our lives to protecting others—protecting mortals who caused an uprising when they last knew about our existence."

Hero pulled him closer by his blood-stained shirt, his jaw clenching. "I've had enough of your bullshit, Nakamura. The Immortals are lying to you," he grunted, enraged. He held Rane's head and kneed him, smashing his face. Hero flung him back to the ground, admiring his work from above.

Blood dripped from Rane's mouth as he wiped his broken nose. Hero knew it would heal, but he still prayed to the gods that it hurt like a bitch. He'd held back his strength enough so that he wouldn't kill him, but enough to cause severe damage. Rane deserved nothing less.

Wincing in pain, Rane tried to push himself off the ground, his left hand holding his side. "You're going to lose the war. You're going to lose them all."

The doors at the entrance flung open as Elijah raced through with the rest of his team, Diana, and some guards, their faces awash in confusion and shock.

"What's going on here?" Diana demanded.

"Why don't you tell them, Rane," Hero spat, grabbing his body from the ground so he could stand. "He's behind it all—the hallucinations, Poseidon, Nyssa."

"R-Rane? You're the one who told Poseidon? Why?" Cassie asked, her voice just a whisper. Torture, betrayal, and sadness all flashed in her eyes, swirling in a storm. Rane had used her, tricked her, and Hero wanted to say screw the laws and kill him right then and there.

"Why?!" Rane snapped at Cassie, his face covered in blood. "Because you shouldn't have even been born! I'm protecting my people and doing what this Arena has failed to do. And I'm not the only one who thinks that way," he warned as an army of guards seized him. "Your fate is sealed, Cassie. I'm sorry."

Her face morphed into anger, her teeth clenching. "Why get close to me if you hate me so much?"

"He did it so he could take your powers away, like Nyssa. But it didn't work," Hero said, his eyes never leaving Rane.

"In my defense," Rane said, coughing as he grasped his abdomen, "you're the one who asked me to come along to the nymphs with you. You led me to hear the plan, and that's when I realized, I didn't need to get my hands dirty; I just had to ruin any chance of you getting that Elixir. And finally, I succeeded." He paused, and Hero wanted to bash his face in all over again. "It's just ironic that you knew it was me all along, and still . . ."

Cassie froze before turning around to face Hero. "You knew?"

Hero hung his head, sighing. "Once Rane started to point fingers at Titus after the party, Elijah and I knew something was wrong. So, we played along, waiting for him to make his next move so we could finally catch him. We had to trick you all into believing Titus poisoned us, until Eli and I could get a confession out of Rane." Hero just wished that no one had gotten hurt in the process. He would always blame himself for the deaths of those mortals. He'd only brought Rane with them to see the nymphs so he could keep an eye on him, expose him for working on the other side, but instead . . . instead it had brought about a nightmare.

"So, *Rane's* the one who drugged us?" Lukas said, peering over from behind Artemis's shoulder.

"Nyssa's sister, Hana, was more than happy to help me lace the champagne."

Hero watched Cassie's face whitened, and Lukas's eyes widened at Rane's reveal. "Titus—I have to go see him," Lukasgasped. Hero threw him the keys to the cells, and Lukas took off, disappearing through the doors.

Hero only hoped everyone could forgive him. But right now, he had to make sure Rane never saw daylight again.

Elijah trudged toward Rane, grabbed a handful of his shirt, and pulled him close. "Whatever you did to Nyssa's powers, you better reverse it, asshole."

Rane held his hands up and shook his head. "I can't let her see what I'm doing. Tell her I'm sorry, but she was collateral damage. Now, let's go," Rane said, and Hero watched in confusion as the guards holding him released their grip and pointed their weapons at Hero and his team instead. Two more guards appeared from out of the shadows.

Capricorns.

Elijah backed away as Hero's stomach dropped.

One of the guards moved his hand in a circle, creating an emerald portal out of thin air. It whirled beside them, waiting for their escape.

Hero began to sprint toward them, but Diana put her hand out, stopping him. "Let them go," his mother whispered. "They've made it clear which side they're on. They're in clear discord with the Oracle's laws, and their punishment will come; I'll be sure of it." Diana turned to Rane, tilting her chin high. "You have nowhere to hide," she warned, her look as deadly as her words.

Rane dipped his head, a subtle nod for his group to exit through the portal. "There's a war coming, and I'm choosing the winning side," he said, his foot halfway through the swirling jade. "Oh," he added, taking one last look at them, "there's one more gift I left you. But don't worry, you'll find it soon enough." Rane winked, walking through the portal as it sparked to a close behind him.

Rage built inside of Hero as he turned to face his mother. "Why did you let him go? We had him!" he yelled. *Everything I did . . . all the deceit, all the deaths . . . It was for nothing.*

"Patience," she said, patting her hand against his chest. "There are more things in motion than you can see right now in your anger. We will get our revenge—the right way."

Diana turned to face the rest of his team, their faces reflecting the anger he felt. "We should all get some rest. Rane will get what's coming to him. I promise you, the sun does not shine in the deepest parts of the Underworld." Diana clapped her hands, dismissing them.

"Nyssa's room. Now," Artemis ordered them.

They all walked back toward their quarters without a single word, until the door to Nyssa's room closed behind them. As the nurses had promised, Nyssa was lying there, her eyes wide as she took them in.

Elijah rushed to her bed, running his hand over her hair. She smiled back at him. "I'm so, so sorry," he choked. "Rane did this. And it's all my fault. We should have said something before."

Nyssa's brows furrowed as she shook her head. "Rane? No. He couldn't have .. .Wait—you're serious?" They all nodded. Then her eyes narrowed, and she turned more fully to Elijah. Even though it wasn't directed at him, Hero felt her glare deep in his soul. "You mean to tell me that you guys suspected my cousin the entire time—and didn't say *anything*?"

"I'm so sorry, Nys," Elijah said, his eyes fixated on the floor. Eli then filled her in on everything Rane had done, and what had happened in the prison just now.

Nyssa huffed. "'Sorry' doesn't fix this! And now we can't even see what he'll do next or where he could be!"

Hero took a deep breath. They had royally messed up this time, and he didn't know how they could recover. "We weren't one hundred percent sure it was him at first," he said, attempting to take some of the weight off Elijah's shoulders. "And we certainly didn't think he would be working for Poseidon."

Cassie. She had barely said a word throughout all of this. He looked over at the silver-haired beauty standing there, hugging herself as the tears fell, and his heart ached for more reasons than one. "I'm so sorry, Cassie," he said, moving toward her slowly. "I had no idea how far he would take this. Please believe me, I would've never let him do anything to you. Or you, Nyssa," he said, turning to his friend.

The remorse was almost too much to bear. The only thing keeping him upright was the knowledge that everyone he loved was alive, and as safe as they could be, even if hurt or injured.

If Cassie wouldn't be the ruin of him, he himself certainly would be.

"But it still happened," Artemis said through gritted teeth.

The door creaked open as Titus poked his head in. Relief flooded through Hero as he saw his best friend enter, his name cleared. Lukas followed in silence behind him. "Well, did the plan work?" Titus asked, looking around the room at all the upset and angry faces.

Artemis spoke first. "We're so sorry for not believing you, Titus. When Hero said you confessed to poisoning us to get to Cassie, we didn't know what to think." She shot daggers at Hero with her eyes.

"It's okay." Titus shrugged. "It's my fault for being such a great target. And it means our plan went better than expected."

Nyssa blew out a breath, all eyes going to her. "My thoughts just caught up with me. How did Rane even take away my powers? I didn't think that was possible."

Hero ran his hand through his hair and sighed. "I have no idea, but he said he tried it on Cassie too, and it didn't work."

"He crafted everything perfectly," Lukas said, his voice cracking. "He probably even tried to direct a Seeker to the Arena to possess Quinn, hence Nyssa's vision."

"Luckily, he failed," Artemis sneered.

"He still got away," Elijah said. He leaned down, muttering something into Nyssa's ear before he pulled away, his eyes wide and apologetic. Nyssa placed her hand in his, rubbing her thumb on his palm.

"I'll make sure he'll pay for all of it, no matter what," Hero said, his voice cracking. "I should have known better."

Artemis lifted a brow. "It was stupid, yes. But what Rane did, his actions—they're not your fault, Hero."

Titus and Elijah came up beside him, placing a hand on each shoulder. "We were all a part of this plan," Titus said. "If you're to blame, then we're all to blame. But seriously," he said, addressing the group, "Poseidon would have retaliated no matter what."

The weight on Hero's heart lessened at Titus's words, but he knew his guilt wouldn't go away any time soon. He'd get his retribution. He had to.

"At least he was exposed for what truly he is," Nyssa said, turning to face Hero and Titus, pointing between the three friends. "But next time you guys decide to play spy, involve us. Or just let us handle it."

Artemis snorted. "Yep. We would have done it so much better than you three idiots."

A chuckle sounded from where Cassie stood.

Hero shot his attention toward her—and everything else around him faded. Not one wisp of silver hair remained on her head, a darkness swirling around her instead.

Cassie's dark side crossed her arms as she smirked at them. "Hello," she said wickedly, her purple eyes shining in amusement. "It's nice to finally meet you all."

CHAPTER 36

VERKLEMPT

(ADJ.) COMPLETELY OVERCOME WITH EMOTION

Hero's heart tightened as he stared at what used to be Cassie, all the light once inside her was suddenly *gone*. His first reaction was to reach for his weapon, but then he caught himself. It was still *Cassie,* he reminded himself. It was still the girl whose dimple showed when her happiness was true, the girl whose temper and mood could change in a second, the girl who had shone a bright light into his life the moment she walked into it. He had to find a way to get to her, and remind her of it.

"I've been stuck in Cassie's mind forever," Cassie's dark side groaned as she stretched. "It feels good to finally be in control."

Hero sneered. He glanced at Titus, who crossed his arms, his body stiffening. They nodded as though they could read each other's thoughts; some days, it honestly felt as though they could.

"We want our friend back," Titus jeered.

"Oh, you two are friends now?" she gasped, feigning surprise. "That's sweet. Come on, guys, I just want to talk." She took a seat on Nyssa's purple lounge chair, crossing her legs. "I mean, I'm so much more fun than her. Wouldn't you rather have me on your team against Poseidon?"

"We'd rather fail than ever have you," Nyssa said, stepping out of her bed.

Her expression darkened. "Wrong answer." She pushed herself from the chair and strutted toward Nyssa.

"Don't you dare take one more step," Elijah all but growled, throwing himself in front of Nyssa, flames roaring up his arms.

She sighed, pausing on her warpath. "I did your girl Cassie a favor. She couldn't handle the deaths of those mortals at the diner. She recognized the pictures of the victims. And then the whole thing with Rane—whoops! After his fun little betrayal, all her hopes of getting rid of me . . ." She smiled wickedly, making Hero's fists tighten. "Gone."

"Cass," Hero said, his eyes flicking to hers. "I know you're in there, and if you can hear me, our hope isn't lost. Remember your mental training. Lock her in the cage and throw away the—"

"Don't!" She hissed, her eyes narrowing as she started after him.

"Hey, evil twin?" Artemis flipped her dagger in her hand. "Over here." She grinned, planting her feet, ready for a fight.

Cassie's dark side looked over her shoulder, falling for his sister's antics. She pulled out the dual daggers from her thigh harness, flicking them in the air before catching them.

From the corner of his eye, Hero saw a flash of green appear as Elijah guided Nyssa through a portal—escaping. It was for the best. Nyssa was still too weak from Rane's attack to fight, and because of that, Elijah would be too distracted.

His attention was drawn back to Artemis and Cassie circling each other like lions in a cage. Hero knew his sister would always have the upper hand in a fight, but if something happened to Cassie . . .

Cassie lunged at her as Artemis blocked the attacks, their blades clashing together in unison. She fought rough, every bit different from how *he* had taught her to fight. But Artemis was ruthless, and no matter what Cassie threw her way, she took it, learned from it, and fought back harder. Artemis flung her foot into Cassie's stomach, making her stumble back, allowing Artemis the millisecond she needed to take full control. She swept her leg across the floor, knocking Cassie to the ground, sending her daggers flying from her grip. Artemis kicked them out of her reach before grasping Cassie by the throat. She struggled for breath, her face turning blue, and Hero's heart nearly stopped.

"Don't hurt her!" Hero yelled, stretching toward them, ready to break up their fight no matter what it meant.

Artemis shot her head to the side, staring him down. "She'll heal." She scowled, her hand remaining clenched on Cassie's throat.

Cassie fought back as hard as she could, clawing and kicking at Artemis, but his sister dodged what she could and took the other blows with an unamused look on her face.

Then, something changed. Cassie pulled her hand back, gasping, holding it as if she didn't have control over it. Her eyes found his, the violet hues flashing with silver torment.

"Artemis, let go!" Hero demanded, knowing *his* Cassie was fighting her way out. *You can do this, Cass,* he prayed. *I believe in you.*

With a roll of her eyes, Artemis released her hold.

Cassie sputtered, moving to the side, toward one of her daggers.

Hero stepped closer, calling out to her, "Cass, it's me. It's Hero. You're stronger than this. Fight it." He held out a hand for her to grab, to pull herself out of the darkness with.

"She doesn't want to fight," Cassie spat at him.

"Yes, she does," Hero stated, his hand still out, waiting for her to come back to him. "I know her, and you're wrong. She's not weak. In fact, she's one of the strongest people I know. And it's only a matter of time until she defeats you."

"I'm not going back into that cage!" In one fast motion, she pushed herself up from the floor and lunged at Hero.

He grabbed her arm, flipping her around so her back slammed against him. Her body heaved, but he held on tight, refusing to let go. The memory of their first training session flashed into his mind, the way her touch had lit him on fire.

He spun her back around, watching how her face twisted with darkness—not one hint of the girl he knew. But as soon as her eyes met his, they snapped shut. He watched breathlessly as her face changed in delicate motions. The strands of onyx faded back into the glistening silver, her face transitioned back to rosy and pure, and her body fell into him. Cassie, *his* Cassie, blinked herself back to reality, her eyes widening with sheer panic, tears dripping down her cheeks.

"I'm so sorry," she wept, gripping his shirt.

"It's okay. You're okay. You came back." Hero wrapped his arms around her, and he swore he would never let go again. He wanted to make all the pain she would ever suffer disappear. Pride surged through his veins as he held her shaking body tightly, not letting go until she was ready.

Cassie watched the embers frolic in Hero's roaring fireplace, drawing the blanket closer to herself with shaking hands. She ignored the few sparks flying out onto the carpet before her, too numb to care. The past few days had been too much for her, and the darkness she had pushed back for so long waited patiently in its cage to take over again. Regaining control over herself was one of the hardest battles she'd ever fought. Calling it "overwhelming" merely scratched the surface.

She'd just begun to understand this world, to fit in with her team . . . her friends. But now, it seemed as though it could all fall apart at any moment. The Twin Cup was lost, and now all hope of getting the Elixir had disappeared too, along with all the deceit Rane had put her through.

But he was right: she was the Gemini, a ticking time bomb waiting to kill everyone in the Arena. She'd just proved it an hour ago. Tonight had been a close call, and she just was lucky that Artemis was the better fighter, but if Cassie had access to her shape-shifting powers . . . The premonition that her dark side had showed her all those weeks ago flashed in her mind again. The piles of bodies . . . If Cassie failed to keep it under control, her dark side would be unstoppable—a shape-shifting murderer, able to transform into anything. The perfect weapon.

Cassie had no idea what to do now. Poseidon knew their plan to get the Elixir. People had died. Her dark side had escaped. And whatever Rane had done to Nyssa, it didn't even work on Cassie.

All her options, all the ways she would have defeated the monster inside her: gone.

Hero drew the curtains, tearing her from the shadows wrapping around her soul.

"Rane was on Poseidon and Zeus' side long before anyone learned of your existence," Hero said finally, his voice soft. "None of this was your fault. It was the gods' and Rane's, and whoever else helped them. That's it."

He didn't get it. *He* wasn't the reason people would die; she was.

"I could hear her thoughts," Cassie muttered. "I could feel what she wanted to do. She wanted bloodshed and revenge, murder and pain. I can't be responsible for that."

Hero exhaled sharply. "We'll find a way. I'll fight tooth and nail for you to survive, for your dark side to never come out again, and I know everyone on the team will say the same."

"I can't have any more people die for me!" she argued back. "I mean, I tried to kill your *sister*!" Cassie wanted to hold it all together, but the world was crumbling around her. "I never wanted this," she sobbed. It was hopeless. How could they find the Elixir now? Without it, she was lost. *They* were lost.

"That wasn't you." He walked closer to her, crowding her vision with his body, and with it, she felt a small bit of ease for the first time that night. "Even when I got scared and pushed you away, I never once stopped thinking about how fierce and capable you are, how utterly amazing you are. If anyone can find a way to get through this, it's you." He paused. "It's us. Together."

His words lightened her. Tears dropped down her face, and her head fell into her hands. "But how? What *can* we do?"

"Hey," Hero comforted her, "we'll figure it out." He enveloped her in a hug, and she melted into his body, fitting perfectly, a missing puzzle piece.

After a moment, she pulled back as he did, slowly, as though time had stopped just for them. His arms were still wrapped around her, and the heat of his touch burned with passion, devotion, and all her dreams combined. Their foreheads touched, and Cassie's heart quickened. She wanted him so badly. . . She wouldn't let her doubt get in her way any longer.

Hero's lips parted slightly, as though he, too, were opening to her. She tilted her head, closing the gap between them.

The kiss was soft at first, as though they were both afraid the moment could shatter in seconds. Then she felt Hero's hand move to her neck, pulling her in deeper, and heat flared to life inside her. She moaned softly into his mouth, and he seized the opportunity, his tongue sweeping across hers. Her hands trailed across his chest to his shoulders, feeling the muscles play beneath her fingers. The realization that she finally had what she yearned for warmed her entire soul with starlight.

Hero pulled away gently, his forehead still touching hers. "I want you to know, I'm all in. I want you, and I'm not going away." His lips reached hers again for one more soft kiss.

Cassie shut her eyes and breathed in the moment. Those words . . . He was all the proof she needed that light existed in the world, and no matter what darkness lurked inside her, he still wanted her.

"I'm all in, too, Hero," Cassie whispered, pushing Hero down gently and climbing on top of him. She tugged his shirt up as her mouth began to travel from his lips to his neck, then down his muscled torso.

Hero lifted her face up to meet his. "We don't have to do that now," he said, his eyes softening. "All we have is time."

Cassie pushed herself off of him, turning her back to him. *"All we have is time."* Rane had said that to her after he'd tried to kiss her—right before he also tried to seduce her and kill her. Her breathing quickened.

"Hey, hey, I'm sorry. I didn't mean to upset you," Hero said, placing a hand on her shoulder to try to get her to turn around. "I just didn't want to take advantage of you after a bad night."

She leaned into his touch, relishing the peace it gave her.

Hero isn't Rane. This isn't the same thing.

"No, it's not that. It's just something Rane said," Cassie mumbled.

"I'm so sorry about Rane." Hero sighed, taking her hand in his, warming it. "I hate him so much for everything he did to you. To all of us."

"Me too."

Rane's last words echoed in her ears next: *"There's one more gift I left you."* He could have just been trying to scare them, but Cassie had to be careful and keep an eye out for whatever else he could've done. What else could he have ruined for her? "I can't understand how someone could betray us like that. Betray his cousin, even—someone he's supposed to love. I just wish you would have told me. I don't want there to be any secrets between us."

Hero stilled at her words, his shoulders tensing. "Neither do I." He blew out a breath. "I have something to take care of real quick. Are you okay if I go? I promise I'll be back soon."

"Sure," Cassie said, but she wondered why he'd leave now. "Is everything okay?"

Hero planted a kiss on her lips, and one on the top of her head as he rose. "As long as I have you, everything is okay." He shot her one last loving smile before he left.

Cassie sat on Hero's bed, pulling her knees to her chest. Even though the past few days had overwhelmed her more than anything she'd ever experienced, and she felt so mentally and physically exhausted that all she wanted to do was sleep, she couldn't help the smile forming on her lips.

Her eyes drifted to the sketchbook on Hero's bedside table, open to a drawing of her—one of her dancing in the dress he had gifted her. The perfect dress from the perfectly imperfect man.

Hero. He was all in, and so was she. Her heart had never been so full.

The door opened.

"Oh, Cassie. Sorry, I thought Hero was in here."

Cassie turned around to see Titus standing there, half in the room. He seemed so young in the moment, his face hopeful, and his voice trembling ever so slightly. "Actually, since you're here, can I talk to you?"

She nodded, gesturing for him to enter the room fully.

He cleared his throat, tugging at the collar of his shirt. "I wanted to apologize. I'm sorry for making you feel unwelcome."

"Titus . . ." she tried to cut him off, but he put up his hands to stop her.

"There was a reason Rane blamed it on me, and why you all believed him. He saw how I treated you, and knew I'd be an easy target." He paused, biting the side of his lip. "I think I needed this, in all honesty, to see what a jerk I was being. I was trying to protect the ones I love, but by doing so, I was hurting them."

Cassie exhaled deeply as she took in his words. She hated being the reason Hero and Titus fought, and now that she'd taken the time to process that Rane had betrayed them, not Titus, a staggering weight was lifted from her. "Thank you for saying those things," she began. "But it was never your fault. Rane did all of this.

I'm just sorry none of us saw it—well, apart from Hero and Eli. Even if you guys' plan sucked." She chuckled, moving to sit on the edge of the bed as she played with the sleeves of Hero's sweater, which he'd given her after she'd turned back. It mimicked his hug wrapped around her.

"I genuinely thought everyone believed I was the one to poison you all, until Hero and Eli told me their plan afterward. But there's still tension there . . ." he mumbled, rubbing the back of his neck as he glanced down.

"We all fell under Rane's manipulations," Cassie said, knowing she might have fallen under them more than anyone, aside from Nyssa. "And you should go talk to the others about that tension. I know they miss your friendship."

"You may have a fifty-fifty chance of becoming an evil killing machine, but you do give pretty good advice," Titus joked, running a hand over his head.

Cassie laughed, a flutter of heat returning to her with each chuckle. "Go on. Go talk to Hero and Elijah. Sort your bromance stuff out." She shooed him out of the room.

The moment he closed the door behind him, her eyes dropped. It had been a grievous day, one in which she ached for a taste of her old normal life back—but that was a life she would never be able to go back to.

At least she had Hero by her side now. Not as a friend; no. They were all in.

She made one last note in her mind to see her dad . . . She had to find a way to see him. She didn't know if Hero would even agree with her going to see him—it would probably be too dangerous—but she'd do it anyway.

As soon as she lay back in his bed, wrapped in his covers, Cassie succumbed to the magnetic pull of her eyelids, heavy with sleep.

At some point in the night, she felt the mattress dip, and a warm body wrapped around her. The familiar smell of mint and pine filled her senses as she moved back against him. Hero kissed her cheek as he settled a hand on her hip.

In that moment, all Cassie felt was *calm*.

CHAPTER 37

NOCTURNUS

(ADJ.) BELONGING TO THE NIGHT

The glimmering moon shone above Hero through the domed ceiling. It was the only time he could be alone with his mind: the stark of midnight. He didn't even want to entertain the mere idea of losing Cassie. It seemed a too far away thought, yet all the while so incredibly real and possible that he felt as though he could drown.

Hero worked through the motions, each swing of his sword steadying his mind. He needed this after what'd happened with Cassie: to think.

He wanted her so immensely—but that damned prophecy. . . He had to find a way to stop it. He could never make her feel the way she had just then, how betrayed, how drained of the *want* of life she was. Above all, he didn't want to keep this from her.

But if Cassie ever found out about the prophecy, if she was to be the ruin of him—or worse, the death of him—what would it do to her? He didn't know how she would react. He might trigger her dark side, plunge her into a hole not even he could drag her out of.

He'd spent hours last night scouring the library for anything on how to break a prophecy. He couldn't think around her until he found some answers, but they all led to a dead end. His only reward had been curling up beside her when his eyes finally gave out on him.

But she couldn't know. Not yet. He had to protect her, keep her from this. At least until after he found a way to get rid of it.

I have to find a way. I have to.

"Need a sparring partner?" a voice sounded behind him, and his thoughts vanished like smoke.

Hero glanced over to where Titus stood, leaning against the entrance of the empty training room, and heaviness released from his shoulders. He wanted his brother back, his best friend back.

Hero lifted the sides of his mouth as much as he could manage. "Thought you'd never ask."

"Thought you'd never let me," Titus countered. His words were testing, to see if the strength of their relationship had lasted through the past weeks.

"I know we only had a few minutes to talk about our plan the other night, but I never once thought you would hurt her. Your typical broodiness and attitude are the furthest you'd go with her." He chuckled as he walked over to the row of swords mounted on the wall, throwing one to Titus.

"Well, if it puts your mind at ease," Titus replied, whipping the sword around in adjustment, "I had a chat with her last night. She's the one who told me to come talk to you."

Hero raised his eyebrows, blinking. "Really?"

"Yep. I've apologized for my attitude and all." He smiled. "In fact, you could say we're becoming friends."

"Thank you," Hero breathed out, "so much." He knew how much that gesture meant for Titus, and it felt like he was peering into the version of his friend he'd known before everything had happened.

Hero clasped his hand onto Titus's forearm as he did the same. "Now, I'm going to kick your ass."

Titus let out a deep chuckle and took a step back, readying his sword. "You're on, Stamos."

With each swing, it was as though they had an unspoken conversation, filled with apologies, laughter, anger, and brotherhood. Each clash was a joke, and each block was a promise.

"You guys having all the fun without me?" Elijah appeared in the doorway, grinning crookedly.

Titus stopped, his sword hanging by his leg. "Never." He smiled, but his expression quickly fell. "I'm sorry we couldn't save Nyssa's powers."

Elijah's jaw clenched, his face turning cold. "Rane played us all. But after what he did to Nyssa, if I ever see him again, I'm melting his face into the ground."

Hero patted Eli on the back, passing him a sword. "And we'll hold him down for you." He walked backward, putting space between himself and his brothers. Swinging his own sword around, he narrowed his eyes playfully at them, seeing who would bite first. His bet: Elijah.

"The only rule is," Titus said, cracking his neck, "no powers allowed. If I see one glimmer of gold from you, Stamos, I'll send a ball of water over you every time you get dressed."

Hero laughed, holding a hand over his abdomen. "I promise I'll keep my strength matched with you guys. And that means no fire, Eli."

Elijah jumped onto a table, waving the sword about manically. "Fine, but I don't know how to use this thing!" he shouted.

"One way to learn." Hero chuckled, bending his knees before he launched up on the table next to him. Titus joined seconds later.

Elijah whipped his head back and forth from where Hero stood in front of him, and Titus behind him. "My name is Elijah Drakos. You killed my lover. Prepare to die!" he jeered, jabbing the sword toward Titus.

"You butchered the line." Titus rolled his eyes, not even wavering at Elijah's attempts.

"I'll butcher *you*!" Elijah tilted his chin forward, his blond hair shifting out of his face as he grinned at Titus.

Hero wiped the sweat off his face, sitting on the ground next to Titus. He peered over at Elijah, sprawled out like a starfish across the floor, panting while laughing at himself.

"You talk to Lukas yet?" Hero asked Titus before taking a sip of water.

"No," he replied. "I don't know what to say to him."

"Maybe that you're sorry for leaving him?" Elijah piped up, lolling his head to the side to look at them. "But I'm sure he understands that you had to look for Serena." *His sister.*

"It's not that part that hurt him." Titus paused as if to relieve the agonizing memory. "I think it's that I never came back to him afterward. I cut him off."

"Just prove to him you're not going to leave again," Hero said, glancing at him.

Titus gave a small smile. "Speaking of, how is your obvious crush on Cassie going?"

Hero couldn't help the smirk crawling across his face. "We're together."

Elijah gasped, sitting up. "Um . . . Excuse me. When did this happen?"

"Last night." Hero grinned, but then his expression grew serious. "There's something else I should tell you guys, though. About a prophecy." He glanced at his friends, who stared back at him curiously. "But you have to promise not to tell Cassie, and not to judge her for it."

"We're all ears, man," Elijah assured him, nodding.

Titus clasped Hero's shoulder. "And we're not judging."

Hero took a deep breath. "There's a prophecy Apollo warned my mom about years ago. About a Gemini and a Leo fated to be together—pulled to each other through a divine connection." He paused for a moment, collecting himself. ". . . But the Gemini is also supposed to be the ruin of the Leo."

A stiff silence hung in the air. Titus finally said, "You've been keeping that a secret all this time?"

Hero's shoulders slumped. "I didn't want this to be anyone else's burden but mine. I only told Artemis because she caught me destroying my punching bag."

Titus shook his head. "Fuck, dude. I'm so sorry."

"The word 'ruin' is so vague, though," Elijah said, as though he could argue with the prophecy, with Apollo. "Could she kill you or something?"

"I don't know. I guess I'll find out." He shrugged, wishing the heaviness on his chest would release with the motion. "Which is why I need to find a way to stop it from happening, to cross it off whatever record of prophecies the Immortals keep. Cassie would be devastated if she ever found out, or if it ever happened."

"You think you can stop a prophecy from coming true?" Titus asked, pulling his mouth to the side.

"I don't know. My mind's a mess," Hero groaned, leaning back on his wrists. "After Rane came, I realized how much I didn't want to lose her, but I'm no better than him if I don't at least try and save her from this. And save me too."

Elijah placed his chin in his hand. "Hell, if Nyssa told me she'd be the ruin of me, I'd lie back and watch it happen with her by my side."

Hero glanced between Elijah and Titus. "But do you guys think there's hope? That I can really stop this, and I'm not just being ignorant?"

"I guess sometimes you gotta take the leap," Titus said, speaking to himself as well as Hero. "It's clear that you guys have a rare connection; we can all see it. And she fits right into our misfit team. I can't imagine her *not* being here now. If she makes you happy, then I'm happy for you."

"We'll just keep you guys on murder-suicide watch," Elijah joked, dodging Hero's slap.

Hero rolled his eyes, but a smile lurked on his face. "Funny. But thank you. I'm going to find a way. But if all else fails, all that matters is that I'm with her." And as much as it should have scared him, a wave of serenity washed over him, the tide finally pulling back the truth. His heart, his fallen star.

"We're with you every step of the way." Elijah beamed.

"Drinks at Psyche? Kalix might know a way to break the prophecy." Titus paused, looking Hero in the eye with a silent apology. "And it's been too long."

"Nowhere I'd rather be." Hero smiled broadly, throwing his arms around his brother's shoulders.

CHAPTER 38

RETROUVAILLE

**(N.) THE JOY OF MEETING OR FINDING SOMEONE AGAIN
AFTER A LONG SEPA- RATION; REDISCOVERY**

The wind whipped Cassie's long silver hair around her shoulders in the courtyard of the Arena as she waited for Lukas to arrive. She'd gone to him yesterday, behind Hero's back, and asked him to create a portal for her so she could check on her dad, to make sure he was all right, and to finally tell him what was going on.

Luckily, Lukas had agreed, with the condition that if she didn't return in an hour, he'd tell everyone where she'd gone.

Cassie squinted to try to make out the two figures walking toward her. If any of the Zodiacs asked why she was standing out here, she would just say that she needed some fresh air. Most of them didn't talk to her anyway—a perk and a disadvantage of being the one illegal Gemini allowed to exist.

A slim tattooed body came into view, his mocha hair ruffling in the wind. *Lukas.* Her heartbeat quickened when she spotted the taller person trudg-

301

ing behind him. The curly dark hair was all too familiar. *Hero.* Her chest tightened, and she wondered if he was mad at her for not telling him, or if he'd try to stop her.

Cassie swallowed, waiting for Hero to get near enough for her to state her case, to explain why she had to go. If Lukaswouldn't make the portal, she'd just find someone else to do it.

Hero gave her a weak smile, cocking his head to the side, waiting for an explanation.

Pushing her shoulders back, she said, "I need to see my dad." Her feelings for Hero aside, she had to do this, even if he didn't agree. "I have to make sure he's okay. Poseidon attacked the diner we went to almost every Sunday. What if he does it again?" Cassie had kept all this a secret from her dad for so long, but now her lies were catching up with her. She had to come clean.

"I know," Hero said, rocking back and forth on his heels. "Even if I don't entirely approve, I know no matter what I say, you're going to do it anyway. I'm just here to follow your lead."

Lukas thinned his lips. "I'm sorry for telling him, but I wanted you to be safe," he admitted, shoving his hands into the pockets of his skinny black jeans. "After what happened the other night."

When my dark side came out.

"I get it," Cassie said finally. "And thank you, both, for helping me." Her heart swelled at the fact that Hero had come to be with her, even though her stomach felt queasy from trying to keep it from him. "Lukas, can you still make us a portal for an hour?"

He nodded. "Of course. Just think about your home, and you'll be there."

A bead of sweat traveled down her forehead, one she hoped wasn't visible to anyone else. Cassie had only been through a portal once, when she went to see the nymphs, but Rane and Hero had taken the lead. This would be the first time she'd be in control of where they went.

Lukas held out his palm in front of him, his other hand acting as a guide next to it as he moved it around in a circle. What began as a spark of green floating in the air quickly grew into a wondrous emerald portal, acting as a gateway into physical space. Cassie blinked to adjust to the luminous glow as Hero stood next to her, holding her hand.

They stepped into the portal.

Think of home. Warm cinnamon, mom's flowers, the creaking of the porch . . . Dad.

Cassie and Hero landed on the front lawn of her childhood home as the portal behind them swirled shut. She didn't know if she would ever get used to her mind and body warping when traveling through a portal, but the familiar tepid summer breeze and the sound of birds chirping in the distance made it hard to care.

Not a single car passed by, and the sound of swords clanking together felt like a distant memory. Only bliss awaited her here. The scent of freshly cut grass and the crisp farmland air of Napa Valley infiltrated her senses.

No cloud could be spotted in the sky as Cassie held her arm in front of her face to shield herself from the sun. Her eyes finally settled on the house she'd grown up in, the house in which she held some of her fondest memories. She would sit for hours on their porch swing, writing hundreds of stories in her little pink diary as her dad mowed the lawn, joining her on occasion to listen to her latest adventure. They called their house the White House, thanks to its paint job. It also made Cassie feel important, as though something about this house was special. And it was. It was *home*.

She glanced at Hero, who was silently waiting for her. She took a deep breath, dipping her head at him to signal her readiness.

The familiar tiny rocks crunched beneath her black boots as she walked toward the house, the wooden steps creaking as she approached the door. She swallowed hard, her throat dry as she knocked twice. Cassie could hear the heavy footsteps as her dad neared, studying the rusted handle as it bent.

The door swung open.

Her dad had more wrinkles and whiter hair than the last time she'd seen him, which made her heart ache in ways she couldn't explain. But he was still the man who'd raised her and helped her through everything in life. And now she stood there, ready to break his heart with the truth.

Her dad shot out the door faster than she'd expected any fifty-something man to do, flinging his strong arms around his daughter as he lifted her into the air. The smell of his cologne shaped a liquid memory, the oaky, wooden scent wafting through her nose, welcoming her home to the familiarity of him. Her eyes watered. She hadn't had much time to think about her dad, what with her dark side and all, and she hadn't realized how much she'd missed him until this moment.

"Oh my, Cassie." He put her at arm's reach and looked at her, his smile covering his whole face. "What are you doing here?" he asked, shaking his head as though he couldn't quite believe it.

Cassie's heart fluttered in her chest. "I had to make sure you were alright after what happened at Jessie's diner." She oversaw his expression, how his happiness turned to sadness.

He grabbed the dark blue baseball cap off his head and tapped it against his chest. "I think a phone call could've done it, kiddo, but I'm glad you're here," he said. "It's a real shame, what happened at Jessie's. Lost some real good people in that freak accident. They're saying it was a gas leak," he muttered, his voice shaking. "But apart from not hearing from you much over the past few weeks, I've been doing fine. The vineyard's been busy, especially during a summer this nice." He glanced up at the blue skies.

Her dad gestured for her to come in before stopping in his tracks, finally noticing Hero standing behind them. "And who have you brought here? This certainly isn't Stephen!" he joked, reminding Cassie of her ex-boyfriend, another thing she hadn't mentioned to her dad. Stephen was the guy people could bring home to their parents, the straight-A student with perfect hair and a soccer scholarship, all wrapped up as a reminder of her old mortal life, when she had craved a place in the world, a large group of friends who were more like family, and a love that gave her ease and passion all at once. She smiled slightly at the realization that she had found what she was looking for in the most unexpected ways.

"Come on in." Her father gestured for them to come inside.

Hero was the opposite of Stephen. He was unpredictable, passionate, tough, and everything she treasured about the world of the Zodiacs. And he was *hers,* just as the world of the Zodiacs had become hers too.

"John," her father introduced himself, holding his hand out, his light blue eyes shining in the sunlight.

Hero shook it, bowing his head as he did. "Hero."

"Hm. Unique name. So, where did you put your bags? And how did you even get here?" John asked, frowning as he looked for a sign of her car through the screen door—the one she'd sold months ago.

"It was kind of a last-minute trip," Cassie explained, her mouth going dry. She led them into the dining room, knowing they might need to sit down at some point during this conversation. She turned to her father, clasping her hands in front of her. "Dad, what I'm about to tell you is going to sound crazy, but I need you to hear me out and stay calm, okay?"

John nodded, frowning as he blinked, as though to prepare himself. "You can tell me anything, kiddo."

Cassie bit her cheek. All the lies she'd spent months perfectly crafting, the deceit she'd led her father through were about to cascade down like an avalanche, drowning her in ice and truth. But she had to do it.

"Dad, I lied to you. A lot. I haven't been going to school in California anymore. I applied to the University of New Orleans for their summer program, and when I was accepted, I took it, along with their offer to finish my final year with them." Her father's breathing grew louder, but she couldn't bring herself to look him in the eye until she finished explaining. "Then, something happened, on the day of my birthday." She touched her chest, and her dad's eyes went to the spot where the emerald used to hang, his jaw clenching. "Mom's necklace—it burned me. I took it off, and then I started seeing things in the mirror, and *then* I met this group of people—these people with special powers. I know it sounds crazy, but I think it has something to do with Mom. They call themselves the—"

"Zodiacs," her dad interrupted. His face turned white as a sheet of paper, and his eyes stayed fixated in the distance.

Fire surged to her face, her mouth opening. "You know?" *How could he keep this a secret? Did he know I was one of them?* Her breathing grew heavy as she waited for answers.

"Yes, Cassandra," he professed. "Both your mother and I were Zodiacs." He took a seat at their dining table, a round old wooden affair with ring marks scattered about, gesturing for Cassie and Hero to join him. The chairs slid across the flooring before a silence floated around them.

John rested his hands on the table, his thumb rubbing against his palm. "When we found out we were pregnant with you, we were overjoyed. But one summer night in May, your mom started having contractions. It was too early; we weren't supposed to have you for another two months yet." His brows furrowed with the recollection. "We had no other choice but to run away. We couldn't let them take you from us." His deep voice turned sickly. "So, we pretended we lost our baby, and escaped that very night. We left a note saying we were too saddened over what had happened, and that we would take our lives together by the seaside. Your mother gave birth to you the next morning, in the back seat of the car. The birds sang as she screamed, and we knew in an instant we had made the best decision of our lives, because it gave us you." The corners of his mouth lifted as he stared at his daughter.

"We started over. A witch made you that necklace, ensuring you would be guarded from the Zodiac world. It wouldn't keep your powers away forever, but it would help keep them at bay until the day you took it off," he breathed out. "I realized we would have to have this conversation one day. I just wanted to protect you from everything for as long as possible. I lost your mom, and I couldn't lose you too. I'm so sorry you had to find out the way you did, and I'm even more sorry

I wasn't there to help." He reached out for Cassie's hand, squeezing it gently as his eyes watered.

Cassie shook her head, putting her other hand over his. "I'm the one who's sorry. I should've told you about moving; I should have told you about all of it. Things just got so messed up. I didn't know what to do." Tears formed at the corners of her own eyes as she tried her hardest not to let them fall. Hero's knee touched hers beneath the table, a silent acknowledgment that he was there for her.

"Do you still have your abilities?" Hero asked him.

John nodded in response, sniffling as he regained his composure. "I'm a Cancer, but I haven't used my powers in a long while. I still sense them, though," he muttered, examining his hand as it sparked in response, creating what appeared to be a miniature shield. Her dad peered up at her from his seat. "Cassie, I'm so sorry you had to go through all this, and that I never prepared you for it. I assume the Arena knows about you being a Gemini, but at what cost?"

Cassie looked at Hero, whose smile distilled a harmony inside of her, before she turned back to fill her father in on all the details: about her dark side, about having to find the Elixir and the Cup, about Poseidon's attack being her fault. About Quinn, about her team, her friends. The prophecy. The war.

Her dad was in tears by the time she finished, but he hadn't said a word.

She glanced at her watch. They had eight more minutes until Lukas would open the portal again. "You have to come back to the Arena with us. It's not safe for you here anymore," she said, willing her voice not to shake.

John exhaled sharply, running his hand through his short gray beard. "Cassie, if I go back there . . ." He paused, his thoughts wandering. He blinked quickly, his mouth pursing. "Of course I'll go back with you."

Hero cleared his throat. "We better get ready to go soon. Don't worry," he assured them both as he stood, "the Archon will help ensure your safety."

John smiled tightly before rushing off to gather his things.

A silence plunged into the room. "You okay, Cass?" Hero's voice rang in her ears.

Cassie didn't know how to answer. She had been lied to her entire life by the man she trusted most. Betrayal stung her like a thousand wasps, but the guilt she felt for doing the same back to him overwhelmed her, crushed her. She wasn't okay in the slightest.

An emerald spark caught her eye as she glanced out the window.

Time to go back.

Her father now stood behind her, holding an old black leather duffel bag, his tall, lanky body covered in all-black attire, a complete change from the usual flannel and light blue jeans he always wore. He looked like a different person—and she guessed he was.

They stepped out onto the grass as she took one last look at the house behind her. Her mother's plants still grew in their pots, overflowing with color and contrasting beautifully with the white panels of the house. Her dad refused to ever let them die. A lump formed in her throat as she tore herself away, walking out again toward her new life. The only thing that made it possible to leave was the fact that her father was with her every step of the way.

CHAPTER 39

CORDOLIUM

(N.) HEARTACHE; HEARTFELT SORROW

Cassie bit the inside of her mouth, her foot tapping against the floor as she waited for the doors of the mission room to open. Hero had requested a meeting with his mother to discuss the newfound information concerning her father and his safety. She glanced over at her dad, whose eyes were wide as he took in the room around him, as though he belonged there, but not at all.

The doors finally opened as Diana and several guards walked into the room. Diana's eyes shone golden as she passed by a light—a Leo, just like Hero, a true leader in her element. She froze in her path as she noticed them—or rather, *him*.

"Jonathan Castor," Diana gasped, her face draining of color. "You're alive?" She approached him, studying his face like an old painting, memorizing every brittle brushstroke.

John chuckled breathlessly, holding his arms upward in shock. "Diana . . . I never thought I'd see you again!"

309

She took a step back and looked between him and Cassie. "Well, your disappearance makes more sense now." Her eyes fluttered closed for a moment. "I assume Vera is no longer with us." She dipped her head in tribute.

Her dad's face flashed in pain, in grief. "And Archer?"

Diana shook her head, and John cursed.

"Jonathan Castor?" Cassie echoed, ignoring the stitch in her heart at the mention of her mother's name, or of Archer, who must've been Hero's father. She cast Hero a quick glance, noticing the all-too-familiar agony and guilt in his eyes.

"Your true last name." Diana scanned her. "The Castors are one of the founding families of the Zodiacs, like the Stamoses, Hawthornes and Nakamuras."

Cassandra Castor. The name of one of the original Gemini twins—a name she already adored. A founding family. *Family . . .*

"Do we have more family here?" Cassie asked, her eyes wide.

Her father's lips thinned. "I learned that my parents passed a few days short of each other when you were young, but I don't know about your other grandparents."

Cassie faltered at the possibility of her having grandparents, something she'd never had before. And her dad . . . She was haunted by the fact that he'd had to give up his final years with them for her. None of it seemed fair.

Diana's face hardened. "I believe you already know what I have to do by law." She turned back to John, making Cassie's heartbeat quicken. "As much as I do not wish to do this, I have to take you to the Laconia Arena in Greece for a trial, for your betrayal of hiding a Gemini child. I can exert my influence in your favor as much as possible to keep you safe, and I'll arrange a room for you there, much more fitting than a prison cell." Diana paused. "I'm sorry."

Cassie felt as though someone had stabbed her, had robbed her of her ability to even think, to breathe.

"Absolutely not!" Cassie spat at Diana, a fire suddenly roaring inside of her. "What the hell is wrong with you? You guys were friends!" Her ears rang, her vision blurring at the edges. "How shallow of a person could you be to sentence your *friend* and my *father* to a trial, all because of your horrible and selfish laws?" She whipped around to face Hero. "And you!" Tears welled up as she spoke, her voice breaking. "You promised me he would be okay!"

This can't be happening. I can't lose him too. Please . . .

"I didn't know she would do this. I swear it," Hero vowed, begging her to believe him. "Mom, I trusted you with this! You can't take him there," he said, turning to Diana.

"Cassie, it's okay, kiddo," her dad assured her, smiling at her as the guards put their hands on his shoulders. "I knew this would happen; I know the laws. But I needed to make sure you were safe here. Whatever you do, don't give up."

Cassie watched him through blurry eyes, watched how his face softened, and listened to how love and hope swirled through his words. "You're so much stronger than you know. Your mom and I always believed in the best in you. I *will* see you soon!" He shouted his final words over his shoulder as the guards led him out of the room, Diana following silently behind.

Cassie's knees buckled beneath her, and she fell to the ground. She had found and lost her dad within the span of a few hours.

"I'm so sorry. I had no idea my mom would do that. I thought she'd oversee the laws, given everything." Hero shook his head, running his hand through his hair as he paced back and forth.

Deep down, Cassie knew it wasn't Diana's fault, nor Hero's. It all circled back to one person—one *god*. Poseidon was responsible for all of this. And he wouldn't stop until he tormented or murdered everyone who stood in his way.

Cassie couldn't bear for this to ever happen again. She'd already lost so much. Everyone had lost too much.

She had to stop him.

"We have to fight," she said, refusing to look at Hero, knowing she'd break if she did.

Hero froze in place. "What?"

"I want to fight. I want to fight Poseidon. After all," she muttered as she glanced up at him, using his mother's own words, "if you want peace, you have to prepare for war."

CHAPTER 40

CONCILIABULE

(N.) A SECRET MEETING OF PEOPLE WHO ARE HATCHING a PLOT

“I can't ask any of you to come with me, but this is something I need to do,” Cassie said, her voice bold yet callused from a string of rough nights. “Poseidon has to be stopped, and if finding the Elixir can do that, then I have to risk it.”

The air crisped and curled with mist in the morning light, a pink blush casting over her team as they stood on the rooftop—Cassie's new favorite spot.

The rest of them all looked at one another in silent agreement before speaking.

Artemis's husky voice cut through the breeze like a blade. “You're stupid if you think we'll let you do this by yourself. We're a team. Whatever it takes.”

“Even if I don't have my visions anymore, I can still fight,” Nyssa said before sipping her coffee. Even demigods needed their caffeine to stay awake this early. “Whatever it takes,” she echoed.

Hero leaned against the wall in silence, as though he weren't a part of the conversation. Cassie glanced over at him, frowning as she noticed the dark bags under his eyes, staining his pristine face with purple and blue marks. Hero had a habit of messing up, of acting with his heart rather than his head, which was why Cassie thought so highly of him. He was human in all the right ways, and divine in all the others.

She bit the side of her lip. It wasn't Hero's fault her father had to be taken. He hadn't known. Nor was it Diana's fault; they were merely following orders. The real enemy was Poseidon, and the lawmakers, the traders of the Oracle—the same ones who had decided they would prefer to kill her in cold blood than have her try. The same ones who followed what the twelve Immortals told them, what Poseidon had told them about there being no hope for the Geminis. Her blood boiled, then eased as she steadied her gaze on Hero.

"So, what's the plan?" Titus asked.

The water nipped at her skin, sending goose bumps down her legs as she waded in. Cassie sucked in a sharp breath as it lapped against her, the current sluggish but strong, a steady pull that reminded her of the test that lay before her—before all of them.

Water had always been her safe place, for longer than she could remember. Bad day? Shower. Panic attack? Bath. Tough decision to make? Walk in the rain. But now, water was Poseidon's domain, not hers. He controlled it, and if they were to meet with him in battle, he'd have the upper hand. The ability to drown them in his power.

If she wanted to survive, she had to learn how to fight in water. She wasn't confident about it, though. She wasn't weak—her body had been pushed to its limits for awhile now—but there was something terribly unnerving about standing in Poseidon's domain, in his element.

Hero stood ahead of her, already waist-deep in the river they'd chosen just away from the Arena grounds, his dark curls damp, water trailing down his defined bare chest. His golden eyes gleamed in the dimming light of dusk as he watched her, assessed her.

Cassie rolled her shoulders, forcing herself to at least seem relaxed. "You're staring."

Hero smirked. "You're hesitating."

She glared. "I'm *thinking*." And she *was* thinking—thinking about what a terrible decision it was to try to steal something from an already pissed-off god.

"That's your problem," Hero said. He moved before she could react, cutting through the water with lethal speed. Cassie barely had time to dodge him before Hero's arm shot out, fingers curling around her waist as he yanked her forward. The river surged against her legs as she stumbled, nearly falling into him. His breath was warm against her as he held her. "If you overthink it in the thick of battle, you're going to lose. You have to go based on instinct. Every second will be valuable out there, you hear me?"

The protectiveness in his voice raked a shiver down her spine as she nodded.

"Don't let fear control you," he said.

Cassie straightened her spine, swallowing against the pit in her stomach. "I know."

"No," Hero corrected, "you *think* you know. You've never been in a battle like this before."

"Neither have you," she shot back.

"Now you're just stalling," he said, a cheeky grin tugging at his lips.

Cassie barely had time to react before he was on her. His body collided with hers, the force knocking her off balance. Water surged around her as she went under. The warmth of it wrapped around her like a second skin, thick and unrelenting. She surfaced with a sharp gasp, drenched and breathless. She narrowed her eyes at Hero. "You're enjoying this far too much."

Hero tilted his head, a knowing glint in his golden-brown eyes. "Maybe."

Cocky bastard.

Cassie stood, shaking the water off her skin, making a bit too much of a show of wiping the water from her black bikini top. "You want me to stop thinking?" she challenged as she threw her hair back.

She gave Hero no time to react before she moved. She lunged, sweeping her leg through the water, aiming for his. The river slowed her, making her movements heavier, but she adjusted quickly, using the current to amplify her force rather than fighting against it.

Hero faltered as her kick made the landing. His smile at her efforts seemed so pure, his white teeth glistening. "Better."

Cassie smirked, then shoved him.

Hero's back hit the water with a loud *smack*. He stared up at her, blinking, absolutely *drenched*. Cassie had to clamp down her mouth to keep from laughing, until his eyes narrowed into slits.

"Oh, shit," she whispered, already turning to run.

A strong, wet hand wrapped around her ankle and yanked.

Cassie barely had time to shriek before she was dragged under. The water rushed over her, swallowing her whole, stealing the breath from her lungs. The river wrapped around her body like an iron grip, currents curling around her legs, holding her down. Panic surged, her instincts screaming to fight, to thrash—

Then warm hands found her waist, steadying her.

Hero.

Cassie's heart hammered as he pulled her upright, breaking the surface. She gasped, blinking against the water dripping down her face. She barely had time to catch her breath before she realized just how close they were.

Hero's hands hadn't moved. One was still splayed against her lower back, the other pressing into her hip, his grip firm. Protective. *Possessive.* Their bodies were flush, chest to chest, hip to hip, his muscles coiled like a vise beneath soaked fabric. The world around them dimmed. The sound of the river, the birds overhead, the distant hum of the Arena all faded. Cassie swallowed hard, her mind entirely blank. The weight of him, the hard, unyielding press of his body against hers . . . *God.* Her breath hitched.

Hero's chest rose and fell against hers, his hands moving to grip her waist, pinning their bodies together.

She could feel *everything.* Heat surged through her, fire clashing against ice.

Hero's eyes burned into hers, and for a moment, neither of them moved, too afraid to ruin the moment they'd both yearned for.

Cassie's pulse pounded. She'd wanted him so badly for so long. Her legs tightened around his waist. A challenge. A dare.

Hero let out a strangled curse, his grip tightening on her. His restraint cracked.

And then—he kissed her. Not soft, not slow. Hard. Desperate. Starving.

Cassie melted. She arched into him, letting go, letting herself fall.

He pulled her closer, his hands beginning to wander to body. She gasped into his mouth, and he swallowed the sound, deepening the kiss, his tongue stroking against hers, slow and deliberate, like he was trying to memorize the taste of her.

The world around them blurred. There was no battle. No dark side. No impending doom. Only this. Only him. *Only us.*

Cassie's hands slid into his hair, fingers tangling in his damp curls as he kissed her like he was never going to stop. His hands traveled lower, skimming the curve of her hips, slipping beneath the soaked fabric. She shivered. Hero groaned against her lips, his hands tightening as he rolled his hips against hers.

Cassie felt him—*all* of him. Heat pooled low in her stomach, her body igniting, aching, needing.

Hero's mouth left hers, trailing down her jaw, nipping at her throat. Cassie let out a gasp, tilting her head back, giving him more access. He took it. His teeth grazed her skin, then his tongue, then his lips...

Her nails dug into his back. Her body pressed closer, closer . . .

And then—

"My eyes! They're BURNING!"

Cassie and Hero froze, their heavy breaths melting into silence. Cassie barely had time to process before Hero tore himself away from her, spinning toward the shore.

Elijah stood there with his hands over his face, his eyes just peeking through the slits of his fingers. "Is it over?"

Cassie wanted to die of embarrassment.

Hero let out an aggressively deep and pained sigh, dragging a wet hand over his face.

Elijah raised a brow, before raising his hands and mocking their voices. "*'Oh, Elijah, come train with us in the river. It will be good practice. You totally wouldn't be a third wheel...'*"

Cassie groaned, flopping back into the water.

Hero shot Eli a dark glare. "You have the worst timing."

"Nah. I have the *best* timing," he corrected, smirking.

Cassie, still breathless, still shaking, turned to Hero. And he was still looking at her, his golden eyes burning, his chest heaving. He still looked like he wanted to devour her. But now? Now, he had to stop.

Cassie could see how much it killed him. It killed both of them.

Cassie held her breath as she plunged into the water, the chlorine stinging her eyes, but she dove deeper, spotting the golden coin at the bottom of the pool. Her ears clouded with pressure as she swam, her fingers extending as the brush of metal hit her fingertips. Her body flipped around as she used her feet to push herself back to the surface. Gasping for air, she shoved her hair away from her face and bobbed in the pool, peering over at her friends.

She smirked as she lunged her arm out of the water, showing off the coin. Cheers erupted throughout the room, quickly replaced with shushes as they remembered their need for secrecy.

The moon disappeared through the skylight, replaced by the colors of dawn as Cassie floated on her back, absorbing all the power from the moment.

"Well done," Titus said, swimming toward her and stealing the coin. "Now we just have to do it in the sea, dodging a bunch of evil mermaids, and we're all good."

"We haven't been training for weeks for nothing," Elijah said from the side, crossing his arms as he leaned back, his legs dipping in the water.

"My turn!" Nyssa laughed, jumping into the water with her legs tucked into her chest. Elijah fell in after her as Cassie shielded herself from the splash. Quinn and Artemis joined them soon after.

Cassie glided to where Hero sat at the edge of the pool in silence, toying with the strings of his black swim trunks. He'd grown more and more silent, more and more worried as the days past. "Come and join us. We deserve it," she said, her words soft.

"We haven't won yet," Hero said. "Even with this, we're not prepared to take down an Immortal. We have to be extra careful with Poseidon. We can heal from injuries from the Nereids, but a wound from an Immortal *will* kill you."

Cassie understood Hero's worries, but she didn't want to focus on them. She needed hope. She needed to stay strong in the face of death. *Don't give up.* "We can still celebrate the small wins. Swim with me, please?" she asked, looking at him with wide eyes, knowing that she could break him. She took his hand, guiding him in as a siren would.

They floated in the water, Hero's hands finding their way to her waist. "Happy?" he whispered, staring at her intently.

She nodded, giving him a playful smile as she splashed a small wave toward his face. He sputtered in laughter.

Hero pushed his wet curls back. "All in." He smiled at her.

She grinned, heart-warming tranquility stilling inside her. "I'm all in, too, remember?"

Hero gazed at her with such care, such *love.* "It's still sometimes hard to believe." An uneasiness drifted in his eyes, along with a touch of worry. "After the battle, I have something to tell—"

A deep clearing of someone's throat interrupted them. Cassie turned to find Diana standing there, arms crossed as she stared down at them, her nostrils flaring. "Get out of the pool," she demanded, her voice cold and malicious.

The happiness Cassie had felt just moments ago dripped off her, turning into cold, deep, dread.

Cassie shivered at the cool air as she pushed herself out of the pool, finding a white towel to wrap around herself. She couldn't tell if Diana had uncovered their plan, or if she was merely disturbed by their 5:00 a.m. noise. The look on her face remained guarded, as always.

"You honestly don't think I know how to break into someone's phone?" Diana scolded, waving a phone with a picture of Nyssa's face on the screen. "Especially when they leave it lying around so carelessly?"

Diana threw Elijah's phone to his feet, and he scrambled to pick it up.

Her heels clicked against the tiles as she walked back and forth, looking them all up and down. "I had my suspicions about you all recently, but I thought you would have more sense than to go against Poseidon after his threat." Her eyes narrowed at Hero, who stood as straight as a soldier. "You're disregarding my orders and are training for a fight you can never win. Those mortals will have died for nothing if you go and make him angrier. He could retaliate even more."

Hero took a step forward, his jaw clenched. "They die for nothing if we don't fight. I won't allow some terrorist god to get his way. That's not the leader you brought me up to be; that is not who we are. This is our one chance to save Cassie," he said, his voice harsh and filled with rage as he pointed toward her, "to save us all, and we sure as hell are going to take it."

"*Save* her?" Diana huffed, crossing her arms. "You mean you want to risk your life for a ten percent chance that this *girl* can actually survive any of this?"

Hero's muscles bunched as his fists formed at his side. Cassie could see his veins pulsating, his eyes glowing that familiar golden color. "I've trained her. I've watched her fight. She can do this. She's stronger than you think."

Diana stood tall. "I will not ask my soldiers to die for her."

"You don't have to," Artemis's voice echoed through the room. "We have our own."

Diana cackled. "This team here? The Virgo with no visions, the unstable Gemini with no true powers, the Aries who accidentally lights everything on fire? I could go on, but . . . Well, maybe I have failed, because this is not the decision I would have made, or your father would have made," she said sharply before regaining her composure, bowing her head. "I admire your determination, and I *am* sorry to have to do this, but I simply cannot allow this to happen." She waved out the door, signaling something. "Until you are no longer a threat, you will all be placed in a holding cell."

On demand, guards burst through the doors, surrounding them.

Artemis breathed out a laugh as one of the guards grabbed her hands and placed them behind her back, her wet brown hair shifting over her face. "You're going to lock your own kids up?"

"You've given me no choice." Diana's nostrils flared as she stalked toward Artemis, though her hand gently touched the side of her face. "And I worry you won't understand unless you decide to have children of your own, but I am doing this for your own protection."

"Like hell you are!" Hero yelled out, more furious than Cassie had ever seen him.

Cassie's wrists burned as a guard bent her arms back, guiding her and her friends out of the room.

Cassie grimaced. Everything in this room was white and modern. Even the cell bars appeared polished.

Lukas and Titus both had their backs against the wall, sitting near each other, yet keeping a distance. Elijah was laying his head on Nyssa's lap as she played with his hair, just to be that much closer. Quinn was messing around with the material of the white jumpsuits they'd been forced to wear, clearly unamused by how the heavy fabric made her look. Artemis was just sitting there with an emotionless expression on her face.

Cassie pulled at her own collar, scratching at the nape of her neck.

Hero grunted, making one last attempt to break the cell open, with no luck. He sat in a huff, hanging his head in his hands.

An access pad beeped outside their cell, flashing red every few seconds. It was driving Cassie mad.

"It's no use, Hero," Artemis mumbled, dragging a hand over her face. "Only Mom knows the code, and this cell only dampens our powers."

Dampens our powers. Cassie thought back to what Hero had mentioned after the trial, how if things went wrong, they could use something to restrain her, even if it would last a few weeks at best. Cassie didn't fully understand what power had gone into this cell, but a small part of her was relieved that if push came to shove, and her dark side came out, they had a chance against her with this—a chance to bring her back, or to kill her. Though she also felt relieved that they'd decided to help her rather than cast her away in this, or kill her.

"Hey," Cassie whispered to Hero, placing her hand on his arm. "It's okay. We always find another way; this is just the next challenge." She remembered her dad's last words to her. She couldn't give up now.

"I'm sorry you have to go through all this. I just want this for you so much," Hero muttered, leaning forward as he held her face, drawing his thumb over her cheek. If they had been alone, Cassie would have kissed him right then and there.

"At least we're here together," Elijah said, his lips stretched into a thin smile.

Titus scoffed. "Yeah. In a *prison* cell."

"I was being sarcastic."

A chirping sounded from the corner, followed by a white ball of fur prancing at them. "Bones!" Cassie gasped, sitting up as the white cat neared. He carried something in his mouth, something gold that shone as he passed by the streams of lights cascading from the ceiling.

"That's our mother's bracelet," Hero pointed out, his face scrunching in confusion. "I got it for her years ago for Christmas."

"Then why does the cat have it?" Elijah questioned, his eyebrows high.

"Wait . . ." Cassie paused, reaching out to retrieve the item from Bones. He gave it up willingly. *You know more than you're letting on, don't you, Bones?* "I think I know how to get us out of here." She thought back to her first day at the Arena, how she was able to slip into the mind of someone else using an old dress. She'd forgotten about it until now, having been caught up in so much else, but now she wondered if it had anything to do with her abilities.

Although knowing the effect the cell had on the others, something inside Cassie told her to try, to focus and to do it. These bars holding her inside couldn't contain her, or her powers.

Do it.

Cassie shut her eyes, honing in on the jewelry lying in her open palm. Her mind slipped, falling into someone else's. *Diana.* She could see paperwork, a large wooden desk, and a beautiful view of the Arena. A pain shot through her, a dull ache in her heart. *Grief.*

She tried to focus harder, to get into Diana's mind enough to see what the possible PIN code could be. Numbers flew around her, piecing themselves together on a sheet of paper on her desk, forming a pattern. She could see it clearly now.

Cassie twisted her hand, letting the bracelet clang onto the floor, her mind returning to focus.

The rest of the group stared at her, dumbfounded. "Um . . . what just happened?" Elijah asked, blinking. "Did you just use powers in here?" He flicked his fingers, trying to get a flame to appear, but only a tiny ember burst out.

Cassie stood, stretching her hand out as far as it could go, her fingers bristling over the keypad. "I think it's the one part of my Gemini powers I'm able to access," she said. "I did it on my first day here, but I didn't understand it then. I think by holding an object belonging to someone else, I can slip into their minds. And I don't know how I did it in here, I just had this gut feeling that I could."

"Well, that's new," Lukas muttered, shaking his head in amazement.

"I can't get to it," Cassie squeezed out, her body deflating as she released her stretch. She rubbed her arm, now marked red with yet another failure.

Hero stood, wrapping his fists around the metal bars. He sputtered as he forced the metal to alter with all his might, not one bit of his powers being used. No, that was all him. The metal creaked as it bent, but not enough.

Titus stood and placed his hand on the bar below Hero's. "I've spent far too much time down here recently. We're getting out."

The bar bent at last, allowing Hero enough space to shoot his arm out, reaching over to the keypad perfectly. "What's the code?"

"It's 120801," Cassie repeated slowly, her mind flashing back to the numbers shown on the piece of paper on Diana's desk.

"Very original, Mom," Hero sniggered, inputting the code, making Cassie's eyebrows bunch.

"It's the months of our birthdays—mine, Hero's, and Jason's," Artemis explained, the side of her face imprinted with a line from where she rested against the cell door.

All at once, the locks on their cells clicked, the doors swinging open. Artemis caught herself moments before hitting the floor, throwing her hair back as she glared at Hero, filled with annoyance as he shrugged in response.

"Freedom!" Elijah yelled, rushing out of the cell and opening his arms wide as though to embrace the air.

The rest of them hurried out. Cassie knew they had to think of a plan, and fast, before Diana saw them on the security cameras.

As though he had read her mind, Hero stepped forward. "We fight tonight. What do you all need before we go?"

"We need our weapons, and to get out of these hideous things," Artemis said, holding the stiff fabric out from either side of her.

"Lukas?" Hero asked.

He nodded. "I'll portal us back to our quarters, but we have to be quick. You each have ten minutes until I open the main portal to Greece. This is our last chance."

They all agreed before jumping through the portals Lukas made.

Cassie arrived back in her bedroom, Bones jumping out alongside her as the swirling green portal sparked out of existence. She looked around her room, taking it all in for what could be the last time. It was a room once untouched by her, belonging to someone else, and now what she considered to be comfort and home. Parts of her were scattered around, reminders of who lived here now. Her laptop and phone lay at the end of her bed, where Bones also decided to rest for his nap. Spare clothes were draped on the furniture, her books stacked in piles on the floor.

She gazed at the painting hanging at the head of her bed, which she had memorized each stroke of in awe, writing poems about it in her spare time. She had grown to love it in some odd, twisted way, as if a part of the last person who had lived in this room were watching over her, protecting her, wanting a better future for her. She adored the sliver of this world that belonged to her, and she wanted to keep it that way.

Cassie took a deep breath and hurriedly got to work.

She opened her closet door, pulling out a pair of black stretchy athletic leggings Artemis swore by. Cassie paired it with an armored top, which Quinn had spent weeks making for them all. It was a combination of leather and iron, giving them all the protection she could, but with the sleeves long and agile, allowing her the full mobility she needed to fight. She grabbed her thigh harness off the table along with her dual daggers, sliding them into their respective places.

Cassie leaned over to her vanity, pulling a comb through her hair before pushing it back and high, tying it away from her face. She glanced in the mirror, taking in her appearance. She smiled at herself in the reflection, having not seen her dark side since it last came out. She was determined never to let it take control again.

This was her life, her destiny.

She could hear the voices of her team meeting outside in the hall, butterflies erupting in her stomach as she raced to go be with them. Her friends, her team. She opened the door.

They inclined their heads at her. This was it.

Cassie wrapped Quinn in a hug, a whiff of her sweet smell filling her nose. She held onto her extra tight, just in case, not wanting to let go.

"You can do this," Quinn affirmed in her ear.

They pulled back, giving each other a smile, a silent goodbye.

Just then, the doors to their quarters flung open, causing Cassie to jump. Diana stormed in, her guards close behind her. They had to do this now.

Lukas's eyes shone green as he moved his hand to open another blazing emerald portal.

"Stop!" Diana shouted. She had almost reached them.

Nyssa and Elijah jumped in together, Lukas and Titus following. Artemis hesitated for only a moment before running into the portal. Cassie and Hero were the only two left.

"Go," Quinn urged, giving Cassie one last squeeze of her hand. "I can handle her."

Quinn sprinted at Diana, tackling her to the ground, and if they hadn't been about to go into battle, Cassie would have doubled over in laughter at the sight. The guards paused, giving them the perfect amount of time to escape.

Hero and Cassie smiled at each other as they leaped in. Then they traveled through space and time, holding onto each other as they did, until everything stood still.

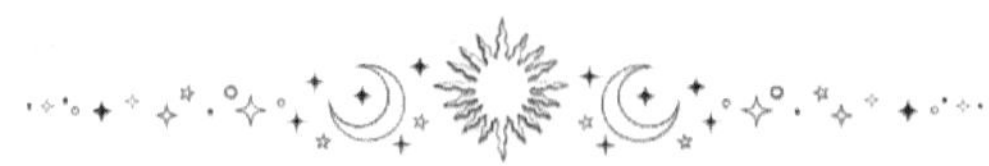

The first thing Cassie smelled was salt.

The air felt moist on her face as she shielded her eyes from the blazing summer evening sun. The sound of waves lapping against the beach filled her ears as she exhaled.

They had made it.

Lukas waved his hand, closing the portal behind him. Cassie's chest tightened. Everything they'd trained for, everything she had been working for, would all be tested now.

She peered around the beach they found themselves on, surrounded by rocks and cliffs. The water shone a pristine blue. She couldn't see any sign of human life anywhere. It was them against the Nereids. Hopefully, they would have the element of surprise.

"Not the way I imagined I'd see Europe for the first time." Cassie chuckled, staring out into the sea. The sky was painted with marigolds and violets, seeming like a dream.

Hero stood behind her. "If we survive this thing, I promise I'll take you back here properly."

Cassie peered over her shoulder, studying him—his tanned skin, his dark, loose curls, his all-consuming brown eyes. "Don't make promises you can't keep."

He half smiled. "I never do."

"The caves are right over there," Titus pointed out, walking up next to them.

Cassie strained her eyes to see a small opening in the rocks. The water chopped against it, and she could almost make out some figures swimming around.

"If we can do this in time, we'll hopefully be able to avoid Poseidon," Hero said. "And remember, the moment, the absolute moment Poseidon makes an appearance—and we can only hope that he doesn't—we get out of there. I'm not risking any of our lives."

"We'll have to swim to the clearing over there and then climb on those rocks," Titus said, pointing at several large surfaces interrupting the path of the sea. "It looks stable enough for us to fight on, and close enough to the cave for us to dive down for the Elixir."

The sand squished beneath the soles of Cassie's boots, her hands going to her blades, finding comfort in them. She was walking into her first real battle. She knew she would have to kill. She knew she would do anything to get the Elixir.

And she knew it would eat away at her soul forever, but the other side of the coin was too dark.

"I am the master of my fate, the captain of my soul," Cassie breathed out, trying to steady herself.

"'Invictus.' William Ernest Henley," Hero said, gravitating to her as if it were the most natural action in the world. Of course he knew the poem. As they shared what might be their final smile, Cassie's eyes teared up.

Her team lined up at the shore, ready to face whatever fate awaited them. "We do this together, or not at all," Nyssaaffirmed, her short black hair flinging back with the ocean breeze.

"Are you ready?" Hero whispered to Cassie, squeezing her hand.

She looked to either side of her, where her team stood, prepared to go to battle for her, making her heart swell with pride. She couldn't let them down.

"As I'll ever be."

CHAPTER 41

THALASSIC

(N.) RELATING TO THE SEA

The harsh wind slammed against the waves, the water sputtering onto her, pushing Cassie back into reality, into the fight that had begun minutes ago when the Nereids appeared from the caves, and all her hopes of gaining the upper hand had disappeared.

Hero had left her side and joined the battle first, the rest of them quickly following.

From the surface, the Nereids looked almost human, aside from the pointy ears and scales decorating their faces and skins. She could also make out the glint of a tail floating beneath them in the water where their legs should be. But these weren't the sweet creatures who helped sailors—not at all. Dozens of them thrashed in the water, viciously baring their razor-sharp teeth at her. Their webbed hands were equipped with claws that scratched at her as though they were starved animals.

Cassie watched in horror as weapons slashed against skin, screeches and grunts filling the air.

Hero fought as though he were the epitome of fatal grace, each swing of his sword an intricate choreography. He kicked a Nereid back as an arrow flung into its chest. Artemis stood on a boulder several feet away, waiting for Hero to line up the Nereids for her to finish off. The two siblings fought together in harmony, as though they were toying with their kills—as though they enjoyed it. The thought made Cassie grimace, but she swallowed it. She had to.

Titus moved swiftly through the water, whirlpools dancing around him, circling some of the Nereids. Cassie's eyes widened at the sight of a Nereid sneaking up behind him, but in a flash of green light, Lukas appeared and plunged his sword deep into its torso, making it shriek in pain before falling back into the sea.

Just then, one of the Nereid's slimy hands wrapped around Cassie's ankle. She flinched as its claws dug into her, her calf seizing as blood dripped down her leg. It tugged on her harshly, and she fell back against the rock. Cassie kicked, her foot pushing into its face as it screeched, but it never once loosened its grip. She whipped out one of her daggers, slashing at it as she used her other hand to cling to the rock. It dodged and swam as though it were a game. *Slimy bitch.*

An arrow shot through its neck, the tip stopping just inches from Cassie's face. Blood sputtered out of the Nereid's limp body as it sank into the depths. Cassie blinked, her stomach rising to her throat.

Artemis lowered her bow, holding out her hand for Cassie to take. "Don't tell me a little mermaid got you down." She smirked, pulling her back up.

Cassie planted her feet, pulling out her other dagger, fully prepared for the next attack. "Thanks," she said. She glanced at her leg, watching as the red slices of skin from the Nereid's claws sewed themselves together again, wishing her pants could do the same.

Nyssa jumped onto the rock, her katana resting in her hands. "You girls alright?" she asked, slicing a head off a Nereid so casually that it sent goose bumps down Cassie's arms.

"Better now." Artemis chuckled, drawing another arrow into her bow.

"Don't you ever run out of arrows?" Cassie questioned, kicking back another Nereid.

Artemis swung around, shooting the same creature in the chest. "A birthday present from Hero. It has a spell on it to replace each arrow I use!" Another arrow flew into the water, into the eye of a Nereid swimming toward them.

Cassie weighed her options on how best to get the Elixir. The sea chopped and pulled violently as her daggers gleamed in the sunlight, as though it were calling her to be the flames, to fight against the darkness.

A Nereid lunged at Cassie, and before she could think, she sliced her weapons across its chest. She shuddered as it wailed before drifting to its watery death. *A horrible way to die.* But today, it was kill or be killed, and she could hold no room for remorse.

The cage rattled in her mind.

She peered behind her at Artemis, who threw one of her many daggers straight through a Nereid's eye, but something else caught Cassie's attention: the cave. They were closer to it than she'd thought, the opening just a short swim away. She could do it.

"Cover me!" she shouted at Nyssa and Artemis, inclining her head toward the entrance.

Nyssa and Artemis glanced at each other, then back at Cassie, grinning. "Let's do it." Artemis released another arrow from her bow, which landed in the arm of a Nereid creeping up next to Cassie, and Nyssa thrust her katana through its skull.

They made a clearing for her, fighting fast and sharp, the Nereids unable to keep up. She had ten, maybe fifteen seconds to jump before they came back with more force.

Cassie shoved her daggers into her harness and dove into the water, the cold slapping her skin. She peeled her eyes open, ignoring the sting from the salt, and remembered her training. She scanned the ocean floor for a glimmer of anything that could be the Elixir, surfacing for air once her chest started to burn.

Arrows flew beside her into the water, hitting Nereids invisible to her. With the girls watching her back, Cassie knew she could focus solely on the mission at hand.

The waves crashed forcefully against the entrance of the cave, the crests like white horses galloping into oblivion. The sea was unforgiving as she swam further, fighting against the pull of the water.

Cassie shivered at the change in temperature as she entered the cave, the water now dull and murky. Wiping her eyes as she broke the surface, she took in her surroundings.

The noise from the battle faded with each stroke of her arms, and she could only hope that she was alone in here. She didn't know if Artemis's arrows could reach such a distance, or if they could even see her now. Glancing over her shoulder, she could see the bright light beaming from the entrance, but no people. No team.

Cassie spotted a cluster of boulders, a flat surface for her to stand on. Her hand was sliced and pinched as she climbed, her knees sliding across the hard rocks, but she pushed herself up, her feet finally on dry land. The sound of her teeth chattering echoed in the cave, and the brisk air on her wet body chilled her bones. Still, nothing could drive her away from her mission. Nothing could stop her now. She glanced toward a ray of light shining through the hole at the top of the cave, her only tether to the outside world.

The Elixir had to be around here somewhere.

Two large rock formations stood tall before her, like skyscrapers. Both were pockmarked with crevices, any of which could contain the Elixir.

From the diagrams Lukas had shown her, she was looking for a small, thin vial, the liquid inside a glowing purple hue—the color of her dark side's eyes. It should be easy to spot, even in the shaded darkness surrounding her.

Making sure no Nereids were waiting for her to jump into the water, she did exactly that. She peeled her eyes open and swam over to the first formation. Her hands rushed around the pebbled exterior, contorting away from the areas of soft algae. She felt around for a pocket or brush of anything out of the ordinary. *Nothing.* She swam to the other side, looking for any sort of glimmer. It was as though the Elixir were playing hide-and-seek with her.

She pushed herself up against the water, breaking the surface tension before she took a deep breath. Giving herself a minute, she eyed the top of the formation for anything, but still saw nothing.

Cassie swam over to the other formation. If it wasn't here . . . *This can't be a waste.*

But if the Elixir is here, why are there no Nereids protecting it?

Pushing away the sensation that something was wrong, she plunged back into the water. Cassie fought the sting of her eyes, keeping them open, desperate to see the violet gleam. Ignoring the fire building in her chest, she swam as far as she could to the bottom of the cave. More nothing. More darkness. She hit her hand against the rock as she screamed, air bubbles rippling around her.

Cassie swam to the surface again, her vision blurring from both salt and desperation.

She went under again. Time passed in waves of eternity and mere seconds all at once.

Cassie searched the entire cave. Once. Twice. Three times. Nothing. It was empty, and she found herself drifting into insanity, repeating the motions over and over again as though this time would be different. That she would see something she had missed before, and it would all be okay, it *had* to be okay. . . It had to.

Her head broke the surface once more, but this time, numbness took over her.

"They're retreating! We have to go!" a frantic voice called out. Nyssa swam to the cave, her black hair sticking to the sides of her face. "Where's the Elixir?"

"I can't find it," Cassie muttered, reality crashing over her as she hopelessly glanced around the cave one last time. *It has to be here. It has to be.*

"We don't have time. Poseidon could show up at any minute," Nyssa urged her, grabbing Cassie's arm and dragging her out. She wanted to fight it. She wanted to keep looking, but the whole thing seemed like a lost cause. The Elixir wasn't here. Maybe the river nymphs had lied to her—a trick. Maybe they were on Poseidon's side too.

The heat returned to her body, her eyes readjusting to the bright light of the outside world.

Her breath caught. The water was inked red with blood.

A stillness drifted in the air; the lapping of the water against itself was the only sound to be heard. She could see Artemis, Lukas, Titus, and Elijah in the distance, but she couldn't spot Hero . . . If something had happened to him, it would've all been her fault. *Please be okay.*

The sun began its descent into the unknown, casting flares of pinks and yellows across the ocean. The beams of light floated over her face. Cassie pulled herself out of the water and pushed herself back onto her feet. She stood, bracing herself, stance wide with her daggers in front of her, just as Hero had taught her all those weeks ago.

A deep exhale fought its way out of her lungs. She could see him in the distance, swimming his way to her. The golden glimmer in his eyes shone miraculously, and her breath caught yet again.

But without warning, the ground beneath her shook, her knees wobbling as she tried to balance herself.

No, no, no, no . . .

The water around them suddenly rose, forming liquid horses that surrounded them. A waterspout swirled up from the sea, a golden trident rising through it. What she could only assume to be the Immortal Poseidon appeared in the midst of the storm, his muscles pulsating with the harsh waves, his body quaking with anger.

They had run out of time.

CHAPTER 42

MANGATA

(N.) THE REFLECTION OF THE MOON ON THE WATER

The god of the sea rose from the turbulent waters as his shadow eclipsed the rocks below. His eyes mimicked the whirlpools, his hair the storm, and his demeanor the unforgiving current—every bit as wicked as Cassie had imagined him to be.

Poseidon gripped his trident in one hand, the other balled into a fist at his side. "I gave you Zodiacs enough warning!" he bellowed, the rocks they stood upon shaking as he did. "Maybe I need to make myself clearer."

Hero stood tall, despite being half the size of the god before him. "We don't bow down to fanatic Immortals with too big of an ego," he sneered.

Poseidon growled before he cut through the water, his arms and legs covered in a scale-like armor that gleamed in the setting sun. Water dripped down his bare torso, curving at each bump of muscle. The Nereids resurfaced, swimming on each side of him, protecting him, ready to die for their master.

337

One swam closest to him, as though she were *almost* an equal, moving carefully behind him. She appeared older than the others, her face more defined and powerful, with a crown resting atop her head, made of shells and seaweed. Yet something else about her caught Cassie's eye: a glimmering purple liquid encased in a delicate bottle hanging around her neck. Then it all clicked. *Poseidon can't keep the Elixir himself, so he trusted it to the Nereid closest to him*—his queen of sorts, she presumed. She had to get to it. There was still hope left.

Cassie tore her attention off the god and back to her friends. They all stood on single bits of the boulder, weapons drawn, faces twisted with fear. Hero's words echoed in her mind: *"A wound from an Immortal* will *kill you."*

She turned around in time to see Poseidon swing his trident at them. She leaped off the side and into the water, hoping her friends managed to do the same. His weapon slammed into the rock, breaking it into pieces.

"My cause is greater than all of you," Poseidon said, his voice deep and commanding. "In time, you'll see that."

Flashes of green light appeared around them as Lukas pushed himself up on an adjacent rock, legs planted wide as his eyes glowed the same emerald color. His hands shook as he opened an array of portals around them, giving them all a chance to escape.

"Let's go! Now!" Hero ordered.

Cassie moved to join them, to leave, but she couldn't. Not with the Elixir, her freedom, right there. She watched as her friends ran and swam to the portals, waiting for them to escape, for them to be safe. She would carry on with the rest alone.

Nyssa jumped first.

Cassie's breath caught as a water horse appeared, knocking her back into the sea. Waves began to rush over the portal, washing it away exactly as water had washed away the effects of the Scorpio poison during the ball.

No, no, no . . .

One by one, each portal disappeared, subject to the same fate as the others. No one had made it through. All her friends, her team . . . they were trapped in a battle with an Immortal.

A knot formed in Cassie's stomach as she looked at Poseidon. His face depicted smugness as he lowered his hands.

"You can't escape your fate," Poseidon said as he lifted his finger at Lukas. Several of the Nereids took off toward him without a second order.

Titus swam faster. He angled his spear, skewering several of them through the side.

Poseidon's face erupted in a fury. He strutted through the sea, the water adapting to his movements. The god flicked his hand, ordering the water around Titus to swirl, entrapping him in a whirlpool. Poseidon peered up to the sky, the liquid conforming to his every command, flinging Titus into the air before it wrapped around his throat.

Cassie gasped as she watched his body wriggle, his hands trying to free himself. The god would kill them if they didn't find another way out of here, but the Elixir still captivated Cassie's mind. She wanted to do both—to come out alive, but not doomed.

Lukas appeared next to Poseidon in a cloud of green smoke, slicing his sword down Poseidon's arm, making him release Titus. Titus fell into the water, his body splattering on the surface as he coughed for air.

"You'll pay for that," the god said through gritted teeth. He examined his cut, which healed twice as quickly as theirs.

Hero and Elijah leaped over to Titus, pulling him onto the rock. Cassie watched in horror to see what Poseidon would do next.

There had to be another way out. They had to find a way for Lukas to open the portals again, to distract Poseidon from seeing what they were doing.

Poseidon's body heaved in anger as he focused on Lukas, swinging him back into the water with the force of his hand. Lukas slammed against the sea, his body sinking.

"Lukas!" Titus yelled, breaking free of his friends' grasp and rushing toward him. He swam through the water faster than ever before, reaching Lukas in seconds and dragging him up for air. Titus placed his hands on either side of his face, trying to wake him. Lukas rolled to his side, coughing out water. As he did, Titus stood, gripping his spear, as though he would take on the god alone for hurting Lukas, no matter the cost.

More and more Nereids emerged to fight, and Cassie's shoulders tightened. Her friends needed to get out of here, and she needed to get the Elixir. *Now.*

Cassie inhaled deeply before diving into the water, pushing herself through the current to the rock Hero fought on. She swam over to him, peeking behind the formation. "Hero!" she whispered harshly, making him turn. "We have to distract Poseidon so Lukas can conjure more portals."

Hero nodded, stabbing his sword through the eye of a Nereid. "Artemis!" He shouted out to his sister, who stood on an adjacent rock, firing arrows at every creature who came her way. He shot her a look, and she grinned.

"Distract and attack," he mouthed to the rest of the team.

Arrows soared through the sky, landing in Poseidon's back, making him turn around.

"That's not very nice, now, is it?" he thundered. He angled his trident at Artemis, plunging it toward her.

"Stop!" Cassie yelled, leaping over to her, but Hero appeared in front of the god, skidding across the rock as he caught his trident by its prongs, his muscles flexing as he held it back. Cassie's breath hitched as she realized Hero's strength could compare to that of a god.

"Don't you dare," Hero grunted, his arms trembling, "touch her." He fell to one knee, a grunted scream releasing as he held it . . . and held it.

Artemis nocked another arrow into her bow, one eye closing as she released. The arrow soared. The god stumbled back, allowing Hero to release his fight with the trident, and Cassie could finally see what Artemis did.

Poseidon pulled the arrow out from his eye in one slimy motion before throwing it aside. He lifted his trident, the blood from his left eye running down his face as it healed. The god roared in anger, his attention entirely on the siblings, who continued to taunt him and throw every bit of force and weapons they had at him.

Distract.

Cassie turned back to Titus and Lukas, dipping her head at them. They had to get the portals back.

Lukas tilted his chin, his hands rising. Portals appeared one by one behind Poseidon as Titus fought off any Nereidscoming their way. "I have a better chance of keeping them standing from the Arena!" Lukas shouted at Cassie.

With one swift motion, Lukas grabbed Titus, pulling them both through a portal, away from the battle.

Two of them had made it to safety. Lukas and Titus would keep the portals up, and make new ones from the other side. But how many of them would make it through?

"Let's go!" Elijah yelled at Nyssa and Cassie, his eyes raging with worry as he pulled Nyssa out of the water from where she had just killed another Nereid.

"You guys go. I can't," Cassie rushed out, pushing herself through the water, trying to stay afloat. "The Elixir—it's right there." She pointed toward the Nereid queen who swam near Poseidon, the Elixir around her neck.

Her attention then set on Hero and Artemis, who fought and fought. But her stomach dropped as something moved under the water, her throat closing as she realized several more Nereids were joining the fight and surrounding them.

Nyssa tried to hide her shivers as she glanced over her shoulder at the Nereids and back to Cassie. "What do you need?" she asked, Elijah nodding next to her.

Cassie gave them as much of a smile as she could muster. They were the two most selfless beings she'd ever met, willing to stay in a battle against a god for the sake of their team. "Help them distract Poseidon," Cassie said. She didn't want to waste any more time. They needed to do this as soon as possible, and if anyone could distract the god, it was the man on fire. "Get him away from the portals."

They set off on their missions, and Cassie jumped into the water, swimming to another boulder that barely showed from the surface.

"Hey! Big dude, over here!" Elijah yelled, waving his arms at Poseidon.

Cassie worked her way through the water to the queen, careful not to draw any attention to herself.

Cassie froze as a shriek left Nyssa's mouth. Her gaze followed as Nyssa fell to her knees, her hands gripping her head in agony. Elijah's face went white as a ghost, and he rushed over to her, guarding her with his body. She screamed even louder as Poseidon held out his hand, twisting it as though he were turning an invisible dial of her pain. Elijah tried to hold onto her tight, his own tears staining his cheeks at her agony.

"I would expect a thank you for allowing Rane to block your powers," Poseidon bellowed as Nyssa remained doubled over. "All this suffering and torment isn't good for a pretty girl like you."

Nyssa stood then, her limbs wobbling with each move, yet she didn't back down, as though she used the pain as strength. "I'm so much more than a pretty face," she muttered through gritted teeth, her back straightening. "Don't you worry." She drew her sword out in one swift motion, lunging at Poseidon. His eyes widened as she drew her blade across his body, the skin on his torso slicing in half. He spewed in anger, ignoring the blood as he flung his hand out once more, making Nyssatumble back over in pain. "So much effort for so little gain."

"Get out of here!" Elijah yelled at Nyssa, his voice full of urgency as she held in screams. "*Please.*"

Cassie hoped Nyssa would listen to Elijah, unable to call out herself. She was too close to the Nereid, too close to the Elixir. Her attention kept switching between Nyssa and the queen.

Nyssa swallowed, her face red with tears streaming.

Flames erupted over Elijah's arms as he ran at Poseidon, gaining his full attention, drawing him away from her. Nyssaglanced between Elijah and the portal opening beside her, pausing before she leaped into the swirling jade. Another weight lifted off Cassie's shoulders.

"I've dealt with Zodiacs like you before," Poseidon bellowed deeply, staring down at Elijah burning in flames before him. "It never ends well for them."

"Oh, really? You've dealt with sarcastic twats who accidentally light everything on fire? Well, please, tell me their names. I'd love to meet with them for brunch," Elijah quipped, loud enough for Cassie to hear and almost chuckle amidst the battle. Elijah snapped his fingers, and within seconds, flames began to dance in wildfires across the shore, angling right at the god and his servants. Screeches echoed through the air, hitting the waves with force.

It was the perfect distraction as Cassie crept up behind the clueless Nereid, holding her dagger high.

But just as she was about to strike, the Nereid queen turned around, gripping Cassie's wrist, making her gasp in pain.

CHAPTER 43

SÉVIR

(N.) TO TAKE MEASURES TO STOP SOMETHING; TO PUT a
N END TO

The creature looked between the weapon and Cassie's eyes before loosening its grip. Its claws then dug into her other hand, where Cassie held her second dagger under the water, as though it knew every move Cassie was going to make before she even made it. Yet what it did next confused her to no end.

The Nereid grabbed her hand, pulling the blade closer to its chest, looking at her—*pleadingly?*

Cassie slipped into its mind as the Nereid held onto her. She saw pain, blood, and torture beyond reason. Poseidon had enslaved this Nereid, Amphitrite, and forced her into many things, including becoming his queen—his toy for deep in the waters as he plotted this war.

Amphitrite showed her what she needed to do. She wanted Cassie to take the Elixir—along with her life. To end her torment, and defeat Poseidon once and for all. To free her sisters from his rule.

344

Cassie pushed back, entering her own mind again. She stared at Amphitrite, who gripped her harder, guiding the weapon into her skin, the first drops of blood rising between them.

"I'm sorry," Cassie whispered, her eyes pricking with tears as she plunged her dagger into the Nereid's heart. A single tear dropped down her scaly skin as Amphitrite stared at the purple sky, a small smile creeping onto her face for the last time.

Cassie unhooked the Elixir from Amphitrite's necklace, laying her body on the water's surface with care as Amphitritetook a final breath, the waves carrying her away, reclaiming her.

Cassie glanced back down at what now rested in the palm of her hand. It was right there, right in front of her: her freedom. She wanted to cry and laugh all at once. All those fights, all those deaths . . . they hadn't been for nothing. Amphitrite was just one more life she had to avenge.

Cassie found Elijah from a distance and nodded at him, letting him know she was okay, that his mission was successful.

"Hopefully see you never!" Elijah stuck his middle finger up at Poseidon as he fell backward and straight into another portal.

Cassie slackened in relief as she saw him disappear back to the Arena. Four of them were safe. Now just she, Artemis, and Hero had to escape.

The waves crashed against Cassie as she pulled herself from the violent sea and onto one of the last bits of rock Poseidon hadn't smashed to pieces. Standing, she placed the Elixir in her harness for safekeeping. She watched Hero and Artemis kill the last Nereid in sight, and as they did, the waves calmed, the tide pulling back. She looked across the water, her heart rising. Poseidon had been there moments ago, but now he was nowhere to be seen.

Then, pure agony struck.

Next, the taste of iron.

Cassie peered down at her stomach to see three pieces of gold stretching through her. They disappeared out of her body as fast as they entered, her mind still trying to process what had happened. Blood gushed out of her as she tried to stop it, but it poured through her fingers like a waterfall.

She turned her head.

Poseidon stared down at her like she was an ant in his way. "You should have never been born," he spat.

His blood-drenched trident swung around for one last assault, knocking her to the ground. The sheer pain overwhelmed her. She could barely taste the red liquid pouring out of her mouth anymore, staining her face and hands.

Her eyes met Hero's from across the sea.

He watched in terror as she fell—first onto her knees, holding her hands over her wounds, as though it made any difference. His eyes never left hers as the color drained from her body. She went limp, falling into the water, lifeless.

His screams were filled with all the rage of the ocean, earthed by the violence of the storm. Hero lunged forward, wanting to run to her, but someone held him back. "Let me go!" he yelled at whoever stood behind him.

"If you go over there, he will kill you too!" Artemis thundered in his ear, holding his arms with all the grip she could muster.

"I don't care!" Hero spat, setting himself free with his immense strength. He couldn't lose her—not now, not ever. *This can't be happening.* He sprinted toward Poseidon, and all he could see was red.

Poseidon lifted his trident to the sky, still drenched in Cassie's blood. The sea moved underneath the god, the water forming above him in a tornado, the force of which flung Hero backward, pinning him in place on the rock. The water sputtered out as Hero tried to shield his eyes, watching as it swallowed Poseidon back into the contentment of his victory.

The sea stilled.

Hero heaved in anger, pushing himself back up. "Why the hell did you do that?" he screamed back at Artemis. He dove into the water, trying to find a glimmer of silver hair.

He surfaced for a quick breath before going back under, searching for as long as he could. He needed to see her, he needed to save her. He couldn't... he couldn't breathe.

As he pulled himself out of the water in failure, his knees buckled, and he screamed out into the ocean, the tears he couldn't let fall edging his eyelids. If he did, it would make this true. She would be nothing but *gone*.

"Hero, stop," Artemis pleaded as his jaw clenched. "It's over."

He...

Couldn't...

Breathe.

"Please don't leave me," Hero whispered into the dark ocean. *This can't be real. She can't be... No...*

Artemis pulled him up to stand, holding him under his arms. "We have to go." His sister's voice shattered through his mind. "More Nereids could come at any minute."

Hero let his body be led by Artemis, too numb to care or think about his surroundings. They found one of the last remaining portals and went through. Hero was deflated, utterly defeated. They had come into this battle together, and now they were leaving broken and bruised—without her.

They landed in the middle of the mission room, the rest of his team rushing to them, asking question after question. Hero's knees collapsed under him, cracking against the marble flooring.

"We thought we lost you guys," Titus breathed, glancing between him and Artemis.

Hero didn't respond. He couldn't respond.

"Are you okay? Are you hurt?" Nyssa said, taking Hero's face in her hands to examine him. She looked between them, backing away as tears formed in her eyes. "Cassie?" she asked, her voice breaking as though she already knew the answer.

Artemis shook her head.

"What happened?" Elijah asked, his voice low and jaw tense.

"Poseidon killed her," Hero mumbled, his body numb. He wanted to die. He wanted the god to die.

He could see Quinn in the corner, falling to the ground as she sobbed. A part of him wanted to comfort her, being possibly the one person who could understand her pain right now. But he couldn't. He couldn't even move.

"It was planned," Artemis said through gritted teeth. "Poseidon disappeared the moment he killed her. It was his plan all along."

"So, that's why Rane took my visions away? He knew that she had to die, and that we would try and stop it." Nyssa wiped her eyes.

"I'll leave a portal open, just in case. You never know," Lukas muttered, giving Hero a tiny smile in what he could assume was pity.

But Hero didn't care. He just wanted her back.

The doors to the room flung open as Diana stormed in, the guards marching behind her. She paused as she gazed around the room, seeing their faces covered in tears and anger. Her head lifted, and she took a deep breath as she waved her hand in the air, signaling the guards to walk back out.

Artemis walked in front of her, blocking her path. "If you're about to say you were right, now is not the time," she voiced sternly.

A flash of sadness showed on their mother's face, but she regained her cold demeanor in moments. Diana stepped around Artemis, approaching Hero. The room fell silent as she stared at him, but he couldn't bring himself to look at her.

"Everyone, go get cleaned up. Leave us." She clapped and shooed them out of the room, his team all shooting him glances as they left, sympathy and sadness dancing in their eyes. He would never get over this, and he knew they understood that. How could he? How could any of them? She was family... *Was.*

A fire burned within him as the doors shut. Hero stood, his legs finding enough strength to support him. "Are you relieved?"

Diana's eyebrows raised, as though she hadn't expected him to speak. "Excuse me?"

"Are you relieved? That Cassie's dead? Now you don't have to worry about your stupid little prophecy." His anger built, and he was unable to contain himself any longer.

"Of course not, Hero," she breathed out, as though she couldn't believe he'd accuse her of such a thing. "Cassie was a strong girl, and she could have been a great advantage in the war. I'm saddened for her, for our people, and for you. I know you cared about her, but we have to move on. All we can do is move on," Diana said, placing her hand on her chest.

"That's just like you, isn't it?" he pressed. "To pretend that nothing bad ever happens? You know, not a day goes by that my heart doesn't burn with shame, that I don't feel so ridden with guilt that sometimes I can't even eat." He paused to catch his breath. "I still carry the weight of Dad's and Jason's death with me, and it stains my heart. I still blame myself for it. And I needed you," he said, his voice cracking. "I needed my *mother* to tell me it was not my fault, and to help me grieve." He knew he shouldn't be saying these things, but red was all he could see, all he could *feel*. "Instead, you turned your pain into power. You busied yourself with being the Archon and turned your back on your children. But I guess I'm not as strong as you are. My pain is *agony*. And now I've lost Cassie, and I no longer wish to breathe," he said, his eyes widening as he pointed at her. "But I blame you for her death. I will not carry around the same weight I do for my dad and Jason; I want *you* to carry that weight. You trained me to be this emotionless man, whose one instinct is to *kill*!" he yelled. "And I lie awake at night, wondering if you had opened your heart to me, just once, then I wouldn't be so messed up."

Out of breath by the time he finished, he stared in a fury at the ground. He was afraid to let go of the anger because the guilt for what he'd said, and the grief of Cassie's death would devour him instead.

Diana merely stood there, taking each word her son spoke with dignity. "It's okay to blame me," she admitted, the normal ice in her voice gone. "I blame myself as well. I always have. Most of all, for how I failed you as a parent."

Her words broke him out of his trance long enough for him to look her in the eyes, glazed and filled with regret.

Before he could even register it, Diana wrapped him in a hug. She wept as she said, "I'm so sorry." She paused, holding her son at arm's length. Patting him on the chest, she nodded. "I'll arrange a funeral service for her. I'll make sure it is as lovely as she was. But you need to rest," she said delicately, but scanned him up and down with worry, though he couldn't imagine he looked worse than he felt.

She led him to his bedroom and sat him on his bed, as if sleep would fix the ache wrapped around his heart. A sting of embarrassment and shame coursed through him. After all, it was his mother who had told him all those years ago, *"Weapons don't weep."*

And there he sat, eyes puffy, cheeks stained.

He watched as her eyes wandered to his bedside table. She lifted his sketchbook as the pencils and charcoal rolled off the sides before flipping through the pages, her mouth falling slightly open. Sketches of Cassie filled every page.

He would find a way to avenge them all. His family, those mortals at the diner . . . *Cassie.* His world broke all over again at the thought of her.

"She truly was beautiful," Diana whispered. "Her loss will be felt by all, but we will not let her die in vain." She brushed his curls out of his face as he let himself embrace his shadows.

The whole day played out like a nightmare, a distant memory that wasn't his. But he knew the truth. He knew their love story was forever lost to the tides.

CHAPTER 44

QUIETUS

(N.) AN END; DEATH

She tried to fight it.

The salt stung her wounds as one last reminder of her death. But Cassie still tried. The blood dripped around her like spilled ink, writing the last moments of her life under water.

The sea was claiming her.

She pushed herself up, fighting against the currents, but it would not let her win. It wanted her to die. It pulled her back into its trap, the waves crashing over her again and again, wearing her down until she surrendered.

Maybe it's for the best.

There would be no more fight, no more strife over her existence. There would be no more looming guilt and anxiety over the duality of herself. She had no more lies to tell, no more stories.

The torture of holding her breath was overcome only by her determination to not inhale the water. Her vision faded, becoming blurrier by the second. Her consciousness began to slip away.

Her lungs burned, and all she could do was scream. Bubbles entrapped the last air to leave her body, floating upward to freedom, leaving her soul behind as a souvenir. She had no more air. Her death was inevitable, piercing her from every side.

Inhale.

The sea finally took her. It infiltrated her body, leaving her with no choice. The water, which now filled her lungs, stung deeper than anything before. It was pure torment.

As she sunk deeper, she finally accepted her death. No calm washed over her, but she was ready. She was prepared to die.

And she did.

CHAPTER 45

ORPHIC

(ADJ.) MYSTERIOUS AND ENTRANCING; BEYOND
ORDINARY UNDERSTANDING

"*The war is coming,*" a familiar voice said, seeming far off in the distance. "*We need you to win. I need you.*"

Golden hair and the tip of an arrow flashed in her mind. She didn't know where she was, but she felt weightless.

Cassie's body convulsed.

Her eyes opened, burning from the salt, but she didn't care. The pain meant she was alive. Her lungs replenished, as though a second chance at life had blown into her.

On instinct, her arms moved, pushing herself upward. Her legs kicked as she fought her way to the surface. The moon glistened as she swam, digging her way through the thick and temperate water.

353

Her first breath of air was heaven. She gasped desperately, trying to get as much oxygen in as she could. Water sputtered in and out of her lips as she tried to stay afloat, the sea's reminder that it could take her again at any moment.

Never again.

She swam in the direction of the waves, praying to whoever listened that she could find some form of land, and fast. Every muscle in her body shook, cramping with exhaustion, too quick for her healing to kick in. Her fingers finally touched the sand, and she could see the end. Her swimming turned to crawling, and she ignored the pain as rocks sliced her hands and knees. At last, she was on the beach.

The water could no longer touch her.

She lay breathless on the shore, letting the sand squish in the crevices of her body, learning her story one grain at a time. Streaks of light decorated the sky, and Cassie stared in wonder at the shooting stars. She had survived. It wasn't as if she'd had a choice in the matter. That was the thing about her. It was in her bones, in her blood, and in her heart. She had survived, and she would keep on surviving.

Cassie pulled herself up, shivering as the cold wind hit her body. Her hair and clothes stuck to her, and she no longer had any shoes on. But if that was the one thing the sea took from her tonight, she didn't care.

Her fingers felt the gashes torn in her shirt by Poseidon's trident. For a moment, she was right back there, peering down at her disfigured body, her blood pouring out. Her eyebrows scrunched together as she searched for her wounds. Her skin was as clear as day, not one imperfection riddling her abdomen, not one trace left of her gruesome murder.

"A wound from an Immortal will *kill you."*

How was she alive? She thought back to the words Apollo had uttered to her, how she would be reborn in the sea. *Was this his plan all along?*

Apollo. His voice . . . He'd said he needed her for the war? Was that a dream?

As she stood, a spark of green caught her eye in the distance. Her pulse stammered, her feet catching up. She ran toward it, shouting for help. Had Hero and

Artemis made it back? Her knees wobbled with each stride, and the cramp in her side built, but she had to keep going.

The swirling jade portal remained wide open, but not one person was in sight. She couldn't decide whether that was a good or bad thing, but she had no more time for thoughts. Her legs had finally carried her to where she needed to be. The whirlpool of light danced in the air, beckoning her.

She stepped through with one thing in mind: she thought of him, she thought of her new life, and she thought of her friends. Then, she spun through space and time, the portal spitting her out onto a cold floor. Unable to stand any longer, she fell to her knees, the portal closing behind her. Try as she might, her eyes would not open. Instead, she welcomed the lull of sleep pulling her in, hoping beyond hope that she was home.

Hero tossed and turned in his bed, plagued with nightmares. Everything was Cassie. She swirled through his mind over and over again as though he were a broken record player. He watched her beam at finding the Elixir, then he watched her die, over and over again—the blood pouring out, the color draining from her face, the lifelessness taking over her body. The way Poseidon threw her life away as he pushed his trident through her, forcing her to spend her last living moments suffocating.

His nightmares turned to dreams as he imagined all the parallel outcomes. The one where he saved her, where he dove in after her and rescued her, just as he had done on the night they first met. Or one where he was the one who died instead of her. He would gladly have given his life if it meant he could see her one last time. Maybe they would die together instead.

Death wouldn't be so terrible with the right company.

He shot upright in his bed, gasping for air. He clasped at his sheets, his shirt soaked through with sweat. For one sweet, grappling moment, he thought it was just that: a dream. But it all came rushing back in seconds, like a storm hailing in his heart.

She was gone.

He would never see her curiously brilliant gray eyes again—the ones that glistened in the starlight. He swore they held the truth of the universe, or at least to his small fraction of it. He would never touch her soft skin; he would never feel her lips against his again. He would never again see the dimple that could light up his whole world in merely a second.

Worst of all, he could never tell her how his heart *ached* for her. That nothing else made sense to him, only her. That she haunted him in the best ways.

The day he'd met her, a spark had begun to grow inside of him, a spark he thought long forgotten. She warmed him, lighting him with flames that could blaze through any battlefield. But he knew that fire would burn out with her gone.

Sitting on the side of his bed, he held his head in his hands. His leg jittered underneath him as he pulled at his hair, wanting to tear it out.

He wanted to die.

At the sudden sound of yelling and running outside his door, he flinched and grabbed hold of the sword he kept hidden underneath his bed. Something had happened. He stood, as if it were the only thing to do. Hero had spent his whole life throwing himself into the actions of others. He hesitated as he arrived at his door, his hand wavering over the doorknob. *No,* he thought. He fought against every instinct he had and sat.

She had died because of *him*. He had pushed for them to fight Poseidon, and he had pushed for them to find the Elixir so quickly. The risks were clear, but the intense desire for her to be okay had consumed him. He *needed* her to be okay.

He was no longer a soldier worthy of battle, of helping.

His ears recoiled over the sounds of screaming, until he heard one word muttered through the voices—a word he hadn't dreamed he would hear right now.

Cassie.

His heart raced. He ran out the door, following the noise of a crowd of Zodiacs through the Arena, shoving his way through them as he neared. All their faces became a blur to him as he scanned for one thing only.

He broke through the sea of bodies, landing in the entrance of the infirmary, freezing as he laid eyes on her. The long flow of silver hair couldn't have belonged to anyone else. It had to be her.

Artemis appeared at his side, gripping his arm as she spotted Cassie too, unblinking.

"Is . . . is she alive?" he managed, unsure if he wanted the answer.

What if they'd just found her body?

Elijah spotted them through the crowd, rushing over. "I don't know how," he said, tripping over his words, "but she found her way back here. Mostly healed. It's a total mystery."

"She's alive," Hero reaffirmed to himself, smiling in disbelief. He moved Artemis out of his way, excusing himself as he ran to her. His stomach turned, his hands trembling.

All that went away the moment he saw her face.

She looked up at him, her soft eyes widening with each slow blink.

He reached out as though he were touching an angel, rubbing his thumb across her cheek. He stared at her, not entirely sure if he could believe she was lying there in front of him.

"Italy," she croaked out.

He shook his head. "What?"

"You said that if we survived, you'd take me to Europe. I want to see Italy first. Then Portugal."

"Cass, I thought I lost you," he sobbed, placing his forehead on hers.

She slowly moved her hand to touch his, giving him as much of a smile as she could. "Guess I'm too stubborn to die," she breathed out in a laugh, her voice raspy from the salt water and a brush with death.

Hero laughed along with her, but it was soon replaced with tears. "Cass, you were gone for hours. I saw you die." He was nearly crazy with how useless and petrified he was with his intense desire for this girl, the one he thought he'd lost for good. "What happened in the water? How did you make it back?"

Her eyebrows bunched together. "I remembered dying. I remember the pain, the torment. I thought it was all over . . . then everything just started back up again. It was like my life pressed pause, then went back to play," she said, her words slow and her voice rough. "I don't understand it."

"What matters is that you're back, and you're safe. We'll find another way to get the Elixir. This isn't over," he muttered, tucking a stray piece of hair behind her ear.

Cassie smiled to herself before lifting herself into a sitting position. She groaned as she leaned down, her hands moving to the spot where Hero had watched Poseidon's trident go right through her. He shivered at the memory.

Cassie reached down to her thigh and undid her harness. The Elixir popped out, dropping into her open palm.

Hero's shoulders sagged, his mouth gaping. "You did it." Hero beamed, relief consuming him. She placed it in his hand, and he, in turn, placed it carefully on the table next to her for safekeeping, staring at it in awe. He'd assumed the Elixir was lost to the sea after Poseidon had . . .

A voice squeaked out, "Cassie?"

Hero turned to see Quinn, who stood with her hand over her mouth, tears streaming from her green eyes and down her brown cheeks. He wondered if they'd stopped since he'd last seen her. He tore himself away from Cassie, still lingering close, unable to fully let her out of his sight.

Quinn ran to her and enveloped her in a hug. His chest tightened when Cassie winced, but she held onto Quinn anyway, burrowing into her shoulder.

"I thought you died," Quinn sobbed.

"I'm here. I'm okay," Cassie cooed. She pulled back after moments of hugging her friend, looking at them all. "My dad . . . Does he know?"

Nyssa came forward and placed her hand on Cassie's. "I don't think anyone has had the chance to tell him yet. It was too fresh. We were all still processing."

"He's going to freak when he finds out," Cassie said, shaking her head.

Titus walked closer to them, his deep voice bellowing as he smiled. "It's good to see you, Cassie."

Hero watched as Cassie smiled back at his brother, holding the hands of Quinn and Nyssa as she looked around at her friends, who surrounded the same bed he'd placed her on several months ago, when she had no idea that this world even existed. And as he did, it was as though he had been pulled from the darkness, from the shadows, and back into the sun. He wanted to draw out this moment forever, to never forget it.

Her eyes stopped on his, and he could have sworn his heart stopped with them.

"One down, one to go." She smiled, glancing back at the Elixir on the table.

"If we need to follow you into another battle, so be it," Hero declared, never taking his sight off the beautiful marvel before him. "But we are going to find the other half. Whatever it takes. We're a team."

"More like family," she whispered, gray eyes holding him captive, and he wished they'd never let him go again.

CHAPTER 46

LATIBULE

(N.) A PLACE OF SAFETY AND COMFORT

Her throat closed, tightening. She was back there—underwater.

Poseidon pulled her deeper, her surroundings inking darker and darker, guided only by the light of his trident, covered in her blood, her death.

He took her to his kingdom, where he would keep her body as a trophy, a constant reminder that he had killed her, murdered her in front of the man she loved.

His brown hair floated in her mind, his golden eyes shining. And then she saw him.

Hero lay there at the bottom of the sea—dead.

Cassie tried to swim to him, but no matter how hard she tried, she failed. The water moved like cement, enveloping her, trapping her.

He was dead, and she could do nothing to stop it. It was inevitable.

Cassie shot out of the bath, clawing at her throat as she screamed.

Strong arms pulled her body from the water, the air hitting her skin in a stream of shivers.

"You're okay. You're okay. I got you," Hero's voice shushed her, holding her tight against his chest. Grabbing a towel from the wall rack, he wrapped it around her, covering her. Dropping to the floor with her still in his arms, her body draped over his lap, he held onto her, and he didn't stop until the shivering faded.

He stared down at her, worry dancing in his eyes. "What happened?" He ran his hand through her wet hair, his brows furrowed.

"I don't know." She gripped his shirt as though he were an anchor, her one hope in the world. "I closed my eyes for one second, and I was back there, underwater. It happened all over again, but worse. You were there too. You were dead, and there was nothing I could do to save you," Cassie sobbed into his chest.

His body stilled for a moment. "You always save me. Now let me save you," he said as he picked her up and carried her back into her room. He placed her gently on the bed in a seated position as she clung to the towel for warmth.

Hero rummaged through her drawers, pulling out a set of blue sweats. He leaned down before her, putting one leg through the pants and then the next, sliding them onto her body. He stood, unwrapping the towel from her torso before pushing her arms up, tugging the sweatshirt down her body, covering her fully.

"I could have done that myself," Cassie mumbled, a small smile nudging her lips. She loved the way he took care of her, the gentleness of his touch.

"I know." He smirked before settling on the other side of the bed. "Come here," he said, lifting his arm for her. Cassie pushed herself closer toward him, placing her head on his chest. She couldn't put her finger on why she'd felt drawn to Hero from the moment she'd met him, but she couldn't be more grateful to have him. He held the key to her comfort, her calm.

Cassie closed her eyes, checking on her mental shields one more time. She ran her hand across the bars of the cage as her dark side sat there, face filled with arrogance. But it was locked up, safe.

Her eyes fluttered open again to see Hero. There had been a moment when she didn't know if she would ever see him again, or be back in this room.

His hair had grown out a bit since she'd first met him. Now, it was a few inches off his shoulders, the ripples so beautiful. His stubble was also now more of a short beard, and she liked it. But she had an inkling that she'd like him no matter what.

She glanced around her room, the blaring light of the TV in front of her on pause, the damp towel on the floor, making her smile. Shivering at the thought of the infirmary bed she'd spent the first day recovering in, she was thankful to have finally convinced the nurses to let her heal in the comfort of her own room.

The infirmary. She breathed out a small chuckle as she thought way back to her first day at the Arena, waking up in that room, terrified and confused, arming herself with a shoe. To think that she'd wanted nothing to do with this world that day baffled her now. Now, she had a new name, a new life, and a new family.

She quickly learned that home was not a place, but rather people, things, and memories. She had a home wherever she went, as long as her heart followed. She had a place in this world. She had a family; she had friends. She was no longer a little girl peering into the world through the window. Now, she stood tall in the middle of it, enjoying every bit of warmth setting her body on fire.

Four small paws leaped onto her lap. "Hey, Bones," Cassie muttered, gliding her hand over his soft white fur. Bones purred. The cat hardly left her side, not that she minded the constant company. They were connected in a way, both having shown up at the Arena at the same time. He'd even helped them escape for their battle with Poseidon. *A guardian angel.*

She didn't know if she even deserved one. Cassie had promised herself that she would never lie to her father again, and here she was, pretending like the battle with Poseidon hadn't happened, that they'd found the Elixir another way—that she hadn't died and come back to life in some mysterious way.

She was alive and fine after all, wasn't she? The one comfort she had was knowing that her dad was being treated with respect, in his own room, instead of a dark and dreary cell. Diana had made sure of it, which made it hard for Cassie to stay mad at her.

"What's got that beautiful mind of yours turning?" Hero questioned.

"My dad," Cassie sighed. "I know I have to tell him what happened sooner or later, but I . . . He has enough on his plate with the trial. I don't want him to worry."

"You'll tell him when you're ready. When you're both ready," Hero mumbled into her hair, laying more gentle kisses from her head to her cheek. But with her time running out with her dark side, she didn't know if she had a moment to get ready. She'd spent too much time lying to her dad, and she didn't want to do it any longer. Not when she didn't know how much longer she had.

The war. . .

"The war is coming. We need you to win. I need you." Those words flashed in her mind—Apollo's words.

"Hero?"

"Yes?"

"I think Apollo saved me," she whispered.

Hero's body shifted under her. "What?"

"I heard his voice, when I died, or *thought* I died," Cassie said, toying with the grooves of the fabric of his shirt. "I heard him say he needed me, and then my eyes opened. Do you think he healed me or brought me back to life?" she questioned, shaking her head. "Do you think that's even possible?"

"I think there's a lot of unanswered questions about you," Hero said after a beat. "I don't know why you're alive, why you have powers no Gemini has ever had before, why you were able to use your powers in the cells, or why Rane couldn't take your powers away, but we'll find out." He held her chin, moving her face toward his. "I promise. And if you need a break from all this for a few days, to stop your mind from turning and to just *live,* then that's what we'll do. We could have a party, we could go drinking in town, we could stay in and eat our worries away . . . anything you want."

Cassie considered it for a moment. Hero was right; she did need a break from everything, and a distraction was just what she needed. And, in true Zodiac fashion, she said, "A party sounds fun. As long as no one spikes the drinks with Scorpio poison."

Hero crinkled his nose. "I'll hire taste testers."

Cassie laughed, digging her face into his chest.

She'd begun to see her life like the phases of the moon: sometimes she'd be broken, less than, and sometimes she'd be whole. She found peace in it, because she knew the only difference was that, unlike the moon, the tides of her life were not predictable. But that was okay, because no matter how far she might sink beneath the waves, she had proved to herself that she would always come back up for air.

Her fight was half over. She had the Elixir now, and even though she'd died getting it, it just made her want the Cup that much more. Having tasted bitter death and being gifted with a second life, she wanted to fight. She wanted to get the Cup, and she would find it, no matter what the cost.

Cassie wanted to live, not just survive.

CHAPTER 47

OSSIFY

(V.) TO BECOME RIGID OR INFLEXIBLE IN HABITS,
ATTITUDES, OR OPINIONS

Hero knocked at the tall door of his mother's office.

He stared at the painted plank of wood before him, mesmerized by the slightest sliver of oak poking through the white. He waited, his stomach curling into a ball as he anticipated the door opening at any second. He waited to hear the clicking of heels, and then the disappointed sigh that would follow once she saw him.

But the sounds, the opening . . . never came.

He pushed the door open himself, walking in.

The room was empty, emphasizing just how large it was. A large wooden desk sat in the middle. He traced the material with his fingers, thinking about how he longed for the day when this would be his, when he would sit here and lead these people into a better life. In truth, this was his favorite place in the whole Arena.

He walked over to the window, his thoughts consumed with *her*. He thought about how much she loved the view from his balcony, and how much she would, in turn, love this view even more. Two dreams were flowing through his life, and he hoped one day they'd meet.

The door behind him creaked open, but he continued to face the outside world, not ready to pull his attention away from the scenic gardens. He spotted a gardener, planting fresh flowers while tearing the older ones out. Although only small imperfections could be seen in them, they had to go.

Diana cleared her throat, making him flinch. "I used to stand right there and watch you, Jason, and Artemis play out in the gardens." His mother's voice held a different tone than he'd grown used to; he'd almost forgotten what she sounded like as his mother and not his Archon. "She was just a little girl, but you two boys always made sure she felt included. I hoped one day you would do the same—that you would stand here and watch your kids play in the flowers." She walked up beside him, placing her hand on his back. Faint, but there.

"I will still be the next Archon," Hero insisted. He wanted to be the next leader. He yearned for that position because he knew he could guide his people fairly. But he wanted *her* at his side as he did it.

"The people in this Arena have always admired you, followed you, but don't be fooled into thinking that can't change. Although Cassie is everything you'd ever want by your side . . ." She paused. "She can and will be the ruin of you, taking innocent lives down with her."

Hero's back stiffened as he used his shoulder to push his mother's hand off him. "I think you're wrong. She's more than these prophecies." *In so many ways.*

Diana nodded, lifting her fingers to guide a curl away from his face. "She *is* special. I'll give you that. Nobody heals from an injury from an Immortal. Even I have no idea how she is still living and breathing. And to learn she is of Castor blood . . ." Diana's voice trailed off into thought, and she took a deep breath. She turned back to Hero. "You could be the best Archon this Arena has ever seen.

Better than myself, than anyone before me, because you lead with your heart." She glanced out of the window and sighed.

A flash of worry coursed through Hero's body, and he wondered what kind of test his mother was giving him. "You taught us that emotions were a weakness." He cocked his head to the side, staring at Diana.

"I did," she confessed, looking Hero in the eyes, "because after I lost both my son and the love of my life, I became weak. I failed as a leader, and as a mother. I never wanted you to experience that kind of pain. I wanted you to become the best Archon you could ever be, and have the brightest future possible, without grief on your shoulders. To thrive in this world without ever knowing pain. I never want you to feel the way you did last night." Her eyes were now filled to the brim with tears, and all Hero wanted was to make it go away, to comfort his mother and make it disappear.

Hero swallowed the knot forming in his throat. "When Dad and Jason died, I felt that pain. The grief, the guilt. But it has never been my weakness. It has always been my strength."

"And for that, I am so proud of you." Diana cupped his face, blinking away the tears. "But I cannot forget this prophecy. I can't lose you too."

"I love her," he said finally, his heart choosing for him. He would no longer push himself to the side for the sake of others, from the words of others. This was his own destiny, his fate. "And I want to be with her. The prophecy won't come true. I'll make sure of it. You won't lose me." Kalix, his excommunicated friend who knew everything about everything, had agreed to investigate it for him, to try and find ways to break it. So far, it was only dead ends, but Hero wouldn't falter.

"I wish you were right, my boy," Diana said, her voice shaking, and Hero could have sworn he saw a small tear fall down her cheek. His heart felt crushed; he needed the conversation to change, to shift his mother's attention away from his possible death, from what his heart chose.

"What's the next step for Cassie?" Hero asked, his posture straightening.

His mother took the bait. "We need to find her the Twin Cup, if she has any hope at all of eradicating that darkness. She trusts you the most, obviously, and as you two have created a unique bond." She shut her eyes for a moment, as though the words pained her. "She will need all the support she can get if she is to survive, but she will also need to remain in hiding. The entire Arena was vetted after Rane's attack, so we know the Zodiacs here are on Athena's and Apollo's side, but I've placed us on lockdown. No one can enter or leave unless they have direct permission from me. You will be allowed to do whatever missions are necessary to find the Cup, but if you run into any trouble, you hide her. No one can see her, understand?"

Hero nodded. These were orders from his Archon, not his mother. Their previous conversation was thrown away like a piece of paper, as he wanted it to be.

"Can the Immortals prevent a soul from passing over into the Underworld?" Hero asked, thinking back to his conversation with Cassie this morning.

Diana hesitated for a moment. "Do you think that's what happened to Cassandra?"

"She thinks it might be." He frowned, trying to make sense of it himself; he'd hoped his mother might have a clue. "I trust her intuition, but I wanted to confirm if it's ever been done before."

Diana shook her head and glanced back out the window. "Not that I'm aware of, but the Immortals are known for their deceit and their lies. I wouldn't rule it out." She clicked her tongue. "I had a meeting with Jonathan," she said, moving her hand in circles as if to keep her thoughts running. "He told me about a witch named Marie who helped him disappear for so long, and who fashioned the necklace Cassandra wore to keep her from our world. If I were you, I would look into her, but report back to me with any findings. Oh, and . . ." she continued, turning to her desk as she picked up what looked like a small purple stone fashioned into a bracelet. "Have Cassandra wear this. It will protect her from Virgos' visions worldwide, further securing her invisibility."

Hero dipped his head at his mother's commands, took the jewelry, and turned to the door. The prophecy still cast a weight on his shoulders, but he would bear if it meant he could be with Cassie. And he would do everything he could to stop it from coming true.

He didn't want to waste another moment in the shadows of his doubt. He wanted her, despite everything. Maybe this was his final challenge, his final hurdle to overcome before letting himself be with her, to admit what he had known all along: he loved her.

And he would always choose her.

Hero clinked his knife against his glass, waiting for the hum of joyful chatter to die down before speaking. He cleared his throat, raising his flute of champagne. "To Cassie: may she forever beat the odds!"

The room erupted back into noise, everyone voicing their agreement before taking a sip of the sparkling wine.

Hero gazed at her from afar, watching as she played with the amethyst stone now around her wrist. The extra layer of protection it gave her settled him a little bit more. He allowed his heart to swell at her beaming smile as she laughed and talked with her friends—their family.

He'd grown into the habit of checking whether she was happy or not, noticing if she laughed at the same jokes he did, and whether her smile reached her eyes. Her happiness seemed as though it could be the singular most important thing in his life, and he wished that it would never change.

Cassie drew a hand down her dress, another one he'd asked Quinn to make for her from the sketches he drew. This one was black and studded with shimmering diamonds. She looked like the night sky, all the constellations flowing together perfectly.

Hero walked back to his team and placed a hand on the curve of Cassie's back. She sunk into his touch.

"If I've learned one thing throughout my time here, it's that Zodiacs like to drink," Cassie mused as they all stood together.

"We're basically just certified alcoholics running around killing demons." Elijah chuckled, the sound filling Hero's ears with joy. Beauty permeated the room at that moment, when all his friends lived in harmonious peace, happy and healthy and alive. Such moments seemed rare these days, and Hero wanted Cassie to live every last one of them.

Elijah made some joke, and Cassie let out a peal of musical laughter, one which sounded so full of life. To Hero, she would forever be an emblem of life, filled with fierce bravery and light, a beautiful reminder of what they were all fighting for. There could be no way she would adhere to what the prophecy claimed her to be: a beacon of death—his death. No, Cassie had beaten it herself, and he would find a way to do the same. He would go to the ends of the universe if it meant they could be together. They would win this war, and they would win their freedom.

Cassie's back stiffened against his palm. "I'm going to go get some air," she said, smiling up at him. "Watch the stars for a bit."

Hero's heart raced as he watched Cassie pass her glass to a waiter, excusing herself from the party. He'd thrown this entire event for her, decorating it like the night, the perfect reminder of her favorite place in the Arena: his balcony. Despite the terror she'd once had on that same balcony the night Rane had poisoned them, she refused to let it tarnish it. And this was his chance to get her alone, to tell her all the things he had wished to say for months, since the moment he'd first laid eyes on her.

"I need a minute too," Hero explained mindlessly to his friends, not listening to their snarky comments and cheers of joy for him and Cassie. He planted a quick kiss on Artemis's cheek before following to where Cassie had disappeared to moments ago, down the long and narrow corridor to their quarters.

He followed his heart.

CHAPTER 48

NYCTOPHILIA

(N.) LOVE OF DARKNESS OR NIGHT: FINDING
RELAXATION OR COMFORT IN THE DARKNESS

Cassie crept into Hero's room. His door, as he'd promised, was always open for her.

The moon cast a wan light across the floor as she approached his balcony and stepped outside. The stars twinkled and shone, glistening in her wake, reminding her of exactly where she was and who she was. She was the Gemini. She was illegal. And she was *here*, against all odds, against all the gods and the prophecies and the tides.

Months ago, she'd sat on her bed at her old apartment and wished that one day she'd find something *real*. Of course, she didn't expect to have to die to find it, but she had found it, nonetheless. And it warmed her.

"Keep your friends close, for they will keep you warm in turn, and keep you alive."

She knew the Zodiacs as family. They trained with her, laughed with her, and now they would go to war with her. She missed her dad so much, and her mom would always be in her heart, but now she had *more.*

Hero had been unexpected. When she'd first met him, she could see that he was more attractive than most—by far—but she couldn't focus on him when she was trying to fight her way out with a shoe or being kidnapped by Seekers. Yet the more time she'd spent with him, the more those feelings grew. And they grew like a wild garden, flowers and thorns seeping into every crevice, beautiful and passionate. Hero steadied her in such a way that she felt as though the waves couldn't take her; she had two feet on the ground, the roots holding her in place. He steadied her in such a way that she didn't crave to be lost in another world, to lie, to see things as something they were not. She could focus. She could *be.*

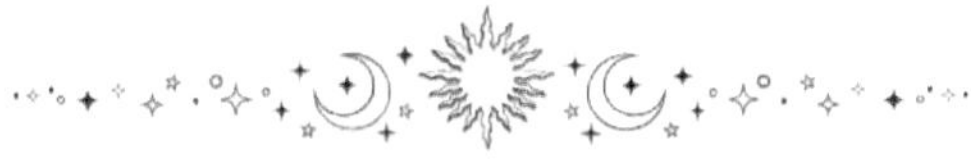

Hero watched as Cassie stood like a silhouette on the balcony of his room. She was his fallen star, a light in his dark life. He spent more time thinking about her than he'd ever care to admit out loud. He dreamed about her, drew her, painted her. He memorized every line on her pale skin as if it was his own unique form of torture.

"The moon's brighter than usual tonight," she remarked as she sensed him.

All he could say in return was a simple, "Yes, it is."

She turned to look at him and smiled, her eyes sparkling in the moonlight. "Sorry. I just needed some air from the party." She turned back around as the words left her mouth, facing the sky again.

"I like you being here, you know that," Hero said, stepping closer to her.

He stayed solid on his decision not to tell her about the prophecy. It was not her burden to bear, but his. She'd made it through a battle with an Immortal; she'd survived a brutal death. He would bear this last thing, so she would not have to. But he needed to tell her one thing first.

"Cassie?" he whispered.

"Yes?"

Running a hand through his hair, he shook his head. "Something happened when I met you. The moment I laid eyes on you, something in me changed. I don't know what exactly, but you brought out a light in me when I was beginning to believe there was none left." He stepped closer to her, enchanted by the way her chest rose and fell more quickly. "I can't promise you everything will be okay, but I'm tired of pretending that I'm not so irreparably in love with you that it hurts to breathe without you." His hands cupped her face as he waited for an inkling of reciprocation. He had handed over his entire heart for her to either keep or throw away, and it was more terrifying than any demon he'd ever slayed.

Cassie's eyes widened, then softened, and she leaned into him. She placed her hand on his face, rubbing her thumb across his cheek as he melted into it. "Hero," she muttered. "You dragged me out of my darkest place and held me until I could see the light again. You steady me," she said, and all Hero wanted was to sweep her up in his arms and never let go. "I love you more than I thought was possible. Even if you make me so mad sometimes . . ." She laughed. "I can't be without you."

His heart leaped in his chest at her words.

"You would think, after all I've done, I'd have many regrets in life," he said carefully, adoring the softness of her cheek beneath his fingers. "But I only have one." He couldn't help himself as his attention slipped to her lips. "I regret that I didn't give myself to you sooner." He closed the gap between them, pressing his lips to hers, gently at first, not wanting to overwhelm her. But her lips moved insistently on his, kissing him back with a fire that matched his own. Her hands wandered all over his muscled body until Hero couldn't contain himself any longer. He ran his hands down her back, to her bottom, and lifted her as she wrapped her legs around his waist.

Hero carried her into his bedroom, blindly shoving the papers and charcoal off his drawing table, and there he sat her down, pushing himself against her as much as he could, intoxicated by the way her body moved against his, clearly wanting him as much as he did her. Cassie tugged at his shirt, and he complied with her wishes, throwing it to the ground. He watched with pure lust as her eyes stalked over his body, eventually meeting his gaze with a devilish look. He smirked, knowing exactly what kind of effect he had on her.

Hero grabbed onto her skin as if she could vanish from him at any moment. It was desperate, exasperated, chaotic. He kissed her deeply, his tongue swirling over hers in unison. Her lips felt like pure ecstasy, and he couldn't get enough. His hands went to her shoulders, sliding the sleeves of her dress off her body, letting it fall to the floor. His eyes grazed over her, taking in every bit of the woman in front of him.

"What do you want, Cass?" Hero breathed out, holding her hips as his lips hovered over hers. He wanted to give her everything she desired, and nothing she didn't. "Is this okay?"

"More," she panted. "I want all of you."

Hero crashed his lips back onto hers, his hands exploring every inch of her. He reached the top of her lacy undergarments, slipping a finger under the material. At the sound of her moan, he ripped them off her, needing her naked beneath him.

Hero lifted her once more and walked toward the bed, their lips melding. He laid her down and took a step back, admiring the silver-haired girl sprawled out on his covers—her soft, delicate curves, her full thighs and beautiful breasts.

Mine.

He watched as she raked her eyes over his body, her hands grasping at his belt and tugging. Needing to be as vulnerable with her as she was with him at this moment, he stripped down to his briefs, then leaned down, holding his body above her and kissing gently. He dragged his finger up the inside of her thigh, watching as she squirmed, her body begging for more. And he did as she wanted, as he always would. His fingers found her, ready for him, and his body reacted to it immediately.

Cassie tugged at his hair, biting his lip as he pushed a finger inside her, his thumb moving over her center. He kissed her down her neck and along the curves of her breasts, his tongue swirling around the peaks. He made his way down her soft stomach, lavishing attention on every curve, and continued further down until his mouth was right above her. "Gods, I've waited forever to taste you," he whispered as she moaned, her hips jolting up.

Kissing her inner thighs softly, he let himself drift over to her, his tongue swirling around her bundle of nerves as she gasped in pleasure.

"Hero, please . . ." She pulled at his hair, but he still wanted more of her. He could have done this forever, hearing the sensuous sounds leaving her mouth, savoring the taste of her . . . He didn't know how he could ever let her go.

She pulled at him harder, and he complied with a groan of disappointment. But he quickly shut up when her hands slid across his torso and under his waistband. He sucked in a breath as she wrapped a fist around him, and he couldn't contain himself any longer. "Say it to me again," he said, his body freezing on top of her.

"Say what?" Cassie panted.

"That you want this. That you want *me*."

"I can't imagine the day I won't," she whimpered. "I want you. I want *all* of this."

He stood, pushing his underwear off his body, and quickly rejoined her, skin on blessed skin. His mouth captured hers as he slid his length into her, both of them moaning in ecstasy.

It was nothing he had ever experienced before, this sensation of being inside someone he loved so immensely. Nothing could compare.

His mouth found her neck, planting kisses, sucks, and bites down its wake. He grabbed onto her, hard enough to make her scream his name, but careful not to bruise her with his strength. Then, he lost himself in her, abandoning everything he had once known with each thrust, giving his heart to her with each moan.

Her back arched as she dug her fingernails into his shoulders. His eyes hungrily watched her as she began to crescendo, then finally erupted in pleasure. Hero found himself obsessed with the sound of her, the feel of her—just *her*.

Cassie wrapped her legs around his back as he moved within her faster, only lifting himself enough to look at her face. He could feel her clench around him, and he knew she was just as close as he was. As she crested the peak again, he felt the heat rising in his own core. Hero shouted her name, crashing headfirst into release, just as she did.

When he was spent, he collapsed atop her, careful not to crush her. He held onto her as though she would fade the moment he let go, allowing himself a few more moments inside her as she ran her fingers down his back.

He eventually lifted himself with all his might, looking into her silver eyes with as much love as he could possibly muster. He leaned down, his lips touching hers once more. The kissing slowed as they lazily melded together as one.

He rolled onto his back, struggling to catch his breath.

He belonged to her. He was entirely hers. He would *always* be hers.

"Come here," he said, nudging her gently toward him. She lay her head against his chest, and his hand went to her hair, running his fingers through the silver threads. "What are you thinking about?" he mused, planting a kiss on the side of her head.

Cassie smiled, her fingers creating circles on his chest. "Just how perfect this moment is. I wish we could just stay here forever."

"No matter what happens, know that how I feel for you will never change." The looming prophecy pounded in his mind and chest, but he shoved it away. "I love you," he muttered into her hair. *My fallen star.*

"I love you too," she said, smiling into his chest.

Screw the prophecies, screw the Immortals, and screw anything or anyone else who dared to get in their way. He wouldn't let anything interfere with their happiness. Not for as long as she wanted him.

And the war . . . He didn't even want to think about the war. Not yet. It would come one day, but for now, all that mattered was Cassie. She was alive and safe, and he'd do everything he could to keep it that way, to make sure they all survived this.

Cassie lifted herself up and kissed him once more, her lips soft and welcoming. Placing his hands on her hips, Hero guided her on top of him, and she sunk herself with ease down onto him once more. He'd meant it when he said he couldn't get enough of her. Yet this time, it wasn't rushed or chaotic, or filled with lust and want. This time they let their bodies become one, gentle and loving. Hero grazed his teeth across her neck as she tilted her head back, rolling her hips on him slowly.

He sat up, bringing her with him. Her legs wrapped around him, and he met her thrusts with his own. With their faces an inch apart, he found himself building to another release, his pace quickening, and with him, she fell too.

She panted into his shoulder, planting small kisses on his skin as Hero tried his best not to flip her over and take her once more. But the urge to just *hold* her took control.

Lying back down, his arms around her, he watched as her eyes fluttered closed. Then his own eyes shut, and he fell asleep easier than he had in years. He dreamed about Cassie as the sun, brightening each path she wandered down, and him as the moon, forever chasing after her. There had not been light in his life before her, the girl who thought herself to be darkness.

Just then, Rane's words broke through his dream, flowing into his mind—words he'd overturned before: *"I left one more gift for you."*

The sound of swords clanking ripped him from his sleep, and he bolted upright in his bed, his heart racing.

Cassie was no longer in his arms.

OF MIRRORS AND ICE

Acknowledgements

Thank you to my parents, who have supported me every step of the way, from plotting the book on a whiteboard, to reading the final edited version. Thank you for believing in me even when I didn't believe in myself. Thank you to my dad, who gave me the idea for the book on a late-night phone call while I was in college, and who hyped it up even before he read a single page. Thank you to my mom, who tells everyone she knows about the book (even when I tell her not to) because she's so proud of me for writing it.

Thank you to all my friends from all over the world who have followed and liked all my random social media posts promoting my book, even before I told any of them about it. I was astonished by the amount of support that I have received from you all.

Kali, my best friend, thank you for always being there. Thank you for making me a better writer, for the countless brainstorming sessions, for giving me harsh feedback when I needed it, for always being there to talk about our latest obsessions, and for the jokes, the laughs, and the cries. I love you, and I can't imagine life without you.

Thank you to my countless beta-readers who have helped me shape my book and bring it from a horrible first draft into something beautiful. I'm sorry you had to sift through my never-ending spelling mistakes and plot holes. I'm very grateful to my editors, especially Robin Fuller, for polishing my book to a publishing standard, and for making it something I was proud to have others read. *Of Stars and Tides* wouldn't be here without you all.

And a final huge thank you to everyone who reads this book. I hope you can find an escape from the outside world within these pages.

I wrote it for all of you.

ABOUT THE AUTHOR

LOCKLYN BLAKE is a neurodivergent author who writes fantasy romance inspired by mythology and astrology. Born in Atlanta, she lived in Brussels and London before moving to Pittsburgh, where she now resides with her dogs. Her love for storytelling came at a young age and continued with her as she achieved a bachelor's degree in English literature. When not reading or writing, she enjoys traveling, art, and her career in event and wedding planning.

Find Locklyn Blake on Tik Tok and Instagram: @locklynblake

Website: www.locklynblake.com